JACK HIGGINS

Jack Higgins lived in Belfast till the age of twelve. Leaving school at fifteen, he spent three years with the Royal Horse Guards, serving on the East German border during the Cold War. His subsequent employment included occupations as diverse as circus roustabout, truck driver, clerk and, after taking an honours degree in sociology and social psychology, teacher and university lecturer.

The Eagle Has Landed turned him into an international bestselling author, and his novels have since sold over 250 million copies and have been translated into fifty-five languages. Many of them have also been made into successful films. His recent bestselling novels include *Pay the Devil*, *Edge of Danger*, *Midnight Runner* and *Bad Company*.

In 1995 Jack Higgins was awarded an honorary doctorate by Leeds Metropolitan University. He is a fellow of the Royal Society of Arts and an expert scuba diver and marksman. He lives on Jersey in the Channel Islands.

D1334741

JACK HIGGINS

THE KEYS OF HELL

DAY OF RECKONING

Grafton

HarperCollins*Publishers*
77-85 Fulham Palace Road
Hammersmith, London W6 8JB

www.harpercollins.co.uk

This omnibus edition published in 2004
by HarperCollins*Publishers*

ISBN 0 007 71198 0

Set in Sabon by Palimpsest Book Production Limited,
Polmont, Stirlingshire

Printed and bound in Great Britain by
Mackays of Chatham plc, Chatham, Kent

THE KEYS OF HELL

*There are no keys to hell –
the doors are open to all men.*
Albanian proverb

MANHATTAN

1995

1

The dream was always the same. Plunging into the marsh, forcing his way through the reeds and mist, pushing the punt hard, Guilio Orsini standing at the front finding the way through and then the engine close by breaking into life and a burst of machine-gun fire.

Guilio went over head-first, always did, and Chavasse floundered through the reeds and the bitterly cold water and then, mysteriously, like a curtain, the reeds parted and there was the lagoon and the boat, the *Buona Esperanza*, and Orsini was at the rail leaning over, a hand outstretched.

'Now, Paul, now.'

And Chavasse reached and the mist seemed to increase and there was the roaring of the engine and the boat slapped away, vanished, and he was alone again.

* * *

Chavasse was subject to dreams of the past, and had always suspected it was a legacy of his Breton father. An old race, the Bretons, an ancient people. But this dream he had not had for some years. Still ... he got off the bed, went to the window of his suite and looked down at Manhattan. The lights sparkled in the evening dusk. He liked New York and always had. There as an excitement there, an infinite probability to things.

When the phone went he answered at once, 'Chavasse.'

'Ah, Sir Paul. Tino Rossi.'

'Good evening, Mr Rossi.'

'Listen, I know we're meeting later for dinner at the Saddle Room, but I wondered whether you'd mind coming round to my apartment at the Trump Tower first.'

'Is there a purpose to this?'

'Well, my lawyer, Mario Volpe, as you may know, is my nephew a couple of times removed. He seems to think there are a few things he could take care of before our meeting. You understand?'

'Perfectly,' Chavasse said.

'I'll send a limousine. Say half an hour?'

'No need. As it's only a couple of blocks, I'll walk.'

'Fine. I'll look forward to seeing you for dinner later.'

Chavasse put down the phone and thought about it, a slight frown on his face, then he went to the wardrobe, took out his rather old-fashioned carpet bag, pulled open a flap in the bottom and produced a short-barrelled Colt, only a .22, but deadly with hollow-point rounds. He checked it out, went into the bathroom and turned on the shower.

In the magnificent sitting room of his Trump Tower apartment Don Tino Rossi replaced the telephone. He was seventy-six years of age and still in good shape, his silver hair almost shoulder-length, his linen suit the best that Savile Row could provide.

The large man in the black suit with the shaven head came forward as the Don nodded, opened a silver box, offered a cigarette and a light. He was Aldo Vinelli, the firm's head of security. Don Tino's nephew, Mario Volpe, stood by the terrace window smoking a cigarette, thirty years of age, medium height, good-looking and like Rossi, impeccably dressed.

'So he's coming.'

'Why wouldn't he?' his uncle asked. 'He doesn't want a car. He's walking.'

'You trust this Chavasse?'

'As much as he trusts me. Our meeting in London made sense.'

'Good. I'll make arrangements.' Volpe nodded to Vinelli. 'I need you.' He went out.

The Don said quietly, 'Aldo, I assigned you to protect my nephew because I trust you and you've done a good job.'

'Thank you, Don Tino.'

'And where does your loyalty lie?'

'With you always.'

'Good.'

The Don held out his hand. Aldo kissed it and went out. Rossi sighed. Strange that facility he'd always had that told him when someone was lying to him. A gift from God really.

* * *

Before it was fashionable, Tino Rossi alone amongst Mafia leaders had realized that life had to change, that the old days were long gone. He had turned the Rossi family to respectability. Real estate developments in New York, the same on the Thames in London. Investments in the electronics industry, shipping, banking. His early start meant that these days his only rivals were the Russian Mafia.

The young man he called nephew, Mario, was an important part of the organization. He'd never known his father, and his mother had also died at a young age. Her widowed sister, Signora Volpe, had brought the boy to New York, raised him in Little Italy. As Don Tino's niece her Mafia connection had assured the success of her café. Mario had gone to Columbia, had taken a law degree. Later, he'd done the same thing at London University and was now indispensable to the family on both sides of the Atlantic for his legal expertise.

He returned to the room. The Don said, 'Is everything in hand?'

'Sure. Look, I'll go with Aldo and monitor him. So he's crazy enough to want to walk alone on a wet night in Manhattan, but that could be asking for it. I mean, this is an older guy. Sixty-five.'

'So I'm ten years older.'

'Heh, Uncle, I didn't mean . . .'

'Make this work, Mario, nothing is more important.'

'You trust this Chavasse?'

'As I told you, no more than he trusts me. Sir Paul Chavasse, knighted by the Queen of England, Mario.'

'So?'

'This man is what? Half English, half French. He speaks more languages than you've had hot dinners. University degrees coming out of his ears. In spite of all that, a killer by nature. For twenty years a field agent for the Bureau, the most secret of British intelligence units. You've seen his record. Shot three times, knifed twice.'

'So he was hot stuff.'

'More than that, Mario, for the past twenty years he's been Belfast Bureau Chief and that's no desk job, not with the IRA and all those other problems. Now he has Eastern Europe on his back. Bosnia, Serbia, Kosova, Albania, and we know who has the greatest input.'

'The Russian Mafia.'

'Exactly, and as they are not *our* friends we can help there. In return, Chavasse will help us.'

'When possible?'

'Of course. Look, I suspended all drug operations there years ago and not for moral reasons as you well know. If idiots want to kill themselves with heroin that's their affair. We make more out of cigarette smuggling from Europe into Britain than we ever would have with drugs.'

'Still illegal.'

'Yes, but as you being an expert in English law know, a drug runner pulls ten or twelve years. Get done, as the English say, for cigarette smuggling and what would your client get?'

'Twelve months and out in six.' Mario Volpe smiled. 'Still illegal, running cigarettes by the millions up the Thames, so where does that leave Sir Paul Chavasse?'

'Exactly as he is. A realist. We're not destroying the lives of stupid teenagers. We aren't harming the widows and orphans. He can live with that as long as we provide the expertise on Eastern Europe that he needs. You'll see that we do.'

'Of course, Uncle.'

'Good boy.' The Don nodded. 'You take care of things. Tell Sir Paul I'll see him later for dinner at the Saddle Room. You'd better go now, you and Aldo, to make sure he gets here in one piece.'

'Uncle.'

Mario Volpe went out. Rain battering the window, Don Tino reached for his unfinished glass of champagne. Such a clever boy. All the virtues really and yet capable of such stupidity. He swallowed the champagne, got up and walked out leaning on his Malacca cane.

When Chavasse emerged from the Plaza Hotel it was raining slightly. He wore a Burberry trench coat in dark blue and an old-fashioned rain hat slanted across his head. Inside, the Colt .22 rested in a special clip. Uncomfortable, but also comforting in its own way. Just a feeling, but that's why he was still here after all these years. He declined the offer of a cab from the doorman, went down the steps and started along Fifth Avenue.

Waiting in a black Mercedes town car, Mario Volpe and Vinelli watched him.

'Let's go, Aldo,' Volpe said, 'and don't lose him.' Not that there was much chance of that as they pulled away from the sidewalk. Not too many people as the rain increased.

Chavasse liked the rain. Somehow you could inhabit your own private world. It was what he called the cinema of the mind time. You considered the facts, tried to make sense, anticipate the other side's next move, and there was certainly more to all this than met the eye. All his senses, the product of forty years of living on the edge, told him that.

Not that he distrusted Don Tino particularly. It was more that he didn't trust anyone. His special kind of life had taught him that. The way Eastern Europe was, the Don could be useful, which was what his meeting with Rossi and Vinelli at the Dorchester Hotel in London had indicated. If a few favours in return was the price, it was worth it, always supposing the price wasn't too high. So Rossi was a gangster. In essence, that was what Chavasse had been for years. You had to be a kind of gangster to be an intelligence agent. All that kept you alive really.

He paused, produced a silver case from an inside pocket, took out a cigarette and lit it in cupped hands. He was standing at the entrance of a darkened mall at the time and for the moment, the sidewalk was clear. As he started forward, a young man darted out of the mall and blocked his way.

'Heh, buddy, you got some change?'

At that moment, another one emerged, his twin, hard-faced in bomber jacket and jeans, only he was holding a Browning pistol.

'This one's got more than change. Let's get him in here.'

He rammed the barrel of the Browning against Chavasse's spine and drove him into the darkness.

All this was seen from the Mercedes.

Volpe said, 'Those bastards. Why the gun?'

There was the sound of a shot. Vinelli braked to a halt and got the door open.

12

* * *

In the mall the one with the Browning rammed it even harder into Chavasse.

'A nice fat wallet here I'd day, so let's stay friendly. You can call me Tommy.'

Chavasse raised his right elbow, struck backwards into the face, turned sideways, pushing the Browning away, grabbed for the barrel, twisted it free and had the gun in his hand.

'You should never get that close to anyone.'

He pivoted, rammed the barrel of the Browning into the back of Tommy's right knee and pulled the trigger. Tommy staggered into the wall and fell down with a cry.

The other one backed away, hands raised.

'Heh, man, don't do it.'

Vinelli arrived, a gun in his hand, Volpe behind him.

They looked at Tommy lying on the ground and Chavasse tendered the Browning to Vinelli.

'Not mine, his.' He looked down at the boy. 'Terrible class of muggers these days. Not too competent.'

Volpe held out his hand. 'Mario Volpe, Sir

Paul. We were worried about you so I figured we'd check the hotel. Aldo recognized you from London, so we were following. I mean, scum like this, what can I say?'

'Not much, I expect. Can we go now?'

'Sure.' Volpe turned to Vinelli. 'Take care of this, Aldo. I'll drive Sir Paul to the Trump, you follow on foot.'

He took Chavasse by the arm and led him away. Aldo turned, reached for the youth who was standing and pulled him close.

'You were supposed to jump him and wait for us to come to the rescue and what do we get? A gun, for Christ's sake.'

'It was Tommy. He's on crack.'

'Really?' Vinelli headbutted him, breaking his nose, sending him staggering.

The youth started to weep, blood everywhere. 'I'm sorry, Mr Vinelli, but what do I do with Tommy?'

'You get an ambulance. Three very large black guys beat up on you, and no fairy stories for the cops or the Rossi family will see to you on a more permanent basis.' He opened his wallet and took out ten hundred-dollar bills. 'I said a grand and

I'm a man of my word.' He dropped the money on Tommy.

'I'll do what you say, Mr Vinelli.'

'You better had, kid.'

Vinelli patted his face, turned his collar up against the rain and walked away.

In the sitting room of the Trump Tower apartment, Volpe helped Chavasse off with his Burberry and placed it on a chair. Chavasse removed the rain hat and put it on the coat carefully.

'Drink, Sir Paul? Martini? Champagne?'

'Irish whiskey,' Chavasse told him, 'Bushmills for preference.'

'Anything. We've got it all.'

'Good.' Chavasse took a cigarette from his silver case. 'And then you can tell me exactly what it is you want.'

Vinelli came in and stood by the door, face impassive. Volpe got the whiskey from the bar by the window and brought it over.

'I don't really want anything, Sir Paul. My uncle and you laid it out pretty clear at your

15

meeting in London at the Dorchester. I mean, even Aldo here met you but I didn't, so I figured it was time. I handle all the family's legal business on both sides of the Atlantic. This whole deal is very important. I wanted to familiarize myself with you.'

'And why would you want to do that?'

'Well, on occasions, we'll be working together, but hell, no problem there. Your record in the intelligence business is amazing.'

'And how would you know that?'

'Bureau records are on file at the Public Records Office in London. Sure, maybe they're on a fifty-year hold, but there are always ways round that. The clerks aren't very well paid. Give them "a few bob" as you Brits say, and it's amazing what you get a copy of.'

Chavasse finished his whiskey. He said calmly, 'What you appear to be saying is that you've been checking up on my past record quite illegally.'

'Yes, but we've got to be careful with the London operation.'

'Does the Don know about this?'

'Of course.'

Chavasse nodded. 'So – where are we at?'

'One case of yours really got to me.' Volpe went to a side table and returned with a file. 'This was so amazing I had it copied. Read it. It's good stuff. I suppose you wrote it originally. I've got phone calls to make to all four quarters of the globe. I'll be about an hour then I'll take you to Don Tino at the Saddle Room. Anything you want, Aldo will get for you.'

He went out and Vinelli stood there, face impassive. 'Another whiskey, Sir Paul?'

'I think champagne might be more appropriate,' Chavasse said in excellent Italian.

'Of course.'

'Is he for real, the boy?'

'He is young.'

Aldo produced a bottle of Bollinger from the bar and Chavasse lit another cigarette, picked up the file and opened it. It was a fifty-page résumé of certain events in Albania in 1965. It was headed 'Bureau Case Study 203, Field Agent Doctor Paul Chavasse'.

Aldo stood at the door, still impassive.

It was very quiet, only rain drumming against the window.

A long time ago, Chavasse told himself, *a hell of a long time ago.*

He started to read.

ROME

MATANO

1965

2

When Chavasse entered the Grand Ballroom of the British Embassy, he was surprised to find the Chinese delegation clustered around the fireplace, looking completely out of place in their blue uniforms, and surrounded by the cream of Roman society.

Chou En-lai surveyed the scene from a large gilt chair, the Ambassador and his wife beside him, and his smooth impassive face gave nothing away. Occasionally, guests of sufficient eminence were brought forward by the First Secretary to be introduced.

The orchestra was playing a waltz. Chavasse lit a cigarette and leaned against a pillar. It was a splendid scene. The crystal chandeliers took light to every corner of the cream-and-gold ballroom, reflected again and again in the mirrored walls.

Beautiful women, handsome men, dress uniforms, the scarlet and purple of church dignitaries – it was all strangely archaic, as if somehow the mirrors were reflecting a dim memory of long ago, dancers turning endlessly to faint music.

He looked across to the Chinese and, for a brief instant, the white face of Chou En-lai seemed to jump out of the crowd, the eyes fastening on his. He nodded slightly, as if they knew each other, and the eyes seemed to say: *All these are doomed – this is my hour and you and I know it.*

Chavasse shivered and, for no accountable reason, a wave of greyness ran through him. It was as if some sixth sense, that mystical element common to all ancient races, inherited from his Breton father, were trying to warn him of danger.

The moment passed, the dancers swirled on. He was tired, that was the trouble. Four days on the run with no more than a couple of hours of uneasy sleep snatched when it was safe. He lit another cigarette and examined himself in the mirror on the wall.

The dark evening clothes were tailored well,

outlining good shoulders and a muscular frame, but the skin was drawn too tightly over the high cheekbones that were a heritage from his French father, and there were dark circles under the eyes.

What you need is a drink, he told himself. Behind him, reflected in the mirror, a young girl came in from the terrace through the french windows.

Chavasse turned slowly. Her eyes were set too far apart, the mouth too generous. Her dark hair hung loosely to her shoulders, the white silk dress was simplicity itself. She wore no accessories. None were needed. Like all great beauties, she wasn't beautiful, but it didn't matter a damn. She made every other woman in the room seem insignificant.

She moved towards the bar, heads turning as she passed, and was immediately accosted by an Italian Air Force colonel who was obviously slightly the worse for drink. Chavasse gave the man enough time to make a thorough nuisance of himself, then moved through the crowd to her side.

'Ah, there you are, darling,' he said in Italian. 'I've been looking everywhere for you.'

Her reflexes were excellent. She turned smoothly, assessing him against the situation in a split second and making her decision.

She reached up and kissed him lightly on the cheek. 'You said you'd only be ten minutes. It's really too bad of you.'

The Air Force colonel had already faded discreetly into the crowd and Chavasse grinned. 'How about a glass of Bollinger? I really think we should celebrate.'

'I think that would be rather nice, Mr Chavasse,' she said in excellent English. 'On the terrace, perhaps. It's cooler there.'

Chavasse took two glasses of champagne from the table and followed her through the crowd, a slight frown on his face. It *was* cool on the terrace, the traffic sounds muted and far away, and the scent of jasmine heavy on the night air.

She sat on the balustrade and took a deep breath. 'Isn't it a wonderful night?' She turned and looked at him and laughter bubbled out of her. 'Francesca – Francesca Minetti.'

She held out her hand and Chavasse gave her one of the glasses of champagne and grinned.

'You seem to know who I am already.'

She leaned back and looked up at the stars. When she spoke, it was as if she were reciting a lesson hard-learned.

'Paul Chavasse, born Paris 1928, father French, mother English. Educated at Sorbonne, Cambridge and Harvard universities. PhD Modern Languages, multilingual. University lecturer until 1954. Since then . . .'

Her voice trailed away and she looked at him thoughtfully. Chavasse lit a cigarette, no longer tired. 'Since then . . . ?'

'Well, you're on the books as a Third Secretary, but you certainly don't look like one.'

'What would you say I *did* look like?' he said calmly.

'Oh, I don't know. Someone who got about a lot.' She swallowed some more champagne and said casually, 'How was Albania? I was surprised you made it out in one piece. When the Tirana connection went dead, we wrote you off.'

She started to laugh again, her head back, and behind Chavasse a voice said, 'Is she giving you a hard time, Paul?'

Murchison, the First Secretary, limped across the terrace. He was a handsome, urbane man, his face bronzed and healthy, the bar of medals a splash of bright colour on the left breast of his jacket.

'Let's say she knows rather too much about me for my personal peace of mind.'

'She should,' Murchison said. 'Francesca works for the Bureau. She was your radio contact last week. One of our best operatives.'

Chavasse turned. 'You were the one who relayed the message from Scutari warning me to get out fast?'

She bowed. 'Happy to be of service.'

Before Chavasse could continue, Murchison took him firmly by the arm. 'Now don't start getting emotional, Paul. Your boss has just got in and he wants to see you. You and Francesca can talk over old times later.'

Chavasse squeezed her hand. 'That's a promise. Don't go away.'

'I'll wait right here,' she assured him, and he turned and followed Murchison inside.

They moved through the crowded ballroom into the entrance hall, passed the two uniformed footmen at the bottom of the grand staircase and mounted to the first floor.

The long, thickly carpeted corridor was quiet, and the music echoing from the ballroom might have been from another world. They went up half a dozen steps, turned into a shorter side passage and paused outside a white-painted door.

'In here, old man,' Murchison said. 'Try not to be too long. We've a cabaret starting in half an hour. Really quite something, I promise you.'

He moved back along the passage, his footsteps silent on the thick carpet, and Chavasse knocked on the door, opened it and went in.

The room was a small, plainly furnished office, its walls painted a neutral shade of green. The young woman who sat at the desk writing busily was attractive in spite of her dark, heavy-rimmed library spectacles.

She glanced up sharply and Chavasse smiled. 'Surprise, surprise.'

Jean Frazer removed her spectacles. 'You look like hell. How was Albania?'

'Tiresome,' Chavasse said. 'Cold, wet and with the benefits of universal brotherhood rather thinly spread on the ground.' He sat on the edge of the desk and helped himself to a cigarette from a teak box. 'What brings you and the old man out here? The Albanian affair wasn't all that important.'

'We had a NATO intelligence meeting in Bonn. When we got word that you were safely out, the Chief decided to come to Rome to take your report on the spot.'

'Nice try,' Chavasse said. 'The old bastard wouldn't have another job lined up for me, would he? Because if he has, he can damn well think again.'

'Why not ask him?' she said. 'He's waiting for you now.'

She nodded towards a green baize door. Chavasse looked at it for a moment, sighed heavily and crushed his cigarette into the ashtray.

The inner room was half in shadow, the only light a shaded lamp on the desk. The man who stood at the window gazing out at the lights of Rome was of medium height, the face somehow ageless, a strange, brooding expression in the dark eyes.

'Here we are again,' Chavasse said softly.

The Chief turned, took in Chavasse's appearance and nodded. 'Glad to see you back in one piece, Paul. I hear things were pretty rough over there.'

'You could say that.'

The older man moved to his chair and sat down. 'Tell me about it.'

'Albania?' Chavasse shrugged. 'We're not going to do much there. No one can pretend the people have gained anything since the Communists took over at the end of the war, but there's no question of a counter-revolution even getting started. The *Sigurmi*, the secret police, are everywhere. I'd say they must be the most extensive in Europe.'

'You went in using that Italian Communist Party Friendship cover, didn't you?'

'It didn't do me much good. The Italians in the party accepted me all right, but the trouble started when we reached Tirana. The *Sigurmi* assigned an agent to each one of us and they were real pros. Shaking them was difficult enough, and the moment I did, they smelt a rat and put out a general call for me.'

'What about the Freedom Party? How extensive are they?'

'You can start using the past tense as of last week. When I arrived, they were down to two cells. One in Tirana, the other in Scutari. Both were still in contact with our Bureau operation here in Rome.'

'Did you manage to contact the leader, this man Luci?'

'Only just. The night we were to meet to discuss things, he was mopped up by the *Sigurmi*. Apparently, they were all over his place, waiting for me to show my hand.'

'And how did you manage to get out of that one?'

'The Scutari cell got a radio signal from Luci as the police were breaking in. They relayed it to Bureau Headquarters here in Rome. Luckily for me, they had a quick thinker on duty – a girl named Francesca Minetti.'

'One of our best people at this end,' the Chief said. 'I'll tell you about her one of these days.'

'My back way out of Albania was a motor launch called the *Buona Esperanza*, run by a man named Guilio Orsini. He's quite a boy. Was one of the original torpedo merchants with the Italian Navy during the war. His best touch was when he sank a couple of our destroyers in Alexandria harbour back in '41. Got out again in one piece, too. He's a smuggler now. Runs across to Albania a lot. His grandmother came from there.'

'As I recall the original plan, he was to wait three nights running in a cove near Durres. That's about thirty miles by road from Tirana, isn't it?'

Chavasse nodded. 'When Francesca Minetti got the message from Scutari, she took a chance and put it through to Orsini on his boat. The madman left his crewman in charge, landed, stole a car in Durres and drove straight to Tirana. He caught me at my hotel as I was leaving for the meeting with Luci.'

'Getting back to the coast must have been quite a trick.'

'We did run into a little trouble. Had to do the last ten miles on foot through coastal salt marshes. Not good with the hounds on your heels, but Orsini knew what he was doing.

31

Once we were on board the *Buona Esperanza*, it was easy. The Albanians don't have much of a navy. Half a dozen minesweepers and a couple of sub-chasers. The *Buona Esperanza* has ten knots on any one of them.'

'It would seem that Orsini is due for a bonus on this one.'

'That's putting it mildly.'

The Chief nodded, opened the file that contained Chavasse's report and leafed through it. 'So we're wasting our time in Albania?'

Chavasse nodded. 'I'm afraid so. You know the way things have been since the 20th Party Congress in 1956, and now the Chinese are in there with both feet.'

'Anything to worry about?'

Chavasse shook his head. 'Albania's the most backward European country I've visited and the Chinese are too far from home to be able to do much about it.'

'What about this naval base the Russians were using at Valona before they pulled out? The word was that they'd built it into a sort of Red Gibraltar on the Adriatic.'

'Alb-Tourist took us on an official trip on our

second day. "Port" is hardly the word for the place. Good natural shelter, but only used by fishing boats. Certainly no sign of submarine pens.'

'And Enver Hoxha – you think he's still firmly in control?'

'And then some. We saw him at a military parade on the third day. He cuts an impressive figure, especially in uniform. He's certainly the people's hero at the moment. Heaven knows for how long.'

The Chief closed the file with a quick gesture that somehow dismissed the whole affair, placing it firmly in the past.

'Good work, Paul. At least we know where we stand. You're due for some leave now, aren't you?'

'That's right,' Chavasse said, and waited.

The Chief got to his feet, walked to the window and looked out over the glittering city, down towards the Tiber. 'What would you like to do?'

'Spend a week or two at Matano,' Chavasse said without hesitation. 'That's a small fishing port near Bari. There's a good beach, and Guilio

Orsini owns a place on the front called the Tabu. He's promised me some diving. I'm looking forward to it.'

'I'm sure you are,' the Chief said. 'Sounds marvellous.'

'Do I get it?'

The old man looked out over the city, an abstracted frown on his face. 'Oh, yes, Paul, you can have your leave – after you've done a little chore for me.'

Chavasse groaned and the older man turned and came back to the desk. 'Don't worry, it won't take long, but you'll have to leave tonight.'

'Is that necessary?'

The old man nodded. 'I've got transport laid on and you'll need help. This man Orsini sounds right. We'll offer a good price.'

Chavasse sighed, thinking of Francesca Minetti waiting on the terrace, of the good food and wine in the buffet room below. He sighed again and stubbed out his cigarette carefully.

'What do I do?'

The Chief pushed a file across. 'Enrico Noci,

a double agent who's been working for us and the Albanians. I didn't mind at first, but now the Chinese have got to him.'

'Which isn't healthy.'

'It never is. There's a boat waiting at Bari to take Noci over to Albania tomorrow night. All the details are in there.'

Chavasse studied the picture, the heavy fleshy face, the weak mouth – the picture of a man who was probably a failure at everything he put his hand to, except perhaps women. He had the sort of tanned beach-boy good looks that some of them went for.

'Do I bring him in?'

'What on earth for?' The Chief shook his head. 'Get rid of him; a swimming accident, anything you like. Nothing messy.'

'Of course,' Chavasse said calmly.

He glanced through the file again, memorizing the facts it contained, then pushed it across and stood up. 'I'll see you in London.'

The Chief nodded. 'In three weeks, Paul. Enjoy your holiday.'

'Don't I always?'

The Chief pulled a file across, opened it and

started to study the contents, and Chavasse crossed to the door and left quietly.

3

Enrico Noci lay staring through the darkness at the ceiling, smoking a cigarette. Beside him the woman slept, her thigh warm against his. Once, she stirred, turning into him in her sleep, but didn't awaken.

He reached for another cigarette and heard a distinctive rattle as something was pushed through the letter box in the outer hall. He slid from beneath the blankets, careful not to wake the woman, and padded across the tiled floor in his bare feet.

A large buff envelope lay on the mat at the front door. He took it into the kitchen, lit the gas under the coffee pot and opened the envelope quickly. Inside was a smaller sealed envelope, the one he was to take with him, and a single typed sheet containing his movement orders.

He memorized them, then burned it quickly at the stove.

He glanced at his watch. Just before midnight. Time for a hot bath and something to eat. He stretched lazily, a conscious pleasure seeping through him. The woman had really been quite something. Certainly a diverting way to spend his last evening.

He was wallowing up to his chin in hot water, the small bathroom half-full of steam, when the door opened and she came in, yawning as she tied the belt of his silk dressing gown.

'Come back to bed, *caro*,' she said plaintively.

For the life of him, he couldn't remember her name and he grinned. 'Another time, angel. I must get moving. Make me some scrambled eggs and coffee, like a good girl. I've got to be out of here in twenty minutes.'

When he left the bathroom ten minutes later, he was freshly shaved, his dark hair slicked back, and he wore an expensive hand-knitted sweater and slacks. She had laid a small table in the window and placed a plate of scrambled eggs in front of him as he sat down.

As he ate, he pulled back the curtain with one hand and looked down across the lights of Bari to the waterfront. The town was quiet, and a slight rain drifted through the yellow street lamps in a silver spray.

'Will you be coming back?' she said.

'Who knows, angel?' he shrugged. 'Who knows?'

He finished his coffee, went into the bedroom, picked up a dark blue nylon raincoat and a small canvas grip and returned to the living room. She sat with her elbows on the table, a cup of coffee in her hands. He took out his wallet, extracted a couple of banknotes and dropped them on the table.

'It's been fun, angel,' he said, and moved to the door.

'You know the address.'

When he closed the outside door and turned along the street, it was half past twelve exactly. The rain was falling heavily now and fog crouched at the ends of the streets, reducing visibility to thirty or forty yards.

He walked briskly along the wet pavement, turned confidently out of one street into another and, ten minutes later, halted beside a small black Fiat sedan. He opened the door, lifted the corner of the carpet and found the ignition key. A few moments later, he was driving away.

On the outskirts of Bari, he stopped and consulted the map from the glove compartment. Matano was about twelve miles away on the coast road running south to Brindisi. An easy enough run, although the fog was bound to hold him up a little.

He lit a cigarette and started off again, concentrating on his driving as the fog grew thicker. He was finally reduced to a cautious crawl, his head out of the side window. It was almost an hour later when he halted at a signpost that indicated Matano to the left.

As he drove along the narrow road, he could smell the sea through the fog and gradually it seemed to clear a little. He reached Matano fifteen minutes later and drove through silent streets towards the waterfront.

He parked the car in an alley near the Club Tabu as instructed and went the rest of the way on foot.

It was dark and lonely on the waterfront and the only sound was the lapping of water against the pilings as he went down a flight of stone steps to the jetty.

It was quiet and deserted in the yellow light of a solitary lamp and he paused halfway along to examine the motor cruiser moored at the end. She was a thirty-footer with a steel hull, probably built by Akerboon, he decided. She was in excellent trim, her sea-green paintwork gleaming. It wasn't at all what he had expected. He examined the name *Buona Esperanza* on her hull with a slight frown.

When he stepped over the rail, the stern quarter was festooned with nets, still damp from the day's labour and stinking of fish, the deck slippery with their scales.

Somewhere in the distance the door of an all-night café opened and music drifted out, faint and far away, and for no accountable reason Noci shivered. It was at that moment that he realized he was being watched.

The man was young, slim and wiry with a sun-blackened face that badly needed a shave. He wore denims and an old oilskin coat, and a seaman's cap shaded calm, expressionless eyes. He stood at the corner of the deckhouse, a coiled rope in one hand, and said nothing. As Noci took a step towards him, the door of the wheel-house opened and another man appeared.

He was at least six feet three, his great shoulders straining the seams of a blue pilot coat, and he wore an old Italian Navy officer's cap, the gold braid tarnished by exposure to salt air and water. He had perhaps the ugliest face Noci had ever looked upon, the nose smashed and flattened, the white line of an old scar running from the right eye to the point of the chin. A thin cigar of the type favoured by Dutch seamen was firmly clenched between his teeth and he spoke without removing it.

'Guilio Orsini, master of the *Buona Esperanza*.'

Noci felt a sudden surge of relief flow through him as tension ebbed away. 'Enrico Noci.'

He held out his hand. Orsini took it briefly and nodded to the young deckhand. 'Let's go, Carlo.' He jerked his thumb towards the companionway. 'You'll find a drink in the saloon. Don't come up until I tell you.'

As Noci moved towards the companionway, Carlo cast off and moved quickly to the stern. The engine burst into life, shattering the quiet, and the *Buona Esperanza* turned from the jetty and moved into the fog.

The saloon was warm and pleasantly furnished. Noci looked around approvingly, placed his canvas grip on the table and helped himself to a large whisky from a cabinet in one corner. He drank it quickly and lay on one of the bunks smoking a cigarette, a warm, pleasurable glow seeping through him.

This was certainly an improvement on the old tub in which he had done the run to Albania before. Orsini was a new face, but then there was nothing surprising in that. The faces changed constantly. In this business, it didn't pay to take chances.

The boat lifted forward with a great surge of power, and a slight smile of satisfaction touched Noci's mouth. At this rate they would be landing him on the coast near Durres before dawn. By noon he would be in Tirana. More dollars to his account in the Bank of Geneva, and this was his sixth trip in as many months. Not bad going, but you could take the pitcher to the well too often. After this, a rest was indicated – a long rest.

He decided he would go to the Bahamas. White beaches, blue skies and a lovely tanned girl wading thigh-deep from the sea to meet him. American, if possible. They were so ingenuous, had so much to learn.

The engines coughed once and died away and the *Buona Esperanza* slowed violently as her prow sank into the waves. Noci sat up, head to one side as he listened. The only sound was the lapping of the water against her hull.

It was some sixth sense, the product of his years of treachery and double-dealing, of living on his wits, that warned him that something was wrong. He swung his legs to the floor, reached for the canvas grip, unzipped it and took out a pistol. He released the safety catch and padded across to the foot of the companionway. Above him, the door opened and shut, creaking slightly as the boat pitched in the swell.

He went up quickly, one hand against the wall, paused and raised his head cautiously. The deck seemed deserted, the drizzle falling in silver cobwebs through the navigation lights.

He stepped out and, on his right, a match

flared and a man moved out of the shadows, bending his head to light a cigarette. The flame revealed a handsome devil's face, eyes like black holes above high cheekbones. He flicked the match away and stood there, hands in the pockets of his slacks. He wore a heavy fisherman's sweater and his dark hair glistened with moisture.

'Signor Noci?' he said calmly.

'Who the hell are you?' Noci demanded.

'My name is Paul Chavasse.'

It was a name with which Noci was completely familiar. An involuntary gasp rose in his throat and he raised the pistol. A hand like iron clamped on his wrist, wrenching the weapon from his grasp, and Guilio Orsini said, 'I think not.'

Carlo moved out of the shadows to the left and stood waiting. Noci looked about him helplessly and Chavasse held out his hand.

'I'll have the envelope now.'

Noci produced it reluctantly and handed it across, trying to stay calm as Chavasse examined the contents. They could be no more than half a mile from the shore, no distance to a man who had been swimming since childhood, and Noci was under no illusions as to what would happen if he stayed.

Chavasse turned over the first sheet of paper and Noci ducked under Orsini's arm and ran for the stern rail. He was aware of a sudden cry, an unfamiliar voice, obviously Carlo's, and then he slipped on some fish scales and stumbled headlong into the draped nets.

He tried to scramble to his feet, but a foot tripped him and then the soft, clinging, stinking meshes seemed to wrap themselves around him. He was pulled forward on to his hands and knees and looked up through the mesh to see Chavasse peering down at him, the devil's face calm and cold.

Orsini and Carlo had a rope in their hands and, in that terrible moment, Noci realized what they intended to do and a scream rose in his throat.

Orsini pulled hard on the rope and Noci lurched across the deck and cannoned into the low rail. A foot caught him hard against the small of the back and he went over into the cold water.

As he surfaced, the net impeding every movement he tried to make, he was aware of Orsini running the end of the line around the rail, of Carlo leaning out of the wheelhouse window waiting. A hand went up, and the *Buona Esperanza* surged forward.

Noci went under with a cry, then surfaced on a wave, choking for breath. He was aware only of Chavasse at the rail, watching, face calm in the fog-shrouded light, and then, as the boat increased speed, he went under for the last time.

As he struggled violently, water forcing the air from his lungs, and then suddenly he was aware of no pain, no pain at all. He seemed to be floating on soft white sand beneath a blue sky and a beautiful sun-tanned girl waded from the sea to join him, and she was smiling.

4

Chavasse was tired and his throat was raw from too many cigarettes. Smoke hung in layers from the low ceiling, spiralling in the heat from the single bulb above the green baize table, drifting into the shadows.

There were half a dozen men sitting in on the game. Chavasse, Orsini, Carlo Arezzi, his deckhand, a couple of fishing-boat captains and the sergeant of police. Orsini lit another of his foul-smelling Dutch cheroots and pushed a further two chips into the centre.

Chavasse shook his head and tossed in his hand. 'Too rich for my blood, Guilio.'

There was a general murmur and Guilio Orsini grinned and raked in his winnings. 'The bluff, Paul, the big bluff. That's all that counts in this game.'

Chavasse wondered if that explained why he was so bad at cards. For him, action had to be part of a logical progression based on a carefully reasoned calculation of the risk involved. In the great game of life and death he had played for so long, a man could seldom bluff more than once and get away with it.

He pushed back his chair and stood up. 'That's me for tonight, Guilio. I'll see you on the jetty in the morning.'

Orsini nodded. 'Seven sharp, Paul. Maybe we'll get you that big one.'

The cards were already on their way round again as Chavasse crossed to the door, opened it and stepped into a whitewashed passage. In spite of the lateness of the hour, he could hear music from the front of the club, and careless laughter. He took down an old reefer jacket from a peg, pulled it on and opened the side door.

The cold night air cut into his lungs as he breathed deeply to clear his head, and moved along the alley. A thin sea fog rolled in from the water and, except for the faint strains of music from the Tabu, silence reigned.

He found a crumpled packet of cigarettes in

his pocket, extracted one and struck a match on the wall, momentarily illuminating his face. As he did so, a woman emerged from a narrow alley opposite, hesitated, then walked down the jetty, the clicking of her high heels echoing through the night. A moment later, two sailors moved out of the entrance of the Tabu, crossed in front of Chavasse and followed her.

Chavasse leaned against the wall, feeling curiously depressed. There were times when he really wondered what it was all about, not just this dangerous game he played, but life itself. He smiled in the darkness. Three o'clock in the morning on the waterfront was one hell of a time to start thinking like that.

The woman screamed and he flicked his cigarette into the fog and stood listening. Again the screaming sounded, curiously muffled, and he started to run towards the jetty. He turned a corner and found the two sailors holding her on the ground under a street lamp.

As the nearest one turned in alarm, Chavasse lifted a boot into his face and sent him back over the jetty. The other leapt towards him with a curse, steel glinting in his right hand.

51

Chavasse was aware of the black beard, blazing eyes and strange hooked scar on the right cheek, and then he flicked his cap into the man's face and raised a knee into the exposed groin. The man writhed on the ground, gasping for breath, and Chavasse measured the distance and kicked him in the head.

In the water below the jetty came the sound of a violent splashing, and he moved to the edge and saw the first man swimming vigorously into the darkness. Chavasse watched him disappear, then turned to look for the woman.

She was standing in the shadow of a doorway and he went towards her. 'Are you all right?'

'I think so,' she replied, in a strangely familiar voice, and stepped out of the shadows.

His eyes widened in amazement. 'Francesca! What in the world are you doing here?'

Her dress had been ripped from neck to waist and she held it in place, a slight smile on her face. 'We were supposed to have a date on the terrace at the Embassy a week ago. What happened?'

'Something came up,' he said. 'The story of my life. But what are you doing on the Matano waterfront at this time of the morning?'

She swayed forward and he caught her just in time, holding her close to his chest for a brief moment. She smiled up at him wanly.

'Sorry about that, but all of a sudden I felt a little light-headed.'

'Have you far to go?'

She brushed a tendril of hair back from her forehead. 'I left my car somewhere near here, but all the streets look the same in the fog.'

'Better come back with me to my hotel,' he said. 'It's just around the corner.' He slipped off his jacket and draped it round her shoulders. 'I could fix you up with a bed.'

Laughter bubbled out of her, and for a moment she was once again the exciting girl he had met so briefly at the Embassy ball.

'I'm sure you could.'

He put an arm round her. 'Don't worry, I think you've had quite enough excitement for one night.'

There was the scrape of a shoe on the cobbles behind them, and he swung round and saw the other man lurching into the fog, hands to his smashed face.

Chavasse took a quick step after him and

Francesca caught his sleeve. 'Let him go. I don't want the police in on this.'

He looked down into her strained and anxious face. 'If that's the way you want it.'

There was something strange here, something he didn't understand. They walked along the jetty and turned on to the waterfront. As port towns went, Matano was reasonably tame, but not so tame that pretty young girls could walk around the dock area at three a.m. and expect to get away with it. One thing was certain. Francesca Minetti must have had a pretty powerful reason for being there.

The hotel was a small stuccoed building on a corner, an ancient electric sign over the entrance, but it was clean and cheap and the food was good. The owner was a friend of Orsini.

He slept at the desk, head in hands, and Chavasse reached over to the board without waking him and unhooked the key. They crossed the hall, mounted narrow wooden stairs and passed along a whitewashed corridor.

The room was plainly furnished with a brass bed, a washstand and an old wardrobe. As elsewhere in the house, the walls were white-washed and the floor highly polished.

Francesca stood just inside the door, one hand to the neck of her dress, holding it in place, and looked around approvingly.

'This is nice. Have you been here long?'

'Almost a week now. It's my first holiday in a year or more.'

He opened the wardrobe, rummaged among his clothes and finally produced a black polo-neck sweater in merino wool. 'Try that for size while I get you a drink. You look as if you could do with one.'

She turned her back and pulled the sweater over her head as he went to a cupboard in the corner. He took out a bottle of whisky and rinsed a couple of glasses in the bowl on the washstand. When he turned, she was standing by the bed watching him, looking strangely young and defenceless, the dark sweater hanging loosely about her.

'Sit down, for God's sake, before you fall down,' he said.

There was a cane chair by the french window leading to the balcony and she slumped into it and leaned her head against the glass window, staring into the darkness. Out at sea, a foghorn boomed eerily and she shivered.

'I think that must be the loneliest sound in the world.'

'Thomas Wolfe preferred a train whistle,' Chavasse said, pouring whisky into one of the glasses and handing it to her.

She looked puzzled. 'Thomas Wolfe? Who was he?'

He shrugged. 'Just a writer – a man who knew what loneliness was all about.' He swallowed a little of his whisky. 'Girls shouldn't be on the waterfront at this time of the morning; I suppose you know that? If I hadn't arrived when I did, you'd have probably ended up in the water after they'd finished with you.'

She shook her head. 'It wasn't that kind of assault.'

'I see.' He drank some more of his whisky and considered the point. 'If it would help, I'm a good listener.'

She held her glass in both hands and stared down at it, a troubled look on her face, and he added gently, 'Is this something official? A

Bureau operation, perhaps?'

She looked up, real alarm on her face, and shook her head vigorously. 'No, they know nothing about it and they mustn't be told, you must promise me that. It's a family matter, quite private.'

She put down her glass, stood up and walked restlessly across the room. When she turned, there was an expression of real anguish on her face. She pushed her hair back with a quick nervous gesture and laughed.

'The trouble is, I've always worked inside. Never in the field. I just don't know what to do in a situation like this.'

Chavasse produced his cigarettes, put one in his mouth and tossed the packet across to her. 'Why not tell me about it? I'm a great one for pretty girls in distress.'

She caught the packet automatically and stood there looking at him, a slight frown on her face. She nodded slowly. 'All right, Paul, but anything I tell you is confidential. I don't want any of this getting back to my superiors. It could get me into real trouble.'

'Agreed,' he said.

She came back to her chair, took a cigarette from the packet and reached up for a light. 'How much do you know about me, Paul?'

He shrugged. 'You work for us in Rome. My boss told me you were one of the best people we had out here and that's good enough for me.'

'I've worked for the Bureau for two years now,' she said. 'My mother was Albanian, so I speak the language fluently. I suppose that's what first interested them in me. She was the daughter of a *gegh* chieftain. My father was a colonel of mountain troops in the Italian occupation army in 1939. He was killed in the Western Desert early in the war.'

'Is your mother still alive?'

'She died about five years ago. She was never able to return to Albania once Enver Hoxha and the Communists took over. Two of her brothers were members of the *Legaliteri* in North Albania, which had royalist aims. They fought with Abas Kupi during the war. In 1945, Hoxha called them in from the hills to a peace conference at which they were immediately executed.'

There was no pain on her face, no emotion at all, except a calm acceptance of what for a long time must have been quite simply a fact of life.

'At least that explains why you were willing to work for us,' Chavasse said softly.

'It was not a hard decision to make. There was only an old uncle, my father's brother, who raised us, and until last year my brother was still in Paris studying political economy at the Sorbonne.'

'Where is he now?'

'When I last saw him, he was face-down in a mud bank of the Buene Marshes in Northern Albania with a machine-gun burst in his back.'

Out of the silence, Chavasse said carefully, 'When was this?'

'Three months ago. I was on leave at the time.' She held out her glass. 'Could I have some more?'

He poured until she raised her hand. She sipped a little, apparently still in control of her emotions, and continued.

'You were in Albania not so long ago yourself. You know how things are.'

He nodded. 'As bad as I've ever seen them.'

'Did you notice any churches on your travels?'

'One or two still seemed to be functioning,

but I know the official party line is to clamp down on religious observances of any sort.'

'They've almost completely crushed Islam,' she said in a dry matter-of-fact voice. 'The Albanian Orthodox Church has come out of it a little better, because they deposed their Archbishop and put in a priest loyal to Communism. It's the Roman Catholic Church that has been most harshly persecuted.'

'A familiar pattern,' Chavasse said. 'The organization Communism fears most.'

'Out of two archbishops and four bishops arrested, two have been shot and another's on the books as having died in prison. The Church has almost ceased to exist in Albania, or so the authorities hoped.'

'I must admit that was the impression I got.'

'During the past year there's been an amazing revival in the north,' she said. 'Headed by the Franciscan fathers at Scutari. Even non-Catholics have been swarming into the church there. It's had the central government in Tirana quite worried. They decided to do something about it. Something spectacular.'

'Such as?'

'There's a famous shrine outside the city dedicated to Our Lady of Scutari. A grotto and medicinal spring. The usual sort of thing. A place of pilgrimage since the Crusades. The statue is ebony and leafed with gold. Very ancient. They call her the Black Madonna. It's traditionally said that it was only because of her miraculous powers that the old Turkish overlords of ancient times allowed Christianity to survive in the country at all.'

'What did the central government intend to do?'

'Destroy the shrine, seize the statue and burn it publicly in the main square at Scutari. The Franciscan fathers were warned and managed to spirit the Madonna away on the very day the authorities were going to act.'

'Where is it now?'

'Somewhere in the Buene Marshes at the bottom of a lagoon in my brother's launch.'

'What happened?'

'It's easily told.' She shrugged. 'My brother, Marco, was interested in a society of Albanian refugees living in Taranto. One of them, a man called Ramiz, got word about the Madonna

61

through a cousin living in Albania at Tama. That's a small town on the river ten miles inland.'

'And this society decided to go in and bring her out?'

'The Black Madonna is no ordinary statue, Paul,' she said seriously. 'She symbolizes all the hope that's left for Albania in a hard world. They realized what a tremendous psychological effect it would have upon the morale of Albanians everywhere if it were made public in the Italian press that the statue had reached Italy in safety.'

'And you went in with them? With Marco?'

'It's an easy passage and the Albanian Navy is extremely weak, so getting into the marshes is no problem. We picked up the statue at a pre-arranged spot on the first night. Unfortunately, we ran into a patrol boat next morning on the way out. There was some shooting and the launch was badly damaged. She sank in a small lagoon and we took to the rubber dinghy. They hunted us for most of the day. Marco was shot towards evening. I didn't want to leave his body, but we didn't have much choice. Later that night, we reached the coast and Ramiz stole a small sailing boat. That's how we got back.'

'And where is this man Ramiz now?' Chavasse asked.

'Somewhere in Matano. He telephoned me in Rome yesterday and told me to meet him at a hotel on the waterfront. You see, he's managed to get hold of a launch.'

Chavasse stared at her, an incredulous frown on his face. 'Are you trying to tell me you intend to go back into those damned marshes?'

'That was the general idea.'

'Just the two of you, you and Ramiz?' He shook his head. 'You wouldn't last five minutes.'

'Perhaps not, but it's worth a try.' He started to protest but she raised a hand. 'I'm not going to spend the rest of my life living with the thought that my brother died for nothing when I could at least have tried to do something about it. The Minettis are a proud family, Paul. We take care of our dead. I know what Marco would have done and I am the only one left to do it.'

She sat there, her face very pale in the lamplight. Chavasse took her hands, reached across and kissed her gently on the mouth.

'This lagoon where the launch sank, you know where it is?'

She nodded, frowning slightly. 'Why?'

He grinned. 'You surely didn't think I'd let you go in on your own?'

There was a look of complete bewilderment on her face. 'But why, Paul? Give me one good reason why you should risk your life for me?'

'Let's just say I'm bored after a week of lazing around on the beach, and leave it at that. This man Ramiz, you've got his address?'

She took a scrap of paper from her handbag and handed it to him. 'I don't think it's far from here.'

He slipped it into his pocket. 'Right, let's get going.'

'To see Ramiz?'

He shook his head. 'That comes later. First we'll call on a good friend of mine, the kind of man you need for a job like this. Someone with no scruples, who knows the Albanian coast like the back of his hand and runs the fastest boat in the Adriatic.'

At the door, she turned and looked up at him searchingly. Something glowed in her eyes and colour flooded her cheeks. Quite suddenly, she seemed confident, sure of herself again.

'It's going to be all right, angel. I promise you.'

He raised her hand briefly to his lips, opened the door and gently pushed her into the corridor.

5

The air in the room was still heavily tainted by cigarette smoke, but the card players had gone. In the light of the shaded lamp, a British Admiralty chart of the Drin Gulf area of the Albanian coast was unfolded across the table. Chavasse and Orsini leaned over it and Francesca sat beside them.

'The Buene River runs down to the coast from Lake Scutari, or Shkoder as they call it these days,' Orsini said.

'What about these coastal marshes? Are they as bad as Francesca says?'

Orsini nodded. 'One hell of a place. A maze of narrow channels, salt-water lagoons and malaria-infested swamps. Unless you knew where to look, you could search for a year for that launch and never find it.'

'Anyone living there?'

'A few fishermen and wildfowlers, mainly *geghs*. The Reds haven't done too well in those parts. The whole area's always been a sort of refuge for people on the run.'

'You know it well?'

Orsini grinned. 'I'd say I've made the run into those marshes at least half a dozen times this year. Penicillin, sulphonamide, guns, nylons. There's a lot of money to be made and the Albanian Navy can't do much to stop it.'

'Still a risky business, though.'

'For amateurs, anything is risky.' Orsini turned to Francesca. 'This man Ramiz, what did he do for a living?'

'He was an artist. I believe he did most of his sailing at weekends.'

Orsini looked at the ceiling and raised his hands helplessly. 'My God, what a set-up. That he got you back safely to Italy is a miracle, *signorina*.'

The door opened and Carlo came in carrying cups on a tray. He handed them round and Chavasse sipped hot coffee. He frowned down at the map, following the main channel, then turned to Francesca.

'You say you know where the launch went down? How can you be sure? These lagoons all look the same.'

'Marco took a cross-bearing just before we sank,' she said. 'I memorized it.'

Orsini pushed a piece of paper and a pencil across and she quickly wrote the figures down. He examined them with a slight frown and then calculated the position. He drew a circle round the central point.

'X marks the spot.'

Chavasse examined it quickly. 'About five miles in. Another three or four to this place Tama. What's it like there?'

'Used to be quite a thriving little river port years ago, but it's gone down the slot in a big way since the trouble started between Albania and the satellite countries.' Orsini traced a finger along the line of the river. 'The Buene forms part of the boundary between Albania and Yugoslavia. Most of the main stream's been allowed to silt up. That means you have to know the estuary and delta region well to get as far inland as Tama.'

'But could you get us there?'

Orsini turned to Carlo. 'What do you think?'

'We've never had any trouble before. Why should we now?'

'The pitcher can go to the well too often,' Francesca observed softly.

Orsini shrugged. 'For all men, death makes the last appointment. He chooses his own time.'

'That only leaves the question of the price to be settled,' Chavasse said.

'No problem there,' Francesca put in quickly.

'*Signorina*, please.' Orsini took her hand and touched it to his lips. 'I will do this thing because I want to, and for no other reason.'

She seemed close to tears and Chavasse interrupted quickly. 'One thing I'm not happy about is Ramiz. Are you sure it was his voice on the telephone?'

She nodded. 'He came from the province of Vlore. They have a distinctive accent. I'm sure it was him.'

Chavasse decided that it didn't look too good for Ramiz. The *Sigurmi* had obviously traced them with no difficulty. Maybe they'd recovered Marco Minetti's body or, what was more probable, had got their hands on the people who

70

had passed on the Madonna in Albania itself. Each man had his limits, his specific tolerance to pain. Once past that point, most would babble all they knew before dying.

And it was natural that the Albanians should go to so much trouble to trace the Madonna. Its disappearance must have meant a big loss of prestige politically, and the knowledge that it must still be in their own territory would be an added spur to recover it.

'If Ramiz did make that phone call, it was probably because he was made to. Either that or he was known to have made it.' He produced the slip of paper Francesca had given him at the hotel. 'Do you know this place?'

Orsini nodded. 'It's not far from here. The sort of fleabag where whores rent rooms by the hour and no questions asked.' He turned to Francesca. 'No place for a lady.'

She started to protest, but Chavasse cut in quickly. 'Guilio's right. In any case, you're out on your feet. What you need is about eight hours' solid sleep. You can use my room at the hotel.' He turned to Carlo. 'See she gets there safely.'

He pulled on his reefer jacket and she stood up. 'You'll be careful?'

'Aren't I always?' He gave her a little push. 'Lock yourself in the room and get some sleep. I'll be along later.'

She went reluctantly and Carlo followed her out. When Chavasse turned, Orsini was grinning hugely. 'Ah, to be young and handsome.'

'Something you never were,' Chavasse said. 'Let's get moving.'

It was still raining, a thin drizzle that beaded the iron railings of the harbour wall like silver as they walked along the pavement. The old stuccoed houses floated out of the fog, unreal and insubstantial, and each street lamp was a yellow oasis of light in a dark world.

The hotel was no more than five minutes from the Tabu, a seedy tenement, plaster peeling from the brickwork beside the open door. They entered a dark and gloomy hall. There was no one behind the wooden desk and no response to Orsini's impatient push on the bell.

'Did she give you the room number?'

Chavasse nodded. 'Twenty-six.'

The Italian moved behind the desk and examined the board. He came back, shaking his head. 'The key isn't there. He must still be in his room.'

They went up a flight of rickety wooden stairs to the first floor. There was an unpleasant musty smell compounded of cooking odours and stale urine and a strange brooding quiet. They moved along the passage, checking the numbers on the doors, and Chavasse became aware of music and high brittle laughter. He paused outside the room from which it came and Orsini turned from the door opposite.

'This is it.'

The door swung open to his touch and he stepped inside and reached for the light switch. Nothing happened. He struck a match and Chavasse moved in beside him.

The room was almost bare. There was a rush mat on the floor, an iron bed and a washstand. A wooden chair lay on its side beside the mat.

As Chavasse reached down to pick it up, the match Orsini was holding burned his fingers and he dropped it with a curse. Chavasse rested on one knee, waiting for him to strike another and was aware of a sudden dampness soaking through the knee of his slacks. As the match flared, he raised his hand, the fingers sticky and glutinous with half-dried blood.

'So much for Ramiz.'

They examined the room quickly, but there was nothing to be found, not even a suitcase, and they went back into the passage. High-pitched laughter sounded from opposite and Orsini raised his eyebrows inquiringly.

'Nothing to lose,' Chavasse said.

The big Italian knocked on the door. There was a sudden silence and then a woman's voice called, 'Come back later. I'm busy.'

Orsini knocked even harder. There was a quick angry movement inside and the door was jerked open. The woman who faced them was small, with flaming red hair. The black nylon robe she wore did little to conceal her ample charms. She recognized Orsini immediately and the look of anger on her face was replaced by a ready smile.

'Eh, Guilio, it's been a long time.'

'Too long, *cara*,' he said, patting her face.

'You still look as good as ever. My friend and I wanted a word with the man opposite, but he doesn't appear to be at home.'

'Oh, that one,' she said in disgust. 'Sitting around his room like that. Wouldn't even give a girl the time of day.'

'He must have been blind,' Orsini said gallantly.

'A couple of men came looking for him earlier,' she said. 'I think there was some trouble. When I looked out, they were taking him away between them. He didn't look good.'

'You didn't think of calling the police?' Chavasse asked.

'I wouldn't cut that bastard of a sergeant down if he were hanging.' There was an angry call from inside the room and she grinned. 'Some of them get really impatient.'

'I bet they do,' Chavasse said.

She smiled. 'You, I definitely like. Bring him round some time, Guilio. We'll have ourselves a party.'

'Maybe I'll do that,' Orsini told her.

There was another impatient cry from inside and she raised her eyebrows despairingly and closed the door.

Orsini and Chavasse went back downstairs and out into the street. The Italian paused to light a cheroot and flicked the match into the darkness.

'What now?'

Chavasse shrugged. 'There isn't really much we can do. I know one thing. I could do with some sleep.'

Orsini nodded. 'Go back to your hotel. Stay with the girl and behave yourself. We'll sort something out in the morning.' He punched Chavasse lightly on the shoulder. 'Don't worry, Paul. You're in the hands of experts.'

He turned away into the fog, and as Chavasse watched him go, tiredness seemed to wash over him in a great wave. He walked along the pavement, his footsteps echoing between narrow stone walls, and paused on a corner, fumbling for a cigarette.

As the match flared in his hands, something needle-sharp sliced through his jacket to touch his spine. A voice said quietly, 'Please to stand very still, Mr Chavasse.'

He waited while expert hands passed over his body, checking for the weapon that wasn't there.

'Now walk straight ahead and don't look round. And do exactly as you are told. It would desolate me to have to kill you.'

It was only as he started walking that Chavasse realized the voice had spoken in Albanian.

6

There were two of them, he could tell that much from their footfalls echoing between the walls of the narrow alleys as they moved through the old quarter of the town. The harsh voice of the man who had first spoken occasionally broke the silence to tell him to turn right or left, but otherwise there was no conversation and they stayed well behind him.

Fifteen minutes later, they emerged from an alley on to the sea wall on the far side of the harbour from the jetty. A house several floors high reared into the night, and beside it a flight of stone steps led down to a landing stage.

An old naval patrol boat was moored there, shabby and neglected, paint peeling from her hull. Across her stern ran the faded inscription *Stromboli – Taranto*.

The landing stage was deserted in the light of a solitary lamp and there was no one to help him. He turned slowly and faced the two men. One of them was small and rather nondescript. He wore a heavy jersey, and a knitted cap was pulled over his eyes.

The other was a different proposition, a big, dangerous-looking man badly in need of a shave. He had a scarred, brutal face, cropped hair and wore a reefer coat and seaboots.

He slipped a cigarette into his mouth and struck a match on the seawall. 'Down we go, Mr Chavasse. Down we go.'

Chavasse descended the steps slowly. As he reached the landing stage, the little man moved past him and led the way to the far end, where he opened a door set in the thickness of the wall. A flight of stone stairs lifted into the gloom and Chavasse followed him, the big man a couple of paces behind.

They arrived on a stone landing and the little man opened another door and jerked his head. Chavasse moved past him and stood just inside the entrance. The room was plainly furnished with a wooden table and several chairs. A narrow iron bed stood against one wall.

The man who sat at the table writing a letter was small and dark and dressed in a suit of blue tropical worsted. His skin was the colour of fine leather, the narrow fringe of beard combining to give him the look of a *conquistador*.

Chavasse paused a couple of feet away, hands in his pockets. Small, black, shining eyes had swivelled to a position from which they could observe him. The man half-turned and smiled.

'Mr Chavasse – a distinct pleasure, sir.'

His English was clipped and precise, hardly any accent at all. Chavasse decided that he didn't like him. The eyes were cold and merciless in spite of the polite, birdlike expression, the eyes of a killer.

'I'm beginning to find all this rather a bore.'

The little man smiled. 'Then we must try to make things more interesting. How would you like to earn ten thousand pounds?'

At the other end of the table was a tray containing a couple of bottles and several glasses. Chavasse walked to it calmly, aware of a slight movement from the big man over by the door.

One of the bottles contained Smirnoff, his

favourite vodka. He half-filled a glass and walked casually to the window, gazing forty feet down into the harbour as he drank, assessing the position of the *Stromboli* to the left, her outline showing dimly through the fog.

'Well?' the little man asked.

Chavasse turned. 'How are things in Tirana these days?'

The little man smiled. 'Very astute, but I haven't seen Tirana in five years. A slight difference of opinion with the present regime.' He produced a white card and flicked it across. 'My card, sir. I am Adem Kapo, agent for Alb-Tourist in Taranto.'

'Among other things, I'm sure.'

Kapo took out a case and extracted a cigarette which he fitted into a holder. 'You could describe me as a sort of middleman. People come to me with their requirements and I try to satisfy them.'

'For a fee?'

'But of course.' He extended the case. 'Cigarette?'

Chavasse took one. 'Ten thousand pounds. That's a lot of money. What makes you think I'd be interested?'

'Knowing who people are is part of my business and I know a great deal about you, my friend. More than you could dream of. Men like you are a gun for sale to the highest bidder. In any case, the money would be easily earned. My principals will pay such a sum in advance if you will agree to lead them to the position of a certain launch which recently sank in the marshes of the Buene River in Northern Albania. You are interested?'

'I could be if I knew what you were talking about.'

'I'm sure Signorina Minetti has already filled you in on the details. Come now, Mr Chavasse, all is discovered, as they say in the English melodramas. According to the information supplied to me by my clients, the body of an Italian citizen named Marco Minetti was discovered on a mud bank at the mouth of the Buene recently after an attempt had been made to smuggle a priceless religious relic from the country.'

'You don't say,' Chavasse said.

Kapo ignored the interruption. 'A few hours earlier, his launch had disappeared into the wastes of the Buene Marshes. Later, a priest and two men were taken into custody by the *Sigurmi* at the town of Tama. Apparently, the priest was stubborn to the end, a bad habit they have, but the two men talked. They named Minetti, his sister and an Albanian refugee, an artist called Ramiz. I was offered what I must admit was a very handsome fee to trace them.'

'And did you?'

'We've been watching Ramiz for weeks, waiting for him to make his move. Incredible though it may seem, he apparently intended to go in again. You see, he was an intellectual – one of those irritating people who feel they have a mission in life.'

'You speak of him in the past tense.'

'Yes, it's really quite sad.' Kapo sounded genuinely moved. 'I decided to have a little chat with him earlier this evening. When Haji and Tashko were bringing him here, there was some sort of struggle. He fell from the seawall and broke his neck.'

'An unfortunate accident, I suppose?'

'But of course, and quite unnecessary. It's surprising how easily one's motives can be misunderstood. I'm afraid an earlier attempt to get in touch with Signorina Minetti also met with a conspicuous lack of success.'

'Which leaves you with me.'

'One can hardly be blamed for thinking it rather more than coincidental that Mr Paul Chavasse of the British Secret Service just happened to be on the spot when the Signorina Minetti needed some assistance.'

Chavasse reached for the bottle of vodka and poured some more into his glass. 'And what would you say if I told you I still don't know what you're talking about?'

'If you persisted, you would leave me no choice. I would have to apply to the *signorina* again, which would distress me greatly.' Kapo sighed. 'On the other hand, women are so much easier to deal with. Don't you agree, Tashko?'

The big man moved to the end of the table, a mirthless grin on his face, and Chavasse nodded thoughtfully. 'Somehow I thought you'd say that.'

He reversed his grip on the bottle of vodka and struck sideways against Tashko's skull. The Albanian cried out sharply as the bottle smashed into pieces, drawing blood, and Chavasse heaved the table over, sending Kapo backwards in his chair, pinning him to the floor.

Haji was already moving fast across the room, a knife in his right hand. As it started to come up, Chavasse warded off the blow with one arm, caught the small man by his left wrist and, with a sudden pull, sent him crashing into the wall.

Tashko was already on his feet, blood streaming down the side of his face. He threw a tremendous punch, and Chavasse ducked under his arm and moved towards the door. Kapo pushed out a foot and tripped him so that he fell heavily to the floor.

Tashko moved in quickly, kicking at his ribs and face, and Chavasse rolled away, avoiding most of the blows, and scrambled up. He vaulted over the upturned table, picked up one of the chairs in both hands and hurled it through the window with all his force. The dried and rotting wood of the frame smashed easily and the window dissolved in a snowstorm of flying glass.

He was aware of Kapo's warning cry, of Tashko lurching forward. He lashed out sideways, the edge of his hand catching the big man across the face, scrambled on to the sill and jumped into darkness.

The air rushed past his ears with a roar, the fog seemed to curl around him; then he hit the water with a solid forceful smack and went down.

When he surfaced, he gazed up at the dark bulk of the house, at the light filtering through the fog from the smashed window. There was a sudden call, Kapo's voice drifting down, and another answered from the *Stromboli*, dimly seen in the fog to the right.

There was only one sensible way out of the situation, and Chavasse took it. He turned and swam away from the landing stage, out into the harbour towards the jetty on the other side. It was perhaps a quarter of a mile, he knew that. No great distance and the water was warm.

He took his time, swimming steadily, and the voices faded into the fog behind him and he was alone in an enclosed world. Everything seemed to fade away and he felt curiously calm and at peace with himself. Time seemed to have no meaning and the riding lights of the fishing boats moored close to the jetty appeared through the fog in what seemed a remarkably short time.

He swam between them and landed at a flight of steps which led to the jetty. For a moment or two he sat there getting his breath and then went up quickly and moved along the jetty to the waterfront.

His first real need was for a change of clothes and he hurried through the fog towards his hotel. After that, a visit to Orsini at the Tabu and perhaps a return match with Adem Kapo and his thugs, although it was more than probable that the *Stromboli* was already being prepared for a hasty exit.

The electric sign over the entrance to the hotel loomed out of the night and he opened the door and moved inside. The desk was vacant, no one apparently on duty, and he went up the stairs two at a time and turned along the corridor.

The door to his room stood open, panels smashed and splintered, and a light was still burning. A chair lay on its side in the middle of the floor and the blankets were scattered over the end of the bed as if there had been a struggle. He stood there for a moment, his stomach suddenly hollow, then turned and hurried back downstairs.

He noticed the foot protruding from behind the desk as he moved to the door and there was a slight groan of pain. When he looked over the top, he saw the old proprietor lying on his face, blood matting the white hair at the back of his head.

7

The landing stage was deserted when Chavasse, Orsini and Carlo drove up in the old Ford pick-up. The big Italian cut the engine, jumped to the ground and went to the head of the steps.

He turned, shaking his head. 'We're wasting our time, Paul, but we'll check the house just in case.'

They went down the steps quickly and crossed the landing stage to the door. It opened without difficulty and Chavasse went up first, an old Colt automatic Orsini had given him held against his right knee.

The door to the room in which Kapo had interviewed him stood ajar, light streaming out across the dark landing. Chavasse kicked it open and waited, but there was no reply. He went in quickly at ground level, the automatic ready.

Vodka from the smashed bottle had soaked into the floor, mixed with blood, and the table still lay on its side. Fog billowed in through the broken window and Orsini walked across, feet crunching on glass, and peered outside.

He turned, respect on his face. 'A long way down.'

'I didn't have a great deal of choice. What do we do now?'

The Italian shrugged. 'Go back to the Tabu. Maybe old Gilberto's remembered something by now.'

'I wouldn't count on it,' Chavasse said. 'That was a hard knock he took.'

'Then we'll have to think of something else.'

They returned to the pick-up and Carlo drove back to the Tabu through the deserted streets. As the truck braked to a halt, Chavasse checked his watch and saw that it was almost half past two. He jumped to the ground and followed the two Italians along the alley to the side door.

There were still a few customers in the bar at the front and, as they walked along the passage, the barman looked round the corner.

'Rome on the phone. They're hanging on.'

'That'll be my call to the Bureau,' Chavasse said to Orsini. 'I'll see what they've got to tell me about Kapo.'

'I'll have another word with old Gilberto,' Orsini said. 'He may be thinking a little straighter by now.'

Chavasse took his call in the small office at the back of the bar. The man on the other end was the night duty officer based at the Embassy. No one of any particular importance, just a good reliable civil servant who knew what files were for and how to use them efficiently.

He had nothing on Kapo that Chavasse didn't already know. Incredibly, everything the man had said about himself was true. At one time a high official in the Albanian Ministry of the Interior, he had been marked down for elimination in 1958 during one of Hoxha's earlier purges. He had been allowed to enter Italy as a political refugee and had since lived in Taranto earning a living as an import-export agent. Presumably on the basis that an Albanian of any description was preferable to a foreigner, Alb-Tourist had appointed him their Taranto agent in 1963. An official investigation by Italian

Military Intelligence in that year had indicated nothing sinister in the appointment.

Chavasse thanked the duty officer. No, it was nothing of any importance. He'd simply run across Kapo in Matano and had thought him worth checking on.

At the other end of the wire in his small office in Rome, the duty officer replaced the receiver with a thoughtful frown. Almost immediately, he picked it up again and put a call through to Bureau headquarters in London on the special line.

It could be nothing, but Chavasse was a topliner – everyone in the organization knew that. If by any remote chance he was up to anything and the Chief didn't know about it, heads might start to roll, and the duty officer hadn't the slightest intention of allowing his own to be numbered among them.

The telephone on his desk buzzed sharply five minutes later and he lifted it at once. 'Hello, sir . . . yes, that's right . . . well, there may be nothing in it, but I thought you'd like to know that I've just had a call from Paul Chavasse in Matano . . .'

Old Gilberto coughed as the brandy caught at the back of his throat and grinned wryly at Orsini. 'I must be getting old, Guilio. Never heard a damned thing. It couldn't have been more than twenty minutes after Carlo had delivered the young woman. One moment I was reading a magazine, the next, the lights were going out.' He raised a gnarled and scarred fist. 'Old I may be, but I'd still like five minutes on my own with that fancy bastard, whoever he is.'

Orsini grinned and patted him on the shoulder. 'You'd murder him, Gilberto. Nothing like a bit of science to have these young toughies running around in circles.'

They went out into the passage, leaving the old man sitting at the fire, a blanket around his shoulders. 'A good heavyweight in his day,' Orsini said. 'One with the sense to get out before they scrambled his brains. Anything from Rome?'

Chavasse shook his head. 'Everything Kapo

said about himself was true. He *is* the Alb-Tourist agent in Taranto, an old Party man from Tirana who said the wrong thing once too often and only got out by the skin of his teeth. According to Italian intelligence, he's harmless and they usually know what they're talking about.'

'That's what MI5 said about Fuchs and look where it got them,' Orsini pointed out. 'Nobody's perfect, and the good agent is the man who manages to pull the wool over the eyes of the opposition most effectively.'

'Which doesn't get us anywhere,' Chavasse said. 'They've gone, which is all that counts, taking Francesca Minetti with them.'

They went into the office at the rear of the bar and Orsini produced a bottle of whisky and three glasses. He filled them, a slight thoughtful frown on his face.

'Whoever took the girl, it couldn't have been Kapo and his men – the time factor wouldn't have allowed it. The men who attacked her on the jetty earlier – what can you tell me about them?'

'Judging by the language the second one used when he tried to stick his knife into me, I'd say he was Italian,' Chavasse said. 'Straight out of the Taranto gutter.'

'Anything else interesting about him?'

'He had a dark beard, anything but the trimmed variety, and his face was badly scarred. A sort of hook shape curving into his right eye.'

Orsini let out a great bellow of laughter and clapped him on the shoulder. 'But my dear Paul, this is wonderful.'

'You mean you know him?'

'Do I know him?' Orsini turned to Carlo. 'Tell him about our good friend Toto.'

'He works for a man called Vacelli,' Carlo said. 'A real bad one. Runs a couple of fishing boats out of here, engaged in the Albanian trade, the town brothel and a café in the old quarter.' He spat vigorously. 'A pig.'

'It looks as if Kapo must have employed Vacelli to get hold of the girl for him,' Orsini said. 'It's the sort of task for which Nature has fitted him admirably. Unfortunately, you arrived on the scene and messed things up.'

'Which doesn't explain why Kapo went to the trouble of having me pulled in for a personal interview.'

'He probably thought he could do some kind of a deal, you made a break for it and he had to leave in a hurry in case you decided to whistle the law down on him. No other choice.'

'And in the meantime, Vacelli and his boys picked up the girl?'

Orsini nodded. 'And Kapo had to leave before they could get in touch with him.'

'So you think Vacelli may still have the girl?'

Orsini opened the drawer of his desk, took out a Luger and slipped it into his hip pocket. He smiled and the great, ugly face was quite transformed.

'Let's go and find out.'

Vacelli's place fronted the harbour on the corner of an alley which led into the heart of the old town. The sign simply said *Café*. Inside, someone was playing a guitar. They parked the pick-up at the entrance and when they went in Orsini led the way downstairs.

There was a bead curtain and the murmur of voices from the bar beyond. The guitar player sat just inside the entrance, chair balanced against the wall. He was young with dark curling hair, the sleeves of his check shirt rolled back to expose muscular arms.

Orsini pulled back the curtain and looked down at the legs sprawled across the entrance. The guitar player made no effort to move and Orsini hooked the chair from under him, the sudden clatter stunning the room to silence.

There was a narrow, marble-topped bar, the wall behind it lined with bottles, and a few small tables and chairs ranged about them. The floor was of stone, the walls whitewashed and there were no more than a dozen customers, most of them men.

The guitar player came up fast, a spring knife in one hand, but Carlo was faster. His hand tightened over the wrist, twisting cruelly, and the youth screamed, dropping the knife. He staggered back against the wall, tears of pain in his eyes, and Orsini shook his head.

'God knows what's happened to the youth of this country. No manners at all.' He turned, looking the other patrons over casually. The bearded man with the scarred face, the one they called Toto, sat at the table by the wall, one arm in a sling.

Orsini grinned. 'Hey, Toto, you don't look too good. Where's Vacelli?'

There was a scrape of a boot on stone and a surly voice growled. 'What the hell do you want?'

Vacelli stood at the top of the flight of stone steps in the corner leading up to the first floor. He was built like Primo Carnera, a great ox of a man with a bullet-shaped head that was too small for the rest of his body.

'Hello there, you animal,' Orsini cried gaily. 'We've come for the Minetti girl.'

Vacelli's brutal face reddened in anger and he obviously restrained his temper with difficulty. 'I don't know what you're talking about.'

'What a pity.' Orsini picked up the nearest chair and threw it at the shelves behind the bar, smashing the mirror and bringing down a dozen bottles. 'Does that help?'

Vacelli gave a roar of rage and came down the steps on the run. Orsini picked up a full bottle of Chianti from a nearby table, jumped to one side and smashed it across Vacelli's skull as he staggered past.

Vacelli fell to one knee. Orsini picked up a

chair and brought it down across the great shoulders. Vacelli grunted and started to keel over. Orsini brought the chair down again and again until it splintered into matchwood. He tossed it to one side and waited.

Slowly, painfully, Vacelli reached for the edge of the bar and hauled himself up. He swayed there for a moment, then charged head-down, blood washing across his face in a red curtain. Orsini swerved and slashed him across the kidneys with the edge of his hand as Vacelli plunged past him.

Vacelli screamed and fell on his face. He tried to push himself up, but it was no good. He collapsed with a great sigh and lay still.

'Anyone else?' Orsini demanded.

No one moved and he turned to Carlo. 'Watch things down here. We won't be long.'

Chavasse followed him up the stairs and the big Italian pulled back a curtain and led the way along a narrow passage. A young woman in a cheap nylon housecoat leaned in a doorway smoking a cigarette.

'Eh, Guilio, have you killed the bastard?'

'Just about.' He grinned. 'He'll be inactive for

quite a while. Time enough for you to pack your bags and move on. There was a girl brought here tonight. Any idea where she is?'

'The end room. He was just going in when you arrived. I don't think he meant her any good.'

'My thanks, *carissima*.' Orsini kissed her lightly on one cheek. 'Go home to your mother.'

Chavasse was already ahead of him, but the door was locked. 'Francesca, it's Paul,' he called.

There was a quick movement inside and she called back, 'The door's locked on the outside.'

Orsini stood back, raised one booted foot and stamped twice against the lock. There was a sudden splintering sound, and the door sagged on its hinges, rotten wood crumbling. He stamped again and it fell back against the wall.

Francesca Minetti stood waiting, her face white. She was still wearing Chavasse's old sweater and looked about fifteen years old. Chavasse was aware of the breath hissing sharply between Orsini's teeth and then the Italian was moving forward quickly.

His voice was strangely gentle and comforting, like a father reassuring a frightened child. 'It's all right now, *cara*. There is nothing to worry about any more.'

She held his hand, gazing up into the ugly, battered face and tried to smile and then she started to tremble. She turned, stumbled across the wreckage of the door and ran into Chavasse's arms.

8

It was just after eight o'clock on the following evening when the *Buona Esperanza* moved away from the jetty and turned out to sea. It was a warm, soft night with a luminosity shining from the water. There was no moon, for heavy cloud banked over the horizon, as though a storm might be in the offing.

Orsini was at the wheel and Chavasse stood beside him, leaning forward to peer through the curved deckhouse window into the darkness ahead.

'What about the weather?' he said.

'Force-four wind with rain imminent. Nothing to worry about.'

'Is it the same for the Drin Gulf?'

'A few fog patches, but they'll be more of a help than anything else.'

Chavasse lit two cigarettes and handed one to the Italian. 'Funny what a day-to-day business life is. I never expected to set foot on Albanian soil again.'

'The things we do for the ladies.' Orsini grinned. 'But this one is something special, Paul. This I assure you as an expert. She reminds me very much of my wife, God rest her.'

Chavasse looked at him curiously. 'I never knew you'd been married.'

'A long time ago.' Orsini's face was calm, untroubled, but the sadness was there in his voice. 'She was only nineteen when we married. That was in 1941, during my naval service. We spent one leave together, that's all. The following year she was killed in an air raid while staying with her mother in Milan.'

There was nothing to be said and Chavasse stood there in silence. After a while, Orsini increased speed. 'Take over, Paul. I'll plot our course.'

Chavasse slipped behind him, and the Italian moved to the chart table. For some time he busied himself with the charts and finally nodded in satisfaction.

'We should move into the marshes just before dawn.' He placed a cheroot between his teeth and grinned. 'What happens after that is in the lap of God.'

'Do you want me to spell you for a while?' Chavasse asked.

Orsini took over the wheel again and shook his head. 'Later, Paul, after Carlo has done his trick. That way I'll be fresh for the run-in at dawn.'

Chavasse left him there and went down to the galley, where he discovered Francesca making coffee. He leaned in the doorway and grinned. 'That's what I like about Italian girls. So good in the kitchen.'

She turned and smiled mischievously. 'Is that all we're good for – cooking?'

She wore a pair of old denim trousers and a heavy sweater and her long hair was plaited into a single pigtail which hung across one shoulder. She looked incredibly fresh and alive and Chavasse shook his head.

'I could think of one or two things, but the timing's wrong.'

'What about the terrace of the British Embassy?'

'Too public.'

She poured coffee into a mug and handed it to him. 'There's a place I know in the hills outside Rome. It's only a village inn, but the food is out of this world. You eat it by candlelight on a terrace overlooking a hillside covered with vines. The fireflies dance in the wind and you can smell the flowers for a week afterwards. It's an experience one shouldn't miss.'

'I'm all tied up for the next couple of days,' Chavasse said, 'but after that, I'm free most evenings.'

'By a strange coincidence, so am I. And I'd like to point out that you still owe me a date.'

'Now how could I forget a thing like that?'

He ducked as she threw a crust of dry bread at his head, turned and went through the aft cabin into the saloon. Carlo had two aqualungs and their ancillary equipment laid out on the table.

'There's fresh coffee in the galley,' Chavasse told him.

'I'll get some later. I want to finish checking this lot.'

He never had much to say for himself, a strange, silent youth, but a good man to have at your back in trouble and devoted to Orsini. He sat on the edge of the table, a cigarette smouldering between his lips, and worked his way methodically through the various items of equipment. Chavasse watched him for a while, then went through into the other cabin.

He lay staring at the bulkhead, thinking about the task ahead. If Francesca's memory hadn't failed her and the cross-bearing she had given them was accurate, then the whole thing was simple. There couldn't be more than five or six fathoms of water in those lagoons and the recovery of the statue shouldn't take long. With any kind of luck, they could be back in Matano within twenty-four hours.

He could hear a rumble of voices from the galley, Francesca quite distinctly, and then Carlo laughed, which was unusual. Chavasse was conscious of a slight, unreasoning pang of jealousy. He lay there thinking about her and the voices merged with the throbbing of the engine and the rattle of water against the hull.

He was not conscious of having slept, only of being awake and checking his watch and realizing with a shock that it was two a.m.

Orsini was sleeping on the far bunk, his face calm, one arm behind his head, and Chavasse pulled on his reefer coat and went on deck.

Mist swirled from the water and the *Buona Esperanza* kicked along at a tremendous pace. There was no moon, but stars were scattered across the sky like diamonds in a black velvet cushion and there was still that strange luminosity in the water.

Carlo was standing at the wheel, his head disembodied in the light from the binnacle. Chavasse moved in and lit a cigarette. 'How are we doing?'

'Fine,' Carlo said. 'Keep her on one-four-oh till three a.m. then alter course to one-four-five. Guilio said he'd be up around four. We should be near the coast by then.'

The door banged behind him and a small trapped wind lifted the charts, raced round the deckhouse looking for a way out and died in a corner. Chavasse pulled a seat down from the wall and sat back, his hands steady on the wheel.

This was what he liked more than anything else. To be alone with the sea and the night and a boat. Something deep in his subconscious, some race image handed on from his Breton ancestors, responded to the challenge. Men who had loved the sea more than any woman, who sailed to the Grand Banks of the North American coast to fish for cod, long before Columbus or the Cabots had dreamed of crossing the Atlantic.

The door opened suddenly as rain dashed against the window and he was aware of the heavy aroma of coffee, together with another, more subtle fragrance.

'What's wrong with bed at this time in the morning?' he demanded.

She chuckled softly. 'Oh, this is much more fun. How are we doing?'

'Dead on course. Another hour and Orsini takes over for the final run-in.'

She pulled a seat down beside him, balanced her tray on the chart table and poured coffee into two mugs. 'What about a sandwich?'

He was surprised at the keenness of his appetite and they ate in companionable and intimate silence, thighs touching. Afterwards, he gave her a cigarette and she poured more coffee.

'What do you think our chances are, Paul?' she said. 'The truth now.'

'It all depends on how accurately your brother plotted the final position of the launch when she sank. If we can find her without too much trouble, the rest should be plain sailing. Diving for the Madonna will be no great trick in water of that depth. Depending on weather conditions, we could be on our way back by this evening.'

'And you don't anticipate any trouble in the Drin Gulf?'

'From the Albanian Navy?' He shook his head. 'From an efficiency point of view, it's almost non-existent. The Russians had a lot of stuff based here before the big bust-up, but they withdrew when Hoxha refused to toe the line. Something he hadn't reckoned on, and China's too far away to give him that kind of assistance.'

'What a country.' She shook her head. 'I can well believe that old story that when it came to Albania's turn God had nothing but trouble left to give.'

Chavasse nodded. 'Not exactly a happy history.'

112

'A succession of conquerors, more than any other country in Europe. Greeks, Romans, Goths, Byzantines, Serbs, Bulgars, Sicilians, Venetians, Normans and Turks. They've all held the country for varying periods.'

'And always, the people have struggled to be free.' Chavasse shook his head. 'How ironic life can be. After centuries of desperately fighting for independence, Albania receives it, only to find herself in the grip of a tyranny worse than any that has gone before.'

'Is it really as bad as they say?'

He nodded. 'The *Sigurmi* are everywhere. Even the Italian Workers' Holiday Association complain that they get one *Sigurmi* agent allocated to each member of their holiday parties. Even at a rough estimate, Hoxha and his boys have purged better than one hundred thousand people since he took over, and you know yourself how the various religious groups have been treated. Stalin would have been proud of him. An apt pupil.'

He took out his cigarettes and offered her one. She smoked silently for a while and then said slowly, 'Last year, two people who were

113

operating temporarily through the Bureau in Rome ended up missing. One in Albania, the other in Turkey.'

Chavasse nodded. 'Matt Sorley and Jules Dumont. Good men both.'

'How can you go on living the life you do? That sort of thing must happen a lot. Look how close you came to not getting out of Tirana.'

'Maybe I just never grew up,' he said lightly.

'How did it all begin?'

'Quite by chance. I was lecturing in languages at a British university, a friend wanted to pull a relative out of Czechoslovakia, and I gave him a hand. That's when the Chief pulled me in. At that time he was interested in people who spoke Eastern European languages.'

'An unusual accomplishment.'

'Some people can work out cube roots in their heads in seconds, others can never forget anything they ever read. I have the same sort of kink for languages. I soak them up like a sponge – no effort.'

She lapsed into Albanian. 'Isn't it a little unnerving? Don't you ever get your wires crossed?'

'Not that I can recall,' he replied faultlessly

in the same language. 'I can't afford that kind of mistake. If it's any consolation, I still can't read a Chinese newspaper. On the other hand, I've only ever met two Europeans who could.'

'With that kind of flair, plus your academic training, you could pick up a chair in modern languages at almost any university in Britain or the States,' she said. 'Doesn't the thought appeal to you?'

'Not in the slightest. I got into this sort of work by chance, and by chance I possessed all the virtues needed to make me good at it.'

'You mean you actually enjoy it?'

'Something like that. If I'd been born in Germany twenty years earlier, I'd probably have ended up in the Gestapo. If I'd been born an Albanian, I might well have been a most efficient member of the *Sigurmi*. Who knows?'

She seemed shocked. 'I don't believe you.'

'Why not? It takes a certain type of man or woman to do our kind of work – a professional. I can recognize the quality, and appreciate it, in my opposite numbers. I don't see anything wrong in that.'

There was a strained silence, as if in some

way he had disappointed her. She reached for the tray. 'I'd better take these below. We must be getting close.'

The door closed behind her and Chavasse opened the window and breathed in the sharp morning air, feeling rather sad. So often people like her, the fringe crowd who did the paperwork, manned the radios, decoded the messages, could never really know what it was like in the field. What it took to survive. Well, he had survived, and not by waving any flags, either.

Then what in the hell are you doing here? he asked himself, and a rueful smile crossed his face. What was it Orsini had said? *The things we do for the ladies.* And he was right, this one *was* something special – something very special.

The door swung open and Orsini entered, immense in his old reefer coat, a peaked cap on the side of his head. 'Everything all right, Paul?'

Chavasse nodded and handed over the wheel. 'Couldn't be better.'

Orsini lit another of his inevitable cheroots. 'Good. Shouldn't be long now.'

Dawn seeped into the sky, a grey half-light with a heavy mist rolling across the water.

Orsini asked Chavasse to take over again and consulted the charts. He checked the cross-bearing Francesca had given him and traced a possible course in from the sea through the maze of channels marked on the chart.

'Everything okay?' Chavasse asked.

Orsini came back to the wheel and shrugged. 'I know these charts. Four or five fathoms and a strong tidal current. That means that one day there's a sandbank, the next, ten fathoms of clear water. Estuary marshes are always the same. We'll go in through the main outlet of the Buene and turn into the marshes about half a mile inland. It's not only safer, but a damned sight quicker.'

The mist enfolded them until they were running through an enclosed world. Orsini reduced speed to ten knots and, a few moments later, Carlo and Francesca came up from below.

Chavasse went and stood in the prow, hands in his pockets, and the marshes drifted out of the mist and their stench filled his nostrils. Wildfowl called overhead on their way in from the sea and Carlo moved beside him and crossed himself.

'A bad place, this. Always, I am glad to leave.'

It was a landscape from a nightmare. Long, narrow sandbanks lifted from the water, and inland, mile upon mile of marsh grass and great reeds marched into the mist, interlaced by a thousand creeks and lagoons.

Orsini reduced speed to three knots and leaned from the side window, watching the reeds drift by on either side. Chavasse moved along the deck and looked up at him.

'How far are we from the position Francesca gave?'

'Perhaps three miles, but the going would be too difficult. In a little while, we must carry on in the dinghy. Much safer.'

'And who minds the launch?'

'Carlo – it's all arranged. He isn't pleased, but then he seldom is about anything.'

He grinned down at Carlo, who glared up at him and went below. Chavasse moved back along the deck and joined Francesca in the prow. A few moments later, the launch entered a small lagoon, perhaps a hundred feet in diameter, and Orsini cut the engines.

They glided forward and grounded gently against a sandbank as Orsini came out on deck and joined them. He slipped an arm around Francesca's shoulders and smiled down at her.

'Not long now, *cara*. A few more hours and we'll be on our way home again. I, Guilio Orsini, promise you.'

She looked up at him gravely, then turned to Chavasse, a strange, shadowed expression in her eyes, and for some unaccountable reason, he shivered.

9

Francesca cooked a hot meal, perhaps the last they would have for some time, and afterwards Carlo and Chavasse broke out the large rubber dinghy, inflated it and attached the outboard motor.

When they went below for the aqualung, Orsini was sitting on the edge of the table loading a machine pistol. The top of one of the saloon seats had been removed and inside the recess was an assortment of weapons: the submachine gun, a couple of automatic rifles and an old Bren of the type used by the British infantry during the war.

'Help yourself,' he said. 'We have a selection to suit all tastes.'

Chavasse picked up one of the automatic rifles, a Garrand, and nodded. 'This will do me. What about ammo?'

'There should be plenty in there somewhere.'

There were three boxes stacked together. The first contained grenades, the second, several pouched bandoliers. Chavasse picked one up and Orsini shook his head.

'That's an explosive we used during the war for underwater sabotage. I've had it for years.'

'A hell of a thing to have people sitting on,' Chavasse said.

Orsini grinned. 'Just the thing for fishing. You stick a chemical detonator in a piece as big as your fist, heave it over the side and wait. They come floating up by the thousand. I'll take some along, just in case we need to do any blasting.'

Chavasse found the ammunition in another box, loaded his Garrand and strapped a bandolier containing a hundred rounds about his waist. He helped Carlo up top with one of the aqualungs and they stowed it in the prow of the dinghy, along with several other items of equipment. As they finished, Orsini and Francesca came up on deck.

She was wearing an old reefer coat of Carlo's against the cold, the sleeves rolled back, and a scarf was tied around her head, peasant-fashion.

She seemed calm, but was extremely pale and there were blue shadows under her eyes.

Chavasse squeezed her hand as he helped her into the dinghy and whispered, 'Soon be over. We'll be on our way out again before you know it.'

She smiled wanly, but made no reply, and he clambered into the dinghy beside her and sat on one side, the Garrand across his knees. Orsini followed, seating himself in the stern. He glanced up at Carlo and grinned.

'If all goes well, we could be back by this evening. Certainly no later than dawn tomorrow.'

'And if it doesn't?'

'You always look on the dark side.'

Orsini pressed the automatic starter and the powerful motor roared into life. Wildfowl rose from the reeds in alarm, the sound of them filling the air. As Carlo released the line, the dinghy moved forward quickly. Chavasse had one final glimpse of his dark, saturnine face scowling at them over the rail and then the marsh moved in to enfold them.

* * *

The reeds lifted out of the mist like pale ghosts on either side, the only sound the steady rattle of the outboard motor. Orsini consulted his compass, turning from one narrow waterway to another, always moving towards the position on the chart that Francesca had given them.

She sat in silence, her hands buried in the pockets of the reefer coat, and Chavasse watched, wondering what she was thinking. About her brother, probably. Of his death and her own struggle for survival in this waking nightmare. The stench of the marshes, heavy and penetrating, filled his nostrils and he hurriedly lit a cigarette.

It was perhaps an hour later that they emerged into a broad waterway and Orsini cut the motor. 'This is as near as I can make it from the position you gave me,' he told Francesca. 'Recognize anything?'

She stood up and gazed around her. When she sat down, there was a troubled look on her face. 'They all look the same, these waterways, but I'm sure this wasn't the place. It was much smaller. I can remember my brother running the boat into the reeds to hide her and then we suddenly emerged into this small lagoon.'

Orsini stood up and looked around, but the reeds stretched into the mist, an apparently impenetrable barrier. He turned to Chavasse and shrugged. 'This is definitely the position he charted, so this lagoon she speaks of can't be far away. We'll have to go looking for it, that's all.'

Chavasse started to undress. 'I hope to God you're right.'

He kept on his shirt, trousers and shoes against the cold, went over the side and struck across the channel. Orsini followed a moment or so later and swam into the mist in the opposite direction.

It was bitterly cold and Chavasse coughed, retching as the strong earthy stench caught at the back of his throat. He swam into the reeds, following a narrow waterway that turned in a circle, bringing him back into the main channel.

He tried another, emerging a few moments later into a shallow lagoon no more than four or five feet deep, and he swam across into the reeds, forcing his way through. Just then, Orsini called through the mist from the other side of the

125

barrier and Chavasse pushed towards him. He came out on the perimeter of a lagoon no more than a hundred feet across, as Orsini surfaced in the centre.

The Italian floated there, coughing a little, hair plastered across his forehead. Chavasse looked down at the launch mirrored in five fathoms of clear water, then did a steep surface dive.

He swallowed to ease the pressure in his ears, then grabbed for the deck rail and hung there. The launch had tilted over on the shelving bottom and he worked his way round to the stern were he found the name *Teresa – Bari* inscribed in gold paint. He had a quick look at the general condition of the wreck, then released his hold and shot to the surface.

He trod water, gasping for air, and grinned at Orsini. 'Good navigating.'

'My mother, God rest her, always told me I was a genius.'

Orsini turned and swam across the lagoon, plunging into the reeds, and Chavasse followed. They emerged into the main channel within sight of the dinghy and swam towards it.

'Any luck?' Francesca asked.

Orsini nodded. 'Just as you described. Without that cross-bearing it would have been hopeless. We could have searched these marshes for a year without finding anything.'

They climbed back into the dinghy and he started the motor and steered for the wall of reeds. For a moment, they seemed an impossible barrier and Chavasse and Francesca pulled desperately with all their strength. Quite suddenly, the reeds parted and the dinghy passed into the lagoon.

Orsini cut the motor and they drifted towards the centre. Francesca gazed over the side, down through the clear water, her face very pale. She shivered abruptly and looked up.

'Will it take long?'

Orsini shook his head. 'We'll fix a line to hold us in position and one of us will go down. With luck we'll be out of here in a couple of hours.' He turned to Chavasse. 'Feel like another swim?'

Chavasse nodded. 'Why not? It couldn't be any colder than it is up here.'

The wind sliced through his wet shirt as he

lifted the aqualung on to his back and Orsini strapped it into place. Francesca watched, eyes very large in the white face, and Chavasse grinned.

'A piece of cake. We'll be out of here before you know it.'

She forced a smile and he pulled on his diving mask, sat on the rail and allowed himself to fall back into the water. As he surfaced, Orsini tossed him a line. Chavasse went under, paused to adjust his air supply, and swam down towards the launch in a sweeping curve.

The *Teresa* was almost bottom-up and he hovered over the stern rail to attach the end of his line and then swam towards the deckhouse, which was jammed against the sandy bottom of the lagoon at a steep angle.

There were jagged bullet holes in the hull and superstructure, mute evidence of the fight between the *Teresa* and the Albanian patrol boat. Some sort of a direct hit had been scored on the roof of the saloon and the companionway was badly damaged, the only entrance being a narrow aperture.

He managed it, pulling himself through by

force, the aqualung scraping protestingly against the jagged edges of the metal. The saloon table had broken free of its floor fastenings and floated against the bulkhead, together with several bottles and the leather cushions from the saloon.

There was no sign of the Madonna or anything remotely resembling it, and he swam towards the door leading to the forward cabin. The roof at this point had been smashed in by what looked like a cannon shell, and a twisted mass of metal blocked the door. He turned and swam out through the saloon, squeezed through the entrance and struck up towards the light.

He surfaced a few feet astern of the dinghy and swam towards it. Orsini gave him a hand over the side and Chavasse crouched in the bottom and pushed up his mask.

'The interior's in one hell of a mess. Stuff all over the place.'

'And the Madonna?'

'No sign at all. I couldn't get into the inner cabin. There's a lot of wreckage at that end of the saloon and the door's jammed.'

'But that is where it is!' Francesca said. 'I

remember now. Marco put it under one of the bunks for greater safety when the shooting started. It was wrapped in a blanket and bound in oilskin against the damp. The whole bundle was about five feet long.'

Orsini pulled a package from under the stern seat. 'A good thing I brought along some of that explosive. You'll have to blast your way in.'

He unfolded a bandolier and took out a piece of plastic explosive shaped like a sausage. 'That should be enough. We don't want to blow the whole boat apart.'

From another bundle he took a small wooden box containing several chemical pencil detonators, each one carefully packed in a plastic sheath.

'How long do these things give me?' Chavasse demanded.

'A full minute. I've got some that take longer, but I left them on the boat.'

'Well, thanks very much, friend,' Chavasse said. 'What are you hoping to do – collect on my insurance?'

'A minute should be plenty. All you have to

do is insert the fuse, break the end and get out of there. I'll go myself if you like.'

'Stop trying to show off,' Chavasse told him. 'In any case, you'll never get that frame of yours in through the saloon companionway.'

He was conscious of Francesca's face, white and troubled, as he gripped the rubber mouthpiece of his breathing tube between his teeth, pulled down his mask and went backwards over the side.

He went down through the clear water quickly, negotiated the companionway with no trouble and moved inside. He jammed the plastic explosive into the corner at the bottom of the door and inserted the detonator carefully. For a moment, he floated there looking at it, then he snapped the end.

The fuse started to burn at once, fizzing like a firecracker, and he turned and swam for the companionway. As he squeezed through the narrow opening, his aqualung snagged on the jagged metal. He paused, fighting back the panic, and eased himself through. A moment later, he was shooting towards the surface.

He broke through at the side of the dinghy

and Orsini pulled him over. There was a muffled roar and the dinghy rocked in the turbulence. The surface of the water boiled and wreckage bobbed up, sand and mud spreading in a great stain towards the reeds.

They waited for fifteen minutes, and gradually the water cleared again and the hull of the launch became visible. Orsini nodded and Chavasse went over the side.

There was still a lot of sand and mud hanging in suspension like a great curtain, obscuring his vision, but not seriously, and he went down towards the *Teresa*.

The explosion had even disturbed the entrance to the companionway, the turbulence blowing the wreckage back out on to the deck, and he passed through the saloon himself with no trouble.

Where the door to the cabin had been, there was now only a gaping hole, and he swam forward, paused for a moment and then moved inside.

The tiered bunks were still intact, but bedding floated against the bulkhead, moving languorously in the water like some living thing. He pushed his way through their pale fronds and looked for the Madonna. It became immediately obvious that he was wasting his time. There was no five-foot bundle wrapped in oilskins as Francesca had described.

The Madonna was carved out of ebony, a heavy wood, but one that would float, and he drifted up through the waving blankets, pulling them to one side, searching desperately, but he was wasting his time.

Back outside, he grabbed for the stern rail and floated there like some strange sea creature, his webbed feet hanging down. Perhaps Francesca had been wrong. Maybe her brother had moved it to some other place in the launch. And there was always the chance that it had been blown clear in the explosion.

He decided to start again, working his way from one end of the launch to the other. But first he had to let Orsini know what had happened.

He surfaced a few feet away from the dinghy and went under again in the same moment. Orsini was standing with his back to him, hands above his head. On the far side of the dinghy was

133

a flat-bottomed marsh punt, an outboard motor at its stern. Its occupants were three Albanians in drab and dirty uniforms, on their peaked caps the red star of the Army of the Republic. Two of them menaced Orsini and Francesca with submachine guns while the third was in the act of stepping across.

Chavasse went under the dinghy in a shallow dive as submachine gun fire churned the water where he had surfaced. His aqualung scraped the bottom of the punt and he reached up, grabbed the thwart and pulled the frail craft completely over.

One of the soldiers sprawled against him, legs thrashing in a panic, and Chavasse slipped an arm around his neck and took him into deep water. His legs scraped painfully against the stern rail of the *Teresa* and he hung on with one hand, tightening his grip.

The soldier's face twisted to one side, hands clawing back, wrenching the breathing tube from his assailant's mouth. Chavasse tightened his lips and hung on. The man's limbs moved in slow motion, weakening perceptibly, until suddenly he stopped struggling altogether.

Chavasse released his grip and the body spun away from him.

The sand at the bottom of the lagoon had churned into a great cloud and he clamped the mouthpiece of his breathing tube between his teeth and struck out for the surface. Above him, there was a tremendous disturbance, limbs thrashing together in a violent struggle.

He came up into the centre of it, pulling his knife from his sheath, and struck out at a dim, khaki-clad shape. The soldier bucked agonizingly, shoving Chavasse away so that he broke through to the surface.

A couple of yards away from him, a fifteen-foot motorboat bumped against the dinghy. He was aware of Francesca struggling in the grip of two soldiers, of Orsini floating against the hull, blood on his face.

A soldier rushed to the rail, machine-gun levelled, and a man in a dark leather coat with a high fur collar ran forward and knocked the barrel to one side, the bullets discharging themselves harmlessly in the sky.

'Alive! I want him alive!'

For one brief moment, Chavasse looked up

into Adem Kapo's excited face, then he jack-knifed and went down through the water, his webbed feet driving him towards the edge of the lagoon. He swam into the reeds, forcing his way through desperately. A few moments later, he surfaced. Behind him, he could hear voices calling excitedly and then the engine of the motorboat coughed into life.

He broke through into the main channel, moved straight across it into a narrow tributary and started to swim for his life.

10

The motorboat turned out of a side channel into the main stream of the Buene River, the dinghy trailing behind on a line. In the stern, four soldiers huddled together, smoking cigarettes and talking in low tones. The bodies of their two comrades, killed in the lagoon by Chavasse, lay under a tarpaulin beside them.

Orsini was handcuffed to the rail and seemed half unconscious, his head roughly bandaged where a rifle butt had struck him a glancing blow. There was no sign of Francesca Minetti, but Adem Kapo paced the foredeck, impatiently smoking a cigarette, the fur collar of his hunting jacket turned up.

Orsini watched him, eyes half-closed, and after a while another man appeared from the companionway. He was as big as Orsini, with a scarred, brutal face, and wore the uniform of a colonel in the Army of the Albanian Republic with the green insignia of the Intelligence Corps on his collar.

Kapo turned on him, eyes like black holes in the white face. 'Well?'

The colonel shrugged. 'She isn't being very helpful.'

The anger blazed out of the little man like a searing flame. 'You said it would work, damn you. That all we had to do was wait and they'd walk right into the net. What in the hell am I supposed to tell them in Tirana?'

'What do you think he's going to do, swim out of here?' The big man laughed coldly. 'We'll run him down, never fear. A night out on his own in a place like this will shrink him down to size.'

'Let's hope you're right.'

Kapo walked across to Orsini, looked down at him for a moment, then kicked him in the side. Orsini continued to feign unconsciousness. Kapo turned away and resumed his pacing.

* * *

As the motorboat rounded a point of land jutting from the mist into the river, Chavasse parted the reeds carefully. He stood up to his chest in water no more than fifteen yards away as it passed, and his trained eyes took in everything – Orsini and the soldiers, Kapo standing in the prow, the cigarette holder jutting from a corner of his mouth.

The most interesting thing was the presence of Tashko. When Chavasse had last encountered him, he had been dressed like any seaman off the Taranto waterfront; now he wore the uniform of a colonel in the Albanian Intelligence Corps, which explained a lot. Beyond him, through the deckhouse window, Chavasse could just see the head and shoulders of Haji, the knife man, standing at the wheel.

The motorboat passed into the mist and he waded on to a piece of comparatively dry land to take stock of the situation. The stench of the marsh filled his nostrils and the bitter cold ate into his bones.

There was a hell of a lot about the whole affair that didn't make sense, but the basic situation was obvious enough. Adem Kapo was no ordinary agent, but someone a lot more important than that. Probably a high-ranking *Sigurmi* officer. He'd have to be to have a Colonel of Intelligence taking orders from him.

In any event, he was a man who knew what he was doing. He'd obviously sailed straight for the Buene from Matano and his twenty-four-hour start had given him the time he'd needed to reach Tama and organize a suitable reception.

The *Buona Esperanza* must have been under observation from the moment it hit the coast, and tracking the dinghy would have been no great trick to men who knew the marshes.

He wondered what had happened to Carlo. He too was probably on his way to Tama by now. It was the only sizeable town in the area and certain to be Kapo's base.

The engine of the motorboat faded into the distance and he slid into the water and started to swim after it. Within an hour at the outside, they'd be out in force looking for him, probably concentrating their search towards the coast.

Under the circumstances, Tama would probably be a whole lot safer. At least there would be houses scattered along the river bank, and where there were houses there were dry clothes and food. There might even be a chance of doing something about the others, although he didn't hold out much hope of that.

About fifteen minutes later, the air in his aqualung ran out. He surfaced quickly and waded from the river into the reeds. He pulled off his rubber flippers, unbuckled the heavy aqualung and let it sink into the ooze.

He went forward through the reeds and the wildfowl called as they lifted from the water, disturbed by his passing. After a while he came out on higher ground and moved on through the mist, keeping the river on his left.

It was hard going through mud flats and marsh, and he constantly had to wade across narrow creeks, often sinking up to his waist in thick, glutinous mud. The salt water stung his eyes painfully and the intense cold steadily drove every trace of warmth from his body until his limbs had lost all feeling.

He moved into the grey curtain and the ground became firmer and he found himself stumbling across firm sand and springy marsh grass. He paused on a small hillock, head turned slightly to one side. He could smell woodsmoke, heavy and pungent on the air, drifting before the wind.

A narrow arm of the river encircled a small island and a low house looked from the mist. There was no sign of life and no boat was moored at the narrow wooden jetty. Probably the home of a fisherman or wildfowler out at his traps. Chavasse moved upstream, disturbing a wild duck, and walked into the river, allowing the current to sweep him in towards the island.

He landed in the reeds and moved through them carefully, drawing his knife. The house was no more than twenty yards away, a poor-enough-looking place of rough-hewn logs with a shingle roof and stone chimney.

Two or three scrawny hens picked apathetically at the soil and scattered as he moved across the patch of open ground. The back door was simply several heavy wooden planks nailed together, and it opened with a protesting groan as he unfastened the chain which held it.

He moved into a small dark room that was obviously some sort of kitchen. There was a cupboard, a rough table and a pail of fresh water at the side of the door. The living room was furnished with a table and several chairs. There were two or three cupboards, and a skin rug covered the wooden floor in front of the stone hearth on which logs burned fitfully, heavily banked by ashes.

He crouched to the warmth, spreading his hands, and a cold wind seemed to touch the side of his face. A voice said quietly, 'Easy now. Hands behind your neck and don't try anything stupid.'

He came up slowly. There was a soft footstep and the hard barrel of a gun was pushed against his back. As a hand reached for the hilt of the knife at his waist, he pivoted to the left, swinging away from the gun barrel. There was a cry of dismay as they came together and fell heavily to the floor. Chavasse raised his right arm to bring down the edge of his hand.

He paused. His opponent was a young girl, perhaps nineteen or twenty, certainly no more. She wore a heavy waterproof hunting jacket, corduroy breeches and leather knee boots and her dark hair was close-cropped like a young boy's, the skin sallow over high cheekbones, the eyes dark brown. She was not beautiful and yet she would have stood out in any crowd.

'Now there's a thing,' he said softly and sat back. For a moment, she lay there, eyes widening in surprise and then, in a flash, she was on her feet again like a cat, the hunting rifle in her hands.

She stood there, feet apart, the barrel steady on his chest, and he waited. The barrel wavered, sank slowly. She leaned the rifle against the table and examined him curiously. Her eyes took in his bare feet, the shirt and trousers that were clinging to his body.

She nodded. 'You're on the run, aren't you? Where from? The chain gang at Tama?'

He shook his head. 'I'm on the run all right, angel, but not from there.'

She scowled and reached for the rifle again. 'You're no *gegh*, that's for sure. You speak like a *tosk* from the big city.'

Chavasse was aware of the enmity which still existed between the two main racial groups in Albania: the *geghs* of the north with their loyalty to family and tribe, and the *tosks* of the south from whom Communism had sprung.

There were times when a man had to play a hunch and this was one of them. His face split into the charming smile that was one of his greatest assets and he raised a hand as the rifle was turned again.

'Neither *gegh* nor *tosk*. I'm an outlander.'

Her face was a study of bewilderment. 'An outlander? From where? Yugoslavia?'

He shook his head. 'Italy.'

Understanding dawned. 'Ah, a smuggler.'

'Something like that. We were surprised by the military. I managed to get away. I think they've taken my friends to Tama.' She stood watching him, a thoughtful frown on her face, and he made the final gesture and held out his hand. 'Paul Chavasse.'

'French?' she said.

'And English. A little of both.'

She made her decision and her hand reached for his. 'Liri Kupi.'

'There was a *gegh* chieftain called Abas Kupi, leader of the *Legaliteri*, the royalist party.'

'Head of our clan. He fled to Italy after the Communists murdered most of his friends at a so-called friendship meeting.'

'You don't sound as if you care for Hoxha and his friends very much?'

'Hoxha?'

She spat vigorously and accurately into the fire.

11

Chavasse stood on a rush mat beside the large bed and rubbed himself down with a towel until his flesh glowed. He dressed quickly in the clothes Liri had provided: corduroy trousers, a checked wool shirt and knee-length leather boots a size too large, so he took them off again and pulled on an extra pair of socks.

The clothes had belonged to her brother. Conscripted into the army at eighteen, he had been killed in one of the many patrol clashes that took place almost daily along the Yugoslavian border. Her father had died fighting with the royalist party, in the mountains in the last year of the war. Since the death of her mother, she had lived alone in the marshes where she had been born and bred, earning her living from wildfowling.

She was crouched at the fire when he went back into the living room, stirring something in a large pot suspended from a hook. She turned and smiled, pushing back the hair from her forehead.

'All you need now is some food inside you.'

He pulled a chair to the table as she spooned a hot stew on to a tin plate. He wasted no time on conversation, but picked up his spoon and started to eat. When the plate was empty, she filled it again.

He sat back with a sigh. 'They couldn't have done better at the London Hilton.'

She opened a bottle and filled a glass with a colourless liquid. 'I'd like to offer you some coffee, but it's very hard to come by these days. This is a spirit we distil ourselves. Very potent if you're not used to it, but it can be guaranteed to keep out the marsh fever.'

It exploded in Chavasse's stomach and spread through his body in a warm glow. He coughed several times and tears sprang to his eyes.

'Now this they wouldn't be able to offer, even at the London Hilton.'

She opened an old tin carefully and offered

him a cigarette. They were Macedonian, coarse, brown tobacco loose in the paper, but Chavasse knew how to handle them. He screwed the end round expertly and leaned across the table as she held out a burning splinter from the fire.

She lit a cigarette herself, blew out a cloud of pungent smoke and said calmly, 'You're no smuggler, I can see that. No seaman, either. Your hands are too nice.'

'So I lied.'

'You must have had a good reason.'

He frowned down into his glass for a moment, then decided to go ahead. 'You've heard of the Virgin of Scutari?'

'The Black Madonna? Who hasn't? Her statue disappeared about three months ago. Everyone thinks the government in Tirana had it stolen. They're worried because people have been turning to the church again lately.'

'I came to the Buene looking for it,' Chavasse said. 'It was supposed to be on board a launch which sank in one of the lagoons in the marsh towards the coast. My friends and I were searching for it when the military turned up.'

He told her about Francesca Minetti, or as

much as she needed to know, and of Guilio Orsini and Carlo and the *Buona Esperanza*. When he was done, she nodded slowly.

'A bad business. The *Sigurmi* will squeeze them dry, even this smuggler friend of yours. They have their ways and they are not pleasant. I'm sorry for the girl. God knows what they will do with her.'

'I was wondering whether it would be possible to get into Tama,' Chavasse said. 'Perhaps find out what's happened to them.'

She looked at him sharply, her face grave. 'We have a saying. *Only a fool puts his head between the jaws of the tiger.*'

'They'll be beating the marshes towards the coast,' he said. 'That stands to reason. Who's going to look for me in Tama?'

'A good point.' She got to her feet and looked down into the fire, her hand on the stone mantel above it. She turned to face him. 'There is one person who might be able to help, a Franciscan named Father Shedu. In the war he was a famous resistance fighter in the hills, a legend in his own time. It would hardly be polite to arrest or shoot such a man. They content themselves with making life difficult for him – always with the utmost politeness, of course. He hasn't been here long. A couple of months or so. I think the last man was taken away.'

'I could make a good guess about what happened to him,' Chavasse said. 'This Father Shedu, he's in Tama now?'

'There's a mediaeval monastery on the outskirts of the town. They use it as local military headquarters. The Catholic church has been turned into a restaurant, but there's an old monastery chapel at the water's edge. Father Shedu holds his services there.'

'Would it be difficult to reach?'

'From here?' she shrugged. 'Not more than half an hour. I have an outboard motor. Not too reliable, but it gets me there.'

'Could I borrow it?'

'Oh, no.' She shook her head. 'They'd pick you up before you'd got a mile along the river. I know the back ways – you don't.'

She took down an oilskin jacket from behind the door and tossed it to him, together with an old peaked cap. 'Ready when you are.'

She picked up her hunting rifle and led the way

out through the front door and down towards
the river. There was still no boat moored at
the little wooden jetty. She passed it, moving
through dense undergrowth, and emerged on
to a small cleared bank which dropped cleanly
into the water. Her boat, a flat-bottomed marsh
punt with an old motor attached to the stern,
was tied to a tree.

Chavasse cast off while she busied herself
with the motor. As it coughed into life, he
pushed the punt through the encircling reeds
and stepped in.

Liri Kupi certainly knew what she was doing.
At one point, they hit rough water where the
river twisted round sandbanks, spilling across
ragged rocks, and she handled the frail craft
like an expert, swinging the tiller at just the
right moment to sweep them away from the
worst hazards.

After a while, they left the Buene, turning into
a narrow creek which circled through a great
stagnant swamp, losing itself among a hundred
lagoons and waterways.

When they finally came into the river again, it was in the lee of a large island. The mist hung like a grey curtain from bank to bank, and as they moved from the shelter of the island to cross over he could smell woodsmoke, and somewhere a dog barked.

The first houses loomed out of the mist, scattered along one side of the river, and Liri took the punt in close. She produced the tin of cigarettes from her pocket and threw it to Chavasse.

'Better have one. Try to look at home.'

'Home was never like this.'

He lit a cigarette, leaned back against the prow and watched the town unfold itself. There were fewer than five hundred inhabitants these days, that much he knew. Since the cold war had warmed up between Yugoslavia and Albania, the river traffic had almost stopped and the Buene was now so silted up as to be unnavigable for boats of any size.

The monastery lifted out of the mist, a vast sprawling mediaeval structure with crumbling walls, several hundred yards back from the river bank.

The Albanian flag, hanging limply in the rain, lifted in a gust of wind, the red star standing out vividly against the black, double-headed eagle, and a bugle sounded faintly.

A little further along the bank, forty or fifty convicts worked, some of them waist-deep in water as they drove in the piles for a new jetty. Chavasse noticed that the ones on the banks had their ankles chained together.

'Politicals,' Liri said briefly. 'They send them here from all over the country. They don't last long in the marshes when the hot weather comes.'

She eased the tiller, turning the punt in towards the bank and a small ruined chapel whose crumbling walls fell straight into the river. At the foot of the wall the entrance to a narrow tunnel gaped darkly, and Liri took the punt inside.

There was a good six feet of headroom and Chavasse reached out to touch cold, damp walls, straining his eyes into the darkness, which suddenly lightened considerably. Liri cut the motor, and the punt drifted in towards a landing stage constructed of large blocks of worked masonry.

They scraped beside a flight of stone steps and

Chavasse tied up to an iron ring and handed her out. Light filtered down from somewhere above and she smiled through the half-darkness.

'I won't be long.'

She mounted a flight of stone steps and Chavasse lit another cigarette, sat on the edge of the jetty and waited. She was gone for at least fifteen minutes. When she returned, she didn't come all the way down, but called to him from the top of the steps.

He went up quickly and she turned, opened a large oak door and led the way along a narrow passage. She opened another door at the far end and they stepped into the interior of the small chapel.

The lights were very dim and, down by the altar, the candles flickered and the Holy Mother was bathed in light. The smell of incense was overpowering and Chavasse felt a little giddy. It was a long time since he had been in church – too long, as his mother was never tired of reminding him – and he smiled wryly as they moved down the aisle.

Father Shedu knelt in prayer at the altar, the brown habit dark and sombre in the candlelight.

His eyes were closed, the worn face completely calm, and somehow the ugly puckered scar of the old bullet wound that had carried away the left eye seemed completely in character.

He was a man strong in his faith, certain in his knowledge of that which was ultimately important. Men like Enver Hoxha and Adem Kapo would come and go, ultimately to break upon the rock that was Father Shedu.

He crossed himself, got to his feet in one smooth movement and turned to face them. Chavasse suddenly felt awkward under the keen scrutiny of that single eye. For a moment, he was a little boy again at his grandfather's village in Finistere just after the war when France was free again, standing before the old, implacable parish priest, trying to explain his absence from Mass, the tongue drying in his mouth.

Father Shedu smiled and held out his hand. 'I am happy to meet you, my son. Liri has told me something of why you are here.'

Chavasse shook hands, relief flowing through him. 'She seemed to think you might be able to help, Father.'

'I know something of what happened to the

statue of Our Lady of Scutari,' the priest said. 'It was my predecessor, Father Kupescu, who gave it into the charge of the young man who was later killed in the marshes. Father Kupescu has since paid for his actions with his life, I might add.'

'The girl who was with me was the young man's sister,' Chavasse said. 'She was the one who guided us to the position of Minetti's launch.'

Father Shedu nodded. 'She and an Italian named Orsini arrived in Tama earlier this afternoon. They were taken to the monastery.'

'Are you sure?'

'I was visiting sick prisoners at the time, one of the little privileges I still insist on.'

'I'm surprised you're allowed to function at all.'

Father Shedu smiled faintly. 'As you may have noticed, my name is the same as that of our beloved President, something for which the average party member holds me in superstitious awe. They can never be quite sure that I'm not some kind of third cousin, you see. There are things they can do, of course. We had a wonderful old church here. Now, it's a restaurant. They use the altar as a counter and the nave is crammed with tables at which the happy workers can consume *kebab* and *shashlik* to the greater glory of Enver Hoxha.'

'All things in their own good time, Father,' Chavasse said.

The priest smiled. 'As it happens, I *can* help you, Mr Chavasse. Your friends are at the moment imprisoned in the back guardroom, which is inside the inner wall of the monastery. A Colonel of Intelligence and a high *Sigurmi* official named Kapo, who brought them in, left again almost at once with every spare soldier they could lay their hands on.'

'To look for me.'

'Obviously. I shouldn't think there will be more than one man on duty at the guardroom – perhaps two.'

'But how could we get in, Father?' Liri demanded. 'There are two walls to pass through and guards on each gate.'

'We go under, my dear. The good fathers who built this monastery thought of everything. Come with me.'

He led the way out of the chapel and back along the passage to the door that led down to the landing stage. He took an electric torch from a ledge on which an ikon stood and went down to the water's edge. When he switched on the torch, its beam played against the rough walls of the tunnel, which ran on into the darkness, narrowing considerably.

'The monastery's sewage system comes down through here to empty into the river,' he said. 'Not a pleasant journey, I'm afraid, but one that will take you inside the walls without being seen.'

'Show me the way, that's all I ask, Father,' Chavasse said. 'You can leave the rest to me.'

'To require you not to use violence against violent men would be absurd,' Father Shedu said, 'but you must understand that I myself could not possibly take part in any such action. You accept this?'

'Willingly.'

The priest turned to Liri. 'You will stay here, child?'

She shook her head. 'There may be a use for me. Please, Father. I know what I'm doing.'

He didn't bother to argue, but hitched his trailing robes into the leather belt at his waist and stepped into the water on the left-hand side of the tunnel. It was no more than ankle-deep and Chavasse followed along a broad ledge, his head lowered as the roof dropped to meet them.

There was a strong earthy smell and a slight mist curled from the water, fanning out against the damp roof. The tunnel stretched into the darkness and gradually the water became deeper until he could feel it swirling about his knees.

By now the stench was appalling and he stumbled on, his stomach heaving. Finally, the priest turned into a side passage which came out into a cavern about fifty feet in diameter.

It was some three feet deep in stinking water and at least a dozen tunnels emptied into it. The Franciscan waded across and counted from the left.

'I think the eighth will be the one.'

The tunnel was no more than four feet high and Chavasse paused at the entrance and reached out to Liri. 'Are you all right?'

'Fine.' She chuckled. 'The swamps stink worse than this lot in the summer.'

They bent double and went after Father Shedu, who was now several yards ahead. A few moments later, he stopped. Light filtered down through some sort of grille and a short tunnel sloped up towards the surface.

'If I am right,' the priest said, 'we should be in a cell of the old cloisters behind the square containing the guardhouse.'

The tunnel was a good fifty feet in length, the stonework smooth and slippery, making it difficult to climb. The priest went first, Liri next and Chavasse brought up the rear. He jammed himself between the narrow walls, working his way up foot by foot. Once, Liri slipped, falling back against him, but he managed to hold her and they continued.

Above them, Father Shedu was already at the entrance, a large slab which had been carved by some master craftsman into a stone grille. He put his shoulder to it and it slid back easily. He climbed out and turned to give Liri a hand.

Chavasse clambered up after them and found himself in a small crumbling cell with a gaping doorway which opened into half-ruined cloisters, broken pillars lifting into the sky, grass growing between great, cracked stone slabs.

'Through the cloisters and you will come to the square,' Father Shedu said. 'The guardroom is a small flat-roofed building of brick and concrete.' A slight smile touched his mouth. 'From here, you are on your own. There is nothing more I can do for you. As I said earlier, I must not play any active part in this affair. I will wait here.' He turned to Liri. 'You will stay with me?'

She shook her head stubbornly. 'There may be something I can do. Something to help.'

'Father Shedu's right,' Chavasse said. 'You stay.'

'If you want my gun, then you take me.' She patted the stock of the old hunting rifle. 'That's my final word.'

Chavasse looked at the priest, who sighed heavily. 'She's got a will of iron, I'm afraid, and she hates the Reds.'

Chavasse said to Liri, 'You can come as far as the edge of the square. You watch from there while I go in. If anything goes wrong, you'll have plenty of time to join Father Shedu and get clear. All right?'

He moved out across the ruined courtyard and through the cloisters to the crumbling wall on the far side. The square stretched before him, quiet and still. The guardhouse was built against the wall halfway along the other side, just as Father Shedu had described, a difficult place to come at from the front. In the far wall, great double gates leading to the outer square were closed.

Chavasse turned to Liri. 'You stay here. I'm going to work my way round the wall so that I come in from the other side where there are no windows. If anything happens, get out of there fast and back to Father Shedu.' She started to protest, but he pulled the rifle firmly from her grasp. 'Now be a good girl and do as you're told.'

He moved along behind the ruined wall to the point where it joined the other, stepped into the open and ran, half-crouching, until he reached the side of the guardhouse. He paused, conscious of the sweat soaking his shirt, and started forward. At that moment the guardhouse door opened and someone stepped out.

Chavasse heard voices, two men talking. One

of them laughed and a match was struck. He was trapped with no place to run. If one of them took a step to the corner of the building, he was certain to be discovered.

A fresh young voice called, 'Hey, you there! Yes, you, you great ox. Come here!'

Liri Kupi strolled calmly across the square, her hands in her pockets. Her intention was obviously to attract the attention of the guards and she succeeded perfectly. As Chavasse went along the side of the guardhouse, two soldiers moved out to meet Liri.

They weren't even armed and one of them was stripped to the waist, as if he had been having a wash. Chavasse ran forward, raised the rifle and rammed it down hard against an exposed neck. As the soldier crumpled with a groan, the other swung round. Chavasse swung the barrel into the man's stomach. He keeled over, and the butt of the rifled smashed his skull.

Chavasse was already moving towards the door when Liri arrived on the run, her face flushed. 'There can't be anyone else. They'd have come out when I called.'

'Let's hope you're right.'

The outer office was quiet, papers scattering across the desk in the wind which blew in through the doorway. Keys hung on a board on the far wall. Chavasse moved across quickly and opened the inner door. There were only six cells. The first four were empty. Guilio Orsini was in the fifth, sprawled on a narrow bunk, head on hands.

'Now then, you old bastard,' Chavasse said amiably.

The Italian sat up, an expression of astonishment on his face. He jumped to his feet and crossed to the grille. 'Paul, by all that's holy! You go in for miracles now?'

'Ask and ye shall receive,' Chavasse said. 'You'll never know just how apt that quotation is. Where's Francesca?'

'Next door. We've been here ever since we arrived. Kapo took off again in something of a hurry. Presumably to chase you.'

'He's out of luck.'

Liri was beside him with the keys. As she released Orsini, Chavasse was already at the next grille. Francesca Minetti stood there, eyes like dark holes in the white face.

'I knew you'd come, Paul.'

He took the keys from Liri and unlocked the cell. Francesca came straight into his arms. He held her close for a moment, then pushed her away.

'We've got to get moving.'

Orsini was already ahead of them, following Liri, and Chavasse picked up the rifle and pushed Francesca along the passage. The Italian paused in the doorway and looked out into the square.

'Seems quiet enough.'

The noise of the siren rising through the still air was like a physical blow, numbing the senses. Chavasse swung round and saw Francesca on the other side of the room. She had opened a small metal box on the wall and her thumb was pressed firmly against a scarlet button.

He pulled her away so violently that she staggered back against the desk. 'What the hell are you doing?'

In answer, she spat in his face and slapped him heavily across the left cheek. In an instinctive reflex action, he returned the blow with his clenched fist, knocking her to the floor.

She lay there moaning softly and Orsini grabbed Chavasse by the sleeve, pulling him round, 'For God's sake, what's going on?'

A single shot echoed across the square, splintering the doorpost, and Orsini ducked, pulling Liri to the floor. Chavasse looked out through the window and saw a movement on the wall above the great gates. Another rifle shot was followed by the rapid stutter of a submachine gun, and a line of bullets kicked a cloud of dust into the air in a brown curtain.

He smashed the window with the butt end of the hunting rifle, aimed quickly and fired. There was a faint cry and a soldier pitched over the parapet and fell, still clutching his rifle.

One of the two guards lying in the square pushed himself onto his knees, an expression of bewilderment on his face. Chavasse shot him through the head and ducked out of sight as the man's comrades started to concentrate on the window.

He moved to the doorway and crouched beside Orsini and the girl. 'There must be half a dozen of them up there now and more on the way. I'm going to draw their fire. It might give you and Liri a chance. She knows the way. Just do as she says.'

Orsini opened his mouth to protest, but Chavasse was already running into the square. He flung himself down beside the body of the guard he had shot, took aim and started to fire at the men on the wall.

Behind him, Orsini and the girl emerged from the guardhouse and started to run. It was at precisely that moment that the great double doors on the far side of the square swung open. An engine burst into life and a jeep roared through in a cloud of dust. A light machine-gun was mounted on a swivel in the rear, and Colonel Tashko swung it in a half arc, a line of bullets churning the dust into fountains beside Orsini and the girl, bringing them to a halt, hands held high.

Chavasse, the heart freezing inside him, saw a detail of soldiers come through the gate, rifles at the port. In the moment that the jeep braked, slewing broadside on, Francesca staggered past him and lurched towards it. Chavasse jumped to his feet and fired the hunting rifle from the hip as he ran.

His first shot kicked up dirt a foot to one side of her and then something punched him in the left arm, spinning him round, the rifle flying from his grasp. He crouched like an animal, holding his arm tightly, blood oozing between the fingers, and heard boots crunch through the dirt in the sudden silence.

When he raised his eyes, Adem Kapo looked down at him, a slight smile fixed to the small mouth.

12

Rain drifted in through the bars of the window and Chavasse pulled himself up and looked out across the monastery walls towards the river. He was immediately aware of the pain in his left arm and dropped with a curse.

The bullet had passed through cleanly, a flesh wound, and the only treatment he had so far received was to have it bandaged. They were in some sort of store room on the second floor of the main building. Liri Kupi slept in the corner, a blanket hitched over her shoulders.

Orsini crouched beside her to straighten the blanket. When he rose to his feet, there was a strange expression on his face. 'Quite a girl. A pity she had to get mixed up in a thing like this.'

'As I've already explained, she wasn't supposed to.' Chavasse walked to the door and peered through the grille at the guard outside. 'God, what a fool I've been and I never saw it.'

'Francesca?' Orsini shook his head. 'I still can't believe it.'

'She said the Madonna was in the forward cabin and it wasn't, and remember we had to blast our way in. How do you get round that?' He kicked a packing case savagely. 'The little bitch. That night outside the Tabu when she was attacked. They must have been waiting for me to show. The whole thing was laid on for my benefit.'

'But why?' Orsini demanded. 'It doesn't make sense. And what happened to the Madonna?'

'That's one thing I'd like to know myself. That part of the story was genuine enough, because Father Shedu confirmed it. At least they don't seem to have laid hands on him, which is a good thing.'

A key rattled in the lock and the door was flung open. Liri came awake and scrambled to her feet as two soldiers moved into the room, followed by Tashko. He examined the girl and smiled.

'I'll come to you later.'

She spat in his face and he reached out, quick as a snake, and grabbed her shoulder. As Orsini and Chavasse started forward, the soldiers raised their machine pistols threateningly.

Tashko's face was expressionless as his thumb expertly pressed a nerve against bone. Liri's mouth opened in a cry and she crumpled to the floor. He turned to Chavasse, adjusting his leather gloves.

'Karate, my friend. You were lucky with the vodka bottle. Next time, all the luck will be mine – this I promise you.'

He nodded and one of the soldiers grabbed Chavasse by the shoulder and dragged him outside. He had a quick glimpse of Orsini dropping to one knee beside the girl, and then the door closed.

They took him along the wide stone-flagged passage and up a narrow circular staircase at the far end. Tashko opened a door at the top and led the way into a comfortably furnished office.

Adem Kapo sat behind a desk, reading through some papers. He glanced up and a smile flashed across his face. 'You'll never know just how much of a pleasure this is. We've been most anxious to lay hands on you since that little affair in Tirana the other week.'

'*Sigurmi?*'

Kapo nodded. 'My Italian front is only one of many, as I'm sure you'll appreciate.'

'So the business in Matano? It was all a fix? No Ramiz? No Marco Minetti?'

'Ramiz was just a little blood on the floor and a bribe to the young woman who lived across the hall from his room. Minetti was a figment of the imagination.'

'Which explains why Francesca was so insistent that I didn't disclose what was going on in Rome.'

Kapo nodded. 'The story was genuine enough. It was played out by a high-minded young Italian named Carveggio who tried the same trick and got his head blown off for his pains.'

'And the statue?'

'We recovered it from the wreck almost immediately.'

He nodded to Tashko, who went to a cupboard, opened it and took out a shapeless bundle. He unwrapped a grey blanket and set the statue on the desk.

She was perhaps four feet high and carved from a single piece of ebony, her robes inlaid with gold. The features carried an expression of wonderful serenity and peace. It was a supreme achievement by some great unknown artist.

'All right,' Chavasse said. 'In all its essential details, the story handed me by Francesca Minetti was true and it did what it was supposed to do – it got me back into Albania. Which means you went to a hell of a lot of trouble – why?'

Kapo selected a cigarette from a wooden box on the desk and leaned back in his chair. 'As you may know, relations between my own poor country and the USSR and its satellites have somewhat deteriorated over the past few years. In our trouble, only one friend came to our aid – China.'

'How touching.'

'We are a sentimental people, I assure you. We like to pay our debts. The report from our counter-intelligence section, which contained the information that you intended to enter our country as a member of an Italian workers' holiday group, was passed on to Chinese Intelligence

Headquarters in Tirana as a matter of courtesy. They expressed great interest. Apparently you did them some disservice in Tibet last year. Something to do with a Doctor Hoffner, I understand. We promised to let them have you.'

'And then I slipped through your fingers.'

'But not for long, you must agree, and thanks to only one person. An extremely able member of the counter-intelligence section of the *Sigurmi*. Perhaps you'd like to meet her?'

When Tashko opened the door she came in at once. She was still in the clothes she had worn on the boat, but looked different. Harder, more assured.

'Why, Francesca?' he said.

'I am as much Albanian as I am Italian,' she said calmly. 'You can't have a foot in both worlds. I chose mine long ago.'

'You mean you've been working for the other side ever since the Bureau took you on?'

'How did you think our people in Tirana knew you were coming? I only transmitted that radio warning from Scutari because the night duty officer was present when it came in.'

And then it really hit him for the first time.

Someone from the other side had been sitting at the very heart of things, with a top security rating, for two years, passing on the information men had sweated and died for, perhaps even sending them to their deaths.

Something of this must have shown on his face, and she smiled slightly. 'Oh, yes, Paul, I have accomplished great things. Remember Matt Sorley and the Frenchman, Dumont? Neither of them lasted long, I saw to that. And there were others.'

'You lousy bitch.'

'You killed my husband, Paul,' she said calmly, and a cold hatred blazed from her eyes.

'Your husband?' He frowned slightly and shook his head. 'I don't know what you're talking about. In any case, I've seen your personal file. There was no mention of any marriage.'

'Not a difficult thing to keep quiet about if one goes the right way about it. His name was Enrico Noci. You drowned him like a rat in a fishing net. No marks, no violence. Just an accident.'

'Which I must say was really damned ingenious of you,' Kapo put in.

There was obviously nothing more to say and

Chavasse turned from her to the little man. 'What happens now? A quick flight to Peking?'

'No rush.' Kapo grinned. 'We've all the time in the world and there's so much you could tell me. How on earth you managed to get inside the monastery, for example. Of course that was the idea – that you should show up. We were quite certain that a man of your resource and energy wouldn't leave his friends in the lurch, but to be perfectly honest your sudden materialization out of thin air was even more impressive than I'd figured on.'

'A trick I picked up from an old fakir in India years ago.'

'Fascinating. You can tell me all about it when I return. If you can't, I'm sure Tashko can persuade the young lady you picked up on your travels to be more cooperative.'

Chavasse ignored the threat and calmly helped himself to a cigarette from the box on the desk. 'You're going somewhere?'

'Didn't I explain?' Kapo took another cigarette, lit it and tossed the matches across to Chavasse. They might have been good friends enjoying a pleasant conversation. 'It's really rather ingenious, though I do say it myself. At this moment, your young friend Arezzi is sitting on the *Buona Esperanza* awaiting your return.'

Which didn't make sense at all. Chavasse was unable to suppress a slight frown and Kapo smiled. 'Later tonight, I shall take Francesca in the motorboat to within a reasonable distance of the launch. In the grey light of dawn, she will float out of the mist in your dinghy, in a distressed condition, I might add.'

'And with an even more distressing story to tell.'

'Of course. They'll be most upset back in Rome when they hear they've lost the gallant Chavasse and his friend Orsini.'

'And you think they'll accept Francesca back into the fold without a question?' Chavasse shook his head. 'My boss would never believe it. He'll check every step she's taken since she was six months old.'

'I wouldn't be too sure.' Kapo smiled. 'You see she'll have the Black Madonna with her, such a lovely stroke of propaganda against Albania. Everyone will be so pleased.'

And he was right. It was good. Kapo started to laugh and nodded to Tashko. 'Take him back to his friends. I'll deal with him when I return in the morning.'

Chavasse turned to face Francesca. She held his gaze for a moment, then looked away and Tashko gave him a push towards the door. They went down the stairs and back along the corridor.

Just before they reached the store room again, Tashko paused to light a long Russian cigarette. The two soldiers waited respectfully a few paces away, obviously frightened to death of him, and he glared at Chavasse coldly.

'That one up there is a big man with words, but I have a different approach. Soon you will find this out.'

'Why don't you take a running jump,' Chavasse said calmly.

Rage flared in the cold eyes. Tashko took a step forward and restrained himself with obvious difficulty. There was a door to one side of Chavasse and, quite suddenly, the Albanian's right fist shot forward in a straight line in the terrible basic karate blow now known as the reverse punch. The inch-thick centre plank of the door splintered and sagged inwards.

There was a little Japanese professor whose

class Chavasse attended three times a week whenever he was in London, who could do the same thing to three planks at once and he was half Tashko's size. His words echoed faintly like an old tune: *Science, Chavasse-san. Science, not force. God did not intend the brute to lord it over the earth.*

'Try to imagine what that would have done to your face,' Tashko said.

'It's certainly a thought.'

Chavasse moved on along the passage. One of the soldiers unlocked the door and they pushed him inside. As it closed, he looked through the grille into Tashko's cold eyes.

The Albanian nodded. 'I'll be back.'

His footsteps died along the corridor and Chavasse turned to the others. Orsini was sitting by the window, an arm around Liri, and the blanket was draped over their shoulders. It was bitterly cold.

'What happened?' Orsini demanded.

Chavasse told him. When he had finished, Liri shook her head. 'She must be a devil, that one.'

'No, *cara*, no devil,' Orsini said. 'She is like

all her kind, convinced that she alone knows the ultimate truth of things. To achieve it, she believes anything to be permissible.'

'Which doesn't help any of us one little bit,' Chavasse said.

He went and sat on a packing case, turning up the collar of his jacket, and folded his arms to conserve what heat was left in his body, thinking about Francesca Minetti. So Enrico Noci had been her husband? Strange that a woman so obviously intelligent should fall for that sort of man.

Orsini and Liri were talking together in low voices, an intimacy between them. What was it someone had once said? A day told you as much about a person as ten years? Pity they'd had to meet under such circumstances.

How ironic that Guilio Orsini, the man who had penetrated the main harbour at Alexandria on one of the first underwater chariots, who had sunk two British destroyers, survivor of one desperate exploit after another through the years, should end like this because he had been touched by the apparent sorrow of a young girl. Life could be puzzling, all right. After a while, his head dropped forward on his breast and he slept.

13

Chavasse was not certain what had caused him to wake up, and he lay for a moment, staring through the darkness, conscious of the ache in his cramped muscles, of the bitter cold. His watch was still functioning and the luminous dial told him that it was two a.m. He sat there for a moment, aware of the wind howling across the square outside, and got to his feet.

There was movement in the corridor, and when he looked out through the grille he could see the sentry standing in front of his chair, a look of abject terror on his face. Colonel Tashko confronted him, hands on hips.

'So. You were sleeping, you worm.'

His hand lashed forward, catching the unfortunate sentry across the side of the face, sending him back across his chair with a crash. As the man scrambled to his feet, Tashko booted him along the corridor.

'Go on, get out of here! Report to the guard-house. I'll deal with you later.'

Orsini and Liri, awakened by the disturbance, came to the door. 'What is it?' Orsini demanded.

'Tashko,' Chavasse told him briefly. 'I think he's drunk.'

The Albanian moved to the door and looked through the grille at Chavasse. His tunic hung open and underneath he was naked to the waist, great muscles standing out like cords.

He unbuckled the black leather holster at his hip and took out a Mauser, then unlocked the door and opened it slowly. Liri took a step forward towards Orsini, whose arm encircled her at once.

'How touching,' Tashko said.

'It's been a long day and we'd like to get a little sleep,' Chavasse said. 'So kindly state your business and get the hell out of here.'

'Still full of fight?' Tashko said. 'That's the way I like it. Let's have you outside.'

'And what if I tell you to go to hell?'

'I shoot the girl through her left kneecap. A pity to waste good material, but there it is.'

Orsini took a step forward, but Chavasse pushed him back. 'Leave it, Guilio. My affair.' He moved into the corridor and Tashko slammed the door and locked it. 'I don't think Kapo's going to like this. He's saving me for Peking.'

'To hell with Peking,' Tashko said. 'In any case, I'm in charge now. Kapo and the girl left half an hour ago.'

He sent Chavasse staggering down the corridor and followed three feet behind, the Mauser ready for action. They went down a spiral staircase at the far end, turned along a broad stone passage and descended a flight of stone steps that seemed to go down forever.

At the bottom, Tashko produced his keys and unlocked an oak door, bound with bands of iron. Chavasse moved in and Tashko flicked a switch and locked the door behind them.

They stood at the top of a flight of broad stone steps and beneath them in the dim light of a couple of electric bulbs was an amazing sight. A great Roman plunge bath, perhaps a hundred feet long, stretched into the gloom flanked by broken pillars and the stumps of what must have been at one time well-proportioned colonnades. There was a strong sulphurous smell and steam drifted up from the water.

'Amazing what they got up to, the Romans,' Tashko said. 'Of course, the mediaeval fathers who built this monastery weren't too keen on such pagan survivals. They simply built over it.'

They went down the steps and crossed a cracked tessellated floor. The pool was about six feet deep, the water very still, and the face in the brightly coloured mosaic that was its floor gazed blindly up at him out of two thousand years of chaos.

'It's fed by a natural spring,' Tashko said. 'One hundred twenty degrees Fahrenheit. Quite pleasant. They say it's good for rheumatism.'

As Chavasse turned slowly, the Albanian slipped off his tunic and let it drop to the floor. He held up the keys in one hand, the Mauser in the other, then tossed them into the centre of the pool with a quick gesture.

'There's nothing to help you this time, my friend.'

So that was it? Was it simply a case of personal vanity on the part of a man so proud of his brute strength that he couldn't bear to be beaten by anyone? Chavasse stumbled back, as if panic-stricken. If Tashko thought him an easy mark, he might still do something stupid.

The Albanian moved forward, arms at his side, and laughed harshly. In the same moment he delivered a tremendous reverse punch, a karate blow that takes the uninitiated unawares because it is delivered with the hand that is on the same side as the rear foot.

Chavasse crossed his hands above his head to counter with the X-block, the *juji-uke*, and delivered a forward elbow strike in return that caught Tashko full in the mouth.

The Albanian staggered back, blood spurting from his crushed lips, and Chavasse grinned. 'A *gyaku-zuki* and badly delivered. Is that the best you can do?'

Tashko's face was twisted by anger, but he immediately dropped into the defensive position, adopting the cat stance, arms down inviting combat. Chavasse moved in, his right forearm vertical, the left protecting his body. They circled warily and Tashko made the first move.

He pushed the heel of his palm at his opponent's face, and as Chavasse blocked it, delivered a lightning punch to the stomach. Chavasse turned sideways, riding most of the force, and at the same moment fell to one side and delivered a roundhouse kick to the groin. The Albanian keeled over and Chavasse, throwing caution to the wind, raised a knee into the descending face.

He realized immediately that he had made a bad mistake. A blow that would have demolished any ordinary man only succeeded in shaking the Albanian's massive strength, and great hands clawed across his body, grabbing for his throat.

The lights seemed to be very far away and there was a sudden roaring in his ears, and through it he seemed to hear the professor's monotonous, sing-song voice. *Science – science and intelligence will beat brute force.*

He summoned every effort of willpower and spat full in that great stinking face and Tashko recoiled in a reflex action that was as natural as breathing. Chavasse stabbed upwards with stiffened fingers at the exposed throat and Tashko screamed and staggered back.

Chavasse rolled over several times and came to his feet as the big man lurched towards him, hands extended, all science forgotten. Chavasse ducked in under the hands, delivering a fore-fist punch, knuckles extended, and it sank into the muscles beneath Tashko's rib-cage. He started to fall and Chavasse raised his knee into the descending face, throwing him back.

Tashko swayed on the edge of the pool, his face a mask of blood, and Chavasse jumped high in the air, delivering a flying front kick, the devastating *mae-tobigeri*, into the Albanian's face, knocking him back into the water.

Chavasse followed him in, twisting in mid-air, going under awkwardly, the warm water drawing him down. His hands took the shock against a bearded mosaic face and he surfaced quickly.

Tashko was about twenty feet away, lurching towards the centre of the pool where he had thrown the Mauser, and Chavasse went after him. He scrambled up onto the great back, his hands sliding under the armpits, locking together at the nape of the neck. He started to press and Tashko screamed. All pity dying in him, Chavasse maintained his relentless pressure and the head sank down into the water.

The body bucked and heaved, hands flailing the surface into a cauldron, but Chavasse strengthened his grip and hung on. The end came with startling suddenness. Tashko simply went limp, and when Chavasse released his grip, the body planed down through the water, turning on its back when it reached bottom.

Chavasse took a quick breath and went after the Mauser. The keys were perhaps ten feet away and he had to push Tashko to one side to pick them up. The Albanian's eyes stared into eternity, blood drifting in brown strings from his smashed face, and Chavasse turned and swam for the side.

He sat on the edge for perhaps five minutes, his chest heaving, drawing air into his tortured lungs. When he felt a little better, he got to his feet and mounted the steps. He had to try four keys before he found the right one. As he opened the door, he looked down for the last time at Tashko, who stared up at him, just another figure in the mosaic now. He switched off the lights, closed the door and locked it.

The corridors were quiet and he met no one on his way back. Outside the store room, the chair on which the sentry had been sleeping still lay on its side, and he righted it before slipping the Mauser into his pocket and fumbling with the keys.

As he worked through them, Guilio Orsini appeared at the grille. He glanced up and down the passage and an expression of bewilderment appeared on his face.

'What happened to Tashko?'

'He made a mistake,' Chavasse said, swinging the door open. 'His last. Let's get going.'

He turned along the passage, remembering the way they had come. A stone spiral stair-case dropped to the first floor, another to the basement. All was quiet and he led the way along a narrow whitewashed corridor, pausing to reconnoitre the entrance hall at the end. There was no sentry, but then, why should there be? The building was encircled by two thirty-foot walls, the main gates in each being strongly guarded.

They had explained earlier to Orsini how they had gained access to the monastery and the big Italian followed Chavasse unhesitatingly, the girl at his side.

They kept to the shadow of the wall, skirting the square on the far side of the guardhouse where a light shone in the window, and entered the cloisters through a gap in the ruined wall. It was very dark and Chavasse moved through the pillars cautiously and turned into the passage containing the cells.

He had to try three before he found the one with the grille and it was Orsini who pulled it out, fingers fastening into the latticework like steel hooks.

'I'll go first,' Chavasse said. 'Then Liri. You follow, Guilio, and replace the grille as you come down.'

He shot down the stone chute on his back, forearms raised to protect his face, and landed in the tunnel below with a splash. Liri followed so quickly that she cannoned into him as he was getting to his feet. Orsini joined them a moment later and they crouched in a little group.

It was so dark in the tunnel that they couldn't

see each other's faces and Chavasse said quietly, 'This isn't going to be any picnic. Whatever happens, keep close together. As long as we can make it to the main channel, we can't go wrong because it's bound to flow in the direction of the river.'

'Anything's preferable to what we've just left,' Orsini said. 'Let's get moving.'

Chavasse started along the tunnel bent double, Liri holding on to the tail of his oilskin jacket. It was a strange, claustrophobic sensation, like nothing he had ever experienced before, and yet he wasn't frightened. The darkness was a friend, cloaking their flight, enfolding them in gentle hands, and he was grateful.

A few moments later, they emerged from the tunnel into the central cavern. He stood thigh deep in the stinking water, staring into the darkness.

'Father Shedu counted eight openings to the left from where we came out, Paul,' Liri said.

He nodded. 'Keep behind me, both of you. I've got an idea.'

He took out the Mauser, pointed it at the water and fired. In the single brilliant flash of light, the tunnel openings stood out like dark wounds. He fired again, counting quickly, then started across the pool.

His questing hand found the opening and he grunted.

Fifty yards further on, the passage emptied itself into the main tunnel and he could hear the splash and gurgling of the water on its way down to the river. Already the stench seemed to be lessening, and as he followed the wall Chavasse breathed deeply to clear the heaviness that weighed upon his brain.

The landing stage loomed out of the darkness, light flowing down from the candles burning at the ikon in the niche at the head of the stairs. Liri's punt was still tied to the bottom of the steps, and Chavasse sat on the edge of the landing stage and rubbed the back of one hand wearily across his eyes.

'How much juice you got in that thing? Enough to get us to the coast?'

'I think so. Most of the way, at least.'

'We still need a compass to get back to the *Buona Esperanza*,' Orsini said. 'At least if we're going to go now in the dark.'

'We can't afford to wait till dawn,' Chavasse said. 'That's when Kapo will send Francesca in the dinghy. If we're going to beat them to it, we must go now.'

'Father Shedu will have a compass,' Liri said. 'Wait here. I'll go and get him.'

She mounted the steps and the door closed behind her. Orsini slumped down beside Chavasse. 'Most girls would have had hysterics by now.'

'She'll have to come with us,' Chavasse said. 'She can't stay here.'

'What about an entry permit? I know what it's like for the stateless refugees.'

'Don't worry about that. I know the right people at the Ministry in Rome. We'll even find her a job. She's earned it.'

'Maybe she won't need a job.'

Chavasse glanced at him curiously. 'You make up your mind in a hurry, don't you?'

Orsini shrugged. 'You either know straight away, or it's no good. Of course, I've got twenty years on her.'

'I wouldn't let that worry you,' Chavasse said. 'She knows a man when she sees one.'

He sat there, his left arm aching like hell, his strength slowly ebbing, and after a while the door clicked open and Father Shedu came down the steps with Liri.

'So miracles can still happen,' he said as he moved forward.

'My friend, Guilio Orsini, Father,' Chavasse said. 'I'm glad you kept out of it back there. They still haven't got the slightest idea how we got inside.'

The priest poured brandy into a couple of tin mugs and handed a small basket to Liri. 'This isn't much, I'm afraid. Bread and cheese and some dried meat. The rich, full life is long in coming for the People's Republic.'

'We'll eat it on the way,' Chavasse said. He drank some of the brandy and coughed as it burned its way down his throat.

'Liri has told me what happened in there,' the priest said. 'It pains me to know this woman deceived you.'

'And she'll go on playing the same game unless we can manage to stop her,' Chavasse said. 'Liri thought you might have a compass.'

The priest held one forward, pressing a small

spring so that the lid flew open. Chavasse examined it, noting the inscription 'W.D. 1941' and the official broad arrow.

'British Army issue?'

'A souvenir from another life. Take it with my blessing.' He turned to Liri and placed a hand on her shoulder. 'And what happens to you, Liri?'

'She goes with us, Father,' Orsini said gruffly. 'I'll look after her.'

The priest gazed at him searchingly and then smiled. 'God moves in His own strange ways. Now go, all of you, while there is still time.'

They dropped into the boat and Liri took the tiller. The roaring of the engine seemed to fill the cavern when it broke into life and the boat turned away quickly.

As they moved through the dark entrance, Chavasse glanced back and saw the Franciscan still standing there watching them. A moment later, they swung into the main current and turned downstream through the darkness.

14

The river was angry, swollen by the rains flowing down from the mountains of the north, and it rushed towards the sea with more than usual force.

The frail punt shipped water constantly and Chavasse and Orsini took turns at bailing with an old tin basin. They ate the food the priest had provided and finished the bottle of brandy.

Chavasse sat in the prow, his collar turned up against the spray, and longed for a cigarette. He wondered what Kapo would do. Probably tie up further downriver till dawn. Then he would send Francesca in with the dinghy and Carlo would swallow every damned thing she said.

Perhaps half an hour later, the engine faltered and died abruptly. As the punt started to drift broadside-on in the strong current, Liri called,

'There are paddles under the seat. Keep her head round.'

Chavasse fumbled in the darkness and found two crude paddles. He leaned over the side and dug one deep into the water, using all his strength, and gradually the punt turned into the current.

Orsini scrambled to the stern and, after a struggle, managed to get the engine housing off. He started to try to trace the fault by touch alone, and after a while his sensitive fingers encountered a broken lead to one of the plugs. The wire was old and brittle and crumbled between his fingers, but he eventually managed to link it together and tried the starter. The engine turned over twice, faltered, then rumbled into life and Chavasse rested on the thwart in relief as the punt surged forward.

'Any chance of that happening again?' he called softly.

'I wouldn't be surprised. This must be the one they used on the Ark.'

Orsini stayed at the tiller, nursing the engine along, and Liri moved into the centre and started to bail. It was still quite dark and visibility was almost nil. Only the surge of white water against the bank gave them any kind of bearing.

The bulk of a large island loomed out of the night, and Liri called urgently as Orsini swung the tiller, taking them away towards the centre of the river.

As the current caught them, there was a sudden challenge from the left and Chavasse glanced over his shoulder and saw the motorboat anchored in the lee of the island, a light in her wheelhouse.

He was aware of people moving along the deck, of confused voices, and then a powerful spot mounted on top of the wheelhouse was switched on, the beam splaying out across the dark water. It followed them relentlessly, trapping them in its dazzling beam like flies in a web.

There was an incredulous cry of dismay and Francesca's voice sounded on the cold air like a bugle. 'Kapo! Kapo! Come quickly!'

Chavasse leaned over the side, digging the paddle into the water feverishly as Orsini gave the old motor everything it had. They dipped into the millrace as the current flowed past the final curved point of the island and coasted into darkness again.

A few moments later, the engine of the motorboat rumbled into life and Liri scrambled back into the stern. 'I'll take over now,' she said. 'There's a creek about a quarter of a mile below. If we can reach that, we're safe. It's too narrow for the motorboat to enter. They'll have to stay in the main channel.'

Orsini moved down beside Chavasse, picked up the other paddle and drove it into the water with all his great strength. They were passing through a narrower section of the river now and the flood waters rushed with a mighty roar, drowning the sound of the motorboat's engine. Chavasse stabbed the crude paddle into the water again and again, exerting everything of mind and will in a supreme effort, pushing the tiredness, the fatigue of the past twenty-four hours away from him.

They swung in close to the land as the river broadened, and quite suddenly, as the roaring of the flood waters subsided, the engine of the motorboat sounded close behind.

He glanced over his shoulder, saw the lighted

wheelhouse, the searchlight stabbing out towards them. There was the harsh deadly staccato of a submachine gun and then the punt swerved into the lee of a small island and started to turn.

Reeds swam out of the darkness, and as the beam of the searchlight fell across them, the opening of the creek sprang out of the night. The punt surged towards it, slowed as it slid across a submerged mudbank and then they were through. The machine gun rattled again ineffectually as the reeds closed about them.

Liri reduced speed and they coasted on, brushing against the pale fronds. Gradually, the sound of the river faded. The engine of the motorboat had stopped for a while, but now they heard it start again faintly in the distance and fade downstream.

Orsini laughed shakily. 'A close call.'

Chavasse took from his pocket the compass Father Shedu had given him, and passed it to the Italian. 'You'd better start using this. We haven't got time to hang about.'

Orsini moved in to the stern beside Liri. 'South-southwest must be our general direction. Can we do it?'

'I think so. I know this creek and where it goes. We'll come to a large lagoon soon. We change direction there. But it's possible you might have to get out and push in places.'

'When will it be light?' Chavasse asked.

'An hour, perhaps a little longer. It will be misty, one can always tell.'

'We're in your hands, *cara*,' Orsini told her.

They moved into a large lagoon as she had indicated and turned into a maze of twisting channels. The outboard motor stopped several times as trailing weeds clogged the propeller, and finally it died altogether.

Orsini examined it for several minutes and shook his head. 'That's all, I'm afraid. There's nothing I can do, not under these conditions.'

From then on they used the paddles, and after a while the reeds became so thick that the two men had to go over the side, wading through thick glutinous mud as they forced a way through for the punt, always trying to keep to their general compass bearing.

The swampy water was treacherous and had a way of changing depth without warning. Once, Chavasse stepped into a deep hole and went in over his head. He struggled back with a curse to a comparatively safe footing and scrambled back into the punt as they emerged into another waterway.

Orsini laughed grimly. 'Now this I could do without.'

It was bitterly cold and a damp mist curled from the water. Occasionally, wildfowl fluttered protestingly from the reeds as they passed through, calling angrily to each other, warning those ahead of the intruders.

There was an appreciable lightening of the darkness and a faint luminosity drifted around them. And then they could see the reeds and there was a honking of geese overhead lifting to meet the dawn.

Orsini was pale and drawn, the dark stubble of his beard accentuating his pallor. He looked about twenty years older, his hands shaking slightly in the extreme cold, and Chavasse didn't feel any better. The girl looked healthier than either of them, but on the other hand she hadn't spent the best part of an hour up to her waist in freezing water.

They coasted into a broad channel and Orsini

held up his hand. 'We must be close now. Very close.'

He stood up in the punt, cupped his hands to his mouth and called at the top of his voice, '*Buona Esperanza*, ahoy! Ahoy, *Buona Esperanza*!'

There was no reply and Chavasse joined him. 'Carlo! Carlo Arezzi!'

Their voices died away, and in the grey light they looked helplessly at each other. Liri held up her hand. 'I heard something.'

At first Chavasse thought it was the cry of a bird, but then it sounded again, unmistakably a human voice. They paddled into the mist, calling again and again, and gradually the voice grew louder.

For the last time, Chavasse and Orsini went over the side, forcing the punt through a wall of reeds and then, quite suddenly, they were through and drifting into a familiar lagoon.

At the other end, the *Buona Esperanza* seemed to swim out of the mist to meet them, Carlo Arezzi poised on top of the wheelhouse.

15

It was warm in the cabin. Chavasse vigorously rubbed himself down and dressed quickly in a spare pair of denim working pants and a heavy sweater of Carlo's.

There was a knock on the door and Liri Kupi called, 'Are you dressed?'

She came in carrying a mug of coffee and he took it gratefully. It was scalding hot and the fragrance seemed to put new life into him. 'Best I ever tasted. Where's Guilio?'

'He went up to the wheelhouse. He wanted to chart the course.'

She opened the little box, gave him one of her Macedonian cigarettes and struck a match for him, holding it in her cupped hands.

Chavasse blew out a cloud of smoke and looked at her shrewdly. 'You like him, don't you?'

'Guilio? Who wouldn't?'

'He's got twenty years on you, you know that?'

She shrugged and said calmly, 'You know what they say about good wine.'

Chavasse slipped an arm about her shoulders. 'You're quite a girl, Liri. I'd say he was a lucky man.'

He swallowed the rest of his coffee, handed her the jug and went up the companionway. It started to rain as he went out on deck and the mist draped itself across everything in a grey shroud. Orsini and Carlo were leaning over the charts when he went into the wheelhouse.

'What's the score?' he said.

Orsini shrugged. 'I think we should try the main channel out. It's quicker and we could stand a good chance of getting away with it. It's Yugoslavian territory on the other side and Albanian boats don't like going in too close. If we can get into the open, nothing they've got stands a chance of catching us.'

'Won't Kapo count on us doing just that?'

'Probably. I say we go and find out.'

Chavasse shrugged. 'That's all right by me, but I think it might be an idea to break out a

208

little hardware, just in case.'

'You and Carlo can handle that end. I'll get things moving up here.'

Chavasse and the young Italian went below, opened the box seat and unpacked the weapons. There was still a submachine gun left, a dozen grenades and the old Bren. They went back on deck and laid the weapons out on the floor of the wheelhouse under the chart table, ready for action.

It was just after five a.m. when the engines shuddered into life and Orsini took the *Buona Esperanza* into the mist. Chavasse stood in the prow beside Liri and rain kicked into his face, and the wind, blowing in from the sea, lifted the mist into strange shapes.

The girl stared into the greyness eagerly, lips parted, a touch of colour in each cheek. 'Are you glad to be going?' he said.

She shrugged briefly. 'I'm leaving nothing behind.'

As the light grew stronger, the dark silver lances of the rain became visible, stabbing down through the mist, and somewhere a curlew called eerily. Once, twice, and he waited with bated breath, trapped by a childhood memory. *Once for joy, two for sorrow, three for a death*.

There was no third call, which left them with a little sorrow, but that he could bear. He turned and went back to the wheelhouse.

For half an hour, they moved slowly along the broad channel, crossing from one lagoon into the other, changing direction only once. Visibility was down to twenty yards, but the reeds were falling away now and the channel was widening.

The water began to kick against the hull in long swelling ripples and Orsini grinned tightly. 'The Buene. We're about half a mile from the sea.'

The launch crept forward, the engines a low rumble that was almost drowned in the splashing of the heavy rain. Chavasse examined the chart. The estuary was a mass of sandbanks and the main channel, the one they had used on the way in, was no more than thirty yards. If Kapo was anywhere, it would be there.

A few moments later, Orsini cut the engines

and they drifted with the current. He opened the side window and leaned out.

'We're almost there. If they're patrolling, we'll hear the engines.'

Chavasse went on deck and stood in the prow listening. Carlo and Liri joined him. At first there was nothing, only the wind and the sizzle of rain, then Carlo held up a hand.

'I think I hear something.'

Chavasse turned, signalling Orsini down, and the Italian swung the wheel, taking the boat in to where a low hog's back of sand lifted from the sea. They grounded with a slight shudder and Chavasse ran back to the wheelhouse.

'Carlo thinks he heard something. No sense in running into anything we can avoid. We'll take a look on foot.'

He stood on the rail and jumped, landing in a couple of inches of water. Carlo tossed the submachine gun to him, then followed and they moved into the mist along the sandbank.

It stretched for several hundred yards, in some places water slopping across it so that they had to wade. The noise of an engine was by now quite unmistakable. At times it faded, then a minute or two later grew louder again.

'They must be patrolling the mouth of the channel,' Chavasse said.

Carlo pulled him down into the sand. The motorboat floated out of the mist no more than twenty yards away. They had a quick glimpse of a soldier crouching on the roof of the wheelhouse, a machine pistol in his hands, and then the mist swallowed it again.

They ran back along the sandbank and the sound of the motorboat faded behind them. The mist seemed to be a little thicker and the water was rising, flooding in across the dark spine of sand, tugging at their boots, and the *Buona Esperanza* loomed out of the gloom.

Chavasse waded into the water and Orsini reached down to give him a hand over the rail. 'Are they there?'

Chavasse nodded and explained briefly what they had seen. 'What happens now?'

They went back into the wheelhouse and Orsini leaned over the chart. 'We could return to the marshes. There is a way through, certainly, but it would take many hours with a boat of

212

this size and there is no guarantee. By that time, Kapo could have called in the Albanian Navy, such as it is. They could give us trouble if we ran into them with no way round.'

'Have we any choice?'

Orsini traced finger across the chart. 'There's a channel here. It runs a mile to the southwest, emerging at Cat Island. See where I mean?'

'What's the snag? It looks good to me.'

'As I said earlier, the river isn't used much these days because of the border dispute, and the channels, such as they are, have been allowed to silt up. There's no knowing just how much water there is any more. It's probably shoaled up.'

'Are you willing to try?'

'If the rest of you are.'

There was really no question, Chavasse knew that as he glanced at Liri, and Orsini pressed the starter and reversed off the sandbank. The launch turned in a long sweeping curve and started back up the river.

Orsini leaned out of the side window, eyes narrowed into the mist, and after a while he gave a quick grunt and swung the wheel, taking them between low, humped sandbanks. He reduced speed to dead slow and the boat moved forward as cautiously as an old lady finding her way across a busy street.

Waves slapped hollowly against the bottom, a sure sign of shallow water, and once or twice there was a slight protesting jar and a scraping as they grazed a shoulder of sand. It was perhaps five minutes later that they ploughed to a halt.

Orsini reversed quickly. At first the launch refused to budge and then it parted the sand with an ugly sucking noise. Carlo vaulted over the side without a word to anyone. The water rose to his chest, and as he waded forward it dropped to waist level.

He changed direction to the left and a moment later it lifted to his armpits again. He waved quickly and Orsini swung the wheel, taking the boat after him.

The young Italian swam forward into the shoals, sounding the bottom every few yards, and behind him the *Buona Esperanza* carefully followed his circuitous trail. And then a wave lifted out of the mist, swamping him, and he went under.

He surfaced and swam back to the launch, and when Chavasse pulled him in there was a wide grin on his face. 'Deep water. I couldn't touch bottom. We're through.'

Orsini waved from the wheelhouse and gave the engines more power, swinging the wheel to take them out of the estuary to sea. Fifty yards beyond the entrance the dark bulk of Cat Island lifted out of the mist, and he turned to port. As they rounded the point, the current pushing against them, engines roared into life and a grey naval patrol boat surged out of the rock inlet where she had been waiting.

As she swept across their bows, a heavy machine gun started to fire, bullets sweeping across the deck, shattering glass in the wheelhouse. Chavasse had a quick glimpse of Kapo at the rail, still wearing his hunting jacket with the fur collar, mouth open as he cried his men on.

Carlo appeared in the doorway of the wheelhouse, the submachine gun at his hip, firing as he crossed the deck to the rail. On the patrol boat someone screamed, and Kapo ducked out of sight.

Already Orsini was taking his engines to

full power and from the for'ard deck of the patrol boat another machine gun started to fire, tracer and cannon hammering into the hull of the *Buona Esperanza*, great shudders rushing through her entire frame as she reeled at the impact.

And then they were through, prow lifting over the waves as the patrol boat faded into the mist behind them. Chavasse picked himself up from the deck and gave a hand to Liri. There was blood on her face and she wiped it away quickly.

'Are you all right?' he said.

She nodded. 'A flying splinter, that's all.'

Carlo turned, the submachine gun hugged to his breast. For the first time since Chavasse had known him, there was a smile on his face.

'I gave the bastards something to remember me by.'

Chavasse moved to the door of the wheel-house. The windows were shattered, glass scattered across the floor, but Orsini seemed to be all in one piece.

'I got down quick,' he called above the roar of the engine. 'Did you see Kapo?'

'For a moment there I thought he'd put one over on us. We should have figured on the possibility of him having both exits watched.'

'I hope the swine's head rolls for this.'

As Orsini grinned savagely, the engines missed a couple of times, faltered, tried to pick up, then stopped completely.

The *Buona Esperanza* ploughed forward, her prow biting into a wave, slowed and started to drift with the current.

16

When Orsini got the hatch off the tiny engine room, they could smell escaping fuel at once. The Italian slid down the short steel ladder and Chavasse and Orsini followed him.

Carlo made a quick examination and turned. 'It could be worse. A section of the fuel-intake pipe is damaged. We were lucky the whole damned lot didn't blow sky-high.'

A jagged hole in the steel hull punched by a cannon shell was mute evidence of how the damage had been caused.

'How are we off for spares?' Orsini demanded.

'No problem there, but I'll have to cut a section to the right size and braze it.'

'How long?'

'Twenty minutes, if you all get the hell out of here and leave me alone.'

Chavasse went up the ladder and joined Liri on deck. 'How bad is it?' she asked.

'Bad enough to make us sitting ducks for the next half an hour.'

Orsini scrambled out of the engine room and nodded grimly. 'If the swine doesn't get us now, he doesn't deserve to. We'd better make ready, Paul.'

He broke open a box of cartridges and carefully loaded the submachine gun's one-hundred-round circular clip and Chavasse checked the machine gun and the half-dozen magazines which went with it. Liri scrambled on top of the wheelhouse and kept watch, straining her eyes into the mist.

When he had finished loading the submachine gun, Orsini went below and came back with an old American service-issue .45 automatic. He tossed it to the girl, who caught it deftly.

'Best I can do, but watch it. It has the kick of an angry mule.'

'I've been using guns all my life,' she said, pulling out the magazine and examining it expertly.

Orsini grinned up at her. 'I wonder what

you'd look like in a skirt and some decent stockings and shoes. The thought has great appeal. When we reach Matano, I must do something about it.'

She laughed, her face flushing, and then the smile was wiped from her face. 'Listen, I think I hear them.'

The boat lifted on the swell, waves slapping hollowly against her bows. Chavasse stood at the rail, straining his ears and, in the distance, heard the sound of an engine.

'Come down from there,' he told the girl. 'Go into the wheelhouse and lie flat.'

She did as she was told. Chavasse stood over her, the barrel of the Bren gun poking through one of the windows, and Orsini crouched beside the engine-room hatch.

'Perhaps they're going away?' Liri whispered.

Chavasse shook his head. 'Not on your life. They must have heard our engines stop and they cut their own and listened to see what was happening. Kapo must know that there are only two possibilities. Either we're being picked up by another boat or our engines have packed in.'

The patrol boat came nearer and nearer, obviously beating backwards and forwards through the mist. It passed very close to them indeed, its bow-wave rippling across the water, rocking the *Buona Esperanza* violently. For a moment, Chavasse thought they had been missed and then the engine of the patrol boat lifted and it roared out of the mist.

It swept across their stern, and the air was broken by the sound of violence. The main trouble came from the heavy machine gun mounted in the stern of the patrol boat, its crew couched behind a curved shield of armour plating. In the prow, several soldiers stood at the rail, firing rifles and machine pistols, and Kapo lurked behind them, a revolver in his hand.

Chavasse started to fire, swinging the barrel of the Bren in an arc, and a couple of soldiers stumbled backwards to the deck. He saw Francesca running, head down, and swung the Bren desperately, his bullets chipping the rail beside her head. As his magazine ran out, she disappeared into the wheelhouse.

He ducked, reaching for another magazine, and glass shattered above his head and the walls splintered, rocking to the impact of tracer and cannon shell. As the patrol boat swung away, Orsini jumped to his feet and fired a long burst at the crew of the machine gun in the stern. There was a sharp cry. As the boat disappeared into the mist, one of them lurched to the rail and toppled into the sea.

The sound of the patrol boat faded and Orsini shouted to Liri, 'Keep down. Next time he's really going to mean business.'

The patrol boat circled several times, invisible in the heavy mist, and Chavasse waited impatiently. When Kapo at last made his move, it was from a different quarter. As the boat roared out of the mist behind him, Chavasse frantically swung the Bren round, firing from the hip.

The heavy machine gun in the stern of the patrol boat raked them with a murderous fire, the *Buona Esperanza* reeling at the impact, and Chavasse ducked as he finished his last magazine and portions of the roof disintegrated above his head.

Orsini was still firing, the barrel of the submachine gun braced against the side of the wheelhouse. As the patrol boat veered in a wide arc, cutting across their bows again, Chavasse snatched a grenade from the box beside Liri, pulled the pin and ran out on deck.

For a brief moment, the patrol boat was so close he could see the expressions on the soldiers' faces, and as it swept by he lobbed the grenade over the railing to her stern. It started to roll, one of the soldiers kicked out at it frantically and then it exploded. When the smoke cleared, only the tangled wreckage of the machine gun was left. The soldiers had vanished.

The patrol boat ran on into the mist and there was quiet. Liri got to her feet, blood on her face, and wiped it away with the back of her hand.

'Will they try again?'

'Certain to. They'll be a little more careful next time, that's all.'

Orsini was leaning over the engine-room hatch and he stood up and came towards them. 'Not so good. At least another fifteen minutes.'

They looked at each other without saying

anything, knowing what that meant, and quite suddenly Kapo's voice boomed out of the mist. 'Why don't you give in, Chavasse? You can't hope to get away.'

Liri gave a startled exclamation and Orsini reassured her. 'Don't be alarmed. He's using a loudhailer, that's all. I wonder what the swine's playing at.'

'We're not interested,' Chavasse called.

The engines of the patrol boat roared into life and it erupted from the mist, the men at her rail raking the *Buona Esperanza* with small-arms fire.

Chavasse shoved Liri down against the deck and Orsini crouched beside them, the sub-machine gun chattering angrily. He stopped firing abruptly just as the patrol boat disappeared into the mist.

He checked the magazine, then tossed the weapon into the wheelhouse. 'What about the Bren?'

'Nothing left for that either.'

Orsini went and pulled the small box of grenades from under the chart table. 'At least we've got these.'

'If they come close enough,' Chavasse said.

Kapo's voice drifted out of the mist again. 'It's obvious that you're incapable of moving, Chavasse, but I'll be generous. Give yourself up without any further nonsense and I'll let your friends go free. I give you my word. I'll give you ten minutes to think it over. After that, we'll come and finish you off.'

In the silence that followed, Orsini gave an audible grunt and disappeared down the saloon companionway. When he returned, he carried the spare aqualung.

'Help me get into this thing quickly,' he said to Liri, and turned to Chavasse. 'You'll find some more of that plastic explosive in the saloon, Paul, and some chemical detonators. Get them quickly.'

'What the hell do you think you're playing at?' Chavasse began, but Orsini gave him an angry shove.

'Don't argue. Just do it.'

The Italian was buckled into the aqualung and pulling on his rubber flippers when Chavasse came back on deck with the bandolier of explosive.

'I'm going to have a go at fixing Kapo once and for all,' Orsini said, as he fastened the bandolier around his waist.

Chavasse shook his head. 'You haven't got enough time left.'

Orsini grinned. 'That's what they told me in forty-one when I took a team into Alex. But we got in *and* out and left two British destroyers squatting on their backsides in the mud. I know what I'm doing.'

He pulled his mask down, turned from Liri's white face and vaulted over the rail. He had only a rough idea of the direction of the patrol boat, but he knew it couldn't be far away. He swam very fast, kicking strongly with his webbed feet, and within a couple of minutes had penetrated the mist.

He surfaced gently and looked about him. There was no sign of the patrol boat, but Kapo's voice boomed over him and he saw a dark outline in the mist.

'Five minutes, Chavasse, that's all.'

Orsini went under, swam forward and the keep of the patrol boat loomed out of the water. He worked his way along to the stern, opened

the pouches of his bandolier and squeezed hand-
fuls of the plastic explosive between the propeller and the hull. He was fast running out of time
and he pushed home the detonator, snapped the
end and turned away.

He drove forward, drawing upon his final
reserves of strength, feet churning the water
into a cauldron, and then the hull of the *Buona
Esperanza* seemed to be moving towards him
and he surfaced.

Chavasse leaned over the rail, Carlo beside
him, and they hauled him up on to the deck.
Somewhere, through the roaring in his ears, the
engine of the patrol boat rumbled into life.

When the explosion came, it echoed through
the rain and the screams of the dying mingled
with it. For a long time, debris continued to fall
into the water and then there was silence.

'Holy Mother,' Carlo said in awe. 'She must
have gone down like a stone.'

Orsini slowly unbuckled the straps of his
aqualung. 'How are things below?'

'All finished,' Carlo said. 'We can move out
whenever you're ready.'

Liri was kneeling beside Orsini, her cigarette

tin open. Chavasse dropped beside them, took one and bent his head to the match as it flared in her hands.

Orsini looked at him curiously. 'You're sorry about the girl?'

'Anything she got, she asked for.'

Chavasse turned and stood at the rail, aware of the tightness in his throat that couldn't be logically explained, remembering a gay and lovely girl he had met a thousand years ago at an Embassy party in Rome.

His head was aching and he was tired, damned tired, and she was calling his name over and over again. He closed his eyes briefly. When he opened them again, she came swimming out of the mist.

She had never looked lovelier, her dark hair spreading around her in the water, her eyes large in the white face. As she drifted in, she looked up at him appealingly.

'Help me, Paul! Help me!'

He looked down at her, remembering Matt Sorley, Dumont and all the others, good friends who had gone to a hard death because of her.

Orsini said, 'For God's sake, Paul. Are we animals?'

229

Chavasse turned and looked at him, and the Italian shrugged. 'If you won't help her, I will.'

He started forward and Chavasse shook his head. 'It's my affair, Guilio.'

He reached down and pulled Francesca aboard and she sprawled on the deck, coughing and gasping for breath. 'Thank you, Paul. You'll never regret it, I promise you.'

As she got to her feet, her hand swung up and he was aware of the blade, shining in the harsh morning light. He tried to turn, but he was too late and it caught him in the left side, slicing through flesh, bouncing from the rib cage.

He staggered back, recoiling as much from the cold hatred in her eyes as from the force of the blow, and Orsini cried out in dismay. Chavasse was aware of the knife raised high, gleaming in a ray of early-morning sunlight which at that moment pierced the mist, and then Liri's voice was lifted in a savage cry.

She moved forward, the heavy automatic Orsini had given her in both hands, and one heavy slug after another hammered Francesca back over the rail into the water.

Chavasse was aware of Orsini kneeling beside

him, of Liri throwing the gun far out to sea. He took a deep breath, fighting against the pain.

'I'm all right, Guilio. I'm fine. Just let's get the hell out of here.'

Orsini called to Carlo in the wheelhouse and, a moment later, the engines started and the *Buona Esperanza* moved forward slowly.

They passed through a great, widening circle of wreckage from the patrol boat and Liri, standing at the rail, called out sharply and pointed to the water.

Chavasse shook his head, holding his bunched shirt tightly against his side to stem the flow of blood, and tried to hear what was being said. There was a roaring in his ears and grey cobwebs seemed to be drifting slowly across his field of vision. He was aware that the engines had stopped, that Carlo had joined Liri, and then Orsini went over the rail.

Chavasse leaned over, suddenly faint, fighting hard against the pain. When he straightened, Carlo was lifting the statue of Our Lady of Scutari over the side.

Orsini brought it across and laid it reverently on the deck in front of Chavasse. 'Look, Paul, floating in the wreckage without a mark on her. A miracle.'

Carlo went back into the wheelhouse and started the engines, and Chavasse sat there looking at the statue. He was crying, which was a strange thing and couldn't be explained, and yet somehow the dark serene face smiling up at him seemed to ease his pain.

Above his head, a gull cried sharply, skimmed low over the sea and sped away through the misty rain like a departing spirit.

MANHATTAN
1995

17

In the sitting room at the Trump Tower apartment, Chavasse finished reading the file, closed it and sat back.

Vinelli said, 'Another drink, Sir Paul?'

'Why not?' Chavasse said. 'Champagne will be fine.'

Vinelli went to the bar, opened a fresh bottle. Chavasse took the glass he offered and savoured it. 'Let's have him in, Aldo.'

'As you say.'

It was quiet, only that damned rain drumming on the windows, and then the door opened and Vinelli came in ahead of Volpe.

Chavasse said, 'A hell of a story. I mean, it was really heavy stuff for you to get hold of it.'

'Like I said, those clerks at the Public Records Office aren't the best paid people in the world.'

'So all you had to do was check up on Paul Chavasse and the Bureau, and it was all there?'

'Well, you were a star performer.'

'What can I say? I'd sound modest.'

'What you did – it was better than James Bond.'

'Oh, I don't know. Just another job for the Bureau. That's what it was all about. The name of the game.'

'You may think that, but I'm truly impressed.'

Chavasse said, 'What now?'

'We go to see Don Tino.'

'At the Saddle Room at the Plaza Hotel.'

'Actually, things have changed. The Don would like to see you on the family yacht. It's moored off Pier Ten at the waterfront in Brooklyn. Full crew, great chef. Don Rossi is concerned with confidentiality here.'

Chavasse picked up his rain hat, slanted it across his head and reached for his Burberry. 'So, let's get on with it.'

Aldo got to the Burberry and held it for him. Chavasse said, 'Why, thank you, Aldo.'

Vinelli appeared to hesitate and Chavasse smiled. 'I'm really looking forward to this. I love boats, Aldo.'

* * *

Aldo drove, Chavasse and Volpe sat together in the back of the Mercedes. The rain washed the streets clean of people as they moved towards Brooklyn. Chavasse took out the silver case, selected a cigarette and lit it. He blew out the smoke.

'Yes, fascinating, that file. Of course, Bureau files are on a fifty-year hold so it would be impossible for anyone to take a look. An offence under the Official Secrets Act.'

'Amazing what money can do. People are so corrupt.'

'Oh, I agree totally, but in this case, there's one thing wrong.'

'And what would that be?'

'Bureau Case Study 203, Field Agent Doctor Paul Chavasse. You said I probably wrote it myself. Actually, I did and there's only one problem.'

'Which is?'

'It's been expanded. For instance, the mention of the death of Enrico Noci. You remember that?'

'Sure. Drowned in a fishing net by you and your friends.'

'No, to be correct, executed.'

'Murdered.' There was a sudden violence in Volpe's voice.

'A point of view. He was what you'd call a bad guy, his actions responsible for the deaths of friends of mine. Having said that, the manner of his death wasn't the kind of thing to put in an official report, so under the Chief's instructions, I left it out.' He took out his case and selected another cigarette. 'So how did you find out?'

'From my aunt.' Volpe was shaking a little.

'And that would be Signora Volpe, if I recall your background, Don Tino's niece.'

'Great-niece by marriage.'

'You Italians take family so seriously. So what was Enrico Noci to you?'

'My father – the father you murdered. Something I learned from my aunt's knee.'

'I see.' Chavasse's voice was gentler.

'No, you still don't. Would you like to know who my mother was?'

Chavasse waited for the axe to fall. 'I believe I know.'

'Francesca Minetti.'

'Who, as I point out in my report, gutted me with a rather large knife.'

'Never mind that. Your friend, Liri Kupi, shot her to pieces, you admit that?'

'So?'

'All my life I dreamt of revenge, but these things take time, one step after another. Your friend Orsini married Liri Kupi. Do you remember what happened to them three years ago?'

Chavasse went cold. 'They were killed in a car accident outside Rome.'

'Exactly. Faulty breaks was the conclusion of the police.'

Chavasse managed to stay very calm. 'So, now it's my turn?'

'Precisely.'

'And what will the Don say?'

'That's not important. His time is long past.' He took a Walther PPK from his pocket, rammed it into Chavasse's side and searched him quickly.

'No weapon. That's interesting.'

'I thought I was amongst friends.'

'So did the Don. The biggest mistake of your

life,' Volpe said as the Mercedes moved along the waterfront.

The pier was deserted in the rain, the large motor yacht moored at the far end, a few deck lights on.

'Don't worry,' Volpe said. 'No crew on board tonight. Usually there's a watchman, but I gave him the night off too. Just you, me and Aldo.'

Vinelli pulled in by the gangway, slid from behind the wheel and opened the rear door. Chavasse got out.

'Does this suit you too, Aldo?'

Vinelli said, 'Heh, conversation I don't need. Just get moving.'

Volpe led the way, Chavasse behind him and Vinelli followed, gun in hand. They passed along the deck and came out in the stern, which was illuminated by dim lights. There was a half canopy, rain thudding against it, the railing of the upper deck above.

Volpe turned at the stern rail, put the Walther in his pocket, took out a pack of Marlboros and lit one. 'Over here, Aldo.'

Vinelli moved towards him holding a Browning against his right thigh. Chavasse said, 'So this is it?'

He removed his rain hat and ran his left hand over his face, his right clutching the butt of the .22 Colt in its clip.

'You know what they say in Sicily is true tonight. Paul Chavasse will sleep with the fishes. Just like my mother and father, you bastard.'

A soft voice said, 'Why Mario, what's all this?'

Don Tino Rossi moved out of the shadows of the port deck and confronted him, his face shadowed by a broad-brimmed hat, Malacca cane in one hand, a raincoat draped over his shoulders.

Volpe registered cold shock, started to stammer. 'Uncle, I . . .'

'Never expected to see you here, isn't that how it goes?' Rossi shook his head. 'Foolish boy. I've known all about your plans, every conversation with Aldo here. In my home, you're even wired for sound in the bathroom – on camera – everything. I treated you like a father and how do you repay me? By killing Sir Paul, who is important to all my plans.'

'He murdered my parents,' Volpe said desperately.

'I've known about that for years. So, it was all right for them to kill others, but not to be killed themselves? A point of view, but there is the matter of your intention to kill me. We can't have that, can we?'

'Aldo!' Volpe cried.

Vinelli's hand swept up clutching the Browning, and Chavasse fired through the rain hat and shot him between the eyes. Vinelli dropped the weapon, bounced against the rail and fell on his face.

'Damn you to hell!' Volpe cried, pulling the Walther from his pocket.

There was the muted crack of a silenced AK assault rifle from the rail above, the first shot spinning him round, the second shattering his spine. There was a step on the companionway and two men came down in reefer coats and knitted caps, both holding AKs.

Chavasse said, 'You left it a little late.'

'Oh, I had very confidence in you, my friend, and as I now know you like a brother, even your trick with the Colt in the rain hat was familiar to me.' Rossi shrugged. 'If you hadn't got Aldo, my man would have.'

'So what happens now?'

'My boys will dump them out there, victims of another Mafia feud.' He smiled bleakly. 'Does it give you a problem or can we still deal on London and Eastern Europe?'

'I don't see why not.'

'Good. Then be on your way. If you look over the rail you will notice a Lincoln has pulled in behind the Mercedes. Your bags have been packed and you are booked out of the Plaza.'

'To where?'

'My chauffeur will take you to Westhampton Airport on Long Island where I keep a private Gulfstream that will have you on your way to London before you know it. Goodbye, my friend. This never happened.'

'Oh, yes, it did,' Chavasse said, turned and walked away.

As the Gulfstream climbed out over the Atlantic, Chavasse sat in solitary splendour and asked the steward for a large Irish whiskey, which he drank quickly.

He thought of Enrico Noci, Francesca, Guilio Orsini and Mario Volpe, asleep with the fishes. A long time ago, most of it, a hell of a long time ago, but was anything ever finished? Truly finished? He closed his eyes and leaned back.

DAY OF
RECKONING

When you have sinned grievously,
the Devil is waiting.
Sicilian Proverb

HELLSMOUTH

1

It was the rat, in a way, which brought Blake Johnson not only awake, but back to life. Sitting on the stone seat in the darkness, up to his waist in water, it was astonishing that he'd drifted into sleep at all, and then he'd come awake, aware of something on his neck, and had sat up.

The light in the grilled entrance behind him gave enough illumination for him to see what it was that slid from his left shoulder. It splashed into the water, surfaced, and turned to look at him, nose pointing, eyes unwinking.

It took Blake back more than twenty-five years to when he'd been a young Special Forces sergeant at the end of the Vietnam War, up to his neck in a tidal swamp in the Mekong Delta, trying to avoid sudden death at the hands of the Vietcong. There had been rats there, too, especially because of the bodies.

No bodies here. Just the grille entrance with the faint light showing through, the rough stone walls of the tunnel, the strong, dank sewer smell, and the grille forty yards the other way, the grille that meant there was nowhere to go as he'd found when they had first put him into this place.

The rat floated, watching him, strangely friendly. Blake said softly, 'Now you behave yourself. Be off with you.'

He stirred the water, and the rat fled. He leaned back, intensely cold, and tried to think straight. He remembered coming to a kind of half-life in the Range Rover, the effects of the drugs wearing off. They'd come over a hill, in heavy rain, some sort of storm, and then in the lightning he'd seen cliffs below, a cruel sea, and above the cliffs a castle like something out of a fairy tale by the Brothers Grimm.

When Blake had groaned and tried to sit up, Falcone, the one sitting beside the driver, had turned and smiled.

'There you are. Back in the land of the living.'

And Blake, trying hard to return to some kind of reality, had said, 'Where am I?'

And Falcone had smiled. 'The end of the world, my friend. There's nowhere else but the Atlantic

Ocean all the way to America. Hellsmouth, that's what they call this place.'

He'd started to laugh as Blake lapsed back into semi-consciousness.

Time really had no meaning. His bandaged right shoulder hurt as he sat on the seat, arms tightly folded to try and preserve some kind of body heat, and yet his senses were alert and strangely sharp so that when there was a clang behind him and the grille opened, he sat up.

'Hey, there you are, *Dottore*. Still with us,' Falcone said.

'And fuck you, too,' Blake managed.

'Excellent. Signs of life. I like that. Out you come.'

Falcone got a hand on the collar of Blake's shirt and pulled. Blake went through the opening and landed on his hands and knees in the corridor. Russo was there, a smile on his ugly face.

'He don't look too good.'

'Well, he sure as hell stinks. Wash him down.'

There was a hose fastened to a brass tap in the wall. Russo turned it on and directed the spray all over Blake's body. It was ice cold and he fought for breath. Russo finally switched off and draped a blanket round Blake's shoulders.

'The boss wants to see you, so be good.'

'Sure, he'll be good,' Falcone said. 'Just like that nice little wife of his in Brooklyn was good.'

Blake pulled the blanket around him and looked up. 'You did that?'

'Hey, business is business.'

'I'll kill you for that.'

'Don't be stupid. You're on borrowed time as it is. Let's move it, the man's waiting,' and he pushed Blake along the corridor.

They climbed two sets of stone steps and finally reached a black oak door bound in iron. Russo opened it, and Falcone pushed Blake through into a baronial hall, stone-flagged, with a staircase to the left and a log fire burning on a stone hearth. Suits of armour and ancient banners hung from poles. There was a slightly unreal touch to things, like a bad film set.

'What happened to Dracula?' Blake asked.

Russo frowned. 'Dracula? What is this?'

'Never mind.' Two men were lounging by the fire. Rossi and Cameci; he'd seen their faces on the computer, more Solazzo family hoods.

Falcone pushed Blake forward. 'Hey, I'm with

6

you. Christopher Lee was the best. I loved those Hammer movies.'

Russo opened another black oak door. Inside was a room with a high ceiling, another log fire on a stone hearth, candlelight and shadows, and behind a large desk shrouded in darkness, a shadowy figure.

'Bring Mr Johnson in, Aldo. By the fire. He must be cold.'

Falcone took Blake to the fire and pulled a chair forward. 'Sit.'

The man in the shadows said, 'Brandy, I think. A large one would seem to be in order.'

Blake sat there while Russo went to a side table and poured brandy from a decanter and brought it to him. It burned all the way down and Blake coughed.

'Now give him a cigarette, Aldo. Like all of us, Mr Johnson is trying to stop, but life is short, art long, and experiment perilous. There's Latin for that, but I forget how it goes.'

'Oh, didn't they teach you that at Harvard Law School?'

Blake took the cigarette and light from Falcone.

'As a matter of fact, no. But clever of you. You obviously know who I am.'

'Hell, why carry on like this? Of course I know who you are. Jack Fox, pride of the Solazzo family. So why don't you turn up the light?'

A moment passed, and it did go up and Fox sat there; the dark hair, the devil's wedge of a face, the mocking smile. He took a cigarette from a silver case and lit it.

'And I know you, Blake Johnson. You came out of Vietnam with a chestful of medals, joined the FBI, and saved President Jake Cazalet from assassination when he was still a Senator. Shot two bad guys and took a bullet. Now you run the Basement, downstairs at the White House, as a kind of private hit force for the President. But unfortunately, Blake' – he paused to take a puff – 'I don't think Cazalet can save you now.'

Blake snapped two fingers at Falcone. 'Another brandy.' He turned to Fox. 'There's an old Sicilian saying, which you might appreciate, since I know you have a Sicilian mother. When you have sinned grievously, the devil is waiting.'

Fox laughed. 'Would your devil be you or Sean Dillon?'

'Take your pick. But God help you if it's Dillon,' Blake told him.

Fox leaned closer. 'Let me tell you something,

Johnson. I *hope* it's Dillon. I've been waiting a long time to put a bullet in his brain. And in yours.'

Blake said, 'You killed my wife.'

'Your ex-wife,' Fox said. 'But it wasn't personal. She got too close, that's all. I wish you could have understood that.' Fox shook his head. 'You've caused me a lot of grief. Now you'll have to pay for it.' Fox smiled. 'I hope Dillon *is* stupid enough to come. Then I'll have you both.'

'Or we'll have you.'

Fox said to Falcone. 'Take him back.'

He turned down the light, and Russo punched Blake in the belly. Blake doubled over and they took him out between them, feet dragging.

NEW YORK

IN THE BEGINNING

2

It was a wet March evening in Manhattan when the Lincoln stopped at Trump Tower, the snow long gone, but replaced by heavy, relentless rain. Jack Fox sat in the rear, Russo at the wheel, Falcone beside him. They pulled in at the kerb and Falcone got out with an umbrella.

Fox said, 'You're okay for a couple of hours.' He took a hundred dollar bill from his pocket. 'You two go and eat. I'll call you on my mobile when I need you.'

'Sure.' Falcone walked him to the entrance. 'Please convey my respects to Don Solazzo.'

Fox patted him on the shoulder. 'Hey, Aldo, he knows he has your loyalty.'

He turned and went in.

The maid who admitted him to the top floor apartment was very Italian, small and demure in black dress and stockings. She didn't say a word but simply took him through to the enormous sitting room with its incredible view of Manhattan, where he found his uncle sitting by the fire reading *Truth* magazine. Don Marco Solazzo was seventy-five years of age, a heavyweight in a loose-fitting linen suit, his face very calm, and his eyes expressionless. A walking stick with an ivory handle lay on the floor beside him.

'Hey, Jack, come in.'

His nephew went forward and gave him a kiss on each cheek. 'Uncle, you look good.'

'So do you.' The Don offered him the magazine. 'I read the piece. You look nice, Jack. Very pretty. Savile Row suits. Big smile. They talk about the hero stuff, decorated in the Gulf War, that's all good. But then they have to mention the other stuff. That in spite of a name like Fox your mother was Maria Solazzo, the niece of Don Marco Solazzo. God rest her and your father. That isn't good.'

Fox waved his hand. 'It's innocuous stuff. Everybody knows I'm related to you. But they think I'm legit.'

'You think so? This journalist, this Katherine Johnson, you think "innocuous stuff" is all she's after? Don't delude yourself. She knows who we are, in spite of our Wall Street interests. So we're

14

respectable – property, manufacturing, finance – but we're still Mafia, that's what gives us our power. That side is not for people such as her. No, she's after something – and you . . . you're a good boy. You've done well, but I'm not a fool. I know, beside the family business, that you have this factory in Brooklyn, the one that processes cheap whisky for the clubs.'

'Uncle, please,' Fox said.

The Don waved his hand. 'A young man wanting to make an extra buck I understand, but sometimes you're greedy. There's nothing I don't know. Your dealings with the IRA in Ireland, for instance, that underground dump they have for the weapons they won't hand over. The weapons you supply them. Your trips to London to the Colosseum.'

'That's our flagship casino, Uncle.'

'Sure, but while you're there, you organize armed robberies with our London connection. Over a million pounds cash two months ago from a security van.' The Don waved him back. 'Don't annoy me by denying it, Jack.'

'Uncle.' Fox tried to sound contrite.

'Just remember your true purpose. The drug business is no longer growing in America. You have to encourage its rise in Russia and the Eastern European countries. That's where growth lies. Prostitution, leave to our Russian and Chinese friends. Just take a percentage.'

'As you say, Uncle.'

'Anything else is okay, but Jack, no more doing things behind my back.'

'Yes, Uncle.'

'And this reporter, this Johnson. Have you gone to bed with her? The truth, now.'

Fox hesitated. 'No, it hasn't been like that.'

'Then like what? Why should she be interested in making you look good? She's in it for more. I'm telling you, she's hiding something. This piece, it's not so bad, all right, but what's next? What's behind the front?' The Don shook his head. 'She flattered you, Jack, and you fell for it. You better find out what she really wants.'

'What would you advise, Uncle?'

'Turn over her apartment. See what you can find.' He reached for a pitcher. 'Have a martini and then we'll eat.'

Terry Mount was very ordinary-looking, small and wiry, the kind of youngster who could have been a delivery boy for some deli. He was, in fact, a highly accomplished burglar and boasted that there was no lock he couldn't open. He'd served time only once, and that was as a juvenile. His very ordinariness had saved his hide on many occasions.

A nice touch two nights before had netted him fifteen thousand dollars, which he'd just picked up from his fence, so he was feeling good, sitting in a bar, relishing the whisky sour the barman was creating, and then a heavy hand touched his shoulder.

Terry turned and his stomach churned. Falcone smiled. 'Terry, you look good.'

Russo leaned against the bar, his usual dreadful self, and Terry took a deep breath. 'Aldo, you want something?'

'Not me, but the Solazzo family would like a favour. You would never say no to the Don, would you, Terry?'

'Of course not,' Terry gabbled, reached for the whisky sour and swallowed it in one gulp.

'Only in this case, it's Jack Fox who wants the favour.'

Which was enough to almost give Terry a bowel movement. 'Anything I can do.'

'That goes without saying.' Falcone patted his cheek and said to the barman, who was looking wary, 'Give him another. He's going to need it.'

The barman said, 'Now, look, I don't want any trouble in here.'

Russo leaned over the bar, his face full of menace. 'Make him the fucking drink and shut up. Okay?'

Hurriedly, the barman did as he was told, his hands shaking.

Jack Fox was in the sitting room of his Park Avenue townhouse, on the second floor, enjoying a light lunch of champagne and smoked salmon sandwiches, when Falcone brought Terry Mount in.

'Why, Terry, you look worried,' Fox told him. 'Now why should that be?' He bit into a sandwich, then Falcone took a wad of money from his pocket. 'Aldo, have you won the lottery or something?'

'No, Signore, but I think Terry has. There's fifteen grand here.'

Fox nodded to the champagne bucket and Falcone poured him another glass. 'Terry, I think you've been a naughty boy again.'

'Please, Mr Fox, I'm just trying to make a buck.'

'And so you shall.' Fox smiled. 'Two grand, Terry.'

Terry's eyes rolled. 'And what do I have to do for that?'

'What you do best.' Fox pushed a piece of paper across that had been lying on the table. 'Katherine Johnson. Ten Barrow Street. Just on the edge of the Village. You'll toss her place this afternoon.'

'But that doesn't give me time to prepare.'

'For what?' Fox said coldly. 'It's a small town-house. She won't be there. You boast that you can break in anywhere.'

Terry licked his lips. 'What do I do?'

'She's a magazine reporter, so you'll probably find an office, a computer, a VCR, all that stuff. Bring whatever disks you find. Bring the videos on her business shelf.'

Terry said, 'People keep videos all the time. I mean, do I bring all of them?'

'Be sensible, Terry,' Fox said patiently. 'I'm not looking for *Dirty Harry* or *She Wore a Yellow Ribbon*. Just use your brain, such as it is. The boys will take you, they'll wait and bring you back. Anything you've got, I want by five o'clock. I'm sure you won't disappoint me.'

Terry's feet hardly touched the ground as Falcone pushed him outside.

He went to Barrow Street wearing a bomber jacket that said 'Smith Electronics' on the back. He didn't bother with the front door, after three rings got no reply, but went down to the basement. There were double deadlocks, but they both responded to his touch.

He found himself in a laundry room and moved upstairs to the entrance hall. There was a parlour, dining room and kitchen, so he tried the stairs, the only sound disturbing the quiet the grandfather clock ticking in the hall. The first door he tried was the study. He saw shelves crammed with books and videos, a computer next to two video and disk machines, and a multiple tape recorder. He switched them all on and removed everything he found in them, placing his haul in the carry bag that hung from his left shoulder. He opened drawers and found more disks and cassettes, which he also took.

The rest really was frustrating. Rows of movies on video, rows of instructional tapes. He was sweating now and swung at the shelves and scattered videotapes across the floor.

Okay. So he'd done what Fox wanted. Time to go. There were some bottles on a side table, and glasses. He poured some bourbon, savoured it, and left by the same route, locking the basement door before returning to Falcone and Russo.

*   *   *

When they arrived at the Park Avenue townhouse, Fox was waiting eagerly. He took the disks and tapes Terry Mount offered and said to Russo, 'Look after him.' He turned to Falcone. 'You stay. It could be bad.'

'Then it's bad for both of us, Signore.' They had been friends since boyhood.

Fox started checking the disks, mostly work notes, letters, accounts, and quickly discarded them. Then he started on the tapes Mount had found in the tape recorder, and on the second struck pure gold.

At first, the sounds were of an innocuous conversation about family business and so on. The woman's voice was very pleasant and intimate, and the man's . . .

Falcone said, 'Jesus, Maria, Signore, that's you.'

There were restaurant sounds in the background, a little music. Fox said, 'She was recording us.'

Suddenly, the tape changed. Now, the woman was clearly making notes to herself.

'There can be little doubt that Jack Fox, in spite of the war hero and Wall Street image, is nothing less than the new face of the Solazzo family and the new Mafia. I'll lull him to sleep with the first article in *Truth* and then hit him hard with the rest. There might even be a special on the Truth Channel

21

in this. I've just got to take it easy, and flatter him. His vanity should take care of the rest.'

Fox switched off the machine. 'The bitch.'

'So it would appear, Signore. What should we do?'

Fox got up, went to the sideboard, and poured a glass of Scotch. He turned. 'I think you know, old friend.' He went to the telephone and punched in a number. 'Katherine Johnson, please. Hello, Kate? Jack Fox. Would you be free for dinner tonight? I was thinking about that piece, and, what the hell, there's some more you might be interested in . . . You are? Terrific. Listen, don't bother going home. I'll send a car. You come on over to Park Avenue and pick me up. We've just bought this new restaurant in Brooklyn, and I'd like to check it out. Will you help? . . . Great! I'll send Falcone to pick you up.' He put the phone down, surprised at the genuine regret he felt.

In that evening of dreary rain, darkness already descending, she sat in the rear of the Lincoln, a small, pretty woman of forty, with dark hair and an intelligent face. Russo was at the wheel and Falcone beside him. They reached the Park Avenue house and Falcone called Fox on his mobile.

'Hey, Signore, we're here.' He turned. 'He'll be right down.'

She smiled and took out a Marlboro. Falcone gave her a light.

'Thank you.'

'Prego, Signora.'

He closed the glass divide between them, and a moment later, Fox arrived, wearing a black overcoat. He scrambled in and kissed her on the cheek.

'Kate, you look good.'

The Lincoln took off.

'You look pretty good yourself.'

He smiled amiably. 'Well, here's to a good night.'

At that precise moment, Terry Mount was swallowing another whisky sour in a downtown bar, aware of the bulge that seventeen thousand dollars now made in his right hand breast pocket. He went out into the street, drew up his collar as rain dashed in his face, started along the pavement, and sensed someone move in behind him, and then a needle-point going through his clothes.

'Just turn right into the alley.' He did as he was told, and found himself shoved against a wall. A hand searched. 'Hey, seventeen grand. You were right.'

'Who are you?'

'I'm a big black mother named Henry, and you wouldn't want to meet me in the showers on Rikers Island.'

Terry was terrified. 'I just did what I was told.'

'Which means you know too much. Regards from the Solazzos.'

The knife went up through the breast bone and found the heart, and Terry Mount slid down the wall.

It was early evening and March dark on Columbia Street, Brooklyn, as the Lincoln turned right and pulled on to a pier where a few coastal ships were tied up. Russo switched off the engine. Suddenly alarmed, Katherine Johnson said, 'What is this? Where are we, Jack?'

'This is the end of the line, Signora. You sure played me for a sucker.'

She managed a smile. 'Come on, Jack.'

'Come on, nothing. I've had your house searched. Found your little tape recordings of us. Not that I said anything, but you sure did. Just take it easy and flatter me, huh? You shouldn't have done that to me.'

'For God's sake, Jack, you've got to listen to me.'

'No, I'm done listening. And talking.'

A limousine pulled up behind. Fox got out and said to Falcone, 'Aldo, you make this good.'

'At your order, Signore.'

Fox got in the rear limousine and was driven away.

Katherine tried to open the door, but Russo was there, his great hand raised. Falcone cried, 'Leave it. I don't want bruising.' He found her neck and yanked her forward on her knees on the rear seat. Her skirt rose up.

'Go on, get on with it.'

He held her as she struggled. Russo took a box from his pocket, opened it, and produced a hypodermic. 'You'll like this, girlie. Best heroin on the market.' He jabbed her left thigh, then injected her again, this time in the right buttock. 'There you go.'

She cried out and slumped forward.

Russo patted her. 'Hey, she's not bad looking. Maybe I could do myself a little good here.'

He turned, reaching for his zipper, and Falcone gave him a shove. 'You stupid bastard, that'll blow the whole thing. Come on, give me a hand.'

Grumbling, Russo picked up her feet while Falcone took her arms, and they carried her to the edge of the pier.

'Easy now,' and she was in the water.

'Come on, let's go get a drink.' They walked back to the Lincoln, and a minute later they drove away.

Neither of them noticed Katherine Johnson's purse, where it had fallen out of the car, in the shadows beside a packing case.

The following morning at six o'clock, rain drove in across the East River, rattling the windows of the old precinct house. Harry Parker, brought out of bed only an hour before, drank coffee from a machine and made a face as a woman detective sergeant named Helen Abruzzi came in.

'This is disgusting,' Parker told her. 'Reminds me of why I switched to tea. Okay, what have we got?'

'This kid is called Charlene Wilson. She was working a strip bar not far from here.'

'And doing business on the side?'

'I'm afraid so.'

'What happened?'

'A man called Paul Moody took her home. When we found her, she'd been raped orally, half-strangled, her wrists tied.'

Parker frowned. 'That sounds like those two murders in Battery Park.'

'That's what I thought, Captain, and that's why I phoned you to come here. Charlene got away because he got drunk and fell asleep and she managed to loosen her hands.'

Parker nodded. 'Okay, let me know when the line-up's ready.'

She went out and Parker went to the window, the rain driving against it, and found a Marlboro, having long since stopped pretending to have quit. He lit it and looked out at the river morosely, a huge black man who had started life in Harlem, earned a law degree at Columbia, and then decided to join the police rather than a law firm. He'd never minded seventy-hour weeks, although his wife had, and had divorced him for it.

For three years now, he'd been captain in charge of a special homicide unit based at One Police Plaza. Sometimes he got depressed dealing with one killing after another, in a never-ending series, and when you were close to fifty you began to wonder if there was something better to do. He wondered if Blake had really meant what he'd said that there might be room for him in that special intelligence unit of his in Washington . . .

The door opened and Helen Abruzzi called, 'Show time, Captain.'

The girl in the viewing room was in a bad way, a blanket around her shoulders, her face swollen, one eye black, bruise marks on her neck. Helen stood behind her, a hand on her shoulder, while Parker read the file. He finished, nodded, and she pressed a buzzer. A light flared and five men appeared on the other side. The girl cried out.

'Number three. That's him,' she said and then she broke down.

Compassion didn't come easy at six o'clock in the morning on the East River, but Parker put an arm around her.

'Hey, take a deep breath. I know it isn't easy, but I'll make you a promise. I'm going to take this fuck out.' He squeezed her shoulder and nodded to Abruzzi. 'Take her away, then bring that bastard in.'

He stood at the window, looking down at the water, and after a while the door opened and Helen Abruzzi came in, followed by Paul Moody, cuffed between two police officers.

'And who the hell are you?' Moody demanded.

'Captain Harry Parker. Sergeant Abruzzi's got quite a list of charges against you, Moody, beginning with aggravated sexual assault.'

'Hey, the bitch wanted it. She was into sadomasochism, all kinds of stuff. I mean, I was shocked, man.'

'I'm sure you were, and I was forgetting physical assault on a minor.'

There was silence. Moody said, 'What's this minor crap?'

'Didn't Sergeant Abruzzi tell you? The girl, Charlene Wilson, was fifteen two weeks ago.'

Moody's face paled. 'Now, look, I didn't know that.'

'Well, you do now,' Helen Abruzzi told him.

'Another thing,' Parker said. 'There've been two killings in Battery Park within the last three months, using the same technique you prefer, Moody. Girls tied up, abused, beaten, and young.'

'You can't pin those on me.'

'I don't need to. We have good DNA samples

29

retrieved from Charlene Wilson. We've got the DNA of the Battery Park killer. I'd bet my pension we'll have a match.'

'Fuck you, nigger bastard.'

Moody lunged at him and the two officers restrained him.

Parker said, 'Why, Paul, you should conserve your energy. You're going to need it to keep you going for the next forty years in prison.' He nodded to the officers. 'Get this piece of shit out of here.'

He turned to the window as the door closed. Helen Abruzzi said, 'It's a bad one, sir.'

'They're all bad, Sergeant.' He turned. 'I need air. I'll take a walk if you can find me an umbrella. I'll come back to sign the papers later.'

'Fine, sir.'

He smiled, and suddenly looked charming. 'You've been doing a good job here, Sergeant. I've been noticing. There's an inspector's job coming up, if you'd like a posting to Police Plaza. You deserve it. I can't promise, mind you.'

'I know, sir.'

'Fine. I'll see you later, but ring the front desk and get me that umbrella.'

* * *

It was raining hard on the waterfront. Parker had borrowed a police raincoat with caped shoulders, and carried the umbrella Abruzzi had organized. The rain actually made him feel good, cleared the head. He lit another cigarette, and then an old man was running towards him in a panic.

Parker got his hand up. 'What is it? What's your problem?'

'I need the police!'

'You've found them. What's the problem?'

'My name's Richardson. I'm a night watchman at the old Darmer warehouse there. I was coming off shift and I went to the edge of the pier to toss my butt in the water, and . . . and there's a woman in the water!'

'Okay, show me,' said Parker and pushed him forward.

Katherine Johnson was a couple of feet under dark green water. Her arms floated to each side, her legs were open, the eyes stared into eternity. There was a look of surprise on her face and she was achingly beautiful in death.

Harry Parker took out his mobile and called the precinct. 'This is Captain Parker. I've got a Jane Doe in the water only three hundred yards from you. Let's get an ambulance and back-up out here.'

He stood there, holding his mobile phone, then handed it to Richardson and took off his raincoat. 'Hang on to those.'

He went down a flight of stone steps, waist deep in water, and reached for her. It was stupid, because that was the recovery team's job, but he couldn't leave her there. In a strange way, it was personal.

She was covered for a moment by flotsam, and he went chest deep and pulled her in and above his head. Above him, he heard the sound of vehicles grinding to a halt as the recovery team arrived.

Parker went home, changed, had breakfast at his corner coffee shop – eggs, bacon, English breakfast tea – and returned to his office. But the dead woman's face, the open eyes, wouldn't go away as he phoned Abruzzi.

'What's happening with the Jane Doe I found?'

'She's at the morgue. They've brought in the chief medical examiner. I believe he's doing the post-mortem himself later this morning.'

'I'll be down. Tell him I'm coming.'

When Harry Parker arrived at the office of the chief medical examiner, Dr George Romano was eating a sandwich and drinking coffee.

'Harry, my man, what's new?'

'This Jane Doe from the river. I took her out.'

'So you're feeling personal about it, right?'

'Something like that.'

'I'm about to finish the post-mortem. I was just taking a break. What do you want to know? Did she fall or was she pushed?'

'Something like that.'

'Okay, Harry, join me, 'cause this one stinks.' Romano drained his coffee and led the way out.

They went into the post-mortem room, where two technicians waited, suitably gowned. Romano held up his arms and one of them helped him into a robe. He went and scrubbed at the sink.

'There she is, all yours, Harry.'

Katherine Johnson lay on a slanting steel operating table, her head on a wooden block. She was naked, the Y cut of the preliminary vivid against her pale skin. Romano held up his hands and one of the technicians pulled on surgical gloves for him. There was a cart loaded with instruments and a TV video recorder on a swivel.

Romano said, 'Tuesday, March 2, resuming post-mortem Mrs Katherine Johnson, 10 Barrow Street, Greenwich Village.'

'Hey, what is this?' Parker demanded.

'Didn't you know?' Romano looked surprised. 'The guy who found her, Richardson? He was hanging around and discovered her purse. She must have dropped it when she went over the pier. Plenty of ID.'

'Okay. Fine. Let's get on with it. Why did you say this stinks?'

'She's a nice lady, well nourished, good condition, about forty years of age.'

'So?'

'So she died of a massive heroin overdose. Enough to kill her twice over. It doesn't fit. Someone like her, in her condition? Plus, someone on that stuff at a high level would have needle sores all over. She only had two – the recent ones. One in the left thigh, the other in the right buttock. And what was she doing in the water?'

'Accidentally overdosed and fell in?'

'Maybe. But I doubt it. Like I said, she wasn't an addict. And another thing. Her medical insurance card was in her purse and I checked it out. She was a lefty.'

'So?'

'Harry, with the greatest will in the world, I can't see a left-handed person injecting herself in the side of the right buttock. It's possible but unlikely.'

He reached for a De Soutter vibratory saw.

'So you're saying she was stiffed by someone?'

'Harry, like you, I've spent years in the death business. You get a smell for it. Yes, I'd say someone wasted her.'

'Which means I've got a murder case on my hands.'

'I'd say so. Now I'm about to take off the skullcap, so if you're not too happy about that, I'd leave.'

'Excellent advice. I'll take it,' said Harry Parker, and he turned and left.

He found his way to Abruzzi's office. She was seated at her desk, working away.

'I hear you turned up ID on the Jane Doe,' he said. 'Let me see.'

'It's an interesting one. She's a reporter for *Truth* magazine, named Katherine Johnson. I did a computer printout. Divorced, no children. Her husband was a guy called Blake Johnson, FBI.'

Parker's mouth went dry. 'Blake Johnson?'

'That's right. You know him?'

'We've worked together. Except he isn't FBI anymore. He works for the President.'

'Jesus, is this a hot one, Captain?'

'I'd say as hot as they come. You zip your mouth tight, Sergeant.'

'If you say so.'

'Jesus,' he said again. He looked at her. 'You

wouldn't happen to have a bottle of anything here, would you, Sergeant?'

She hesitated, then took a half-bottle of Irish whiskey from a drawer in her desk. 'For medicinal purposes,' she said.

'And sometimes we need it. Sergeant, you're working for me now. I'll take care of things with your lieutenant. The first thing I want you to do is call the White House and ask for a woman named Alice Quarmby. Got that? That's Johnson's assistant. I need to talk to her.'

He turned to the window, stared out, and took another swig from the bottle. Abruzzi called to him, he turned and took the phone.

'Alice? Harry Parker. Is Blake there?'

'He's with the President, Harry.'

'Damn.'

There was a pause. 'Is it important?'

So he told her.

In the Oval Office, President Jake Cazalet sat at his desk, Blake Johnson on the other side, as they reviewed the latest intelligence reports on the Irish peace process. The President's favourite Secret Service man, Clancy Smith, a tall, black Gulf veteran, stood by the door. The phone rang and Cazalet picked it up.

'Alice Quarmby, Mr President.'

'Hello, Alice, you want Blake?'

'No, Mr President, I need you.'

He straightened, aware from the tone of her voice that something was very badly wrong.

'Tell me, Alice.'

She did, and a minute later he replaced the phone and turned to Blake, genuine pain on his face, for this was a man he liked more than most, a man who had helped save his beloved daughter's life, who had saved the President himself from assassination.

Blake, sitting there in shirtsleeves, papers in front of him, said, 'What's the problem, Mr President? What did Alice say?'

Cazalet stood up and walked to the window, watching the rain drifting across Capitol Hill. He summoned up all his strength and turned.

'Blake, you're a true friend and one of the finest men I've known, and I'm going to hurt you now in the most terrible way. At least, thank God, it's me.'

Blake looked puzzled. 'Mr President?'

And Cazalet gave him the dreadful news.

When he was done, he ordered, 'Whisky, Clancy, a large one.'

Clancy was at the sideboard at once and back within seconds with a crystal glass half-filled with bourbon. He handed it to Blake, who stared at it, frowning, then swallowed it whole. He put the glass down on the desk.

'I'm sorry, Mr President. This is quite a shock. Although my wife and I were divorced, we've always stayed close, and now I . . . May I phone Alice back?'

'Of course. Use the anteroom for privacy, then we'll talk.'

'Thank you.' Clancy opened the door and Blake went out.

'Clancy,' Cazalet said, 'I need a cigarette.'

Clancy found a pack, shook one out, and gave it to him. 'Mr President.'

Cazalet inhaled deeply. 'These got me through Vietnam, Clancy. Blake, too, I suspect. What about you? In the Gulf?'

'Long days of boredom, broken by moments of sheer terror? Yes sir, a cigarette came in handy now and then.'

Cazalet nodded. 'Old soldiers, the three of us.' He sighed. 'He doesn't deserve this, Clancy. If there's anything we can do for him, I'd appreciate it.'

'My privilege, Mr President.'

Twenty minutes later Blake returned, his face grey, eyes burning.

'Is there anything I can do to help, Blake?'

'No, Mr President, except with your permission I need to get to New York now.'

Cazalet turned to Clancy Smith. 'Make the call and get the Gulfstream ready to take Blake to New York immediately.'

'You got it, Mr President,' and Clancy went out fast.

Cazalet turned to Blake. 'My friend, do you have any kind of idea what happened?'

'No, Mr President.' Blake pulled on his jacket. 'But I intend to find out. And with Harry Parker helping me, that's just what I'll do.' He held out his hand. 'Many thanks, Mr President, for your understanding.'

He turned and went out.

3

___

In Parker's office at One Police Plaza, Blake listened to the whole story. When the police captain was finished, Blake nodded.

'I'd like to hear what Romano said from his own mouth, then I'd like to see where it happened.'

'Be my guest.' Parker picked up the telephone. 'Have my car at the front entrance in five minutes.'

Shortly thereafter, still in the rain, that bad March weather, they stood on the edge of the pier with umbrellas and looked down into the water covered with scum and flotsam.

'She was there by the steps,' Parker told him. 'The night watchman saw her. I happened to be walking along.'

'And you pulled her in.'

'I couldn't leave her.'

Blake nodded. 'Let's go and see Romano.' He turned and walked away.

At the morgue, Romano was in the chief medical examiner's office, drinking minestrone soup from a plastic cup and eating French bread. Parker made the introductions.

Romano said, 'I'm really sorry.'

'Just tell me what you told Harry.'

Romano did.

'So she was murdered?'

'In my opinion, and for what it's worth, yes.'

'But why?' Parker demanded. 'And what would a nice middle-class lady with an apartment in the Village be doing in Brooklyn under these circumstances?' They sat silent for a moment. 'You never had any children, did you, Blake?'

'No.' Blake shrugged. 'It wasn't possible. She was sterile, so she concentrated on her career, and I concentrated on mine. We just kind of drifted apart. But though we got divorced, we never lost touch. We were always concerned friends.' He turned to Romano. 'I'd like to see the body.'

'No, you wouldn't.'

'Yes, I damn well would.' At that moment Blake looked every inch the Vietnam veteran.

Parker put a hand on Romano's shoulder. 'George, I'd say we should indulge the man.'

'Okay, let me phone down.'

She lay on one of the tables under the hard white light. There were enormous stitched scars where Romano had opened her up, the same scar around the skull.

Blake felt incredibly detached. This creature had been the love of his life, his wife, his support in many bad times, and now . . .

He said, 'I was never all that religious, but human beings are pretty remarkable. Einstein, Fleming, Shakespeare, Dickens. Is this what it ends up as? Where's Kate? This isn't her.'

'I can't give you an answer,' Romano told him. 'The essence, the life force – it just goes. That's all I can say.'

Blake nodded slowly. 'I'll tell you one thing. She deserved better, and someone should pay for this.' His smile was the most terrible thing Parker had ever seen when he said, 'And I'm going to see that they do.'

Back at Parker's office, there was a message for him to phone Helen Abruzzi.

'What's new?' Parker asked.

'Well, we checked out Katherine Johnson's house, and it's been burgled.'

'Damn,' Parker said. 'Okay, we'll be right there.' He turned to Blake and explained. Blake said, 'Let's take a look.' Helen Abruzzi was already there ahead of them when they arrived.

'There's no sign of forced entry, but the study upstairs has been ransacked. It's hard to tell what's been taken.'

She led the way, opened the study door, and entered. The scene of devastation was evident, videotapes scattered all over the place.

Parker said, 'Anything in the machinery?'

'Not a thing. No disks, no tapes, no copies, nothing in the computer.'

'That smells, for starters.'

Blake said, 'Somebody was after something, Harry, that's obvious, and probably found it. The thing is, what and why?' He turned to Abruzzi. 'Have the crime scene people finished here?' She nodded. 'Then could you get your people to look at these tapes littering the floor, Sergeant? You never know. You might turn up something.'

'I'll see to it, sir.'

Blake started down the stairs, and Parker said, 'Now where?'

'*Truth* magazine. I want to see Kate's editor, find out what she was working on. You don't

44

have to come. You've got other cases on your hands, Harry. I can handle this on my own.'

'Like hell you will,' Harry Parker told him. 'Let's get going.'

The editor of *Truth* magazine, Rupert O'Dowd, was the kind of middle-aged journalist who'd seen it all, been there, and done that, and he had little residual faith in human nature. Nevertheless, sitting in his office in shirtsleeves, he reacted with horror to the suggestion that Katherine Johnson had been murdered.

'Please, tell me, what can I do to help?'

'You can tell us what she'd been involved in lately,' Johnson said. 'Was she working on anything special, anything dangerous?'

O'Dowd hesitated. 'Well, there's a question of journalistic ethics here.'

'And there's the question of my wife being murdered by the administration of a massive heroin dose, Mr O'Dowd. So don't play around or I'll make you wish you'd never been born.'

O'Dowd put up a hand. 'Okay, okay, you don't have to come down hard.' He took a deep breath. 'She was working on a big Mafia exposé.'

There was silence. Parker said, 'Isn't that old stuff?'

'Only because the Mafia wants you to think that. Let me explain. The ruling power in the Mafia, the Commission, right? It called a halt to mob killings in New York in 1992 because of the bad publicity.'

'So?'

'So they started again last year. Five stiffed in Palermo a month ago, three in New York, four in London. But it's all different, all back-room stuff you can't connect to them. They've gone legit. They don't figure in *Forbes* magazine, but they're easily the biggest company structure in Europe. The drug market in America is saturated, so they've moved to Eastern Europe and Russia, but now they do it behind an elaborate façade.'

'So what are you saying?' Blake asked.

'That the days of men in gold chains have gone. Now they wear good suits and sit next to you in the Four Seasons or the Piano Bar at the Dorchester in London. They are into construction, property development, leisure, TV. You name it, they do it.'

There was a pause. Blake said, 'So where did my wife fit in to all this?'

'As I indicated, these days the new image is everything. The most influential Mafia group right now is the Solazzo family. Don Marco is the old devil who runs things, but he has an extraordinary nephew named Jack Fox. Fox's mother was Don Marco's niece, so the good Jack is half and half, though he sounds very Anglo-Saxon. He was a young Marine in the Gulf, a decorated war hero, Harvard Law School, and now he's the respectable face of the Solazzos.'

'And how does this affect Katherine?'

'She managed to get into a relationship with Fox. She was intending to produce a devastating series, not only for *Truth* magazine but also for our TV side.' There was silence, then O'Dowd said, 'She wanted to get behind that acceptable face of the Mafia and expose it.'

'Which meant showing the reality behind Fox,' Parker said.

'And he couldn't have that.' Blake nodded. 'So now we know.' He stood up and said to O'Dowd, 'Play this down. Trust me. Give us time and you'll get the story Kate wanted.' He held out his hand. 'A bargain?'

'It sure as hell is.'

On the way downstairs, Parker's mobile rang. He answered and nodded. 'We'll be there.' He turned to Blake. 'Abruzzi. She's sorted out the videotapes. Wondered if you'd like a look.'

'Why not?' Blake said.

The study at Barrow Street was much more ordered now, the videotapes arranged neatly on the shelves.

Helen Abruzzi said, 'I've put the movies on the top two shelves, the language courses and self-help tapes on the bottom two shelves.' She turned to Blake. 'There is one that refers to you, sir. That's what I thought you'd want to know.'

Blake said, 'What do you mean?'

'The label says: Blake's parents.'

Blake was silent for a moment. 'My parents died when I was very young. I never knew them. And my wife knew that better than anyone. I'd appreciate you turning that tape on, Sergeant.'

He sat down, Parker stood behind him, and the screen flickered.

'This is just a fail-safe, Blake, my darling, in case anything goes wrong. As someone who was the pride of the FBI and whatever you get up to there at the White House, I know you'll find this one way or the other.' She smiled at him. 'These are bad people that I'm trying to expose, the Solazzo family. Don Marco's like Brando resurrected for

Godfather IV, cold, calm, and businesslike, even while he seems like your favourite grandfather.'

'Jesus!' Harry Parker said.

'But Don Marco is old-school. Jack Fox is different. The genuine all-American hero and Wall Street golden boy. You'd think he was some Boston blue blood, but instead he's a cold-blooded psychopath, the worst of them all. Get in his way and you're dead. Well, I'm going to get *him*. Lull him to sleep with the first article, then wham! He'll never know what hit him.'

Blake hammered a clenched fist on a coffee table and Helen Abruzzi stopped the tape.

'What in the hell are you doing?'

'I'm giving you a chance to breathe deeply. I'm also finding you a drink. Trust me, sir.'

Parker put a hand on his shoulder. 'She's right, Blake.'

Helen Abruzzi returned with a glass. 'Vodka, it's all I could find. It was in the freezer.'

'That's what she liked, cold vodka.' Blake drank it down. 'Okay, let's get on with it.'

The screen flickered again. 'I was real lucky. I found a guy called Sammy Goff, who used to do accounting work for Jack Fox. Nice guy, very gay and very ill. AIDS, which is why Fox threw him out. I was having lunch with Fox in Manhattan one day. He left early, and Goff came up to me. "You look like a nice lady," he said, "so watch it. He's not good for you."'

A telephone sounded in the background and she went to answer it and returned.

'Okay, Goff was dying and bitter. I cultivated him, and with three martinis in him he sounded off good, and what he told me was special. Here's the lead. Fox is front man for the family. Smart, very clever, but he's always pushing for more. He's played the market with family money and lost, particularly with the Asian crisis. How much the Don knows about this is unknown to me. He's getting by because he's responsible for the Solazzo flagship casino in London, the Colosseum. The cash flow from that is critical to him. He can't milk the family's large interests, the drug market in Eastern Europe and Russia, for example, but he has personal cash flow that helps keep him afloat. There's a warehouse in Brooklyn called Hadley's Depository. The one thing they store there is whisky. Cheap liquor. The booze is watered down and then sold to the clubs at a huge profit margin.'

Parker said, 'I can't believe the Don doesn't know.'

Blake waved a hand and Katherine continued. 'Another sideline in London is he's been involved with some heavy gangsters called the Jago brothers. Armed robbery, that kind of stuff, Sammy Goff said, always a source of instant cash. Fox's bad investments in the Far East are draining him. More serious, he's been into arms dealing, too, specifically for the IRA. He helped somebody called Brendan Murphy, a real hard-liner who didn't like the peace process, not only to buy arms but to build a concrete bunker in County Louth in the Irish Republic. There's everything there from mortars to the kind of machine gun that can shoot down an Army helicopter. Oh, and lots of Semtex.'

'My God,' Helen Abruzzi said softly.

'Goff told me there was also some link with Beirut via Murphy. Arms for Saddam, that sort of thing. He didn't have many details on that. The other thing he told me was that Fox doesn't own a London house. He usually stays in a suite at the Dorchester, but he does have an indulgence. An old castle and estate in Cornwall, in England. Very rural, very remote. Believe it or not, it's called Hellsmouth. Somewhere near Land's End.'

A telephone sounded in the background again.

There was some confusion. She was off-screen, then back quickly.

'It's a hell of a story, thanks to Sammy Goff. However, although I'd like to expose it, Blake, life is uncertain, and the other day poor dying drunken Sammy was the victim of a hit-and-run driver. Now, was that an accident? I don't think so. He just knew too much.'

The screen seemed to jump and her voice scrambled for a moment. Things returned to normal. She smiled brightly.

'So there you are, my darling Blake. I'd like to believe the good guys win, but life can be such a bitch. If you're watching this, that probably means that the bad guys won this time.' The smile slipped for a moment, then came back, a little more tentative this time. 'Take care, and remember, in spite of everything, I've always loved you.'

Helen Abruzzi switched off. Blake sat there, eyes dark. 'I'd appreciate you running that back, Sergeant.'

'It's evidence, sir.'

'Just get the man a copy,' Parker told her.

Blake got up and walked to the window. After a moment, he turned. 'Okay, Harry, arrange a meeting with the bastard.'

'I'll have to check with the District Attorney.'

'Try the Pope if you like, but I want to face Jack Fox.'

'Maybe you should take time, sir,' Abruzzi told him.

Blake took a document from an inside pocket and unfolded it. 'You've never seen one of these, Sergeant. Harry has. It's a Presidential warrant. You belong to me, not NYPD, and so does he. Now let's get moving.'

It was the following morning when Parker picked up the Buick at the Plaza Hotel. The woman in the rear of the police car was very personable, around forty and smartly dressed, a briefcase on the floor beside her.

Blake sat in front and Parker said, 'Assistant District Attorney Madge McGuire.'

She shook hands as they drove away. 'I understand you're FBI, Mr Johnson.'

'Used to be.' He turned to Parker. 'Did you tell her?'

'How could I?'

Blake took out his Presidential warrant and passed it across. Madge McGuire read it. 'Jesus Christ.'

She handed it back and Blake put it in his pocket. 'So, what do you think?'

'We're wasting our time. Dammit, Mr Johnson, we all know the reality, but we can't prove it. You'll see – Fox will be all sweetness and light: any way he can help, he will, but when we finish we'll be no better off than when we started. His attorney, Carter Whelan, will be there, by the way. That one is a serpent.'

'Fine by me.'

'Okay. I'm bound by that warrant, but let me do my job, Mr Johnson.'

'Be my guest.'

When they got there, Fox was sitting behind a desk, wearing an excellent navy blue suit, his hair swept back from his handsome face. The man who sat beside him, Carter Whelan, was small, balding, and wore a black suit.

'I'm Madge McGuire, Assistant District Attorney, and this is Captain Harry Parker.'

'Pleased to meet you, Miss McGuire. I'm sure you know my attorney, Carter Whelan. And you are aware, I'm sure, that I'm an attorney myself. May I ask who this other gentleman is?'

'Blake Johnson, also an attorney,' Blake told him. 'I believe you knew my wife.'

Whelan said, 'He's no right to be here.'

Fox cut in. 'I've no objection. I was distressed to know of Katherine Johnson's untimely end. You have my sympathy.'

Parker said, 'Evidence would suggest that Mrs Johnson's death was no accident. Could you assist us in that matter, sir?'

Whelan said, 'Jack, you don't need to answer any of this.'

'Why not?' Fox shrugged. 'I've nothing to hide. I knew Katherine Johnson, gave her interviews, and she did an article about me for *Truth* magazine. It's in the latest edition. Quite flattering, actually.'

'Except for the references to the Solazzo family.'

'Just how well did you know her, sir?' Parker asked.

Fox said, 'I knew her well.'

'How well?'

Fox seemed to struggle with himself. 'All right, we had a brief affair. It only lasted a few weeks, and I didn't want to mention it, because I didn't want to damage her reputation in any way. For God's sake, the lady is dead.'

It was an impressive performance.

Madge McGuire said, 'Did you ever know her to use heroin?'

Fox struggled with himself again, got up, went to the window, turned, face working. 'Yes, once. I caught her at her apartment. I was shocked, tried to remonstrate. She said she'd only just started and promised to stop, but . . . I guess she didn't.'

Whelan said, 'She was obviously not very practised with it and must have accidentally given herself too much, or had a particularly lethal batch.'

'Still, there are certain anomalies,' Parker told him.

'Which have nothing to do with my client.' Whelan turned to Madge McGuire. 'Are we finished here?'

'Yes,' Madge said. 'That'll do for now. Thank you for your cooperation.'

She stood up, and Fox said, 'Hasn't Mr Johnson anything to say?'

Blake stood up, face pale, eyes very dark. 'Not really. It's all pretty clear,' and he turned and walked out.

In the car, Madge said, 'There's no case, people. It's not even worth trying to bring one. He just

gave the explanation for the lack of track marks –
she'd just started shooting and didn't know what
she was doing.'

'But if she'd shot up before, wouldn't there be
some tracks?'

'If it was only a few times, not necessarily.
Whelan would laugh it out of court, Mr Johnson.
There's evil here and we don't know the half of it,
but there's nothing we can do,' Madge told him.

'It gets harder the older I get.' Parker shook his
head. 'I've been a cop long enough to know when
something stinks, and this surely does.'

Blake lit a cigarette and leaned back. 'But what
about justice?'

'What do you mean?' Madge asked.

'What happens if it isn't done, and the law doesn't
work? Is someone entitled to take the law into his
own hands?'

'Well, I know one thing,' Parker told him. 'It
wouldn't be the law they were taking.'

'I suppose not.'

'What will you do, Blake?'

'Go back to Washington. See the President.
Arrange a funeral.' The car pulled in at the Plaza.
He shook hands with Parker and turned to Madge.
'Many thanks, Miss McGuire.'

He got out and went up the steps to the hotel. As the car moved away, Madge said, 'Are you thinking what I am, Harry?'

'If you mean, God help Jack Fox, yes.'

At the office, Fox waited for a computer printout he'd ordered on Blake Johnson. It finally appeared and he was reading through it when there was a knock on the door and Falcone entered.

'Just checking, Signore. Is there anything I can do?'

Fox passed him the printout. Falcone read it. 'Quite a record.'

'It sure as hell is. War hero, FBI, took a bullet saving the President. But there's a block there. What's he been doing lately? I'll have to get my top people to work on it.'

'Is he a threat?'

'Of course he is. He didn't believe me for a moment about his wife. Aldo, I've stared at the face of the enemy in Iraq, and I know what I saw in Blake Johnson's eyes. There was no rage in them, only revenge. He'll be coming, and we must be ready.'

'Always, Signore.'

Falcone went out, and Fox went to the window as a flurry of sleet brushed across Manhattan. Strange, he wasn't afraid. He was excited.

4

Fox had an impeccable source when it came to computer-accessing: an ageing lady named Maud Jackson, who was a retired professor in communication sciences at MIT, seventy years old – and a confirmed gambler. A nice Jewish widow who lived in Crown Heights, she was always chronically short of money, because she was an easy mark and liked the game anyway.

Fox met her in a local bar by appointment. She sat there, sucking on a cigarette and drinking Chablis, while he told her about Blake Johnson.

'The thing is, there's a block on the guy.'

'Like any roadblock, Jack, it's made to be gone around.'

'Exactly, and who better than you to do it?'

'Flattery will get you everywhere, but if this guy used to be FBI and there's a block, this is serious stuff.'

She took out another cigarette and he gave her a light, revolted by the thinning dyed red hair, the cunning old eyes, but she was a genius.

'Okay, Maud, I'll pay you twenty thousand dollars.'

'Twenty-five, Jack, and happy to oblige.'

He nodded. 'Done. There's only one problem. I want it, like, yesterday.'

'No problem.' She swallowed her Chablis and stood up and nodded to Falcone. 'Now, if this big ape will take me home, I'll get on with it.'

Falcone smiled amiably. 'My pleasure, Signora.'

It took her no more than three hours of devious double play to make her breakthrough and there it was: Blake Johnson, ex-FBI, now Director of the Basement for the President, and what a treasure house that turned out to be. The President's personal hit squad, and such an interesting cross-reference to London. It seemed that Johnson was very cosy with the British Prime Minister's personal intelligence outfit, led by one Brigadier Charles Ferguson, its muscle supplied by an ex-IRA enforcer named Sean Dillon. It was all there, past exploits, addresses, homes and phones. She telephoned Fox and asked to be put through.

'Jack, it's Maud.'

'Have you got something?'

'Jack, I don't know what's going on, but what I've got is pure dynamite, so don't screw with me. Just send Falcone round with thirty thousand in cash.'

'Our deal was for twenty-five, Maud.'

'Jack, this is better than the midnight movie. Believe me, it's worth the extra five.'

'All right. I'll have him there in an hour.'

'And, Jack, no rough stuff.'

'Don't be stupid. You're too important.'

An hour and a half later, Falcone returned with the printout. What Fox didn't know was that Falcone had stopped on the way and had the printout copied.

Fox read the printout – Johnson's background, the London end of things, Ferguson, Dillon, the computer photos – and shook his head.

'My God.'

'Trouble, Signore?'

'No, just rather startling information. The old bitch did well. Read it.'

Falcone already had, but pretended to again. He nodded and handed the printout back, face impassive. 'Interesting.'

Fox laughed. 'You could say that. This Dillon.'

He shook his head. 'What a sweetheart. Still, it's always useful to know what you're up against.'

'Of course.'

'Good. You can go. Pick me up at eight for dinner.'

Falcone left, and was at Don Marco's apartment at Trump Tower half an hour later, where the old man read the copy of the printout with interest and checked the photos.

'You've done well, Aldo.'

'Thank you, Don Marco.'

'Anything else you find out, tell me at once.'

He held out his hand and Falcone kissed it. 'As always.'

Brigadier Charles Ferguson's office was on the third floor of the Ministry of Defence, overlooking Horse Guards Avenue in London. He sat at his desk, a large, untidy man in a crumpled suit and Guards tie, working his way through a mass of papers.

The buzzer rang and he pressed a button. 'Is Dillon here?'

A woman's voice said, 'Yes, sir.'

'Good. Come in.'

The door opened. The woman who entered was perhaps thirty, wore a fawn trouser suit and horn-rimmed glasses, and had cropped red hair. She was Detective Superintendent Hannah Bernstein of Special Branch and allocated to Ferguson as his assistant. Many people had underestimated her because of her looks, and they'd come to regret it. She'd killed four times in the line of duty.

The man behind her, Sean Dillon, was no more than five feet four or five, with fair hair almost white. He wore an old leather jacket, dark cords and a white scarf. His eyes held no colour, but his mouth was lifted with a perpetual smile that said he didn't take life too seriously. Once an actor, and later the most feared enforcer the IRA had ever had, he had been working for what had become known as the Prime Minister's Private Army for several years.

'Anyone heard anything?' Ferguson asked. 'We keep getting rumours about secret IRA gun caches, but no specifics. Sean?'

'Not a peep,' Dillon told him.

'So what's next, sir?' Hannah Bernstein asked.

The phone rang on Ferguson's desk. He answered it and his face showed considerable surprise. 'Yes, sir. Of course . . . well, would you like to talk with

him directly? He's right here . . . Just one moment.'
He held the phone out. 'Dillon? President Cazalet
would like a word.'

Dillon frowned in surprise and took the phone.
'Mr President?'

'This is a bad one, my fine Irish friend, involving
Blake Johnson. Just listen . . .'

A few minutes later, Dillon relayed the news to
Ferguson and Hannah Bernstein. He walked to the
window, looked out, and turned.

'The funeral's the day after tomorrow. I'm going,
Brigadier.'

Ferguson raised a hand. 'Sean, the three of us
have all been to hell and back with Blake Johnson.
We'll all go. We owe him that.' He turned to
Hannah. 'Order the plane.'

Katherine Johnson's funeral at the crematorium
two days later was singularly unimpressive. Taped
and fake-sounding religious music played, and a
minister who looked as if he'd hired his costume
from a TV wardrobe company threw out plati-
tudes.

Ferguson, Dillon and Hannah arrived halfway
through the ceremony, just in time to see the coffin

slide through the plastic curtains. The only other people there were the funeral staff and a couple of people from *Truth*. Blake distributed dollars, turned, and found his friends. His face said it all.

Hannah Bernstein embraced him, Ferguson shook hands; only Dillon stood back, very calm. He inclined his head and walked out.

They stood on the step, the rain driving in, and Dillon lit a cigarette. 'I've heard what the President had to say, now I want it from you. You've saved my life on a number of occasions and I've saved yours. There are no secrets between us, Blake.'

'No, Sean, no secrets.'

'So let's collect the Brigadier and Hannah and go and sit in the limousine and we can all hear the worst.'

Blake told them everything, including all that Katherine had relayed to them on the videotape. Afterwards, they all sat silent for a moment. 'From my point of view, the arms-dealing with the IRA, the Brendan Murphy business, that's the worst,' said Ferguson, shaking his head. 'And the Beirut connection, working for Saddam. We've got to do something about that.' He turned to Hannah. 'What are your thoughts, Superintendent?'

'That Fox has problems. He's skimmed money

from the Commission, he's fiddling from the London casino, the Colosseum. Beirut and Ireland are desperate attempts to make cash.'

'And those hits with the Jago brothers are even more desperate,' Dillon said.

'Do you know them?' Ferguson asked.

'No, but I'm sure Harry Salter does.'

'Salter?'

Hannah said, 'You know him, sir. A London gangster and smuggler. Owns a pub at Wapping called the Dark Man.'

'Ah, I remember now,' Ferguson said.

'He's into warehouse developments by the Thames, also running booze and cigarettes from Europe.'

'But no drugs and no prostitution,' Dillon reminded her.

'Yes, an old-fashioned gangster. How very nice. He only shoots his rivals when absolutely necessary.'

Dillon shrugged. 'Well, they shouldn't have become gangsters then. I'm sure he'll help us with the Jago brothers and with Fox, though. He has a good team – his nephew, Billy Salter, Joe Baxter, Sam Hall.'

'Dillon, these people are real villains,' Hannah said.

'Compared to Jack Fox, they're sweetness and light.' And then Dillon smiled. 'Except that if you push them hard, they'll be Fox's worst nightmare.'

There was a pause. Ferguson said, 'Yes, well, we'll see. We'll talk about it more on the way back to London.'

Dillon said, 'Not me, Brigadier. I haven't had a vacation in two years. I think it's about time I took one.'

Ferguson said, 'Sean, you're not getting into one of your moods, are you?'

'Now, do I look that kind of fella, Brigadier?' He kissed Hannah on the cheek. 'Off you go. I'll see you in London. I'll drive back with Blake.'

She frowned. 'Now, look, Sean . . .'

'Just do it,' he said, turned and walked towards Blake Johnson's limousine.

Driving back to Manhattan, Dillon closed the sliding window partition.

'I take it we're going to take Jack Fox to the cleaners.'

'You say we.'

'Don't mess with me, Blake. If you're in, I'm in, for more reasons than we need to state.'

'Nobody should die like she did, Sean. Can you imagine? A dark, rainy night on the waterfront? Forced into taking that massive overdose?' He shook his head. 'I'll see Fox in hell, and don't talk to me about the law and all that kind of crap. I'm going to take him down in whatever way I have to, so my advice to you is to stay out of it.'

Dillon pulled open the panel and said to the driver, 'Pull over for five minutes and pass the umbrella.'

The man did as he was told, and Dillon got out and opened the huge golfing umbrella as Blake joined him. They stood by the wall and looked out at the East River. Dillon lit a cigarette.

'Listen, Blake, you're one of life's good guys, and Jack Fox is one of life's bad guys.'

'And you, Sean, what are you?'

Dillon turned, his eyes blank, face wiped of all emotion. 'Oh, I'm his worst nightmare, Blake. I was engaged in what I saw as war for twenty-five years with the Brits and the IRA. Fox and his fucking Mafia think they're big stuff. Well, let me tell you something. They wouldn't last five minutes in Belfast.'

'So what are you saying?'

'We take this animal out, only we do it my way. It's too easy to shoot him on the street. I want this to be slow and painful. We destroy his miserable little empire bit by bit, until he has nothing left. And then we destroy him.'

Blake smiled slowly. 'Now, that I would like. Where do we begin?'

'Well, according to Katherine, there's this place called Hadley's Depository in Brooklyn where they process cheap liquor.'

'So?'

'So let's take it out.'

'You mean that?'

'Sure. Just the two of us.'

Blake's face was pale with excitement. 'You really mean this?'

'It's a start, me old son.'

'Then you're on, by God.'

Hadley's Depository was beside a pier close to Clark Street on the river in Brooklyn. It was eleven o'clock that night, black rods of March rain falling, as Dillon and Blake drove up in an old Ford panel truck and parked at the side of the road.

They stood by a wall and Dillon lit a cigarette

as they looked the place over. 'This shouldn't be hard,' he said. 'You, me, and no one else. An in-and-out job.'

'There's just one thing, Sean. I don't want any victims here.'

'No problem. If there's a night shift, we leave it. If there's just security, we'll handle them. There'll be only one victim here, Blake: Jack Fox and his income from the booze business.' He laughed and hit Blake on the shoulder. 'Hey, trust me. It'll work.'

The following day, Blake went through files and accessed city and police records to find out everything he could about the Hadley Depository. When he saw Dillon for lunch at a small Italian family restaurant, he was quite strong again, probably because he had an end in view.

'It's funny, but this place has no record. Not even a hint with the police.'

'So Fox is a clever bastard. Do you have any details on how it operates?'

'I know the security firm who handles it. Two men guard the place. On the other hand, since the warehouse is not what it seems to be, who knows? They could have a night shift.'

'We'll see.' Dillon smiled, looking like the Devil

himself. 'No waiting, Blake. We go in and stiff the place. Give Fox something to think about.'

'When?'

'Tonight, for God's sake.'

Blake said, 'You're right. To hell with him.'

It was midnight when they drove up to Hadley's Depository in the old Ford. Blake was driving and pulled into a side turning. Both he and Dillon wore dark pants and sweaters. Now, as they sat there, they pulled on ski masks, and Dillon took a Browning out of a handbag and stuffed it into the waistband of his pants at the rear.

'Bring the other bag,' he told Blake. 'The Semtex pencils. Let's move it.'

There was a nine-foot wall. He cupped his hands, helped Blake over, then passed the bag, reached for an outstretched hand, and scrambled over himself. They crouched on the other side, as it started to rain.

'Okay, let's do it,' Dillon said.

There were indeed two security guards in a small, lighted office off a courtyard. Dillon and Blake moved in through factory doors which, surprisingly, had been left open. Inside the main building, they saw an extensive range of equipment, obviously all of importance to the racket that was going on there. Great vats, stacks of bottles, many with exotic labels.

Dillon pulled one up. 'Highland Pride Old Scots Whisky.'

'Believe that, you'll believe anything,' Blake told him.

'Okay, so let's get on with it.'

Dillon opened the bag that hung from his shoulder. He took out several Semtex primer pencils Blake had obtained for him, ran round the main area, and placed them.

'How long?' Blake asked.

'Ten minutes. Let's get those guards out and move on.'

The two security guards were playing Trivial Pursuit when the door opened and the men in hoods slipped in. Dillon relieved them of their guns.

'If you want to live, move fast and make it to the street.'

They didn't argue, did exactly as they were told, and a few moments later were out of the front gate. Just after that, the Semtex timers exploded and the whisky in the vats caught fire.

Dillon caught the nearest guard by the collar. 'Listen, here's a message. It isn't for the police.

It's for Jack Fox. Tell him, this is just the beginning, for Katherine Johnson. Got that? Okay, now run for it.'

Which they did.

Dillon and Blake drove some little distance away and parked, watching the flames and waiting for the fire department.

Blake said, 'Funny, but I didn't feel guilty.'

'Why should you? Fox is a murdering bastard.'

'I work for the President, Sean. You work for the Prime Minister.'

'I don't care about that. One way or another, Fox goes down.'

The following morning, Jack Fox was at Trump Tower, summoned there by a phone call from Don Marco. The old man sipped coffee by the fire.

'A bad night, I hear, Jack.'

Fox hesitated, then decided that at least some sort of truth was the best way to handle it.

'Yes, Uncle. The whole place was destroyed by fire. Thank God there is the insurance.'

'But only the equipment, Jack, not on a couple of million in booze.' The Don shook his head. 'It's very unfortunate. Still, these things happen.

Have you anything to add? Anything you wish to tell me?'

Fox hesitated, then said, 'No, Uncle.'

'Fine. I'll see you again.'

Fox went out. After a while, Falcone looked in. 'Don Marco.'

'Has he gone?'

'Yes.'

'Good. Bring the security guard in. My nephew failed to mention him, Aldo.'

'A matter to be regretted, Signore.'

'But you did, Aldo, and I'm grateful.'

He poured another cup of coffee, and a moment later Falcone brought in the security guard.

'Your name?' Don Marco asked.

'Mirabella, Signore.'

'Good, a fellow countryman. Now tell me what happened.'

Which Mirabella did.

Don Marco said, 'Tell me again what he said, the man in the hood.'

Mirabella clutched his cap in his hands. 'He said, this isn't for the police. Tell Jack Fox, it's just the beginning. For Katherine Johnson.'

'Good, thank you.' Don Marco looked at Falcone. 'Take care of him, then come back.'

Perhaps twenty minutes later, Falcone returned. The Don stood at the window, fingering a Cuban cigar. Falcone offered a light. Don Marco smiled.

'You're a good boy, Aldo. Your father was one of my most trusted people until those Virelli swine murdered him on that Palermo trip. He was always loyal, and loyalty is everything.'

'Absolutely, Don Marco.'

'So where does loyalty lie? You and my nephew, you were boyhood friends.'

'Please, Don Marco.' Falcone held up a hand. 'My loyalty is to you, above everything else.'

Don Marco patted his chest. 'You're a great comfort to me. You will attend to Jack's requirements, that goes without saying, but you will tell me everything that goes on, won't you, Aldo?'

'Always, Signore.'

'Good. Now be on your way.'

Jack Fox, in the Grill Room of the Four Seasons, sat with the great and the good and the not-so-good, drank champagne, and tried to come to terms with what had happened the previous night. The interview with Mirabella had been particularly unnerving, and he hadn't mentioned it to his uncle, for obvious reasons. Falcone and Russo stood against the wall.

A waiter appeared. 'Sir, your guests are here.'

'My guests?' Fox looked up, and Dillon and Blake appeared.

Falcone stepped forward and Fox waved him away. They sat down, and Dillon reached for the champagne bottle. He sampled it, shook his head, and said to Blake, 'The man has no taste.'

Fox said, 'Okay, get on with it. I know who you are. You're Blake Johnson and you work for the White House, and you're Sean Dillon. You used to be IRA, but now you work for the Prime Minister.'

'My, you are well informed,' Blake said.

'That's because I can access anything. The trouble with computers is that all you need is the right kind of genius to break into them, and I have mine. So, you fuck with me and you'll wish you'd never been born.'

'And we'll return the favour to Don Solazzo.' Dillon shrugged. 'And by the way, no one "used to be" IRA. Once in, never out. I'm really bad news, son. You know why? Because I don't care whether I live or die.'

'Maybe I can do something about that.'

'The British Army and the SAS couldn't catch

him in twenty years,' Blake said, 'so I doubt you'll have much luck. In fact, you're already running out of luck, aren't you, Jack? We know you front for the Solazzo empire. But you also have a personal sideline, a cheap liquor still in Brooklyn. Or at least you used to.'

'Hey,' Dillon said. 'Isn't that the place that got blown up last night? What a coincidence.' He smiled beautifully. 'Well, that isn't going to help the cash flow.'

Fox said, 'I don't know what you're talking about. That had nothing to do with me.'

'Oh, I believe it did,' Blake told him. 'And then there's all that family money you lost in the Asian banking collapse, money you didn't have the right to invest. Unless Don Marco knew and approved of it all? Which I doubt.'

Fox said calmly, 'What are you getting at?'

'That you're in deep shit with Don Marco unless you come up with some very considerable cash very soon.' Dillon smiled. 'And we intend to see that you don't get it.'

Fox turned to Falcone. 'Aldo, break this little bastard's right arm for me.'

Falcone moved forward, and Dillon's left foot flicked as he kicked the Sicilian under his right kneecap. At the same moment Blake took a Walther from under his jacket and laid it on the table. Falcone was down on one knee, grabbed for the table, and pulled himself up. Russo had a hand on the gun under his left shoulder.

'Is this what you want?' Blake asked. 'A gunfight at the OK Corral?'

'Not really,' Fox said. 'Let's leave it to a more appropriate time. Just go.'

'Our pleasure.' Blake stood up, and Dillon rose beside him.

'I have a line for you that I remember from some old movie I saw on television. To our next merry meeting in hell.'

'I look forward to it,' Fox told him.

They turned and went out.

Falcone said, 'They knew about the Depository.'

'So did a lot of people. It was an open secret. How many clubs did we deal with? A secret's only a secret when one person knows it.'

'You think they know about anything else?'

'No, they were just bluffing. Come on. We have to leave for London soon.' Fox drained the champagne in his glass and made a face. 'You know, that little bastard was right. This stuff is bad.'

*　　*　　*

80

In the bar at the Plaza, Dillon and Blake were sharing a pot of tea and Irish whiskeys when Ferguson and Hannah Bernstein appeared.

'My goodness,' Ferguson said. 'Here you two sit enjoying yourselves, when according to Captain Harry Parker somebody torched up Mr Jack Fox's illegal liquor still last night.'

'Do you tell me?' Dillon shook his head. 'Isn't that dreadful.'

'Are you coming home, Dillon?'

'Why not? I think I'm done with business here for the moment.'

'I would point out that when I saved you from the Serbs and took you on board, I offered to clear your rather terrible slate.'

'So you did.'

'But, on the other hand, you still haven't learned to behave yourself.'

'That's the Irish for you.'

Ferguson said, 'Sean, you still work for me. Use your judgement, but please keep me informed.'

'Jesus, Brigadier, I won't let you down. There's only one thing.'

'And what would that be?'

'I intend to totally destroy Jack Fox and the Solazzo family. In Ireland, London, Beirut –

wherever it takes me.' Dillon turned to Blake. 'Is that okay with you?'

'It sure as hell is. I'll see the President tomorrow and retire if I have to.'

Dillon turned and smiled at Ferguson. 'There it is, Charles.'

Ferguson smiled. 'Wonderful. Absolutely delicious.' He smiled, then didn't. 'In this case I actually approve of what you're up to. You will use Superintendent Bernstein as your connection. The full facilities of the department will be available.'

He stood up, and Dillon said, 'It's the grand man you are, Brigadier!'

'Well, I *am* half Irish.'

'I'll get on with it, then.'

'All the way. Finish Fox and the family.'

'Consider it done.'

'There is one thing. It's disturbing that Fox knows so much about us. What was it he said? You can access anything with the right kind of genius?'

'That's right.'

'Well, I know such a genius in London.'

Hannah Bernstein smiled. 'Roper, sir?'

'Exactly. See that the introductions are made at the right time, will you, Superintendent?'

She nodded.

'Good. Well' – he stood up – 'time to go. We'll see you later, Superintendent?'

They left. Dillon turned to Blake. 'You didn't figure much in that. What happens now?'

'I've got to clear myself with the President.'

'Then what?'

'Let's hit the bastard in London.'

'Sounds good to me.'

Cazalet had gone down to his old family house on Nantucket. Blake couldn't wait for his return, so he ordered a helicopter on departmental authority and flew down.

The President was walking the beach with his beloved flatcoat retriever, Murchison, followed by Clancy Smith. The surf roared, the sky was grey, a little rain drifted in, and the President read for the fifth time the fax he'd received from Harry Parker. There was a roaring in the distance. Clancy had a hand to his ear and mumbled into his mouthpiece. He looked up. 'Helicopter, Mr President. It's Blake.'

'Good. Let's go back to the house.'

They were halfway there when Blake appeared.

'Give us a little space, Clancy,' the President said.

They walked along the edge of the surf, Murchison running in and out. Cazalet said, 'Idiot. I'll have to hose him down.'

'I know. Sea water isn't good for his skin.'

Cazalet waved to Clancy, who lit a Marlboro away from the wind and handed it over.

Cazalet passed the fax to Blake. 'I'm afraid I leaned on your friend Harry Parker. I asked what was happening with this whole unhappy business.'

'And he told you.' Blake smiled. 'Well, he would. After all, I placed him under Presidential warrant. So, you know everything, Mr President.'

'Yes. A bad business. But it's wonderful that Brigadier Ferguson and Superintendent Bernstein flew over to support you.'

'And Sean Dillon.'

'As always!' Cazalet smiled. 'You know, it's a remarkable coincidence, that fire destroying Fox's warehouse like that.'

'Mr President . . .'

'No, Blake, let me speak. You've been looking tired lately. I think you need a break. Let's see what a month does. You should travel. Get to London, Europe. See some sights. Hmmm? Any departmental facilities you need are yours.'

'What can I say, Mr President?'

Cazalet said, face hard, 'Nothing at all. If you and Dillon can take those bastards down, then it'll be better for all of us.' He smiled crookedly. 'However, it would seriously inconvenience me if you didn't return from your vacation in one piece.'

'Yes, Mr President. I'll see to it.'

'Good.' Cazalet flicked his cigarette into the surf. 'Now, come back to the house for lunch and then, on your way.'

At Don Marco's apartment at Trump Tower, the old man listened as Falcone related what had happened at the Four Seasons.

Don Marco nodded. 'What does my nephew intend?'

'We're going to London, landing at Heathrow.'

'He's using the Gulfstream?'

'Yes, Signore.' Falcone hesitated. 'You don't know this?'

'Oh, I'm sure he'll tell me when he's ready. You have my coded mobile number. Keep me informed. I wish to know what he's up to at all times.'

He held out his hand, Falcone kissed it and withdrew. Don Marco rose, went to the piano, and picked up a photo of Jack Fox, the war hero in his Marine uniform.

'What a pity,' he said softly. 'All the virtues, as well as vanity and stupidity.'

He replaced the photo on the piano and went out.

LONDON

5

The following morning, Ferguson's plane landed at Farley Field, with the usual pilots, Flight Lieutenants Lacey and Parry, in the cockpit. A Flight Sergeant Madoc had also been on board, to see to the passengers' wants.

It was March weather again, the rain driving in towards the waiting Daimler. Madoc produced an umbrella as the four of them – Ferguson, Dillon, Bernstein and Johnson – went down the steps and led the way. They scrambled into the Daimler, and Ferguson leaned out to the two pilots.

'It could be a busy time ahead, so don't make plans.'

They both smiled. 'Excellent, sir,' Lacey said.

'Just one thing, Lacey. I do think you should wear correct uniform.'

Lacey was staggered. 'Brigadier?'

'Check the promotions list out today. I put you

89

up for Squadron Leader, and for once the Ministry of Defence has acted sensibly. In addition, in view of recent hazardous pursuits at my behest, you've both been awarded the Air Force Cross.'

They stared at him. 'Good God, sir,' Parry said. 'Sincere thanks.'

'Nonsense. Go and have a drink on it.'

Ferguson closed the door, and the chauffeur drove away.

Dillon said, 'I always knew it. At heart, you're a sentimentalist.'

'Don't be stupid, Dillon, they've earned it.' Ferguson turned to Hannah. 'We'll drop these two off at Dillon's house, then carry on to my place in Cavendish Square. I suggest you contact Roper as soon as possible to arrange a meeting.'

Blake said, 'Could someone tell me about this Roper guy?'

'Well, you recall the White House Connection and Lady Helen Grant? She wanted to know how to work the computer field in a nefarious way,' Hannah told him. 'She asked the London branch of her organization for help and they sent Roper.'

'A remarkable man,' Ferguson said. 'He was a captain in the Royal Engineers, a bomb disposal expert, awarded the Military Cross and the George

Cross, and then he got careless. A silly little car bomb in Belfast ended him up in a wheelchair. Computers became a whole new career for him, and he proved to have a real genius for them. As Lady Helen Grant found out.'

Blake was silent, remembering Lady Helen and the White House Connection case that had so nearly ended in disaster. So Roper had been her computer man.

'I look forward to meeting him,' Blake said.

The Daimler turned into Stable Mews, and Dillon and Blake got out. Hannah said, 'I'll contact Roper straight away.'

Blake carried the bags, and Dillon unlocked the door at the mews house and led the way in. It was small, Victorian, with Turkish carpet runners and wood block floors. The living room was delightful, sofa and chairs in black leather placed among scattered rugs, a superb painting over the fireplace.

'My God, that's fabulous,' Blake said.

'A great Victorian painter, Atkinson Grimshaw. Liam Devlin gave it to me. Remember him?'

'How could I forget? He saved our bacon. Is he still around?'

'Ninety years old and pretending to be seventy-five. Come on, I'll show you your room. Then we'll go to the King's Head on the other side of the square for what we call great pub grub in England.'

'Sean, I know what great pub grub is. It's usually the best food in London. So lead the way.'

As they were sitting in the King's Head, drinking Guinness and eating shepherd's pie, Dillon's coded mobile rang faintly.

Hannah said, 'I've contacted Roper. He lives on Regency Square, only half a mile from you.'

'Shall we go round?'

'No, he said he prefers the exercise. He operates one of those state-of-the-art electric wheelchairs. He hates being regarded as a cripple.'

'I hear what you're saying, dear girl.'

'He'll see you at Stable Mews at two-thirty.'

'We'll be there.'

'Another thing. I put out a search on the Special Branch computer. Guess who's arriving at Gatwick this evening? Jack Fox, Aldo Falcone and Giovanni Russo.'

'As Ferguson would say, quite delicious. This should prove interesting.'

He put the phone down, turned to Blake, and filled him in.

An hour later, at Stable Mews, it was Blake who happened to be at the sitting room window and looking out into the street, when he witnessed the arrival of the strange young man in the electric wheelchair. The man wore a navy blue reefer coat, a white scarf at his throat. When Blake went into the hall, Dillon already had the door open.

'Ah, Mr Dillon. I've seen your face on my computer. Roper's the name.'

He had hair to his shoulders, hollow cheeks and very blue eyes. His face was a taut mask of scar tissue, the kind you only got from burns.

'Come in,' Dillon said cheerfully.

'Only if you help me over the step. It's the one thing these gadgets can't manage.'

Dillon obliged, then pushed him along the hall into the kitchen, Blake following.

Roper said, 'What I could really do with is a nice cup of tea.' He turned to Blake. 'Lieutenant.'

Blake smiled. 'Should I say "sir"?'

'Of course. I outrank you.'

Forty-five minutes later they'd filled him in on everything they needed from him. Roper said. 'Fine. I'll go into everything. The Solazzo family, Jack Fox, the Colosseum operation, these Jago brothers. Oh, and this Brendan Murphy. I remember the name from my Irish service. A hard man, as I recall.'

'No, a fanatic, Brendan,' Dillon said. 'I had dealings with him in the old days. Hates the peace process, and now we hear he's into arms dumps – and possibly worse, this hint of an involvement with Saddam in Beirut.'

'So I'll access Army HQ at Lisburn, the RUC, the Garda in Dublin, maybe the Security Services.'

'You can do that?' Dillon asked.

'Dillon, I can even access your lot, and Ferguson probably knows that. I'm the hand of God, so leave it with me.'

'Okay,' Blake said. 'But in case you don't know, Fox turns up in London this evening, plus his two minders.'

'Falcone and Russo.' Roper smiled tranquilly. 'Mafia hard men. Ireland was my business for eleven years and terrorists were my enemy, but in a strange way you can empathize with your enemy, both IRA and Loyalists. These two wouldn't last half an hour in Derry or Belfast.'

'So, what happens now?' Blake asked.

'Well, from what I've been told, you want to see the Colosseum severely damaged.'

'Exactly.'

'Good. Then wheel me out into the street and I'll go home and organize it.'

Blake said, 'You'll be able to do it, then?'

Roper nodded. 'No problem. God wouldn't have given some people brains if He'd wanted the scum to inherit the earth.' He turned to Dillon. 'I'll see you at six at my place in Regency Square. You will then put into operation what I tell you to. Is that acceptable?'

'Bloody cheek,' said Dillon, but then he smiled. 'I'm sure it will be, so let's get on with it,' and Dillon wheeled him out.

Roper's apartment in Regency Square was on the ground floor, with a slope to the front door for his wheelchair. Everything from the bathroom to the kitchen had been designed for a handicapped person. In what would have been the sitting room was a kind of computer laboratory, with every kind of equipment on view on a workbench.

He answered the door when Dillon, Blake and Hannah Bernstein arrived. 'Ah, there you are.'

He led the way through to the sitting room. 'Here we are, then.' He tapped a keyboard and the screen started to fill. 'Colosseum Casino, Smith Street. General Manager, Angelo Mori. Minders, Francesco Cameci, Tino Rossi.' Photos appeared. After a while, he tapped again and ground plans came up.

'Lots of security,' Blake said.

'Not if you know your way in.'

'So what would be the point?' Dillon asked.

'A top casino stands on its reputation. The slightest hint of scandal, and the Gaming Act enters into it and the place can be closed down.'

There was silence. Dillon said, 'And how do we achieve that?'

'Tonight will tell you, if you do what I say and go in hard.'

'You mean go in feloniously, Captain,' Hannah said.

'That sums it up. You want this bastard, we go for the throat.'

Dillon said, 'That suits me, and as the Superintendent knows, I've been guaranteed the full co-operation of the Department by Brigadier Ferguson, so let's hear what you have in mind.'

'It's very simple. What's one of the oldest games of chance in the world? They loved it at the height of the Roman Empire. They still love it.'

Blake smiled. 'Craps.'

'Exactly. You simply throw the dice and pray the right number comes up. People can't resist.'

Dillon said, 'So what do you want?'

'Dice, old boy. Steal me some dice.'

'Why?' Blake asked.

'Because every casino has its own made to order. Unique. Of course, once I have them at my workbench I make a slight adjustment, put a spot of lead inside, and they become what's known in the trade as loaded dice. Now, if the house is using loaded dice, the punters are bound to lose.'

'But how do you make the house actually use the loaded dice?' Blake asked.

'That's the whole point about having house dice. You or Dillon join the crowd making a wager. When your turn comes and the dealer gives you the dice, you palm them and use the ones I've doctored. They'll have the house logo on them, so everyone will assume they're the real thing. Of course, it will be necessary to bring this unfortunate situation to the attention of the other gamblers. The results could be devastating for the casino.'

'You wicked man, you,' Dillon said.

'You or Blake, I think, should be the ones. I wouldn't dream of asking the Superintendent.' He smiled at Hannah. 'I happen to know you're Jewish Orthodox, with a rabbi for a grandfather.'

She smiled. 'My grandfather might surprise you. His poker is deadly.'

Dillon said, 'Sounds good to me. So what's the plan?'

At ten o'clock that evening, Jack Fox arrived at the Colosseum, backed by Falcone and Russo. He was stopped at the door by a large man in evening dress.

'Membership card, sir.'

'I don't need one. I own this casino.'

'Very funny.'

The bouncer put a hand on Fox's shoulder and Russo said, 'You want me to break your right arm? You just made the biggest mistake of your life.'

'Signor Fox, what a pleasure,' a voice called, and Angelo Mori, the general manager, rushed down the stairs, followed by his two minders. 'Is there a problem?'

'Hell, no,' Fox said, and smiled at the bouncer. 'What's your name?'

'Henry, sir.' He looked very worried.

'You're doing a good job, Henry.' Fox took out

his wallet, extracted a fifty-pound note, and slipped it into Henry's breast pocket. 'In fact, you're doing a great job. Anyone else comes in and says they own the joint, kick them in the balls.'

There was sweat on Henry's forehead. 'Yes, sir, anything you say.'

Inside, the main room was crowded, every kind of game in progress. Fox nodded approvingly. 'Looks good. How's the cash flow?'

'Terrific.'

Fox turned to Mori's minders, Cameci and Rossi. 'You two behaving yourselves?' He used Italian.

'Absolutely,' Rossi told him. 'Don Marco is well?'

If this seemed overly familiar, it wasn't. Rossi came from the same village as the Solazzo family, close to Corleone in Sicily.

'He is very well,' Fox continued in Italian. 'And I appreciate your concern.' He turned to Mori. 'We just flew in, and I'm starving. The restaurant is still open, I trust.'

'For you, it never closes, Signore.'

'Excellent. Louis Roederer Cristal, nineteen-ninety, smoked salmon, scrambled eggs, chopped onions. I've got to watch my health.'

'But you look wonderful, Signor Fox.'

'Hell, I'm the only man in here tonight who took a bullet in the left side in the Gulf War, Angelo. I've got to be careful.'

They moved through the main room and entered the small restaurant. Mori led the way to a corner booth.

'Is this satisfactory, Signore?'

'Excellent. Put Falcone and Rossi at the next table. They'll probably stuff themselves with spaghetti bolognese, but anything they want, they get.'

'Of course.'

'Another thing. I'm expecting the Jago brothers, Tony and Harold.'

'Yes, they phoned.' Mori looked pained.

Fox laughed. 'They're terrible people, I know. Think they're the reincarnation of the Kray brothers, fell in love with their legend years ago, but the Kray brothers were special. The Jagos will never match that. Still, they're working with us. When they arrive, wheel them in.'

Mori departed. Fox took out a cigarette and Falcone gave him a light. 'Trouble with these English bastards, Signore?'

'No. They've seen too many gangster movies, but they have their uses. Nothing you and Russo can't handle. Now get me a martini.'

Half an hour later, just as he finished his scrambled eggs, the Jagos arrived. Harold, the elder, was forty, just under six feet, hair already greying, face pock-marked. Tony was thirty, smaller in every way, his right cheek disfigured by a razor scar. The one thing they had in common was the beautifully tailored Savile Row suits that both wore.

'Jack, it's good to see you.' Harold shook his hand.

'Join me,' Fox said. 'As you say in London, I may be able to put a bit of business your way.'

'Anything,' Harold said with enthusiasm. 'I mean, that security van tickle was magic.' He turned to Tony. 'I mean, it really was, wasn't it, Tony?'

Tony, a hard little bastard who was English enough not to like foreigners, said, 'If you say so, Harold.'

'Well, he does,' Fox said dryly, and snapped a couple of fingers at Falcone. 'The briefcase.'

Falcone had been carrying it all evening. He took it from under the table and passed it across. Fox gave it to Harold.

'It's all in there, page by page. I'll leave you to put the team together.'

'But what is it?' Harold demanded.

'That new development at Wapping. St Richard's Dock. The White Diamond Company.'

Harold was horrified. 'That's impossible. It's a fortress.'

'Yes, well, they forgot one thing. London's riddled with underground rivers and tunnels, some of them hundreds of years old, and one of them happens to be under St Richard's Dock. It's all in the file. Read it over and we'll talk again. If you're not interested, I'll get someone else.'

It was Tony who said, 'How much?'

'Ten million basic, maybe more. You get forty per cent.'

'Fifty,' Tony answered.

Harold said, 'Shut your mouth,' and turned back to Fox. 'I'll read the file, but I can tell you now we're in, Jack. Leave the team to me.'

'Good man.' Fox smiled. 'Now, let's have a bottle of champagne on it.'

The casino closed at two in the morning; by three all was quiet, with only a security guard in the office by the main entrance, watching TV.

Along the street beside the basement entrance was a grey British Telecom van. The rear door opened and Blake Johnson, wearing a hard hat and yellow oilskins, got out, carrying two grappling hooks, and lifted a manhole cover in the pavement. Dillon passed him an inspection lamp and a red warning light saying: Danger. Men at Work. He then passed some canvas screens and an awning against the rain. There was an army of wires and switches. Blake tried to take an interest.

Inside the van Roper, in a wheelchair, sat opposite a very simple-looking computer set-up. Dillon, in black tee shirt and jeans, crouched beside him. Roper punched the keys.

'How's it looking?' Dillon asked.

'So far, so good. Don't worry, the great Roper is never wrong.' There was the sound of a car slowing outside and he raised a hand. 'Wait.'

Blake looked out from under the awning, the rain pitiless. The police patrol car slowed, the driver leaned out.

'What a bloody way to make a living at this time in the morning.'

'You, too,' Blake told him, putting on his best British accent.

The policeman smiled and drove away.

Dillon said, 'Let's do it.'

'Fine. As I told you, I can screw the entire security

system, but only for fifteen minutes, so you'll need to be fast.'

'Hell, I've been all over those ground plans you showed me. I know where I'm going.'

'You better had. I'm starting now, so count to ten and get down to that basement door.'

Various lights flickered on the screen, reds and greens, there came a faint sound, and then Dillon was out of there, past Blake and down to the basement, pulling up his hood.

He had a small flashlight, but really didn't need it, for there were subdued security lights everywhere. He had no worries about cameras. As Roper had told him, they were frozen, too.

Remembering the ground plans from the computer screen, he went up the steps fast, passed through the kitchens, and emerged by the entrance to the restaurant. He could see into the glass office by the main door. The security guard was fiddling with the TV, which had gone off.

Dillon slipped through the shadows into the main gambling room and found the right table. There was a tray of dice on the table, all very neat, but he left them alone, and instead dropped to one knee by the right-hand side of the table, where the dealer stood. There was a stack of dice there. He took six, no more, and put them into his pocket, turned, and went out fast.

The security guard was still arguing with the TV. Dillon slipped through the shadow, went down the steps, and speeded into the basement, closing the door behind him. He stepped past Blake, gave him a thumbs-up, and went into the van. He took the six dice from his pocket and put them on the bench in front of Roper.

'There you go.'

'Thirteen minutes,' Roper said. 'You did well.' He tapped the keys and sat back. 'Everything normal again.'

'Now what?'

'We clear up and get out of here.'

Dillon removed his hood and went out to Blake. 'It worked. I got what he wanted, so let's get moving. I'll help you.'

'Okay,' Blake said.

Dillon collapsed the screens and awning and put them into the truck, while Blake replaced the manhole cover. A few moments later, they drove away, Dillon at the wheel.

At Roper's place in Regency Square, they sat and watched him at the bench examining the dice with an eyeglass.

'Will it be okay?' Blake asked.

'Of course it will, old boy. Being a perfectionist, however, I prefer solitude when engaged in sensitive work, so be good and clear off. You won't be able to use these things until tomorrow night anyway, so I've got all the time in the world.'

Dillon nodded to Blake and they stood up. 'We'll check in tomorrow, then.'

'You do that,' Roper said, ignoring them completely as he picked up a tiny electric drill of the kind used by jewellers.

The following morning at eight, Dillon's phone rang, and Ferguson said, 'As I've had no intimations of disaster, you must have pulled it off last night.'

'Absolutely. We're in Roper's hands now.'

'What are you and Blake up to?'

'We're going to the King's Head for a full English breakfast.'

'I can't wait to join you.'

Which he did half an hour later, accompanied by Hannah Bernstein. They all ordered, and Ferguson said, 'You haven't checked with Roper yet?'

'Give him a chance, sir,' Hannah said, as the waiter arrived with the breakfasts on a large tray.

Dillon said, 'Pass your bacon to me, Hannah. I wouldn't want to put your fine Jewish principles under siege.'

'You're so kind, Dillon.'

And then the door opened with a bang and Roper surged in. 'Smells great.' He turned to the waiter. 'The same for me.'

'I must say, you look astonishingly well,' Ferguson said.

'You mean for a cripple who hasn't been to bed all night?' Roper asked, and took the six dice from his pocket and rolled them on the table. They all came up ones. 'Snake eyes.' He turned to Blake. 'Isn't that what you call them in Vegas?'

'It sure as hell is.'

'Excellent. God help Jack Fox and the Colosseum this evening. I think I'll go and watch.'

'You have to be a member,' Hannah Bernstein said.

'Which, thanks to my computer, I am. In fact, you all are.' The waiter appeared with his breakfast. 'My God, this looks good.' He picked up a knife and fork and got to work. 'I assume it had occurred to you that if Dillon and Blake wanted to create mayhem in the Colosseum tonight, they also needed to be members?'

'Of course it did.' Ferguson smiled. 'And I knew you'd take care of it. It'll be an interesting night ahead of us, I think.'

'You can sure as hell say that,' Blake agreed.

6

Roper's expertise produced plastic membership cards for all of them, plus photos of Rossi and Cameci, the restaurant's minders, to add to those of Falcone and Russo, and that evening, at eight o'clock, they were passed through the door at the Colosseum by Henry, Roper in a light collapsible wheelchair pushed by Dillon.

The main room was already busy, waitresses in minuscule skirts moving through the crowd offering champagne. Dillon took a glass and looked up.

'Any good?' Blake asked.

'If you like sparkling wine, but champagne it's not.'

'Ah, well, Fox will be into profit margins,' Ferguson observed.

They stood in a small group by the bar, and Hannah said, 'There are a couple of villains you're interested in, sir. The Jago brothers, Harold and Tony, at the end of the bar.'

The others took a look. Ferguson said, 'Very unsavoury.'

'Yes, well, we can sort them out later,' Dillon said. 'The thing is, who's going to start the ball rolling?'

'Well, actually, I've had another of my ideas,' Ferguson said. 'We have six dice, so why not two each?'

'Brigadier, I can see why you achieved high command,' Blake told him. 'Agreed, Sean?'

'Why not?' Dillon turned to Roper. 'Here we go. Showtime.'

Roper passed the dice across and Dillon gave the others theirs. 'There you go.'

'Into action, then,' Ferguson said. 'Let's get on with it,' and turned for the dice table. 'Oh, and palm your dice smoothly, gentlemen.'

In the restaurant, Fox enjoyed his scrambled eggs and smoked salmon again and tried a little Krug champagne.

'Great stuff, this,' he said to Falcone. 'But not the vintage. It's the non-vintage that's really special. Different grapes.'

Russo appeared. 'There's a problem, Signore. You remember those two from the Four Seasons in New York, Dillon and Johnson?'

'Yes?'

'They're here now, in the main room.'

'Really?' Fox emptied his glass. 'Well, let's take a look.'

Falcone pulled back the chair, and Fox stood up and walked out into the most active part of the casino.

Russo said, 'Over there, Signore. Next to some woman and another man. In the striped suit, see?'

Fox snorted. 'That "some woman", Russo, is Detective Superintendent Hannah Bernstein of Scotland Yard's Special Branch. And that "another man" is Brigadier General Ferguson, head of a special intelligence unit for the Prime Minister. An absolutely devious old bastard. I guarantee you they're not here for a friendly game of cards.'

'So what do we do, Signore?' Falcone asked. 'Move them out?'

'Don't be stupid,' Fox said. 'This is one of the most prestigious gambling clubs in London. Scandal is the last thing we want. You expect me to expel a brigadier general and his friends? No, we wait and see what they're up to.'

111

The dice table was a popular one, every inch taken up by the crowd standing around. Ferguson said to Hannah, 'Would you like to have a go, Superintendent?'

'No, sir. I don't know craps. It's not one of my vices.'

'Well, it's one of mine,' Blake said. 'Let's do it.'

He had to wait ten minutes for his chance, then took the offered dice and started. Strangely enough, he did quite well for the first three throws, actually won money. Then he palmed the dice and tossed two of Roper's.

'Snake eyes.'

There was a groan from the crowd.

The dealer passed the dice to Dillon, who palmed them for the real article, and made two successful throws. Then, just when he had everything riding on the toss – 'Snake eyes!'

'Hey,' he said ruefully, 'bad luck I understand, but this is diabolical.'

Ferguson moved in. 'Let me try, old boy. Mind you, these dice do seem to have lost their edge.' He turned to the croupier. 'Let me have a new pair.'

The croupier complied. Ferguson rolled and immediately came up with snake eyes. He turned to a military-looking man with a stiff moustache next to him. 'How strange.' He laughed. 'We all keep getting the same thing.'

'Yes,' the military-looking man said slowly. The croupier's rake reached out, but the military-looking man said, 'Not so fast,' and grabbed the dice.

The croupier said, 'I hope monsieur isn't suggesting there could be something wrong?'

'Let's see.'

The man rolled the dice and threw them the length of the table: again, snake eyes. The croupier's rake reached out and the military gentleman beat him to it.

'Oh, no, you don't. That's snake eyes too many times. These dice are loaded.' There was a sudden murmur from the crowd and he turned to an ageing gentleman. 'See for yourself. Pair of ones guaranteed.'

The man threw and the result was clear. The outrage in the crowd was plain to see, and Mori hurried down the steps.

'Ladies and gentlemen, please. A misunderstanding.'

'Are you the manager?' Ferguson demanded.

'Yes,' Mori replied.

'Then oblige us by throwing those dice.'

Mori hesitated. People in the crowd shouted, 'Get on with it.'

Mori threw. The dice rolled. *Snake eyes.*

The crowd roared in anger. The military-looking man said, 'That settles it. Loaded dice, and I've lost a bundle here in the last few weeks. We need the police.'

'Ladies and gentlemen, please,' Mori called.

Fox, Falcone and Russo stayed well to the rear.

Hannah Bernstein moved forward and said to Mori, 'The dice, sir, I'll have them.'

'And who the devil are you?' He was so upset he asked her in Italian.

Hannah replied with fluency in the same language. 'Detective Superintendent Bernstein, Special Branch.' She looked at the dice she picked up. 'I notice that, in accordance with the Gaming Act, these carry the club's registered mark. Do you agree?'

'Well, yes,' Mori said lamely, then added, 'Someone must have substituted false ones.'

The military-looking man said, 'Don't be stupid. What on earth would be the point of a player substituting for the real dice a pair that would make him lose?'

There was a roar from the crowd, Mori sagged

across the table, and Hannah said, 'In accordance with the statutory provisions of the Gaming Act, sir, I must issue an order closing you down until such time as Westminster Magistrate's Court can consider the matter. I believe you also own twelve betting shops in the City of London. Is that so?'

'Yes,' Mori told her.

'I'm afraid they must close, also. Any infringement of this order means a fine of one hundred thousand pounds with further penalties thereafter.'

'Of course.' Mori raised his voice shakily. 'Ladies and gentlemen, I'm afraid we must close by order of the police. Please leave now. Don't forget your things.'

The crowd faded, and at the rear were Ferguson, Bernstein, Dillon, Blake, and Roper in his wheelchair. At the door, Dillon turned and waved to Fox.

'Hey, there you are, old buddy. Have a good night!'

They went out. Fox turned to Falcone. 'I want to know where they go. There must be a couple of young punks available. Not Rossi or Comeci.'

Russo said, 'There's Borsalino and Salvatore in the kitchen.'

'Get them now. I know who most of them are, but not the one in the wheelchair. Then follow him to hell.'

They took Roper from his wheelchair, eased him into the Daimler, and then followed him, after folding his wheelchair.

'Now what?' Blake asked.

'We wait for Fox to react,' Dillon said.

'Shall we eat?' Ferguson asked.

'Not me, Brigadier,' Roper told him. 'I want to check out the computer again. Take me home, then you lot go and enjoy yourselves.'

But already following the Daimler was a very ordinary Ford car driven by a young man named Paolo Borsalino, with his friend, Alex Salvatore, sitting beside him. In Sicilian terms, they were *Piccioti*, youngsters gaining respect, doing the odd killing, climbing up the ladder. Borsalino had acted as executioner three times, and Salvatore twice, and they were eager to do more.

The Daimler stopped in Regency Square, and Dillon got out, set up Roper's wheelchair and helped him into it. They all got out and Dillon took Roper's key and opened his door.

Ferguson said, 'We'll speak tomorrow. Excellent job, Captain.'

'We aim to please, Brigadier.'

Dillon pushed Roper up the ramp into the hall. 'You're a hell of a fella, Roper.'

'Well, considering your background, I take that as a compliment.'

Dillon closed the door and went back to the others. 'Now what?'

'Fredo's – it's round the corner from Cavendish Square. A nice Italian restaurant,' Ferguson said. 'We can have a look at what's next.'

The Daimler drove away, and Borsalino and Salvatore, parked at the end of the square, watched them go. Salvatore said, 'Now what?'

'You watch the car,' Borsalino said. 'I'll be back.'

He walked to the other side of the square and found a corner shop, the kind that stayed open until midnight. The man behind the counter was Indian. Borsalino asked for two packs of Marlboros.

'You know, I saw this guy earlier getting out of a taxi in the square in a wheelchair. I thought I knew him, but I'm not sure.'

'That would be Mr Roper,' the Indian said. 'He was a captain in the Royal Engineers. Blown up in Ireland.'

'Oh, well, I've got it wrong. Thanks, anyway.'

Borsalino returned to the Ford, called Fox on the mobile, and relayed the information, also telling him where they were.

Fox said, 'Stay there. I'll be back.'

At that point, he was still in Mori's office at the casino. He picked up the telephone and called Maud Jackson in New York. It was late afternoon there and she was enjoying a pot of tea and cookies.

Fox said, 'Maud, I'm having serious problems here in London with Ferguson and company. There's a wild card, a British Royal Engineers captain in a wheelchair, blown up in Ireland, name of Roper. I'd like to know who he is right away.'

'Where are you?'

'I'm going back to the Dorchester. We had problems at the Colosseum.'

'Sounds like a bad night. Give me an hour.'

At the Dorchester, in the Oliver Messel Suite, Fox drank Krug champagne and looked across the wonderful London view by night from the terrace. Russo was down in the suite he and Falcone were sharing, but Falcone was standing by, as usual.

'More trouble, Signore?'

'We'll see, Aldo.'

The phone rang and he answered it. Maud Jackson said, 'Boy, do I have a good one for you. This Roper was blown up by the IRA, all right, and now he's a legend – in computers. Jack, if he's into your affairs, you've got serious trouble.'

'Thanks, Maud, you're an angel.'

'Yeah, well, don't forget to send a cheque.'

Fox put down the phone and said to Falcone, 'Take him out.'

'Me personally, Signore?'

'Of course not. Get over to Regency Square. See Borsalino and Salvatore. Give them their instructions. Have them get rid of him. I smell big trouble where he's concerned.'

'At your orders, Signore,' Falcone said. 'I'll leave Russo here.'

He used Fox's Mercedes limousine, driven by Fox's Italian driver, Fabio, closed the screen, and called Don Marco on his mobile and brought him up to date.

'This isn't good,' Don Marco said. 'I'm beginning to smell trouble here myself. Keep me informed, Aldo.'

Falcone found Borsalino and Salvatore in the Ford parked in the square very close to Roper's place. They were, of course, all attention.

'Stay here for the moment. This guy in the wheel-chair? You take him out, but make it look like an accident. You wait if it takes all night. You wait if it takes until tomorrow, but he's finished. *Capisce?*'

'Anything you say,' Borsalino told him.

Falcone left them, went back to the Daimler. Fabio said, 'Back to the Dorchester?'

'No, I'm hungry. Find somewhere close by where we can get something simple. You know, a bacon and egg sandwich.'

'I know just the place, Signore.'

'Good. Then we'll come back and see what the situation is.'

At the computer bank, Roper trawled all the way through from Jack Fox to Brendan Murphy, the pride of the Provisional IRA. There were some fascinating facts there. Then he tried the Jago brothers and found a litany of crime on a Dickensian level. He sat back. *Excellent.*

He checked his watch. Eleven o'clock, and he felt hungry, which was okay, because Ryan's Irish Restaurant on the far side of the square stayed open until one and knew him well.

He eased himself into a raincoat and then transferred to his electric wheelchair and made for the front door.

Rain bounced down. He raised a small telescopic umbrella as he went down the ramp and started along the pavement. Falcone, sitting in the Mercedes, saw him go.

Fabio said, 'Signore?'

'Let's leave it to the boys.'

Roper coasted along, his umbrella raised, a slightly incongruous figure. In the Ford, Borsalino and Salvatore saw him.

'Now what?' Salvatore demanded.

'We take him out,' Borsalino said. 'Come on.'

He was out of the Ford in a second, Salvatore on his heels, and ran after the wheelchair.

'Hey, Signore, you need a hand?'

Roper knew trouble when he saw it, but said, 'No, thanks, I'm fine.'

Salvatore was on one side of the chair, Borsalino the other.

Borsalino said, 'No, really, I think you need some help – like, into traffic. What do you think about that?'

'That really would be unfortunate,' Roper said.

Falcone, watching from the Mercedes, said to

Fabio, 'You've been around the family for a long time. What do you think?'

'That it stinks, Signore. Where do they find these kids?'

'I agree. Just coast along and let's see what happens.'

The end of the square before the main road was dark, and at that moment deserted.

Borsalino said, 'Shit! There's no traffic here. What are we going to do?'

Salvatore said, 'Roll him down the block. We'll find it. You having a good time, my friend?'

'Depends on your point of view.' Roper's hand came out of the right-hand side pocket of his wheelchair, holding a Walther PPK with a Carswell silencer on the end. He jammed it into the back of Salvatore's left knee and pulled the trigger. There was a muted cough, and the Italian cried out and stumbled into the gutter.

Roper turned slightly in the chair, the gun raised, and Borsalino jumped back. 'You really wouldn't have got by in Belfast, old son,' Roper said. 'Not for a minute,' and as Borsalino turned to run, shot him in the back of the right thigh.

They lay together on the pavement. Roper paused and looked down. He took out a mobile phone and dialled nine, nine, nine. When the operator answered, he said, 'There are two men down on the pavement in Regency Square. Looks like a shooting.'

'Your name, sir?'

'Don't be stupid.'

He switched off his coded mobile and moved on.

In the Mercedes, Fabio said, 'My God, Signore, what do we do?'

Already, in the distance, they could hear the sound of a police siren.

'Nothing,' Falcone told him. 'We do nothing.' He watched the two men trying to get up. 'Just get out of here.'

As they left the square, a police car turned in, and as they moved up the main road, an ambulance appeared.

In Ryan's Restaurant, Roper ordered Irish stew and a pint of Guinness, phoned Ferguson on his mobile, and gave him the bad news.

'Where are you?' Ferguson asked, and Roper told him. 'All right, stay where you are. We'll come for you.'

Ferguson put down the phone at his Cavendish Square flat and turned to Hannah, Dillon and Blake. 'That was Roper. He went out for a late meal and two men of Italian persuasion had a go. Told him they'd push him into the late-night traffic.'

'What happened, sir?' Hannah asked.

'He shot them in the legs,' Ferguson said. 'Would you believe that? Left them on the pavement.'

'Frankly, I don't have the slightest difficulty in believing it,' Dillon told him. 'Jack Fox moved fast.'

'So now what?' Blake asked.

Ferguson turned to Hannah. 'Superintendent?'

'I doubt they'll talk, sir, not if they value their lives. And I doubt that this will be the last attempt that Jack Fox makes.'

'You're right,' said Ferguson. 'We'll move Roper to the Holland Park safe house. Anything he wants, you know, all his gadgets and so on, make sure he gets. I think we'll need him. Will you take care of that, Superintendent?'

'As you say, sir.' Hannah went out.

Blake turned to Dillon. 'All right, we've taken care of the casino. What do we hit next?'

Blake turned to Dillon. 'The Jago brothers? The army dump? Beirut?'

'Let's get Roper into the safe house. Once he's got his equipment in order, we'll see.'

At the Dorchester, Fox listened to Falcone's account of what had happened in Regency Square. He actually laughed.

'You mean this fuck in the wheelchair shot them both in the legs?'

'Something like that, Signore.'

Fox shook his head. 'Mind you, with what I've learned about him, I'm not surprised. You can check if he's at his house, but if he's not there, leave it. We've got other things to do.'

'Like what, Signore? I spoke to Mori. The Colosseum will remain closed, as well as the betting shops, until the police and the Director of Public Prosecutions decide what to do, which could take months.'

'We concentrate on other matters. There's the Lebanon connection that Murphy arranged.'

'Beirut, Signore?'

'No, Al Shariz to the south, I believe. Murphy is due in Beirut next week. We'll meet and agree on the goods we're supplying. Forget the casino. There's a fortune to be made there, Aldo, and he pays in gold. I'll see you in the morning.'

Falcone left, went to his room, and phoned Don Marco.

The Don said, 'He's digging himself in deeper, isn't he?'

'Do you want me to do anything?'

'No. Just stay in touch.'

'Of course, Don Marco.'

The Holland Park safe house was an Edwardian townhouse in an acre of gardens surrounded by huge walls. The notice by the gate said Pine Grove Nursing Home, which it definitely wasn't.

Roper was picked up by a contingency squad Hannah had arranged, mostly ordinary-looking young men and women who were actually Special Branch, and always available to Ferguson's demands. Two female sergeants packed Roper's clothes and three men moved equipment, according to his instructions. By one o'clock in the morning, he was in residence at Pine Grove, his various gadgets and computers plugged into sockets in what had been the sitting room.

The police departed, and a small, very pleasant woman said, 'Is everything satisfactory, Major?'

Roper was puzzled. 'Captain.'

'Oh, no, sir. Brigadier Ferguson said Major.'

'And who might you be?'

'Helen Black, sir. Royal Military Police. Sergeant Major.'

'Good God,' Roper said. 'That's an Armani suit.'

'Well, my father left me rather well off.'

'I smell Oxford here.'

'No, Cambridge. New Hall. I worked for the Fourteenth Intel undercover in Derry. You were a bit of a legend.'

'Look where it's got me. A bloody wheelchair, my bits and pieces damaged.'

'Courage never goes out of fashion, sir, in a wheelchair or not. As far as I'm concerned, you're one of the bravest men I've ever met. Now, you're probably peckish. I'll arrange for some sandwiches.'

'Tell me, Sergeant Major, are you my bodyguard? Because there are some pretty bad people out there looking for me.'

'I'm aware of that, sir.' She opened her jacket and revealed a holstered Colt automatic. 'Twenty-five millimetre, with hollowpoint bullets.'

'Well, that should do it.'

She smiled and went out.

Roper phoned Ferguson, in spite of the hour, and when the Brigadier answered, said, 'What's this Major thing?'

'Well, you're still on the Army list. I thought it would give you a bit more authority to promote you. You're established at Holland Park?'

'Yes, with the redoubtable Sergeant Major Black.'

'Redoubtable is right. Inherited money, you know, so she's fairly independent-minded. Her husband's a major in the Blues and Royals. Refused a commission herself. One of the few women to hold the Military Cross. Shot two Provos in Derry. You're in good hands.'

Roper whistled. 'I'd say so. So, what's my next move?'

'I'll put Dillon on.'

There was a pause, and Dillon said, 'Billy the Kid, is that who you are now?'

'Hey, these guys didn't want to play nice, so I figured, stuff them.'

'I'm with you there.'

'So what do you want me to do? Who's next?'

'Well, we've got two choices: the Jagos and Brendan Murphy. What do you know about the Jagos?'

'Not much. They like to knock off security vans.

Really old-time stuff. Sawn-off shotguns, like some British gangster movie. The thing is, finding out about the future plans of such people is difficult,' Roper went on. 'Unless Fox committed his plans to the computer, how would I know?'

'It's all a question of inside information,' Dillon said.

'And where do you get that?'

'The Jagos are gangsters, right?'

'And what does that prove?'

'Set a gangster to catch a gangster.'

'What in the hell are you talking about?'

'Harry Salter. He's a legendary name in London criminal circles. Did seven years for bank robbery in the seventies, never been inside since. He has warehouse developments, property, pleasure boats on the Thames. Still owns his first buy, a pub called the Dark Man at Wapping, by the river.'

'You sound as if you like him.'

'Well, he's saved me in the past and I've saved him. He's a dinosaur, but a very wealthy dinosaur. Even the cops have given up on him. Works with his nephew, Billy, and a couple of minders, Baxter and Hall. All the rest are accountants.'

'So, you'll go and see him?'

'That's my plan.'

'Fine. Keep me posted. Meantime, I'll check out Mr Murphy.' Roper smiled. 'I like to keep occupied.'

'See you sometime tomorrow.'

Roper sat there thinking, then the door opened and Helen Black came in with two toasted bacon sandwiches.

'Will these do?'

'Can't wait. Are you tired?'

'Not particularly.'

'Good, then would you like me to show you just how effective a computer can be if you know what you're doing?'

'What's the object of the exercise?'

'To hunt down a particularly obnoxious piece of Provisional IRA crap called Brendan Murphy.'

'Just a minute. I remember him. Derry, 'ninety-four.'

'And years before that.' Roper tried a sandwich. 'Excellent. Now, follow my instructions and I'll show you what to do.'

7

They all came together at Ferguson's office the following morning. When they were all settled, Ferguson said, 'Bring me up to date, Superintendent.'

'The attackers were a couple of small-time hoods employed at the kitchens at the Colosseum, named Borsalino and Salvatore. They're at Westminster Hospital under supervision. Salvatore has lost his left kneecap and Borsalino has a bullet wound in one thigh.'

'My goodness, Major Roper doesn't play patty fingers, does he?'

'Well, he wouldn't, would he, sir?' she said.

'What's their story?'

'They told the officers in charge of the case that they were attacked by two very large black muggers as they walked through the square. There was a struggle. The rest you know.'

'Nobody's safe from crime today, it seems.' Ferguson turned to Dillon. 'Now what?'

'Blake and I are going to see Harry Salter. I'll put him on to the Jagos, see if he can come up with anything. If there's a big tickle being organized, Salter will get wind of it. He owes me a favour. In fact, he owes Blake a favour. We saved his bacon on a pleasure boat called the *Lynda Jones* downriver from Wapping, when the Hooker mob were going to waste him.'

'Yes, I recall some such thing,' Ferguson said. 'Good. But meantime, what about Brendan Murphy? That's much more worrying.'

'Roper's been working on it,' Hannah said. 'But he says it'd be a lot easier if he had some more information to go on. Is there any way to find out more?'

'Well, I do have a suggestion,' Dillon said. 'While Blake and I go and see Salter, why don't you phone Liam Devlin in Kilrea?'

'Good God,' Ferguson said. 'Is he still with us?'

'He certainly is. Devlin is ageless. He liked you, Hannah, when you met. Tell him the whole story, the works. Ask him to find out what he can about Brendan Murphy. He's still the living legend of the IRA and the best source of information about anything regarding them.'

Hannah turned to Ferguson. 'Brigadier?'

'It makes sense. I have just one suggestion. Don't phone him, do it face to face. Get yourself to Dublin today.'

'If you say so, sir.'

'Yes, I do. So, people, let's get on with it.'

Hannah went back to her office, with Blake and Dillon. She picked up the phone, spoke to Farley Field, and booked the plane.

Dillon said, 'You watch yourself over there, woman. Peace process or no peace process, it's still the war zone.'

'Don't be patronizing, Dillon.'

'There are people there who'd shoot your eyes out if they could.'

She took a deep breath. 'You're right. I'm sorry.'

'Yes. Well, make sure you're carrying.'

'I will.'

'We'll leave you to it.'

He and Blake left. She took her personal notebook from her purse, found Devlin's phone number in the village of Kilrea outside Dublin. It was answered instantly.

'And who would that be disturbing my morning?'

'Hannah Bernstein.'

'Jesus, girl, and what's all this? I hear you've made Superintendent.'

'Mr Devlin, we have a big problem, and we need your assistance.'

'Where's Dillon?'

'Employed elsewhere, together with Blake Johnson.'

'Is that the FBI man Dillon and I went down to Tullamore with, to save Dermot Riley's hide? A good man. All right, give. When can I expect you?'

'I'm leaving now. I could be with you by twelve noon.'

'I'll look forward to it.'

He put the phone down, standing there in his kitchen, and smiled.

Dillon drove down Horse Guards Avenue in the green Mini Cooper.

Blake said, 'So Harry's still working the rackets.'

'Oh, sure, it's in his blood. But like I was saying, it's all smuggling – booze, diamonds, that kind of thing – no drugs. He's an old-fashioned family man, in values, anyway.'

'Aren't we all?'

They reached Wapping and pulled up outside the Dark Man. It was a typical London pub; the painted sign showed a sinister individual in a black cloak.

It was early for the drink trade, noon an hour and a half away, but it was open. They went into the main bar, which was very Victorian, the bottles ranged against mirrors, an enormous mahogany bar smelling of polish, the porcelain beer handles waiting for action.

Three men were in the corner booth, drinking tea and reading newspapers: Billy Salter, Harry's nephew, and Joe Baxter and Sam Hall.

'What's this, a thieves' kitchen?' Dillon asked.

Billy looked up, and a delighted smile appeared on his wicked face. 'Dear God, it's you, Dillon, and our American friend, Mr Johnson. We remember you.'

Baxter and Hall laughed, and Billy said, 'Well, we're not in the nick, and I suppose that's one good thing. What brings you here?' He smiled eagerly. 'Could it be trouble?'

'Why, are you getting bored, Billy?' Dillon asked. 'Let's see Harry and decide.'

'He's down at the boat.'

'The *Lynda Jones*?'

'Sure. Refurbished. His pride and joy. I'll show you. Let's take a walk.'

They went along the wharf, passing a few boats, one or two old barges sunk into the water. It started to rain as they reached the boat. Harry Salter was sitting at a table under an awning, reading *The Times*. Dora, the chief barmaid from the Dark Man, was pouring tea. He patted her ample rear.

'I've said it before, Dora, you've got a great arse.'

'Now, isn't that the poet in him?' Dillon said. 'Such a majestic choice of language.'

Salter looked up and took off his reading glasses. 'Christ, Dillon, it's you.' He glanced at Blake. 'And the bleeding Yank again. Here, what's going on?' The blue eyes hardened in the well-lined face. 'Trouble?'

'Well, let's put it this way. You owe me, and this is payback time. You'd have been dead meat when the Hooker mob had you if Blake and I hadn't stuck an oar in.'

'No problem. I always pay my debts. Anyway, I like you, Dillon. You remind me of Billy here. I mean, you don't give a stuff. Mad as a hatter.'

'Seeking death, you mean,' Dillon asked.

136

'That's it,' Billy said. 'You and me both, Dillon, brothers under the skin. Have we got a problem?'

'Well, if it is, its name is Jago.'

Billy's face turned pale. 'Harold and Tony, those two bastards.'

'You don't like them?'

Salter said, 'Dillon, we're friends, right? I'm doing well on the cigarette run from Europe. There are big profits, with the tax differential. But I've had three cargoes hijacked in two months. I know it's the Jagos, but I can't prove it. So what's your problem?'

'A guy called Jack Fox fronts for the Solazzo family.'

'The Colosseum?' Billy said. 'Hey, we know about them. The Jagos have been running with him. In-and-out jobs, security trucks.'

'Always cash,' Salter said. 'What's your interest?'

'Fox had Blake's wife murdered. She was a reporter who got close, too close, so he had her wasted.'

'Jesus,' Salter said. 'The fucking bastard.' He turned to Blake. 'Look, what can I say?'

'That you'll help us, will do.'

'Well, you can bloody well count on that. What's going on?'

'Fox needs cash flow. You won't have heard yet, but we closed the Colosseum and the betting shops down last night.'

'And how in the hell did you do that?'

Dillon said to Blake, 'Go on, tell him,' which Blake did, and Salter and his boys fell about laughing.

'Dear God,' Billy said. 'I mean, that's beautiful.'

'Yes, but the Jagos were there, and we know Fox needs a big tickle. Eyes and ears, Harry, see what you can find out.'

'We certainly will.' Salter rubbed his hands together. 'Life suddenly becomes interesting again, eh, Billy?'

Billy looked wolfish. 'It certainly does.' He turned to Dillon. 'I'm reading this paperback on philosophy. Pinched it from the hairdresser. Better than a novel. This guy Heidegger. Have you heard of him, Dillon?'

'German. A great favourite of Heinrich Himmler, I believe.'

'Never mind that. This Heidegger says that life is action and passion, and that a man fails to take part in the action and passion of his times at the peril of being judged not to have lived.'

'That's really very erudite, Billy.'

'Don't take the piss out of me, Dillon. I didn't get much schooling and I know I'm a tearaway, but I've got a brain. I like books and I know what erudite means, which is that I'm a clever bastard.'

'I never doubted it.' Dillon took out a card and scribbled numbers. 'My house, my mobile, Ferguson at his Cavendish Square flat. Do what you can, Harry.'

'Sure will, my old son.'

Dillon and Blake went to the gangplank and Dillon noticed some air bottles. 'Hey, Billy, you're still at the scuba diving?'

'Master diver now,' Billy said. 'Are you a master diver?'

'As a matter of fact, I am.'

'Oh, go and stuff yourself, Dillon. We'll be in touch,' and Billy went back to his uncle.

The Gulfstream did not carry RAF roundels, so when it landed at Dublin Airport it was simply directed to an area that handled private planes. Flight Sergeant Madoc got the door open. Like

Lacey and Parry, he wore the kind of navy blue uniform used by flight crews throughout the world. He put an umbrella up against the driving rain.

'There's a limousine by the hangar,' Madoc said, and led the way towards a black Mercedes.

But there was another vehicle waiting there, a Garda police car, a uniformed officer at the wheel, a large man in a fawn Burberry trenchcoat and tweed cap sitting beside him.

He got out, smiling. 'Dan Malone, Special Branch, chief superintendent. We've never met.'

'Ah, you outrank me, sir.'

'Heard they've put you up to Super. I bet the boys at Special Branch at Scotland Yard didn't like that.'

'Malone? That's a good Irish name. We have a Detective Sergeant Terry Malone in Special Branch.'

'My nephew. English mother, born in London. Can we have words, away from the pride of the RAF here?'

They moved out of the rain into the hangar, and he took a cigarette from a crumpled pack. 'Do you use these things?'

'No.'

'Good for you. You'll live longer than me. Listen, we're all together these days, what with Europe and the peace process. And I know all about you, Superintendent, just like most of Dublin Special Branch. Your reputation precedes you. Ferguson's and Dillon's, too.'

'What are you trying to say?'

'That we're not looking the other way where the IRA is concerned. On the other hand, if Ferguson's sent you over, something's up. I'll be honest with you. I leaned on your driver, who told me he was to take you to Kilrea, and that means only one thing. You're going to see Liam Devlin, the old sod.'

'Ah, you like him, too?'

'Yes, damn you, I do. So – is there something I should know about?'

'I'm seeking information.'

'Is this a hot one?'

'It could be.' She took a chance then. 'One cop to another?'

'One cop to another.'

'Does Brendan Murphy mean anything to you?'

'That bastard? Dear God, is he in this?' He frowned. 'But he wouldn't be in this jurisdiction. He's always stayed north of the border. What is this?'

'This is just a rumour right now. Could be an

arms dump in County Louth. Could be an Arab terrorist connection in Lebanon.'

'So that's why you've come to see Devlin?'

'That's right. If anyone will have heard a whisper, it'll be him.'

'No doubt about that.' Malone frowned. 'You'll keep me informed?'

'Of course. We might even need your good offices.'

'Fine. I'll hear from you, then.' He walked her back to the limousine and opened the door. 'And watch your back, peace or no peace.'

'What peace?' she asked, got in the limousine, and closed the door.

It was just after noon when she reached Devlin's Victorian cottage next to the convent in Kilrea village. She told the driver to wait, went up the path, and knocked on the door. It opened and he stood there, an ageless figure in black Armani slacks and shirt, his hair silver, his eyes very blue, a man who still held literary seminars as a visiting professor at Trinity College, but also a lifetime member of the IRA who had killed many times.

'Jesus, girl, you look wonderful.' He embraced her. 'You look grand. Come away in.'

'You're not looking too bad yourself.'

He led her to the sitting room.

He turned. 'Would you like a drink or something?'

'No, I'd like to get on with it.'

She sat down and he took the opposite chair. 'Get on with it, then.'

'Do you know a man called Brendan Murphy?'

His face hardened. 'Is that dog in this?'

'A bad one?'

'As bad as they come.' He took a cigarette from the old silver case and lit it. 'You'd better tell me.'

When she was finished, he sat there, frowning. 'Yes, that sounds like Murphy.'

'I was thinking. Where would Murphy get the kind of money he'd need to pay for an underground arms bunker and weaponry?'

'Drugs. Protection. This early release of prisoners the government's been doing has handed Ulster back to the Godfathers on both sides, Loyalist and Catholic.'

'Have you any information on what Murphy could be up to?'

'Only in general. The word is that he did time in Libya, not only in training but also working for various Arab outfits. He'll be the one supplying the contacts for Fox in this Lebanon business.'

'Nothing more specific?'

He shook his head, then his eyes narrowed. 'However, I might know somebody who could help. But I want your word as regards confidentiality.'

'IRA?'

'Exactly.'

She nodded. 'My hand on it.'

He reached for the phone. 'Let's see.'

In Dublin, Michael Leary was just pulling on his raincoat to go out when the phone rang.

'Leary,' he said.

'Michael, my old son, Liam Devlin.'

'Jesus, Liam, my heart's sinking already, because that can only mean you want something.'

'And don't I always? I'll meet you at the Irish Hussar for a snack, and I'll have a Special Branch superintendent with me.'

'What? The Garda I don't need.'

'No, this is the Scotland Yard variety, name

of Bernstein. A woman with brains and beauty, Michael. Works with Sean Dillon.'

'My God.' Leary groaned. 'I don't want to know.'

'You'll love it, son. See you soon,' and Devlin put the phone down.

In Hannah's limousine on the way to Dublin a short while later, Devlin pulled the glass screen across and filled her in on Michael Leary.

'A nice lad. He went to Queen's University, Belfast. Read English literature. Taught for a while.'

'And then took up the glorious cause.'

'He had his reasons.'

'But an educated man taking up guns and bombs.'

'You mean all members of the IRA should be off a building site and wear hobnailed boots? Hannah, after the Second World War the Jews who fought to create Israel, the members of Irgun and the Stern gang, used guns and bombs, and many of them had been to the finest universities in Europe.'

'Point taken.'

He found a cigarette and opened his window to let the smoke blow away. 'I might also mention, with my usual modesty, that I was educated by Jesuits myself and took a first class honours degree at Trinity.'

'All right, I surrender. I can't talk. I've killed

people myself. It is just that I don't like bombs.'

'And neither do I.'

'So, more about Leary.'

'Michael was on the active list for years. We worked together, except that he liked the bombs more than you or I do. He was running one in a truck over the border to Ulster, and it went off. Killed the two men with him and took off half of his left leg. The good news was he was still in the Republic, so he didn't end up in the Maze prison.'

'So his active career was over?'

'Oh, he ran the Dublin intelligence section for the chief of staff, but once the peace process started he'd had enough. He knows Dillon well, from Derry in the old days, when they were facing soldiers.'

'And now what?'

'He writes thrillers. The kind you see on the stalls at airports, and doing well.'

'Good God.' She frowned. 'Will he help?'

'Let's put it this way: he's like a lot of people these days. Big for peace. We'll see.'

Devlin directed the driver to a quay on the River Liffey, where they parked outside the Irish Hussar.

'It's a favourite with good Republicans and Sinn

Fein supporters, and the food is excellent,' Devlin told her.

The bar was very old-fashioned with mahogany and mirrors, bottles offering every kind of drink. It was busy, people sampling good simple pub food. Leary sat in a booth in the far corner. He had a pint of Guinness at his right hand, a plate of Irish stew in front of him.

'Don't get up,' Devlin told him. 'This is my friend Hannah, so let's start with that.'

Leary looked at her, a good-looking man of forty-five, black hair streaked with silver. He hesitated, then held out his hand. Hannah also hesitated, then took it.

'Sit down.'

'The stew looks good,' she said, as a waitress appeared. 'I think I'd like to sample that.'

'And you, Professor Devlin?' the waitress asked.

'Ah, now you're stroking me.' He turned to Hannah. 'Eileen's a student at Trinity. For her sins, she comes to my occasional seminars.'

'Nonsense, you're the best, everyone knows that,' Eileen said.

'Which gets you an A for your next essay. An all-day breakfast for me. A grand old playwright and novelist called Somerset Maugham once said

147

that to dine well in England you should eat breakfast three times a day. Bushmills Whiskey for me,
my love.'

'A mineral water would do fine for me,' Hannah
said.

'Still writing through the night, Michael?'

'The leg, Liam. Hurts like hell at night, so I can't
sleep and I refuse to take the morphine.'

'I'd stick to the Bushmills if I were you.'

Eileen brought the drinks and departed. Leary
went back to his stew. 'So, what's it about?'

'Brendan Murphy. Friend of yours?'

'Nobody's friend, that one. As far as I'm concerned, he's a gangster. A disgrace to the movement.'

'Would the chief of staff share your view?'

'Certainly. All the old hands want peace to work,
Liam, except for people like Murphy . . .'

'Who have a vested interest in keeping things
going,' Hannah said.

'Exactly. Splinter groups like the Continuity IRA,
the Real IRA, they all have other agendas.'

The breakfast and the Irish stew arrived and they
started to eat.

'And where would Murphy be now?' Hannah
asked.

'God knows, Superintendent.' Leary pulled up short. 'As you must know better than most, these days in the Republic, Ulster, and the UK, they're letting them out, not locking them up. Murphy can come and go as he pleases. He's only in trouble if he crosses the line with the Provisional IRA.'

'Would he be dealt with?'

'Certainly. No question. We're an army, Hannah, with rules and regulations. Now what's all this about and why should I help?'

'Because fifteen years ago I saved your life in County Down after you were shot. Got you over the border.'

'Liam, I paid off on that one when you, Dillon and that Yank were after Dermot Riley, and I told you he was back and probably at the farm at Tullamore, and down you went.'

'And you told the chief of staff, who sent Bell and Barry down. Two walking ape men. They tortured Bridget Riley, with cigarette burns on the face.'

'And Dillon killed Bell and you shot Barry in the back. We got it all from Dermot.'

'Yes, disgraceful in a man of my age.' Devlin nodded. 'All right, tell him, Hannah.'

Which she did. The underground bunker in County Louth, Fox, the Lebanese connection. Everything.

Leary sat there frowning, then said, 'Let me make one thing clear, and I'm speaking for Provos in general here. We won't give up our arms. History has shown that to be an unwise thing to do.'

'So, you're happy to think that this bunker might exist and Murphy's in charge.'

'No, I'm damn well not, and the chief of staff won't be pleased.'

'You'll tell him?' Hannah asked.

'I have no choice.'

'Ah, well, for once, you've got something in common, you two,' Devlin said. 'So what can you do, Michael?'

'We can trawl County Louth, but it's a hell of a lot of county and Murphy has a lot of hard-line friends there, so I'm not hopeful.' He frowned suddenly. 'I've just thought of something. Sean Regan. Remember him, Liam?'

'From Derry,' Devlin said. 'Shot a military policeman and cleared off to America. As I recall, the peeler recovered.'

'That was two years ago. Regan came back and was working with Murphy in Europe. Apparently, he was on a plane from Paris to Dublin three weeks ago that was diverted to Heathrow because of fog.

His name came up on the computer security check and he was lifted.'

'I wonder why I don't know about this.' Hannah frowned.

'Well, according to my information, the Secret Intelligence Service picked him up at Heathrow on one of their special warrants and spirited him away. I'd have thought you'd have known that. Don't your departments share information?'

'Only some of the time.'

Devlin turned to Hannah. 'What do you think?'

'If Regan's been working for Murphy, he might well know something. Frankly, it's our best lead.'

'I can't see that there's anything else I can do,' Devlin said. 'Michael here will spill the beans to the chief of staff, and if I do get any crumbs from the table, I'll let you know.'

They got up and walked to the door. Outside, Leary shook Hannah's hand. 'Superintendent, it was a sincere pleasure, but don't let's make a habit of it,' and he walked away.

Devlin smiled. 'A decent enough stick. Anyway, back to the airport in that grand limousine of yours. I'll drop you off and the driver can take me back home.'

*　　*　　*

Leary sat in the parlour of the chief of staff's sub-urban home, and the great man listened while his wife served tea and scones.

'Did I do right?' Leary asked.

'Of course you did. Murphy's a poisonous animal. I've no time for him and neither has the Army Council.'

'So what do we do?'

'I'll have our people check out things in Louth, although I don't expect much from that.'

'So?'

The chief of staff smiled. 'If Ferguson's on this case with Sean Dillon . . .' He smiled. 'Well, for once we're on the same side. Sean can do our dirty work for us.'

At the airport, Hannah's limousine drove into the hangar where Lacey and Parry waited. The Gulfstream was outside in the rain. As Hannah and Devlin got out, the Garda police car returned and Malone emerged.

'Liam, you old sod,' he said.

'And stuff you, too,' Devlin said genially, and they shook hands.

Malone said, 'Anything come up?'

Hannah looked uncertain, and Devlin said, 'Go on, he's on your side.'

She told him about the meeting with Leary.

Malone said, 'So anything Murphy's involved with certainly isn't official with the IRA.'

'What about this thing with Sean Regan?' she asked.

'Not a word, and I'd have known.'

'So somebody's playing silly buggers,' Devlin said.

Hannah nodded. 'I'll have to sort that out when I get back.' She held out a hand. 'Liam, you're a treasure.'

'Hell, you can do better than that, girl.' He kissed her. 'Take care, and tell Sean to watch his back.'

'That's something he's good at. Goodbye, Superintendent.'

Lacey and Parry were already inside, and Flight Sergeant Madoc gave her a hand up the steps. The door closed, the engines turned over, the Gulfstream moved away.

'A hell of a woman,' Malone said.

'You can say that again.' Devlin smiled. 'Now you can dismiss your car, join me in my luxurious limousine that the good Superintendent has loaned

153

me, and we'll return to the Irish Hussar, where you can buy me a very large Bushmills.'

'Me, in that hotbed of Republican gunmen?'

'I seem to recall that your younger brother, Fergus, was one.'

'We don't talk about that.'

'As I said, the Irish Hussar.' Devlin smiled. 'It will do my reputation no end of good being seen in the company of the police. A great comfort to me.'

The Gulfstream climbed steadily out over the Irish Sea, and Hannah called Ferguson on her Codex Four.

'Ah, there you are. How did it go?'

She brought him up to date, Regan included. 'So there you are, sir. We should have been told. There is supposed to be interdepartmental cooperation.'

'Not with the Secret Intelligence Service, as long as Simon Carter is Deputy Director. Leave it with me.'

He sat there at his desk, thinking about it, then picked up the phone and spoke to Dillon, who was in the outer office with Blake.

'Get in here. I've had the Superintendent on the line and we could have a problem.'

8

Dillon and Blake listened as Ferguson related Hannah Bernstein's adventures. When he was finished, Blake said, 'This is surely unacceptable, one major intelligence department hugging secrets to itself that could be of possible crucial importance to others.'

'Yes, well, Carter's always been good at doing his own thing, and to hell with anyone else.'

'Seems to me it's time to remind Carter,' Ferguson said, 'that the particular circumstances of my position as head of the Prime Minister's personal security service give me extraordinary powers. Including over him.'

'That I'd love to see,' Dillon told him.

Ferguson smiled, picked up his phone, and dialled a number. 'Ah, that you, Carter? Look, something's come up and I need to see you. I want your input on something before I speak to the Prime Minister . . . Yes? Good. I'll see you at the Grenadier in St James's in thirty minutes.'

'Nothing like being decisive,' Blake said.

'Well, as you Yanks say, you ain't seen nothing yet. Order the car, Dillon, I'll find a warrant or two, and we'll be on our way.'

The Grenadier was a pleasant traditional London pub, with old-fashioned dark oak booths. Carter was already there in a corner, sipping a glass of sherry. A small, pale-faced man with white hair, he reacted angrily at the sight of Dillon.

'Really, Ferguson, I've told you before. I object to this murderous swine's presence.'

'Well, take it up with the Prime Minister. He employs him.'

'God save your honour,' Dillon said cheerfully. 'It's a blessing, the grand man like yourself allows me in the same room.'

'Oh, go to hell.'

Ferguson said, 'You'll remember Blake Johnson.'

'Yes, the American.' Carter offered a reluctant hand and turned to Ferguson. 'So what is this?'

'An IRA renegade named Brendan Murphy's up to no good, and I need to know what it is.'

'Nonsense, that's old hat, Ferguson. Murphy isn't a problem any longer, not since the peace process overwhelmed the land.'

'It's the great liar you are,' Dillon told him, and turned to Blake. 'This is the Deputy Director of the Security Services, a faceless man who never worked in the field himself.'

'Damn you, you Irish swine.' Carter was furious.

'Now, that's a racist remark,' Dillon said. 'I could take you to the tribunal.'

'Exactly,' Ferguson agreed. 'And as my sainted mother was Irish, then as a half-Irishman I take it very personally.'

'I'd say you've just insulted his mother's memory,' Blake put in.

'Could we get on with it?' Dillon asked. 'You lifted a man named Sean Regan at Heathrow three weeks ago, when his plane to Dublin was diverted because of fog. Why?'

'Don't be stupid, Dillon. He shot a military policeman in Londonderry a couple of years ago and fled. The policeman nearly died.'

'So you're going to stand Regan up on trial at the Old Bailey?' Ferguson asked.

'We might.'

'But you won't, because of the peace process. We're letting them out of prison now, not banging them up.'

Carter was strangely confused. 'Come on, Ferguson, we're in the hands of our political masters.'

'Not as far as I'm concerned. We're in the hands of the law. The truth is, you're holding Regan to squeeze anything you can out of him in case it may be of future use.'

'So what?'

'Not any more. Where are you holding him?'

'Wandsworth.' Carter answered as a reflex.

'Not any longer.' Ferguson produced a paper from his inside pocket. 'That's a warrant from me as head of the PM's security squad, authorizing me to, as quaint legal language has it, take possession of one Sean Regan.'

Carter was outraged. 'Now, look here, Ferguson.'

'No, you look here. The difference is that I *did* serve in the field. I was an eighteen-year-old second lieutenant in the Hook in Korea in 'fifty-two, and I've seen more villains here than you've had breakfasts. So don't argue. Just countersign the order. Here's my pen.'

He offered it and Carter took it, hand shaking, and signed the document. 'My turn will come, Ferguson.'

'I don't think so.' Ferguson blew on the ink. 'Now go away.'

Carter suddenly looked helpless, got up, and stumbled out. Blake said, 'Why is it I don't feel sorry for him?'

'Because he isn't worth it,' Ferguson said. 'So, gentlemen, Wandsworth Prison next stop.'

Ferguson, Dillon and Blake waited in the interview room at Wandsworth until the door was opened, and the kind of prison officer who looked as if he'd been a sergeant in a Guards regiment pushed Regan in.

Dillon said, 'Good man yourself, Sean.' He turned to the others. 'Always gave us a problem, the two of us being Sean.'

Regan said, 'Jesus, is that you, Dillon?'

'As ever was. Come to take you away from your cell and the stench of the lavatory buckets. This is Brigadier Charles Ferguson, your new boss. The other fella is a Yank, and FBI, so watch it.'

'What in the hell is going on?'

Ferguson turned to the prison officer. 'Give us a moment.'

'Certainly, sir.'

The man went out, and Dillon said, 'Brendan Murphy. We know you've been part of his outfit.'

Regan was thrown, but tried to brazen it out. 'I haven't seen Brendan in years.'

'So Carter didn't manage to wheedle anything out of you?'

'I've said I don't know what you're talking about.'

'Don't waste my time,' Ferguson told him. 'You shot a military policeman in Derry two years ago and fled to the States. Since then, you've worked for Murphy in Europe.'

'It's a lie.'

Dillon said, 'Don't be stupid. You shot a peeler. All right, he didn't die, but at the Old Bailey you'll pull ten years for attempted murder. Imagine Wandsworth or maybe Parkhurst, year after year. You'd be afraid to take a shower.'

'No.' Regan was shaken. 'Mr Carter said if I cooperated I wouldn't do time.'

'Yes, well, unfortunately, I'm in charge now,' Ferguson told him. 'Now make your mind up. A comfortable safe house where you'll fill us in on Brendan Murphy's doings, or a very unpleasant future.'

Regan, in despair, said, 'Brendan would cut me to pieces. He's a sadist.'

'Which is why we'll have to take good care of you.'

He nodded to Dillon, who knocked on the door, which opened and the prison officer appeared. Ferguson took his warrant out.

'Take this prisoner to his cell, allow him to collect his belongings, then present this document to the Governor, authorizing his release into my custody.'

'Certainly, Brigadier.'

Regan was pushed out, and Ferguson turned to Dillon and Blake. 'So, we take him to Holland Park, where you, Dillon, will squeeze out the last drop of juice.'

'My pleasure, Brigadier,' Dillon said.

They delivered Regan to Holland Park and drove in through the electronic gates. The security guards wore neat navy blue blazers and flannel slacks.

'Nursing home? What is this?' Regan asked.

'It's a fortress,' Ferguson told him. 'And the gentlemen in blazers are all military police. There's no way out of here, as you'll find for yourself.' He turned to Dillon. 'Let Helen settle him in and feed him. You and Blake stay. I'll be back.'

His Daimler drove away. They took Regan up the steps between them, his wrists still manacled. The door opened and a very large man appeared.

'Mr Dillon, sir.'

'Another one for you, Sergeant Miller, one Sean Regan. He shot a Royal Military Policeman in Derry two years ago.'

'That would be Fred Dalton.' Miller's face was like stone. 'He survived, but had to take a medical discharge. Oh, I'll take good care of you, Mr Regan.'

He reached for Regan's left shoulder with a hand the size of a meat plate, and Helen Black came down the hall stairs.

'Is this the prisoner, Sergeant Miller?'

Miller got his feet together. 'Yes, ma'am.'

'Good. Room ten, unpack him, then we'll have sandwiches and tea in the parlour.'

'As you say, ma'am.'

Regan turned. 'What is this? Who's she?'

'Sergeant Major Black, and don't be a male chauvinist, Regan,' Dillon said. 'She shot two Provos in Derry and holds the Military Cross.'

'Fuck you, Dillon.'

162

'That's bad language in front of a lady. We can't have that, can we, Sergeant?' he asked Miller.

'We certainly can't, sir.' Miller squeezed Regan's left arm very hard. 'Up we go, there's a good gentleman.'

Blake said, 'Now what?'

'Oh, they have a canteen, a kitchen. We won't starve.' Dillon smiled. 'We'll sort Regan out later.'

Upstairs, Regan was astounded. He had a decent bedroom, a bathroom, a view of the garden, even if it was through barred windows. He even had a fresh shirt, blazer and slacks, like the guards'. Miller took him downstairs to a small sitting room, a gas fire flickering in the hearth. There was soup, ham sandwiches and a glass of dry white wine. Miller stood by the wall, enigmatic.

Regan, slightly euphoric at the difference from Wandsworth, said, 'Could I have another glass of wine?'

'Of course, sir.'

Miller poured the glass of Chablis, and behind the mirror Ferguson, Dillon, Hannah – who had just arrived – and Helen Black watched.

Ferguson said, 'You all know the story by now.

This is a bad business, so we make sure he talks. I'd like you to go in, Sergeant Major, and you, Dillon. Facts, that's what I need.'

'Certainly, sir.' Helen Black nodded to Sean. 'Good guy, bad guy, suit you, Sean?'

'Nothing better. Takes me back to my days at the National Theatre.'

'Yes, you *have* told us that one before. Let's do it.' She led the way out. 'But follow my lead.'

'Shall I leave, ma'am?' Miller asked, as they stepped into the room.

'No, I might need you, Sergeant.' Her voice was different and very hard. 'This is a Provisional IRA gunman. He crippled Fred Dalton. Do you think Fred was his first?'

'I doubt it, ma'am,' Miller said coldly.

'Right, but I'd like you to manacle him, Sergeant. Once a killer, always a killer.'

'Certainly, ma'am.'

'Now, look here,' Regan protested.

'Just hold out your wrists and be a good boy.'

Regan was sweating and very, very worried. He'd had three weeks in Wandsworth, with the lavatory bucket, the twice-a-week showers, the unwelcome attentions of certain wild-eyed prisoners, and others: basic English criminals who didn't like the

IRA. The contrast of his treatment at the safe house spoke for itself. In a way, he'd thought he was going to be all right, but now he had this woman who looked like his elder sister, acting like the Gestapo.

She unbuttoned her jacket, revealing the holstered Colt. 'Now then, let's get started.'

Roper had joined the group on the other side of the mirror. 'She's really very good.'

'Outstanding,' Blake agreed.

'And still won't take a commission,' Ferguson said.

'You can't buy her, sir,' Hannah put in.

'I know,' Ferguson sighed. 'Very depressing.'

And then, Helen Black started to work.

The change was astonishing. This pleasant, decent Englishwoman seemed to take on a new persona.

'I've been fighting people like you for years. The bomb and the bullet, women and kids – you couldn't care less. I shot dead two of your bastards in Derry. They were parking a van with fifty pounds of Semtex on board outside a nurses' hostel. Well, we couldn't have that, could we? I took a bullet in the left thigh, got the bastard who did it, then sat up and got his friend in the back as he ran away.'

Regan was terrified. 'For Christ's sake, what kind of woman are you?'

She grabbed his jaw and shook his head painfully from side to side. 'The Apache Indians used to give their prisoners to their women to go to work on. I'm *that* kind of woman.'

'Excellent,' Ferguson said. 'She should be at the National Theatre herself.'

'You crippled a comrade of mine. Fred Dalton.' She took out her Colt and touched him between the eyes. 'These are hollowpoints, you scum. I pull this trigger and your brains are on the wall.'

'For God's sake, no,' Regan cried.

Dillon caught her wrist and turned the gun. 'No. Sergeant Major, this isn't the way.'

She turned, as if in fury. 'I'll be back.' She walked out.

Regan was shaking. Dillon said to Miller, 'Uncuff him, Sergeant, he isn't going anywhere.'

'As you say, sir.' Miller got out a key and unlocked the manacles. Dillon opened his old silver cigarette case, took out two cigarettes, lit them, and gave Regan one.

'There you go, just like in *Now Voyager*.'

Regan was shaking. 'What in the hell are you talking about?'

'Never mind, Sean, I've a weakness for old movies. Now listen. Me, I got smart. I could have faced a Serb firing squad, but Ferguson is an extraordinarily powerful man. He saved my life, and in return I dropped working for the glorious cause and work for him instead. Which means I'm alive.' Regan was trembling, and Dillon turned to Miller. 'A large brandy, Sergeant.'

'Certainly, sir.'

Miller opened a cupboard and returned with a glass, which Regan emptied at one throw. He looked up at Dillon. 'What do you want?'

'What's best for you. Look, Ferguson's in charge now, and you did shoot that fella, Dalton. Peace process or not, he'll make you stand up in court if he wants to.'

On the other side of the mirror, Ferguson said, 'In you go, Sergeant Major.'

Helen Black went back into the sitting room, a document in one hand. 'All right, I've had enough. It's back to Wandsworth for you, you bastard.'

Regan simply fell apart. 'For God's sake, tell me what you want, just tell me.'

'Excellent,' Roper said. 'Pure Gestapo. They used physical abuse much less than people realized. Didn't need to. They just messed with their heads.'

Ferguson said to Hannah, 'We won't overwhelm him.' He turned to Roper. 'You and Blake stay here. You come in with me and do your Scotland Yard bit, Superintendent.'

Ferguson walked in with Hannah and said to Miller, 'Give him another brandy, Sergeant.'

'Sir.' Miller did as he was told, and Regan took the glass with shaking hands and drained it.

'Do I have a deal?'

'That depends on what you have for me.'

Regan looked at Dillon, who said, 'The Brigadier's a hard man, Sean, but a moralist. If he says it, he means it.'

Hannah said, 'Mr Regan, I'm Detective Superintendent Bernstein of Special Branch. I'd be interested to know if you can assist us in our inquiries regarding the activities of one Brendan Murphy.'

Regan said, 'What do you want to know?'

'I understand there's an underground concrete bunker somewhere in County Louth.'

'Semtex, machine guns, mortars,' Dillon said. 'Enough to start a civil war. Where is it, Sean?'

Regan said, 'Close to Kilbeg.'

'Jesus, son, there are Kilbegs all over Ireland.'

'Well, this one is in Louth, like the Superintendent says, just south of the border in the Republic and south of Dundalk Bay. Near Dunany Point. Very remote.'

'I know that area,' Dillon said.

'You wouldn't last long, Dillon. They're a funny lot. Strangers stand out like a sore thumb.'

Ferguson said, 'Let's be specific.'

'When I fled to the States, I was helped by a wealthy Irish American group who were a bit radical. Didn't approve of peace. I brokered a big financial deal for Brendan. The idea was to prepare for the future, the next war.'

'Which explains the bunker,' Ferguson said.

'But where did the arms come from?' Dillon asked.

Behind the mirror, Roper was making notes.

'Oh, that was a Mafia connection. Brendan had worked with them in Europe. A fella called Jack Fox.'

'Fronting for the Solazzo family?' Hannah said.

'Well, I always figured he was fronting for himself. He supplied the arms.'

'Anything else?' Hannah asked. 'Lebanon, for example?'

'Christ, is there nothing you don't know?'

'Get on with it,' Dillon said.

'Murphy was trained in Libya years ago, has

strong Arab contacts, can even get by with the language, enough to order a meal, anyway.'

'So?' Ferguson asked.

'Well, Fox controls the Solazzos' drug operations in Russia, so he has big contacts. Murphy has the Arab link.'

'Which Arab link?'

Regan hesitated. 'Saddam. Iraq.'

'That's nice,' Dillon said. 'What's intended?'

'There's a freighter down from the Black Sea next week. Called the *Fortuna*. If it's on time, it's due at a place called Al Shariz, south of Beirut, next Tuesday.'

Dillon took over. 'Russian crew?'

'No, Arab. All Army of God.'

'And the cargo?' Regan hesitated. 'Come on, what's the bloody cargo?'

'Hammerheads.'

There was a pause, and Hannah turned to Ferguson. 'Hammerheads, sir?'

The door opened and Blake entered. 'Sorry, Brigadier, but I know all about those. They're short-range missiles mounted on a tripod that only take two minutes to erect. Their range is three hundred miles. Nuclear-tipped. They wouldn't take out Israel or Jordan completely, but Tel Aviv wouldn't look too good.'

Ferguson turned to Regan. 'Have you told me the truth, told me everything?'

Regan hesitated again. 'When the boat gets in, the *Fortuna*, Brendan will be on board. Fox meets them, gets paid in gold. Five million.'

'Dollars or pounds?' Dillon asked.

'How the fuck would I know? Paid on the boat is what I heard, because they want to arrange another consignment a month later.'

'And all this is true?' Ferguson asked.

'Yes, damn you.'

Ferguson turned to Helen Black and Miller. 'Send him back to his room.'

They took Regan out between them, and Roper came in after they left.

'I've had a thought,' he said. 'I've got details of Fox's Gulfstream. It's parked at Heathrow, as I recall. Let me check its movements.'

They followed him to his ground floor suite, where all his equipment had been set up. Roper started on the computer, fingers deft on the keys.

He grunted. 'Fox has a slot booked out of Heathrow for Monday morning, destination Beirut.'

'Wonderful,' Dillon said. 'Regan was telling the truth.'

'So what now, sir?' Hannah asked.

Ferguson said, 'We can't send in the SAS, and we do have other business with Fox. Something more subtle is needed.'

Hannah said, 'The Israelis wouldn't like this, Brigadier.'

'Exactly what I was thinking.' Ferguson turned to Dillon. 'You went to Beirut the other year with the Superintendent here. Stayed at the Al Bustan.'

'How could I forget it? It overlooks some excellent Roman ruins.'

'You remember my man there, Walid Khasan?'

'Very well. Lebanese Christian. He and the Superintendent got on rather well. Which is not surprising, considering that he was actually Major Gideon Cohen of Mossad.'

'Lieutenant colonel, now.'

'Had a nice sister, Anya, I remember. A lieutenant.'

'Captain, now.'

'And there was another one – what was his name? Captain Moshe Levy?'

'Major. Everything goes up in the world, Dillon. Yes, I think Colonel Cohen might be interested. I'll give him a call.'

*　　*　　*

Lieutenant Colonel Gideon Cohen wore uniform only on occasion. Sitting in his office now at the top of a secluded building in Tel Aviv, he was wearing a white shirt and linen slacks, all very unmilitary for a Mossad colonel. Forty-nine years of age, he had olive skin, and hair that was still black and down to his shoulders.

His sister, Captain Anya Shamir, sat at a corner desk, working a computer. She'd been a widow since her husband's death on the Golan Heights.

In the other corner, Major Moshe Levy sat at a second computer. He was in uniform because he'd had a report to make at Army headquarters, and wore khaki shirt and slacks, paratroopers' wings and decorations. The phone on Gideon Cohen's desk rang.

A voice said, 'This is Ferguson. Are you coded? I am.'

'My dear Charles, of course I am.' Cohen waved to Anya and Moshe. 'Ferguson from London.'

He pressed the audio button on his telephone. 'Charles, old boy.'

'Don't call me old boy just because you went to Sandhurst. I'm glad to say I still outrank you.'

'Something special, Charles?'

'Something rotten in the state of Lebanon.'

'Tell me.'

Which Ferguson did.

When he was finished, Cohen said, 'Hammer-heads. We can't have that.'

'Jerusalem wouldn't look too good after one of those.'

'Exactly. Charles, I need to consider this.'

'What you mean is, you need to talk to the general, your uncle.'

'I'm afraid so.'

'That's no problem. But this is a black one, Gideon. Keep it close.'

In his penthouse office, General Arnold Cohen, head of Mossad's Section One, the group with special responsibility for activities in Arab areas, listened gravely.

When his nephew was finished, he said, 'Hammer-heads. This is very serious.'

'So what do we do? Call an air strike on this boat, the *Fortuna*?'

'In Lebanese waters? Come on, Gideon, we're supposed to be nice at the moment while our British and American cousins castigate Saddam.'

'And he's going to send Hammerhead strikes up our backside.'

His sister, Anya, standing with Levy by the window, said, 'Can I make a point, Uncle?'

'Of course you can. You've gotten away with murder with me ever since you learned to speak, so why should this time be different?'

'Why don't we use Dillon, Uncle? He's hell on wheels, that one – remember that job with him in Beirut the other year? He was incredible.'

'She's right,' Levy put in. 'What's important here is disposing of this *Fortuna* boat and its cargo with a minimum of fuss, right?'

'So?'

'So we make it a small-scale operation. With Dillon to call on, the three of us – Anya, Moshe, me – can handle it in Al Shariz. The right equipment, and we can blow the damn boat to hell.'

'He's right,' Gideon Cohen said. 'No adverse publicity. No air strikes.'

'I like it,' the general said. 'Get on with it.'

Ferguson said, 'Fine, Gideon. I'll send over Dillon. Also an American colleague, Blake Johnson, who works directly for the President. You'll find him most useful. I'll put Dillon on.'

A moment later, Dillon said in bad Hebrew, 'How are you, you lying dog?'

'Dillon, we seem to have business together.'

They switched into English. 'I'm not sure how we'll do this,' Dillon said. 'If we're to blow this *Fortuna* out of the water, we'll need mines, Semtex, some scuba equipment.'

'We'll take care of it. We'll keep it low-key. Myself, Levy, my sister. With you and this American, that's five. We don't want to draw attention, although things have changed since you operated in Beirut, my friend. It's not quite the war zone it used to be. People are trying to build up the infrastructure again, tourism and so on.'

'Where would Fox stay? Beirut?'

'No, there's an old Moorish palace in Al Shariz which has been refurbished as a hotel. I'd say he'll be there. It's called the Golden House.'

'No good for us, then.'

'No problem. We'll come up on a motor yacht, like tourists. You and your friends can stay on board.'

'We can't exactly sit in the bar at the Golden House, though. We don't want Fox to know it's us. It'd be much better if he thought it was an Israeli job.'

'Do you recall my sister Anya?'

'How could I forget? She played a lady of the night better than a lady of the night.'

'Enough to ensnare this Fox.'

Dillon laughed. 'Enough to ensnare friend Fox.'

'You and Johnson, Levy and myself, we'll stay on our boat, the *Pamir*, well out of the way. Anya can squeeze what she can out of the guy. We'll send the *Fortuna* down when we're ready.'

'You Israelis are such morally committed people,' Dillon said. 'But you'll sink that boat, crew and all, without a flicker.'

'Not even half a flicker,' Cohen said. 'See you soon.'

Dillon hung up, and Ferguson said, 'So, here we go again.'

Hannah Bernstein said, 'What about me, sir?'

'Not this one, Superintendent. Dillon and Blake, plus our friends from Mossad, are enough. What I'd like you to do is get a little more basic with friend Regan as regards the bunker in County Louth.' He turned to Roper. 'I'm sure the Major here will be more than willing to help.'

'A pleasure, sir,' Roper said.

'Sorry, Hannah, I'll have to love you and leave you.' Dillon turned to Blake and smiled, a strange excitement there. 'Here we go, old buddy, back to the war zone again.'

LEBANON

AL SHARIZ

9

Brendan Murphy leaned over the rail of the small coastal freighter, the *Fortuna*, and watched the distant lights of Syria. The ship was Italian-registered and had definitely seen better days, but under its battered exterior the essential bits, the engines, were in excellent condition. They'd left the Black Sea two days earlier and had made good time.

The man who approached him, wearing a seaman's reefer coat, held a cup of coffee in one hand, which he passed to him. His name was Dermot Kelly and he had unfashionably Irish blond hair and a hard, pocked face. He lit a cigarette.

'Jesus, Brendan, they're all fugging Arabs, this crew. If I light up in the saloon, they glare at me. Lucky I brought a bottle on board.'

'Fundamentalists,' Murphy said. 'Army of God, this lot. They're just waiting for death in the service of Allah, so they can go to Paradise and have eternal pleasure and all those women.'

'They must be crazy.'

'Why? You mean we're Catholics and we're right, and they're Muslims and they're wrong? Come off it, Dermot.'

An Arab, in a reefer coat the same as Kelly's, came down a ladder from the bridge. He was the captain and his name was Abdul Sawar.

'How's it going?' Brendan demanded.

'Excellent. We'll be on time.'

'Well, that's good.'

Sawar said, 'Any problems?'

'Well, I miss bacon and eggs for breakfast,' Kelly told him.

'We do our best, Mr Kelly, but some things are not possible.'

'Well, you'd probably have a problem in reverse in Dublin,' Kelly told him.

'Exactly.'

Sawar went back up the ladder, and Murphy said, 'Don't stir the pot, Dermot. You can't expect good Irish bacon on an Italian boat crewed by Arabic fundamentalists off the coast of Syria.'

'All right, so I'll just think of the money.'

'The gold, Dermot, the gold. Speaking of which, we'll check it out.'

He led the way to the stern of the ship, and went down a companionway to a rear saloon. There were two cargo boxes wrapped in sacking.

Dermot lit a cigarette. 'They look like shite to me.'

'Five million in gold, Brendan.'

'How do we know?'

'Because Saddam wants another cargo next month, so he won't screw around with this one.'

'Do you think it's all going to work?'

'Like a Swiss watch. Fox will be on a plane. We'll offload the gold, and take it to the airport at Beirut, where the right officials have been bribed. The plane is routed to Dublin, but it puts down at an old air force base in Louth on the way. We unload our half and Fox carries on, announcing a mid-air change of destination.'

'Where will he go?'

'Supposedly Heathrow, but on the way there, when the plane is in uncontrolled air space, he'll put down on this estate nearby in Cornwall, called Hellsmouth. There's an RAF aerodrome there from the Second World War. The runway's a bit rough, but it can take a plane like the Gulfstream.'

'Sounds good to me, Brendan.'

'And me, Dermot.'

The other man smiled, took a half bottle of Paddy whiskey from his pocket, unscrewed the top, and drank deeply. He passed it across.

'Well, here's to Irish bacon and eggs, soda bread and rain.' He smiled. 'I miss the rain, Brendan. The good Irish rain.'

Gideon Cohen, his sister and Moshe Levy had left a yachting marina on the coast near Haifa in a forty-foot boat of a kind regularly rented by tourists interested in diving. There were stocks of air bottles in the stern, bunks for seven people below, a good kitchen galley, every convenience.

Cohen's passport was British, in the name of Julian Grant; his sister and Levy had become a Mr and Mrs Frobisher, also British. Their background being impeccable, and Lebanon desperate for tourist money, they'd had no trouble getting the necessary visas, and pushed towards Al Shariz through the late afternoon.

Cohen was at the wheel, Levy lounging beside him, Anya looking out of the half-open window.

'So, let's go over it,' her brother said. 'You

and Moshe book into the Golden Palace, and do remember, Moshe, this is my sister you're sharing a suite with.'

'How could I forget, Colonel?'

'Fox is booked in with these two hoods, Falcone and Russo. You make yourself available in the bar, Anya, just in case there's information available.'

'Oh, dear,' she said. 'Here I go again. Stage Six at MGM, playing the whore.'

Her brother smiled, and hugged her with his spare arm as he steered. 'No, the good-looking whore.' He shook his head. 'This is a bad one, little sister. We can't make a mistake.'

'Well, at least we have Dillon.'

He laughed out loud. 'My God, yes, the poor old *Fortuna* doesn't know what's going to hit it.'

On the plane on the way to Beirut, Dillon said to Blake, 'So, we're interested in establishing an electronics factory, a joint Anglo-American project, jobs for all. Three days in and out.'

'No problems?' Blake asked.

'Certainly not. They're still trying to build up the country again, while surrounded by people who want to cut each other's balls off.'

'So, we join Cohen's boat, look like recreational scuba divers.'

'And send the *Fortuna* to the bottom. Hammer-heads, the lot,' Dillon said.

'And the crew?'

'Murdering fanatics. If they didn't want the risk, they shouldn't have joined.'

'But, Dillon, there's five million pounds in gold on board.'

'Yes, isn't that, as Ferguson would say, delicious? It also goes to the bottom. A fabulous expression of conspicuous consumption.' He waved to Flight Sergeant Madoc. 'Bring me another Bushmills, I'm celebrating imagining how Jack Fox will feel.'

Fox booked into the Golden House, with Falcone and Russo. He had a nice suite on the first floor – marble, scattered rugs, all very Moorish. He felt good. The Colosseum was a bad memory, and his lawyers seemed to think they might be able to fix things. Whether they did or not, the gold from the *Fortuna* was a certainty. Added to that, the cash Murphy owed him in Ireland from Irish-American arms orders would take the pressure right off.

'Everything okay, Signore?' Falcone asked.

'Couldn't be better. Tonight's the night, Aldo. Gold, there's nothing like it. It's still the one commodity you can rely on. You've checked with the harbourmaster?'

'Yes, Signore, the *Fortuna* is due in at ten. A crew of twelve, all Arab. It left the Black Sea the day before yesterday.'

'Where will they anchor, on the pier?'

'No, it's full. A few hundred yards out in the entrance to the bay.'

'Excellent. I'll have a shower, then dinner. I'll see you later.'

Their plane landed in early evening. Dillon and Johnson booked in as Russel and Gaunt and took a taxi to Al Shariz. On the way, Dillon called Cohen on his mobile.

'Lafayette, we are here. I'm saying that on behalf of Blake.'

'Well, we're here, too. Lower yacht basin. *Pamir*, Pier Three.'

'See you soon.' Dillon switched off his phone and relayed the information to the driver.

On the *Pamir*, Cohen looked through a pair of Nightstalker glasses and watched the *Fortuna* drop anchor. He said to Anya, 'Off you go. All I want to know is what he's up to. It could give us a clue to his movements.'

'Sure,' she said.

'Another thing.' He was strangely awkward. 'Duty is duty, but you're my beloved sister. Don't get close to this one. He's bad news.'

She kissed his cheek. 'Hey, little brother, don't worry.'

She booked into the hotel, changed, then went down to the bar, resplendent in a black mini dress, her dark hair to her shoulders, and looking terrific. She sat at the bar, and Fox, over by the window, Falcone and Russo at the next table, saw her at once. He nodded to Falcone, got up, went to the bar, and sat next to her.

'Hi, there.'

'An American!' She smiled. 'What are you doing here?'

'Investigating tourist prospects,' he said glibly. 'What about you?'

'Oh, I'm over from London with my husband, on the same errand.'

'Your husband?' Fox was disappointed.

'Yes, well, he's been called to Tel Aviv. Left me on my own for three days.'

Fox put his hand on hers. 'That's terrible, a nice-looking lady like you all on her own. But you've got me now. Have you eaten?'

'No.'

'Well, join me.'

Which she did, for a sumptuous meal, part Arab, part European, and lots of Cristal champagne. She endured his questing hand on her thigh and waited. Finally, Falcone, who had stood by the window, answered a mobile, came over and whispered.

Fox squeezed her thigh. 'Listen, I've got to go.'

'What a pity.'

It was ten o'clock. He said, 'I'll be a couple of hours. Will you still be here?'

'Of course. I'll see you.'

He went out with Falcone. She followed, and stood in the shadows of a palm tree and shrubbery while they talked on the terrace.

'The *Fortuna* is in, Signore.'

'Good. We offload the gold in two hours.'

'There's just one thing I don't understand,' Falcone said. 'These Hammerheads are short range?'

'Absolutely.'

'So if we're talking Iraq, I'm puzzled. I mean, we're off the coast of Syria, so they can't be fired from Iraq.'

'Aldo, you don't get the point. They're very easy to set up and fire. The *Fortuna* is going to be a gun platform. The entire crew, as you know, is Army of God. All they want to do is take out Tel Aviv. Jerusalem, they're funny about. After all, it's the second most important Muslim city.'

'My God, they're animals, these people.'

'Depends on your point of view. Now let's get moving.'

Anya called her brother on her mobile and relayed the information. Gideon said, 'Right, get out of there now. I'll expect you within the next half hour.'

On the *Pamir*, Dillon, Blake, Cohen and Levy were sitting under the stern awning having a look at the harbour chart when Anya arrived. She paid off the taxi and stepped over the rail.

'Jesus, woman,' Dillon told her. 'You look like page sixty-four in *Vogue* magazine. You should be a young Jewish mother having babies and making your husband's life miserable. Instead, you're still going around shooting bad guys.'

'It's my nature, Dillon. Who's your friend?'

'Blake Johnson. Former FBI and works for the

President now, so let's have some respect here.'

She shook hands with Blake. 'Nice to meet you,' she said and turned to her brother. 'As I told you, I overheard Fox talking to one of his men on the terrace. The gold is definitely on board, as well as the Hammerheads. The worrying thing is that the boat is to be used as a gun platform, with Tel Aviv a possible target.'

'Not if we blow that thing out of the water.'

'I couldn't put it better myself,' Dillon told him.

'And sooner rather than later,' Blake put in. 'The boat's here, and Fox will want it offloaded as soon as possible. We know from Roper that he has a return slot booked for seven o'clock tomorrow.'

'Right, then let's get on with it.' Cohen turned to Dillon. 'How do we do this?'

'Well, you remember in 'ninety-four in Beirut, when we blew up the *Alexandrene* with all that plutonium on board?'

'You mean, *you* blew up the *Alexandrene*,' Anya said.

'And how did you do that?' Blake asked.

'Took a shallow dive, went up the anchor chain, created a little mayhem, dropped a block of Semtex in the engine room, and that was that.'

Cohen said, 'Sounds good to me.'

'A one-man show?' Blake said. 'I don't like it.'

'Blake, Vietnam was a long time ago.'

'Stuff that kind of talk, Sean. We go in together.'

Dillon sighed. 'All right, it's your funeral.' He looked out as orange flickered on the horizon, and in the distance the security lights gleamed on the *Fortuna*. 'Let's get on with it. Time to save the free world again.'

Falcone, Russo and Fox went out to the *Fortuna* in a water taxi and pulled up to a steel stairway at the side of the ship. Fox told the boatman to wait and led the way up to where Brendan Murphy, Dermot Kelly and Captain Sawar waited. Fox and Brendan embraced.

'You're looking good,' Murphy said.

'And you, old buddy, and you'll have an even broader smile when you know what's on shore and on its way to my plane.'

'Come and have a look.'

Murphy led the way down to the stern saloon, where the two cargo boxes waited.

'Five million, Jack,' he said. 'It makes me feel God is on my side.'

'That's because you're Irish, you daft bastard,' Fox said. 'Let's go and have a drink and then we'll offload this lot. I've got a water taxi waiting.'

Beside the *Pamir*, an inflatable waited, Dillon and Blake aboard in black dive suits with a single air bottle each, weight belts around their waists. Each had a dive bag with a Browning Hi-Power with a Carswell silencer inside. Dillon also carried two three-pound blocks of Semtex, with three-minute timer pencils.

Gideon Cohen said to his sister and Levy, 'I'll take them out. You wait here and be ready for sea.'

Anya hesitated, then picked up an Uzi submachine gun and stepped in beside Dillon and Blake.

'Not this time. You might need back-up and Moshe is better with the boat than I am.'

Cohen sighed. 'You're a great trial to me. Okay, take the Nightstalker and monitor what happens.'

They moved out into the harbour and floated to a halt a hundred yards from the *Fortuna*.

Dillon said, 'Here we go,' and pulled down his diving mask and reached for his mouthpiece.

At only ten feet, there was enough illumination from the security lights to give the water a kind of glow. He paused beside the steel stairway, released his jacket and air tank, and took the Browning from his dive bag and cocked it. His face half-covered by his diving hood, he surfaced, Blake beside him, and an Arab seaman appeared at the top of the stairway. Dillon shot him instantly, the Browning near noiseless, tumbling him into the water, and started up. Blake, somewhere behind him, had another problem.

The Arab who crewed the water taxi had been shocked to see Dillon surface and kill the seaman. He tossed his cigarette into the water, stood up, and Blake, with no options, had to shoot him.

On deck, it was quiet only for a moment, then voices called. On the bridge, Captain Sawar moved out on to the flying bridge, a machine gun in his hands.

'Selim, are you there? What is it?'

Dillon called in Arabic, 'It's Mossad, you dog. We've come for you.'

Sawar fired his machine gun blindly down into the darkness of the deck, and Blake, scrambling up beside Dillon, fired back, shattering a window up there. Fox and Falcone and Russo, who were on the bridge, ducked down.

Fox said, 'What the hell gives?'

'Israelis. Someone down there said Mossad.'

'Cover me,' Dillon said to Blake, and ran crouching through the dark to the engine room hatch, pulled it back, took out the two blocks of Semtex from his dive bag, activated the timing pencils, then dropped them down and closed the hatch.

As Dillon ran back to rejoin Blake, who was firing up at the bridge, Sawar made a bad mistake. He switched on more security lights. Dillon and Blake ducked behind a lifeboat, as Sawar fired his machine gun again, and there were cries from members of his crew as they surged on to the aft deck from below, all armed.

Sawar fired repeatedly, Falcone and Russo joining in, and Anya, crouched in the inflatable, sprayed the deck and bridge with fire from her Uzi. Sawar took a bullet in the head and went down. Fox and his two men crouched, Falcone with blood on his face from a glass splinter.

'Now get out of it, Blake,' Dillon said. 'They're three-minute timers, remember. Take the port side. There's another lifeboat there that will give us some protection.'

Anya looked through the Nightstalker. 'I can see them. They're sliding to the port rail,' she said to Moshe Levy.

'Well, they would. Dillon will have planted the Semtex. There's maybe two minutes left.'

'Then get moving.'

He pushed the engine up to top speed, and went round the prow, Anya still firing up on the side deck and bridge, and Dillon and Blake jumped. Fox, peering out of a side window, saw them go, saw the inflatable surge on. Anya tossed a line, Dillon and Blake grabbed it, and the inflatable vanished into the darkness.

'They've jumped ship, Signore,' Falcone said. 'They didn't stay long.'

And Fox, his senses sharpened by years of hard living, jumped to an immediate conclusion.

'That's because they accomplished what they came here to do. Let's get out of here now!'

He scrambled down the ladder and they followed, running into Murphy and Kelly on the side deck.

'What the hell is going on?' Murphy demanded.

'Mossad. They've planted explosives. Move it!'

'Christ.'

They went down the steel stairway fast and crowded into the water taxi. Fox started the engine, Falcone and Russo threw the dead Arab into the water, and Fox took the boat away fast.

They were perhaps a hundred yards away when the explosion took place. The deck lifted, the bridge buckled, flames shot up into the night. Two or three men jumped from the stern, then the *Fortuna* seemed to break in half and went down very fast indeed. There was burning oil, faint screams.

'Shall we go back, Signore?' Falcone asked.

'What for? All I want to do is get back to the airport and get out of this fucking place. Take over.'

He lit a cigarette as they moved towards the pier. Murphy said, 'It's all gone, not just the missiles but the gold.'

'I know. Isn't life hell?' Fox had an insane desire to laugh.

'But how did they know?'

'This is the Middle East, Brendan. The Israelis have had considerable experience at giving the Arabs a hard time. You think they can't find out what Saddam is up to? You think their friends everywhere from London to Washington can't find out?' He tossed his cigarette into the water. 'On top of that, the bastards can fight.'

'All that gold. I can't believe it.'

'Well, better get used to it.'

'Back to Heathrow now?'

'No point sticking around here. Do you and Kelly want a lift?'

'No, we're going to Paris, then Dublin.'

They crashed on to the pier. Fox had left a limousine with an Arab driver waiting. He said, 'I'm going back to the Golden House to pack and move on. Do you want a lift there, at least?'

'No, we'll get a taxi and go right to the airport.'

'No luggage – you lost it all on the boat. They'll think that's funny.'

'I know this place. There's a late-night bazaar. We'll pick up some stuff. No problem.'

'Good.'

They moved away from the others to the end of the pier. Murphy said, 'Christ, I needed that gold.'

'So did I,' Fox said.

'So what will you do?'

'I've something laid on in London that should take care of things.'

'Jesus, do you need a hand?'

'Not this time. What about you?'

'Back to Kilbeg to reflect. I'm not broke.'

'You still owe me on a lot of that equipment in the bunker. I know you've got at least a million on hold there.'

'I know, I know. A few bank raids will take care

of the expenses, and the war will start again soon anyway.'

Fox held out his hand. 'Good luck. Stay in touch.'

'I will.'

They went back to the limousine, Fox, Falcone and Russo got in, and it drove away.

Murphy smelled the warm air, the aroma of spices. 'Disgusting, this place, Dermot. Let's go home to some civilization.'

Blake had a bullet crease on his right shoulder. Anya gave him first aid. On the *Pamir*, there was a certain jubilation.

Dillon and he changed, then went into the saloon. Moshe Levy was pouring wine into glasses, and Anya came in from a shower in a towelling robe, drying her hair.

'Where's Gideon?' Dillon asked.

'Making a phone call.'

Gideon was talking to his uncle at his apartment in Tel Aviv. General Cohen listened and slapped his thigh. 'Marvellous. What a coup.'

'Dillon and Blake Johnson are returning to London soon.'

'Well, tell them they go with my blessing. And Anya, she is well?'

'She should get a medal. She was wonderful.'

'Mossad doesn't give medals, you know that. But I *will* give you all a nice dinner.'

In Beirut, Fox, Falcone and Russo boarded their plane, discreetly observed by Lacey and Parry, who had been supplied with photos. The plane rose steadily to fifty thousand feet and turned into the Mediterranean. Russo sat at the back and a woman flight attendant offered drinks and a menu. Fox waved her away.

Falcone sat opposite him. 'Now what, Signore?'

'I don't know, Aldo. I've just lost a fortune. Murphy's lost a lot, and he owes me God knows how much for those arms in that bunker in County Louth. The Colosseum is closed down.' He took a deep breath. 'We've only got the Jagos left and that White Diamond Company job. Ten million. Four to them leaves me with six.'

The attendant handed Falcone a vodka martini. He savoured it and said, 'Why not the full ten, Signore? Why not all the proceeds? Russo and I could handle it. It'd go a long way to making up what you just lost.'

Fox tasted his glass of champagne. 'You really are a very bad man, Aldo. But I like it.'

Falcone smiled, recalling his conversation in the washroom at the airport with Don Marco on his mobile. He'd recounted the whole sorry affair.

Don Marco had said, 'It just gets worse. If I didn't know better, I'd say it was Dillon and Johnson again. But you say it was the Israelis?'

'No doubt about it. They identified themselves.'

'It's like he was snakebit. All right, Aldo, watch out for him, okay?'

Remembering, Falcone said, 'The Jagos. They're animali, Signore. As I say, let Russo and me take care of them.'

'It's certainly an interesting thought.' Fox smiled. 'We'll see.'

In London, Ferguson listened to Dillon on his Codex and nodded. 'What an absolutely marvellous result. Our friends at Mossad have performed magnificently, but you and Blake haven't done too badly, either.'

'Why, Brigadier, praise from you is praise indeed.'

'Don't let it go to your head, Dillon. We'll see you soon.'

He sat there by the fire in his flat, thinking about it, then called for his Daimler, got a coat on, and told his driver to take him to Pine Grove, where he knew Hannah Bernstein was working on Sean Regan. Helen Black greeted him and took him to Roper's suite, where the Major sat at one of his screens, Regan on one side, Hannah on the other.

'Well, children, you'll be delighted to know that Al Shariz has resounded to a most satisfactory explosion. The SS *Fortuna*, crewed by Army of God fanatics, is no more. Not only the Hammerheads, but the five million in gold, which was supposed to have been split between Murphy and Fox, has gone down, thanks to Czechoslovakia's gift to the world, Semtex, in one hundred fathoms of water.'

'Holy Mary,' Regan said.

'A moment, Brigadier.' Roper punched at the keys and checked his screen. 'Two hundred fathoms, actually. There's a trench in that harbour. Be a little difficult to retrieve, anyway.'

'What next, sir?' Hannah asked. 'Kilbeg?'

'How far have we got?'

'Oh, Sean's being very cooperative. I'm assembling a ground plan,' Roper said. 'Would you like to see?'

'No, let's wait for Dillon and Blake.' He turned to Hannah. 'Any word from Salter?'

'No, sir.'

'I think I'll go and see him.'

'Do you want me to come, sir?'

Ferguson shook his head. 'No, you continue here with Regan and the Major.' He turned to Helen Black. 'How would you fancy an excursion into the London underworld, Sergeant Major?'

'Why, I can't think of anything I'd like more, Brigadier.'

'Good, let's be on our way, then,' and Ferguson led the way out.

LONDON

10

Salter and Billy were in the Blind Beggar, one of London's most famous pubs, in its heyday the haunt of gangsters such as the Kray brothers, the Richardsons and others. It was crowded and busy at that time in the evening, although a lot of the crowd were tourists, for organized trips were very much a part of the scene.

Salter waved to a small man, an albino in a black tee shirt and suit. 'One of the best lock and safe men in the business, Billy. Manchester Charlie Ford. The big black guy with him is Amber Frazer. Very good with his hands, though, mind you, he's got a brain. They're an item.'

'What do you mean, an item?' Billy asked.

'You know, gay. Homosexual.'

Billy shook his head. 'Well, all I can say is they're missing out on a damn good thing.'

'Takes all sorts, Billy. We'll have him over.'

He beckoned, and Ford approached, with Frazer by his side. 'Charlie, my old son, and Amber.' Salter shook hands. 'My nephew, Billy. Watch yourselves. He's a right villain.'

'Aren't we all?' Ford said.

'Join us for a drink. I might be able to put a bit of business your way.'

He'd already heard that Ford and his friends were booked up, but was testing the water.

'What are you suggesting, Harry?' Ford asked.

'Well, I'm organizing something big. I won't say what, but I'd need a top man with your skills, and let's face it, Charlie, you *are* the top man.'

'When are we talking about?'

'Next couple of weeks.'

'No way, Harry, I mean, next month could be all right, but I'm booked right now.'

'Well, good for you. It's a nice one, I hope.'

'Very nice, Harry, very special.'

'Say no more. What I don't know, I can't talk about.' He kept the façade going. 'What about Phil Shapiro?'

'Got turned over last week. They're holding him at West End Central. You could try Hughie Belov. Mind you, he claims to be retired, but he taught me a lot. Depends on what you're offering.'

'Thanks for the idea,' Salter told him.

At that moment, the Jago brothers walked in and stood at the end of the bar. Ford said, 'Got to go, old son. See you around.'

'Take care,' Salter told him.

Ford and Frazer joined the Jagos. Billy said, 'That settles it, I'd say.'

'Yeah. But we still need to know exactly what they're up to.'

'How do we do that?'

'The old-fashioned way. Follow them to see where it leads. Come on.'

Baxter and Hall waited in the Range Rover parked up the street. Salter said, 'Don't bother with me, I'll get a taxi. You wait with Billy. The Jagos are inside, with Manchester Charlie Ford. When they come out, follow them. You've got those night glasses in the glove compartment, Joe, the Russian things.'

'Sure have, Harry.'

'Get on with it, then,' and Salter walked away.

It was half an hour later that the Jagos emerged, with Ford and Frazer. They went up the street to a Ford station wagon, got inside, and drove away. To Billy's surprise, they were aiming for home territory, Wapping. There was plenty of late evening traffic and Baxter stayed well back. The station wagon finally turned into a narrow road between old warehouses, mostly refurbished.

'St Richard's Dock,' Baxter said. 'They turned all the old warehouses into offices and such last year.'

'Any housing, apartments?' Billy asked.

'No.'

'Then what the hell are they up to? Pull in at the end of the street and give me those glasses.'

Baxter parked in the shadow of a wall and they got out. Billy focused the glasses, as the Jagos and the other two got out and went down stone steps to the shingle beach beside the river. They started to walk, and Billy watched, for they were clearly seen in the strange green glow of the glasses.

'The tide's out,' Hall said. 'Otherwise, they'd be swimming.'

'They've disappeared,' Billy said. 'We'll wait.'

It was ten minutes later that the Jagos and the others reappeared and walked back along the beach. They climbed the steps, got in the station wagon, and drove away.

'Okay,' Billy said. 'Get the torch from the Range Rover, Joe, and we'll take a look.'

He found what he was looking for with no

trouble, an arched entrance to a tunnel, dark and wet, lichen growing over the ancient stoneware. There was a damp river smell to everything. He led the way, probing the darkness with the torchlight, and came to a huge rusting iron grille gate. There was a lock, everything corroded tight.

'So what are they up to?' Baxter asked.

'God knows, but we'll find out. Back to Harry,' and he turned and led the way out.

In his personal booth at the end of the bar at the Dark Man, Harry Salter sipped beer and listened. 'St Richard's Dock. I've got a piece of that, Billy.' He called to Dora and she came round the bar. He put an arm round her waist. 'Have a look in the file in my office, love, St Richard's Dock.'

'Anything for you, Harry.'

'Yes, I know that, only just get me the bleeding file.'

She was back in a couple of minutes. He opened the file, took out a plan and checked it. 'Two merchant banks, estate agent, property developers, two restaurants, the White Diamond Company.' He sat back. 'Jesus Christ, no, they couldn't. I mean, a place like that these days. It's state-of-the-art security. The bleeding works. I can't believe this.'

Strangely, it was Billy who said, 'Just take it slowly, Harry. Let's consider what they were doing on the beach in that tunnel.'

'You're right, Billy, you're learning.' He turned to Hall. 'Have a look in the saloon bar. See if that old geezer Handy Green's in. He usually is. Used to be a barge captain. There's nothing he doesn't know about the river – more than me, and that's saying something.'

Hall went off, and returned a moment later with an ancient and wizened man, all shrivelled up inside a reefer coat and jeans.

Salter said, 'Handy, my old son. Come and join us for a drink. I think you might be able to help me.'

'Anything, Harry, anything I can do, you know that.'

'The thing is, Handy, I've got a problem. You know St Richard's Dock?'

''Course I do, Harry.'

'They've redeveloped all the warehouses, offices, all that.'

'Finished it last year. I used to work the boats, the old sailing barges from there when I was a kid.'

'There's an interesting thing,' Harry said. 'Billy

happened to be on the beach there and noticed the entrance to a tunnel.'

'Well, he would, if the tide was out. If the tide's in, the entrance is covered. It's called St Richard's Force.'

'What the hell is that supposed to mean?' He took the large brandy Dora brought and gave it to the old man.

'Oh, it's a medieval thing. Force meaning pressure, and when the tide goes up, the water goes in that tunnel like you wouldn't believe.' Handy swallowed his brandy greedily. 'The thing is, Harry, it's an interest of mine, London under the ground. There's tunnels from Roman times, Norman times, Tudor sewers, then the Victorians covered everything up. I mean, all these modern multi-storey buildings and office blocks haven't the slightest idea of how many tunnels and sewers go through their foundations.'

'And you do?'

'Always been an interest of mine.'

'And St Richard's Dock?'

'Riddled, Harry, it's like a honeycomb down there.'

'Are you sure?'

'Harry, I've got old books with maps, Victorian.'

'Really?' Salter turned to Billy. 'Do me a favour, Billy, take Handy round to his place and get these books. I'll phone Ferguson, tell him what we've got.' Which he did, and Ferguson, alerted on his mobile, returned to Pine Grove.

An hour later at Pine Grove, Handy Green sat with Roper and showed him some very interesting plans in some very old books. Roper checked the information, then got to work. Ferguson and Salter watched with Billy. Baxter and Hall were in the canteen. The screen came alive with ground plans.

'Extraordinary,' Roper said.

'What is it?' Ferguson asked.

'A network of Victorian tunnels and sewers adjacent to the St Richard's Dock infrastructure. There are places where you'd only need a sledge-hammer to smash through Victorian brick into the St Richard's basement.'

'So what's that bleeding mean?' Salter demanded.

Roper said, 'Let me check the St Richard's specifications.' His fingers moved on. Finally, he nodded. 'Interesting. State-of-the-art security, but it's all external. If you come up like a mole, you're home free.'

'That's it, it must be,' Salter said.

'I'd say.' Roper turned to Ferguson. 'Brigadier?'

'Looks like it, but when are they going to do it, that's the thing.' He turned to Salter and his nephew. 'Will you stay on the case? We know the place, but we need to know the time.'

'Well, I don't think it's on Tuesday, if you follow me. Not from what Manchester Charlie Ford indicated. It'll be a week to two weeks.'

'Well, do what you can.'

'A pleasure, Brigadier. It makes a change being on the right side for once. Come on, Billy, we'll leave and take Handy with us. Tell you what, we'll keep an eye on the beach.'

They left, and Ferguson said to Roper, 'Do you have anything for me on County Louth?'

'I've extracted everything I can from Regan. From what I've surmised, I've done a breakdown on the Kilbeg place. Do you want a quick look?'

'If you like.'

When Roper was finished, Ferguson sat there thinking about it. 'A tricky one.'

'Very.'

'But I think it should be done sooner rather than later, in view of what's happened.'

'I'd be inclined to agree.'

'Let's have something in the canteen and wait for Dillon and Blake.'

'Just one thing, Brigadier.'

'Feel free.'

'I'm an old Irish hand, and I tell you now, there's no way you can drive into that coastal area of County Louth and pretend to be tourists.'

'Yes, I can see that. You're suggesting a sea approach?'

'It's the only way.'

'Show me County Down, Louth, the Scottish coast.'

Roper tapped it up obediently. 'There you go.'

Ferguson said, 'What would you say about Oban on the west coast there? Would that be a suitable point of departure?'

'Perfect, Brigadier.'

'Excellent.' Ferguson took out his mobile and called Hannah Bernstein at the office. 'Dillon not in yet?'

'Just landed at Farley Field, sir.'

'Good. I want him down here, Blake, too. Things are moving, Superintendent. We're going to make an Irish expedition. Speak to transportation. A motor cruiser, that kind of thing.'

'Certainly, sir. Home port?'

'Oban. Any equipment Dillon needs, we'll call him when he arrives. Make the meeting here and come yourself. I'm sorry, but I may have to put you in harm's way again.'

'It's what I'm paid for, sir.'

Dillon and Blake wolfed bacon and eggs and listened to Ferguson and Roper.

Hannah said, 'I think it might be useful if Dillon and Sergeant Major Black had another chat with Regan, sir, just to make sure he's being honest.'

'A sensible idea,' Ferguson said. 'Let's do it.'

They went up to Roper's suite first and he showed them the situation at Kilbeg on the screen. 'It's very remote, a village on the coast, population a hundred or so. Scattered farms, hard-line Catholic Republicans. You couldn't move an inch without the whole countryside knowing.'

'So it's got to be by sea,' Ferguson continued.

Dillon nodded. 'That's right. We'll go under cover of darkness. Do a frogman job, if necessary.'

'Transport's already arranged a suitable boat from Oban,' Hannah said, 'called the *Highlander*.

They'll need to know what equipment you want as soon as you can.'

'No problem. I'll draw up a list. Are you coming, Blake?'

'I sure as hell am.'

'Also the Superintendent,' Ferguson said. 'I want an official police presence.'

Dillon sighed. 'At it again, Hannah, trying to get your head blown off. What is it, guilt?'

'Get stuffed, Dillon.'

'Hey, for a nice Jewish girl with a Cambridge degree, that really is elegant.'

She laughed in spite of herself. 'Now what?'

'Oh, let's look at the map again.'

Roper went over it. 'There's this old abbey which is the entrance and cover, but the interesting thing is this rural farmhouse to the east. That's an emergency exit. Regan says they only keep a couple of guys in the bunker as caretakers. Murphy turns up occasionally. He's the local hero.'

'Fine,' Blake said. 'We go in and blow it to hell.'

Ferguson nodded. 'Let's have Regan in for interrogation. You, Sergeant Major Black, Dillon. The same variety hall act, just in case there's something he forgot.'

When Sergeant Miller brought in Regan, Dillon

was sitting by the fire. 'Ah, there you are, Sean. They tell me you've been very helpful.'

'I've done all I've been asked.'

Behind the mirror, Ferguson, Blake, Hannah and Roper watched. Suddenly, Roper said, 'He's lying, the bastard's lying.'

'How do you know?'

'Body language, instinct. I don't know, but there's something he hasn't told us.'

'Right, Sergeant Major,' Ferguson told her. 'Put the boot in.'

She burst through the door a moment later, boiling over with rage. 'I'm sick of lies, Dillon. This little sod's lying through his teeth. There are still things he hasn't told us.'

She took out her silenced Colt, and Miller, playing his part, caught her wrist. 'No, ma'am, that's not the way.'

The Colt discharged into the ceiling and Regan cried out in terror.

'All right, anything – anything you want.'

Dillon shoved him down into a chair.

'Okay, we've got Kilbeg, the bunker, the village, even the old granite quarry pier below the cliff. But what did you leave out?'

Regan hesitated, and Helen Black said, 'Oh,

this is a waste of time. Let's send him back to Wandsworth.'

'No, for God's sake.'

'There's something. What is it?' Dillon demanded.

'It's the money. Brendan has one of those safes in the floor of the bunker office. He's supposed to have a million pounds in there, proceeds of bank raids, exploitation, that kind of thing.'

'So?' Helen Black demanded.

'He owes that to Fox for arms supplies.'

'Really,' Dillon said.

'Only he's lying. He keeps fobbing Fox off. He's got nearly three million in there.'

Dillon almost fell about laughing. 'Jesus, you mean you're telling me that if we blow the place up, we'll not only be stiffing Murphy, but also Fox? That's beautiful.' He turned to the mirror. 'Isn't that a joy, Brigadier? Come on in.'

Ferguson came in, with Hannah and Blake. 'Very naughty, Regan. Still playing stupid games.'

'Yes, he's an untrustworthy sod,' Dillon said. 'In the circumstances, I think I'd like to take him along.'

'Really?'

'Just in case of problems. What if there's more he hasn't told us?'

Ferguson nodded. 'Yes, I take your point. Would you agree, Superintendent?'

'Well, she'll need to, as she'll have to take care of the bastard.'

'What are you getting at?' Hannah asked.

'There's no sense in wasting time. If you get the quartermaster to fill my order and have the boat ready, Blake and I will fly up later this afternoon. There is an RAF base near Oban. We'll get things shipshape. They'll fly back and pick you up in the morning and do the return journey. We'll do the trip tomorrow afternoon and hit Kilbeg tomorrow night.'

'You're not wasting time, are you?' Ferguson said.

'Can't see much point, Brigadier.'

'Fine by me.'

'There's just one thing,' Dillon said. 'Blake took a bullet at Al Shariz.'

'Hell, it's a crease only. Anya fixed it.' Blake was indignant.

'Blake, if we do have to go in underwater, it isn't on.'

'So what you're saying is you want another diver?' Ferguson said. 'It's a bit short notice, but if I phone Marine Headquarters they could possibly find someone from the Special Boat Squadron.'

'No good. They cut their hair, those boys, they'd never pass for locals. Now, SAS at Hereford have plenty of lads who haven't seen a barber in months. That's so they can go undercover in Belfast at a moment's notice and look like they're off a building site.' Dillon smiled.

'That makes sense,' Blake said. 'When you put me in there undercover the other year, I recall it was dicey as hell.'

'So,' Dillon said. 'I've got another diver in mind.'

'Who?' Ferguson demanded.

Dillon told him.

The Brigadier laughed helplessly. 'Oh, I like it. I really do. Do you mind if I come with you and hear him turn you down?'

'No problem, Brigadier, it'll be the best pub grub in London. Meanwhile, though, I want Blake's shoulder checked out by Daz at Rosedene.'

'Rosedene?' Blake asked.

'A private clinic we use near Pine Grove. We have a very nice man, a professor of surgery at London University, who, shall we say, helps us out.'

Ferguson said to Regan, 'Fancy a sea trip to Ireland, do you?'

'I don't have much choice, do I?' But already, his mind was racing.

Ferguson turned to Helen Black and Miller. 'Take him away. The Superintendent will pick him up tomorrow.'

'Fine, sir.' Miller took Regan by the arm and she followed them out.

Ferguson said, 'All right, Dillon, take Blake to Rosedene. The Superintendent will phone ahead and make sure Daz is there. We'll go back to the office. I'll meet you for lunch.' He laughed. 'I can't wait to get his reaction. Hope he's a patriot.'

'People like him usually are, Brigadier.'

Rosedene was an exclusive townhouse in its own grounds. The receptionist greeted Dillon like an old friend, spoke on the phone, and a pleasant, middle-aged woman in matron's blue came out of her office. She had the accent of Ulster, like Dillon, and kissed him on the cheek.

'Have you been in the wars again, Sean?'

'No, Martha, but he has,' and he introduced Blake.

'Well, let's get on with it. Mr Daz is waiting.'

'Mister?' Blake was puzzled.

'In England, ordinary physicians are "doctor", but surgeons are "mister".' Dillon smiled. 'And only the English could explain that to you. In his case, he's also "professor".'

She took them along a corridor and opened the door into a well-equipped operating theatre. Daz, in a white coat, was sitting at a desk reading some papers, a tall, cadaverous Indian with a ready smile.

He got up and took Dillon's hand. 'Sean, it's not you this time. What a change.'

'No, it's my friend, Blake Johnson.'

'Mr Johnson, a pleasure. And what is the problem?'

'A superficial gunshot wound. I mean, it's nothing.'

'It never is, my friend.' Daz turned to the matron. 'Under the circumstances, Martha, I'd rather not have one of the girls in. Would you be kind enough to assist?'

'Of course, Professor. I'll get ready.'

Daz said, 'Stay if you want, Sean.'

Blake, stripped to his waist, stood while Daz and Martha, suitably robed, got to work.

'My goodness, you *have* been to the wars.' Daz probed under the left ribs. 'Bullet scars are always distinctive.'

'Another here,' Martha said. 'Under the left shoulder.'

'Vietnam,' Blake said. 'A long time ago.'

'But not this, I think,' Daz said, as Martha cut away the pad on the right shoulder. He made a face. 'Nasty.'

'Hell, it's nothing,' Blake told him.

Daz ignored him. 'Yes, well, *nothing* requires some very careful stitching. How many would you say, Martha? Fifteen? Perhaps twenty. In the circumstances, I don't think a local anaesthetic will do. We'll need a general. Get Doctor Hamed for me. I know he's here. He can assist.'

'Now, look here, I don't want to be on my back,' Blake said. 'I've got things to do.'

'Not if you have a crippled shoulder for the rest of your life.'

Martha said, 'Do as you're told, Mr Johnson. You're not a stupid man.' She turned to Dillon. 'Leave him to it. Check in this afternoon.'

'For God's sake, Sean,' Blake said.

'No problem. If you're not fit, you can come up to Oban tomorrow with Hannah and Regan.'

*　　*　　*

At that moment, Billy Salter drove up to St Richard's
Dock in the Range Rover and parked. He got out
and walked along the embankment to where an old
Ford van was parked, opened the door, and got in
beside Joe Baxter, who was looking down at the
shingle beach through a pair of old binoculars. He
lowered them.

'What is it?' Billy asked.

'Well, having nothing to do, we checked out that
café where Manchester Charlie Ford has breakfast. The thing is, he wasn't only with the big
beast.'

'Go on, surprise me.'

'Connie Briggs.'

'Well, that's good. He's about the best on any
kind of electronic security system in London.'

'I know, he's a genius.'

'Who else?'

'Val French.'

'Jesus. The big expert with the thermal lance.
Cut up those security boxes on that Gatwick
gold bullion job like sardine cans. We all know
that.'

'So do Scotland Yard, but they couldn't
prove it.'

'So why are we here?'

'They all came down in a Toyota van. We followed. They got out carrying a couple of canvas bags, went along the beach, the tide being out, and went along to the tunnel entrance. Sam's down there now, tucked behind that old wreck.'

Billy took the binoculars, focused them, and at that moment Manchester Charlie Ford and the others came out of the tunnel and went back to the steps up to the dock.

They all got in the Toyota and drove away. 'Give me the torch and let's take a look.'

'Let them go,' Billy said.

The tunnel was damp from the receding early morning tide, the brickwork green, as Billy switched on the torch. The rusting iron grille was there as before. The only difference was that the huge old lock had gone and the gate responded to a strong heave.

'Well, well,' Billy said. 'Let's take a look.'

They followed the tunnel, sloshing through two or three inches of water. It seemed to go on for ever and there were side tunnels.

'All right,' Billy said. 'Enough is enough. We're under the dock and there's nothing important. Let's go back.'

They arrived back at the Dark Man at noon and

found Salter in his usual booth. He listened and nodded.

'Okay, it's on, and it's got to be the White Diamond Company. I'll check with Ferguson.'

At that moment, Ferguson and Dillon walked in.

'I can't believe it,' Billy said. 'We were just talking about you and here you are.'

'Magic, Billy,' Dillon said. 'It's with me being from County Down.'

'What are you after, Brigadier?' Salter asked.

'Cottage pie for lunch and an indifferent red wine would do, for a start.'

'Yes, well we've got news for you,' Billy said, and told him.

Ferguson took out his mobile and called Roper at Pine Grove and relayed the information. 'I'm concerned with timing here. It's just occurred to me. If you could access the White Diamond Company, we might find something is going on.'

'Leave it with me, Brigadier.'

Ferguson put his phone down. 'So, we could be in business, gentlemen. It's an OBE for you, Harry, for services to the country.'

'Fuck off, Brigadier.'

Dora appeared. 'Cottage pie, love, and a bottle of that Krug champagne, as Dillon's here.'

She walked away and Dillon said, 'It's the great man you are, Harry.'

'What are you trying to do, you little Irish git, butter me up?'

'Actually, yes. I need a favour.'

'What favour?'

'I need a master diver, and the only one I know on short notice is Billy.'

Salter was totally shocked. 'You've got to be kidding.'

'No. My American friend Blake took a bullet in the shoulder and won't be too fit. I'm taking a boat into a remote part of the Irish coast, where there's an underground bunker full of the wrong kind of weapons waiting to be used in the next round of the Irish troubles. I intend to blow it to hell, and as friend Fox has a financial interest, I'll get extra pleasure.' He turned to Billy. 'Listen, you young dog, it'll be a good deed in a naughty world. Are you with me?'

Billy had an unholy light in his eyes. 'By God, I am, Dillon. These fucks come over and blow up London. Let's go and blow them up.'

'Billy?' his uncle said.

Ferguson's phone rang. He listened, then said, 'Fine. I'll talk later.' He drank a little champagne.

'That was Major Roper. He's accessed the White Diamond Company's computer. They're receiving a consignment of top-grade diamonds on Thursday. Ten million pounds' worth.'

Dillon said, 'So we know where we are.' He turned. 'Harry?'

Salter said, 'What the hell, we're with you.'

'Excellent.' Dillon smiled. 'It's Scotland for you, Billy, and a nice sea voyage.'

'Christ,' Billy said. 'I get seasick.'

'We'll stop at a pharmacist and get you some pills on the way to Farley Field. That'll be three hours from now, after which you'll be winging your way north.'

'I've never been to Scotland,' Billy said.

'Well, we'll take care of that.' Dillon smiled as Dora brought plates of food to the table.

'Cottage pie and Krug champagne, and God help Brendan Murphy.'

SCOTLAND
IRELAND

11

Blake was flat out when Dillon called at Rosedene to check on his condition. Hannah was with him. Daz was at the university, but Martha was there.

'He'll be fine, but not particularly fit for a while,' she said, and frowned. 'He's not going to get up to any nonsense, I hope, Mr Dillon? I know what your lot are like, and he honestly isn't up to it.'

'I know, Martha. I know. We'll take it as it comes. I'm flying off to Scotland, so keep the Superintendent here informed.'

'Trouble again?' she asked.

'Always is.' He kissed her cheek.

'Oh, well,' she said, and gave him the ancient toast. 'May you die in Ireland.'

'Oh, thanks very much.' Dillon laughed. 'See you soon.'

He and Hannah left.

On the way to the Dark Man, she said, 'It could be a hard one, Sean.'

'I know, and Blake won't be up to it. Frankly, in his condition, he'd be a liability.'

'What do you want me to do?'

'Try and lose him. With luck, you won't have to do much. Maybe Martha could give him a pill.'

'Always the practical one, aren't you.'

'He's a good man, Hannah, I'm the bad one. I don't care about that, but I do care about him.'

'I'll never understand you.'

'I don't understand me. Join the club. I'm just passing through, Hannah, I'd have thought you'd have realized that by now.'

Dillon phoned ahead, and Billy was waiting outside the Dark Man with his uncle, Baxter and Hall.

Harry said, 'I actually care for this young bastard, so bring him back in one piece, Dillon. Notice I didn't say *try*, so don't let me down, because if you come back alone . . .'

'I get the picture,' Dillon said. 'In you get, Billy.'

The driver put the case in the boot and Billy sat in front, nervous and excited. 'Christ, Dillon, what have you got me into?'

'High adventure, Billy. You'll come back and join the Marines.'

'Like hell I will. Independent spirit, me.'

At Farley Field, the department's quartermaster, a retired sergeant major, waited with his list.

'All loaded, Mr Dillon. Walthers with Carswell silencers, three Uzi machine pistols with silencers. Stun grenades, and half a dozen of the fragmentation variety, in case you have trouble, plus the Semtex and timers.'

'What about diving equipment?'

'Standard suits and fins as issued to the Special Boat Service. Our local agent in Oban will put six air bottles in the stern rack. That should suffice.'

'Excellent.' Lacey was already in the Gulfstream with Parry; Madoc waited at the bottom of the steps.

Dillon kissed Hannah on the cheek. 'We who are about to die salute you.'

'Don't be stupid. I'll see you tomorrow.'

'I know, and watch Regan. He's a devious little sod.'

'I thought that was you.'

It was such a stupid remark, and instantly regretted, but Dillon smiled. 'Ah, the hard woman you are.'

He pushed Billy up the steps in front of him, Madoc followed and closed the door, and the Gulfstream moved away.

'Why?' Hannah whispered. 'Why do I say things like that?' And yet she knew that, for her, his past condemned him. All those years as the Provisional IRA's most feared enforcer, all the killing.

She looked up as the Gulfstream lifted. 'Damn you, Dillon,' she said. 'Damn you.'

In his suite at Pine Grove, Roper trawled the computer and came up with results. He checked again, then phoned Ferguson.

'Fox and his two goons are booked into the Dorchester for a week.'

'Anything else?'

'Murphy and Dermot Kelly are booked on an Air France flight from Paris, arriving in Dublin around what the Irish call tea time.'

'Any idea of the onward destination?'

'Come on, Brigadier, it must be Kilbeg. They

think he's Robin Hood up there. If you want to check, why don't you call in a favour from that Chief Superintendent Malone at the Garda Special Branch?'

'What an excellent idea,' Ferguson said.

He thought about it, then rang through to Malone in Dublin. 'Charles Ferguson, Daniel.'

Malone groaned. 'What in the hell do you want, Charles?'

'A favour.'

At Dublin Airport, Murphy and Kelly landed at four-thirty, proceeded through customs with light luggage, went out of the concourse and approached an old Ford saloon car. The driver was named John Conolly, the man beside him Joseph Tomelty; both were hard-line Republicans and had been members of Murphy's group for many years, all boyhood friends. They shook hands with Murphy and Kelly.

'Good to see you, Brendan,' Conolly said. 'Did it go well?'

'A total fuck-up,' Murphy said. 'Couldn't have been worse. Let's get out of it. Make for home and I'll tell you.'

They all got in and drove away, and Malone, sitting in an unmarked car with a driver, said, 'Jesus. Conolly, Tomelty, plus Brendan and Dermot Kelly. The old Kilbeg Mafia. There's no doubt where they're going, but follow at a discreet distance and let's make sure they're taking the right road north.'

Twenty minutes later and well outside Dublin, he tapped the driver on the arm. 'Turn back. It's got to be Kilbeg.'

A few minutes later, as the car returned to Dublin, he called Ferguson on his mobile and told him what had happened.

'So it's Kilbeg?' Ferguson said.

'I'd say definitely. Are you going to give us trouble here, Charles?'

'Don't be silly, Daniel, we're doing ourselves a favour and you a favour. Leave it alone and I'll keep you informed.'

'One more question. Since you're running this, it means Dillon's involved.'

'Obviously.'

'Then God help Brendan Murphy.'

Ferguson put down his phone and turned to Hannah, who had been listening. 'You heard? Murphy and company are on their way to Kilbeg.'

'I'll let Dillon know, sir, in case it affects his plans.'

'It won't make much difference. You know what he's like. He'll go in tomorrow night anyway, Murphy or no Murphy. Just like a bad war movie.'

'I know, sir. He has a kind of death wish.'

'Why?'

'God knows.'

'You really have it in for him, Superintendent.'

'You couldn't be more wrong, sir. Actually, I like him too much. He reminds me of Liam Devlin, that combination of scholar, actor, poet and absolutely cold-blooded killer.'

'Just like Sir Walter Raleigh,' Ferguson said. 'Very bewildering, life, on occasion.'

Dillon and Billy were delivered by an unmarked RAF car driven by two uniformed RAF sergeants named Smith and Brian.

'Checked it out earlier,' Sergeant Brian said. 'That's the *Highlander* two hundred yards out.'

'Well, it doesn't look much to me,' Billy told him.

'Don't go by appearances. It's got twin screws,

depth sounder, radar, automatic steering. Does twenty-five knots at full stretch.'

'Good. Let's get cracking,' Dillon said.

'Right, sir, we've got a whaleboat to take your gear out.'

Forty minutes later, the gear was stowed, everything shipshape. Brian said, 'You've got the inflatable, with a good outboard motor. We'll get back now.'

'Thanks for a good job,' Dillon told him.

The sergeants departed in the whaleboat, and Dillon's mobile rang. It was Hannah Bernstein, bringing him up to date on the Kilbeg situation.

'Murphy being there, will it give you a problem?'

'Only if I can't shoot the bastard. How's Blake?'

'Still on his back.'

'Good, let's keep it that way. We'll see you tomorrow.'

Oban was enveloped in mist, and a fine rain was driving across the water, pushed by a light wind. Above on the land, low clouds draped across mountain tops, but beyond Kerrera the waters of the Firth of Lorn looked troubled.

'This is Scotland?' Billy said. 'What a bloody awful place. Why would anybody come here for a holiday?'

'Don't tell the tourist board, Billy, they'd lynch you. Now, we've things to do. We can go ashore and eat later.'

He laid out the diving equipment in the stern cabin. 'I don't need to explain this to you, you're an expert, but let's check over the arms.'

They laid the Walthers, the Semtex, the Uzis and stun grenades on the main saloon table. 'Let's give you a quick course on the Uzi, Billy. The Walther is simple enough.'

They spent half an hour going over things, then Dillon took one of the Walthers and led the way up to the wheelhouse. There was a flap to one side of the instrument board. He found a button, pressed, and inside was a fuse board. He cocked the Walther, slipped it inside, and closed the flap.

'Ready for action with ten rounds, Billy. Remember it's there. It's what is called an ace in the hole.'

'You think of everything, don't you?'

'That's why I'm still here. Let's go ashore and eat.'

He switched on the deck lights before they left and they coasted to the front at Oban on the inflatable and tied up. There was a pub close by that offered food. They went in, had a look at the menu, and opted for fish pie.

Dillon ordered a Bushmills, but Billy shook his head. 'Not me. I never liked the booze, Dillon. There must be something wrong with me.'

'Well, most things in life are in the Bible, and what the good book says is: wine is a mocker, strong drink raging.' He smiled. 'Having said that, I'll finish this and have another.'

Later, back on the *Highlander*, it started to rain harder. They sat on the stern deck under the awning, and Dillon went through everything from Katherine Johnson's death in New York to Al Shariz.

Billy said, 'These Mafia guys are fucks, Dillon, and Murphy's no better.'

'That about sums it up.'

'So we take them out?'

'I hope so.'

The rain drummed on the canvas awning and Dillon poured another whisky.

Billy said, 'Listen, Dillon, I know a little bit about you, the IRA hard man who switched sides. But every time I ask my uncle how it all happened, he clams up. What's the story?'

Maybe it was the rain, and maybe it was the

whisky, but instead of giving him a hard look and telling him to mind his business, Dillon felt himself talking, the words coming slowly but steadily.

'I was born in Ulster, my mother died giving birth to me – a heavy load to bear. My father took me to London. He was a good man. A small builder. Got me into St Paul's School.'

'I thought that was for toffs?'

'No, Billy, it's for brains. Anyway, I liked the acting. Went to the Royal Academy. Only did a year and joined the National Theatre. I was still only nineteen. My father went home to Belfast and got caught in a fire fight between IRA and Brit paratroopers.'

'Jesus, that was a bastard.'

Dillon poured another whisky, looking back into the past. 'Billy, I was a damn good actor, but I went back to Belfast and joined the IRA.'

'Well, you would. I mean, they killed your old man.'

'And I was nineteen, but they were nineteen, Billy, mostly a lot like you. Anyway, the IRA had access to camps in Libya. I was sent for training. Three months, and there wasn't a weapon I didn't know inside out. You wanted a bomb,

I could make it, any bomb.' He hesitated. 'Only that side I never liked. Passersby, women, kids – that isn't war.'

'That's how you saw it, war?'

'For a long time, yes, then I moved on. I was a professional soldier, so I sold my services. ETA in Spain, Arabs, Palestinians, also the Israelis. Funny, Billy, the job I've just done in Lebanon, blowing up a ship with arms for Saddam. Back in 'ninety-one, I worked for them.'

'You what?'

'Gulf War. I did the mortar attack on Downing Street in the snow. You wouldn't remember that.'

'I bleeding well do. I've read articles. They used a Ford Transit, then a guy on a motorbike picked up the bomber.'

'That was me, Billy.'

'Dillon, you bastard. You nearly got the Prime Minister and the entire cabinet.'

'Yes, almost, but not quite. I made a great deal of money out of it. I'm still rich, if you like. Later, I got into trouble in Bosnia. I was due to face a Serb firing squad, only Ferguson turned up, saved my miserable skin, and in return I had to work for him. You see, Billy, he wanted someone who was worse than the bad guys, and that was me.'

There was a kind of infinite sadness, and Billy surprised himself by saying quietly, 'What the hell, sometimes life just rolls up on you.'

'You could say that. The kid who was an actor at nineteen carried on acting just like in a bad movie, only he became the living legend of the IRA. You know those Westerns where they say Wyatt Earp killed twenty-one men? Billy, I couldn't tell you what my score is, except that it's a lot more.' He smiled gently. 'Do you ever get tired? I mean, really tired?'

Billy Salter summoned up all his resources. 'Listen, Dillon, you need to go to bed.'

'True. It's not much good when you don't sleep very well, but there's no harm in trying.'

'You do that.'

Dillon got up, rock steady. 'The trouble is, I don't really care whether I live or die any more, and when you're into the business of going into harm's way, that's not good.'

'Yes, well, this time you've got me. Just go to bed.'

Dillon went down the companionway. Billy sat there thinking about it, the rain beating down relentlessly, dripping off the awning. He'd never liked anyone as much as he liked Dillon, never admired anyone as much, outside of his uncle, anyway. He lit a cigarette and thought about it and suddenly saw a parallel. His uncle was a gangster, a right villain as they said in London, but there were things he wouldn't do, and Billy saw now that Dillon was the same.

He looked at the bottle of Bushmills morosely. 'Screw you,' he said, then picked it up, and the glass, and tossed them over the rail.

He sat there, the rain falling, feeling curiously relaxed, then remembered the paperback on philosophy, took it out of his pocket, and opened it at random. There were some pages about a man called Oliver Wendell Holmes, a famous American judge who'd also been an infantry officer in their Civil War: *Between two groups of men that want to make inconsistent kinds of worlds, I see no remedy except force . . . It seems to me that every society rests on the death of men.*

Billy was transfixed. 'Jesus,' he said softly, 'maybe that explains Dillon,' and he read on.

He awoke in the morning in the aft cabin, and was lying there, adjusting, when he was aware of a loud cry. He threw aside his blankets and went up the companionway in his shorts. It was still raining relentlessly and mist draped the whole of Oban harbour. As he looked over the rail, Dillon surfaced a few yards away.

'Come on, the water's wonderful.'

'You must be bloody mad,' and then Billy cried out. 'Behind you, for Christ's sake.'

Dillon turned to look. 'Those are seals, Billy. No problem. They're intelligent and curious. You get them a lot around here.'

He struck out for the ladder and climbed it, his shorts clinging to him. There was a towel on the table under the awning and he picked it up.

'What a bleeding place.' Billy looked out across the harbour. 'Does it always rain like this?'

'Six days out of seven. Never mind. Get dressed and we'll take the inflatable and go back to that pub. We'll get an all-day breakfast, just like in London.'

'Well, I'm with you there.'

Hannah Bernstein called in at Rosedene around nine-thirty and found Martha in reception.

'How is he?'

'Not wonderful. The bullet gouged deep. We

thought twenty stitches and ended up with thirty. Look, I don't know what's going on, but he isn't fit to go anywhere. The professor is checking him out now. I'll go and see how he's doing.'

Hannah helped herself to coffee from the machine and was sipping it when Daz appeared.

'Listen, tell me the truth,' he said. 'He's as woozy as hell, yet he keeps trying to tell me he's got important things to do, and I presume by that he means the usual kinds of things you, Dillon and the Brigadier get up to.'

'Absolutely, only this time it's something so dangerous that there's no way he can be involved in his condition. Dillon will handle it.'

'Yes, well, he would, wouldn't he? What do you want from me?'

'I know it sounds unethical, but couldn't you sedate him?'

'Hmm. That might be the best solution.' He turned to Martha. 'He really needs a sound sleep. You know what to do.' He smiled at Hannah. 'If you want to see him, better do it now.'

Blake was propped up, his right shoulder and arm bandaged, and looked awful, his face haggard. Hannah leaned over and kissed his cheek.

'How are you, Blake?'

'Terrible. I just need a rest. A couple of hours, and I'll be fine. When are we leaving?'

'Later this afternoon, but take it easy for now.'

'Christ, it hurts.'

Martha, lurking in the background, came forward with a glass of water and a couple of pills in a plastic cup. 'Here you go,' she said to Blake.

'What are these?'

'Painkillers. You'll feel a lot better soon.'

Hannah held his hand for a while, and slowly it relaxed and slipped away, as he stared blankly at her.

'There he goes,' Martha whispered. 'He'll be asleep for hours.'

They went out and found Daz at reception signing a few letters. He looked up. 'All right?'

'On his way to dreamland,' Martha told him.

'Good. I must go. I've got an operation scheduled at Guy's Hospital.' He smiled at Hannah. 'You'll monitor the situation?'

'The Brigadier will. I'm needed elsewhere.' She nodded to Martha and went out with him to where the Daimler waited. 'Can I give you a lift?'

'I was going to get a taxi, but, yes, a lift would help.'

'Ministry of Defence first, then you belong to

Professor Daz,' she told the driver, and they drove away. 'I hate March weather,' she said. 'Bloody rain.'

'Oh, dear, it's like that, is it?' Daz smiled. 'As may not have escaped your attention, I'm a Hindu, Hannah. Personal vibrations are important to me, and I sense you're up to your neck in trouble again, the Dillon kind of trouble.'

'Something like that.'

'When will you learn?'

'I know. I'm a nice Jewish girl, unmarried, with no kids, but very good at shooting people.'

He took her hand. 'Hannah.'

'No, don't say a thing. Dillon and I will go off and save the world again, only increasingly, I wonder what for.'

In Ferguson's office, she said, 'So what's the situation? Dillon and Billy Salter are fine. They're both master divers and Dillon is an expert boat handler. That leaves me and Sean Regan.'

'And without Blake, you're one short.'

'Exactly, sir.'

Ferguson got up, went to the window, and looked out. He turned. 'This kind of black operation works best without official special forces intervention. That's why I haven't given the Kilbeg bunker to the SAS. It has to be the kind of job that never happened.'

'Yes, I see that, sir. On the other hand, we could do with another gun, just to be on the boat when Dillon and Billy are doing their thing on shore.'

'It's a difficult one. Do you have any thoughts?'

'Yes, I do actually. An excellent gun.'

'And who would that be?'

She told him.

Dillon and Billy were sitting in the window seat at a pub in Oban, just finishing a superb Scottish breakfast of kippers, poached eggs and bacon, washed down with hot steaming tea, when Dillon's mobile rang.

Hannah said, 'Blake isn't good. They've sedated him. He'll be out for hours.'

'So you'll be on your way with Regan?'

'Yes, but Sean, we've got a problem. With you and Billy on land, and me with Regan on the boat, we need another gun. No big deal, just somebody reliable who really knows what he's doing.'

'And who would that be?'

She told him what she'd suggested to Ferguson, and Dillon laughed. 'Why not? There's nothing like a professional soldier. When will you leave?'

'Two o'clock. Be with you about four-thirty.'

'I look forward to it.' Dillon closed his phone and smiled. 'There you go, Billy, you'll have to mind your manners.'

'What do you mean?'

So Dillon explained.

Ferguson accompanied Hannah to Pine Grove when she went to pick up Regan. He was in Roper's suite again, going over a few points, and Helen Black stood by, with Miller.

Roper said, 'Well, I think the bastard's told the truth, or his version of it, anyway.'

'I damn well have,' Regan said.

'You'd better.' Ferguson smiled coldly. 'If not, I'll see you stand in the dock, Regan. Fifteen years.' He nodded to Miller. 'Take him and prepare him to move out. Put the manacles on.'

Miller complied, and Ferguson said, 'Get on with it, Superintendent.'

Hannah said, 'We've got a problem, Sergeant Major. You are aware of most of the facts, but let me summarize. We're sailing to County Louth from Oban late this afternoon. There'll be Dillon and Billy Salter, and me to guard Regan. Blake Johnson is unwell after the treatment for his gunshot wound. We're short a gun.'

'I see.' Helen Black smiled. 'How long have I got to pack?'

'Half an hour.'

'Then I'd better get moving.' She was out of the door instantly.

Later, at the main entrance, Hannah led Regan down the steps and eased him into the Daimler on to one of the extra seats. The driver had put the luggage in the boot and Ferguson stood at the top of the steps with Helen Black, who wore a khaki jumpsuit. They were alone for a moment.

'I'm grateful, Helen.'

'Tony's in Bosnia at the moment,' she said, referring to her husband. 'The Household Cavalry has two troops there.'

'I know, my love.'

'There's no need to worry him, but you'll obviously see to things if anything goes wrong.'

'My dear Helen.' He kissed her cheek. 'Just believe in Sean Dillon. He is a bastard of the first order, but my God, he's good.'

253

'You didn't need to tell me, not with the years I spent in Ulster. See you, Charles, and thanks for asking me to the party.'

At Farley Field, the Gulfstream was ready. Madoc loaded the luggage, then took them in. As Parry and Lacey came on board, Hannah made the introductions.

Lacey said, 'There's a bit of a headwind. It'll be an hour and forty-five minutes, but could run to two.'

He joined Parry in the cockpit, the engines started, and they moved away, taking off very quickly and climbing steeply.

Regan held out his manacled wrists. 'Can I have these off? I'm not going anywhere.'

Helen Black laughed. 'That's true.' She took out a key and unlocked him.

Madoc appeared from the galley. 'Tea, ladies.'

'An excellent idea,' Hannah said.

'Personally, I'd like an Irish whiskey,' Regan told him.

Madoc looked at Hannah, who nodded. 'Give him what he wants, Sergeant.'

Helen Black turned to her. 'Well, here I go, into the war zone again.'

*　　*　　*

As they returned to the *Highlander*, Billy said, 'Jesus, Dillon, not only two women, but both coppers.'

'Yes, Scotland Yard Special Branch variety and Royal Military Police. But remember one thing, Billy: they've both killed more than once in the course of duty. They both know what they're doing.'

'What have I got myself into?'

'Well, as Heidegger said, and you quoted him to me, life is action and passion . . .'

Billy cut in. 'Okay, so it's going to be bleeding active and terribly exciting.'

'You'll love it, Billy,' Dillon said, as they coasted in and he reached for the *Highlander*'s ladder.

12

The rain continued relentlessly. Billy was coiling a rope under the awning when a voice called, '*Highlander*, ahoy.'

Hannah, Helen Black and Regan were standing on the jetty beside a Range Rover, the driver in plain clothes but obviously RAF.

Billy called down the companionway, 'They're here, Dillon.'

Dillon came up on deck and looked across. 'Fine. I'll go and get them.'

The inflatable coasted in at the bottom of the steps and Hannah called, 'Everything okay?'

'Absolutely. Let's have the luggage.'

There were only three bags and the driver brought them down. Regan followed, hands manacled again. He held up his wrists to Dillon. 'I might as well be on a Georgia chain gang.'

'You deserve to be, you shite.' Dillon shoved him

into the boat. 'Go on, get in there.' He turned to greet the women. 'Sergeant Major, Superintendent. A fast boat and a passage by night. Action, passion, we've got it all here.'

'How riveting,' Helen Black said. 'I can't wait,' and she stepped into the inflatable.

Dillon handed the luggage up to Billy, and Helen climbed in, followed by Hannah. Hannah looked around the *Highlander*. 'My God, I must say it looks pretty basic.'

'Underneath its lack of a good paint job, it's superb, so don't worry,' Dillon said. 'Just get settled in, stick Sean in the saloon, and let's get on with it.' He turned to Regan. 'Just remember one thing, we're back with the old movies again: one false move and you're dead.'

'Come on, Dillon, you're going to kill me anyway.'

'Not if you're good.'

They put Regan in the saloon, the two women settled into the aft cabin, and Dillon made ready for sea. He took Billy, Hannah and Helen into the wheelhouse and went over the controls, then showed the women the Walther in the fuse box beside the wheel.

'Just in case.'

The sea was starting to flood in through the entrance to the harbour, and the *Highlander* was rocking from side to side.

Billy said, 'Jesus, I feel terrible,' and he turned, went out on deck, and vomited over the side.

Dillon followed, took a plastic pill bottle from a pocket of his reefer jacket, shook the pills out, and offered them. 'Get them down, Billy. They'll make a difference.'

Hannah said, 'Kindness and consideration from the great Sean Dillon?'

Dillon smiled. 'Sticks and stones, Hannah, not that it matters. We've got to leave if we're to make tonight's schedule, so I've other things to worry about. We'll discuss the plan of attack later. The wind's force five to six at the moment, but it should ease later.'

They left at three, and ploughed out into the turbulent waters, the sea running heavily. Dillon stood at the wheel alone. After a while, Helen Black came in with a mug.

'Tea,' she said. 'I believe that's your preference.'

'It's the grand woman you are.'

'I'm part Irish, too, Dillon, from my father's mother's side. In spite of thirty years of war, it seems we're somehow inextricably mixed.'

'Eight million Irish in the UK, Sergeant Major, and the population of the Republic only three and a half million. It's a puzzle.'

'You and the Superintendent, that's a puzzle, too.'

'She's a hard woman, Hannah, a moralist. She finds it difficult to forgive my wicked past. You, on the other hand, understand perfectly. We've both been down the same road on different sides.'

'Yes. That's the problem, isn't it?' And she left.

Billy turned up an hour later with another mug of tea. 'Are you okay, Dillon?'

'I'm fine, but what about you?'

'The pills worked. It's Regan who's in trouble. You'd better give me some more of those pills.'

Dillon handed him the bottle. 'Take care of it, Billy. Let me know how he is.'

Perhaps half an hour later, Billy came back. 'He's lying down, but I think they're doing the job.'

'Good.'

Billy said, 'Dillon, on the White Diamond job. I've been thinking.'

'Go on.' Dillon turned to automatic pilot and lit a cigarette.

'So they've sliced through the grille entrance and we know those tunnels go right into the St

Richard's Dock basement. Then all you need is a sledgehammer to break through those old brick walls.'

'So?'

'But the vaults. I still don't see how they get past the electronic security.'

'Neither do I. But there must be a sophisticated explanation. It's like computers, Billy. They're state of the art, too, but if you can get in, if you can access the files, then all is revealed.' Dillon smiled. 'Don't worry. Harry's on the case, and so is Roper. They'll come up with our answer. All I'm concerned with now is Kilbeg, and taking you back to the Dark Man in one piece, because if I don't Harry will want an explanation.'

'Hey, stuff that, Dillon. I'll do my thing.'

'Okay, time for truth, Billy. Since Blake isn't here, it's the women I'm leaving behind. I'll need you to go on shore with me. How do you feel about that?'

'Great.' Billy smiled. 'Never better. I'm with you, Dillon, all the way.' And he went out.

It was into early evening when the wheelhouse door opened and there was the smell of fried bacon sandwiches.

'And tea,' Hannah said.

'Now what's a nice Jewish girl doing, giving me bacon?'

She ignored him. 'Where are we?'

'Islay to the east. Rain's a bit squally.'

'Can I take over?'

'No need. I'll go on automatic pilot.'

Dillon checked the course, then locked on. He attacked the sandwiches. 'Fabulous. Any word from London?'

'No.'

He finished the sandwiches and drank the tea. 'There you go. Thanks, love.'

'I really think you should go and lie down for a couple of hours, and let me take over.'

'Hell, what do women know about boats?'

The wheelhouse door swung open and Helen Black came in. 'Don't be a chauvinist pig, Mr Dillon. I don't know if the Superintendent knows boats, but I do. My husband and I race them as a hobby, so do shut up and go and rest. You're going to have a very hard night.'

Dillon raised his hands. 'I give in to this monstrous regiment of women. I'll leave you to it, ladies,' and he went below.

Hannah, too, went, and Helen Black took the

wheel, enjoying it as she always had, increasing speed as heavy weather threatened from the east. She thought about her husband, Tony, serving in the hell of Bosnia with the Household Cavalry. It was a source of hurt that just because the Households were the Queen's personal bodyguard and rode round London in breastplates and helmets on horseback there were those who thought they were chocolate soldiers. In fact, they'd served in the Falklands, in the Gulf War, in Ireland, and in most of the rotten little wars in between.

Her trouble was that she was a woman and she was a soldier and she loved the army. Of course, Dillon had been a soldier too, to be fair. She rather liked him, although he'd been the worst of the enemy.

Against the early darkness she could see the outline of one of the Irish ferries, red and green navigation lights visible. She altered course a couple of points, then increased speed, racing the heavy weather that threatened from the east, and the waves grew rougher.

By now it really was dark, only a slight phosphorescent shining from the sea, and then the door opened and Dillon appeared.

'How are things?'

'A bit rough.'

He tapped the radio, got the weather channel, listened, and added, 'That's okay. The wind's going to drop soon. Why don't you go and get some coffee? I'll hang on, then I'll put her on automatic pilot and we can discuss what's going to happen. An hour, an hour and a half, we'll hit the Louth coast.'

'Fine.' She nodded and went out.

Half an hour later, Brendan Murphy, Dermot Kelly, Conolly and Tomelty arrived at Kilbeg and pulled up outside the Patriot public house. Murphy led the way in, running through torrential rain.

It was a typical Irish pub for either side of the border, with a bar, beer pumps, and a log fire in the hearth. There were only three old men at the fire and the landlord behind the bar, one Fergus Sullivan.

'Jesus, Brendan, and it's grand to see you.'

They shook hands. Brendan said, 'You're dying the death tonight.'

'Well, it's Monday night. What can I do for you?'

264

'Beds for me and Dermot. We've business else-where at the moment. We'll have a drink now and see you later.'

Sullivan poured four Irish whiskeys and a fifth for himself.

'Up the IRA.'

'And confusion to the English,' Murphy said.

A short while later, inside the grounds of the ruins of Kilbeg Abbey, they entered an ancient hall and approached a dark old oaken door at one end banded with iron that looked as if it had been there for centuries. In fact it was a modern replica backed by steel plate of the finest quality. Murphy took a transceiver from his pocket and pressed the button. There was the murmur of a voice.

'Murphy,' he said. 'Open sesame.'

A moment later, one half of the door opened electronically. He and Kelly passed through into a short tunnel and went down a flight of con-crete steps. There was electric light, another door opened, and in moments they were into a concrete corridor, painted white, very functional, and then into the main part of the bunker.

Two men stood waiting: Liam Brosnan, tall, heavily built, with hair to his shoulders, and Martin O'Neill, the direct opposite, small and red-haired.

The only thing they had in common were the AK47 assault rifles they carried.

'Well, at least you're on your toes,' Murphy said. 'Any problems?'

'Only one, Brendan,' Brosnan told him. 'Down at the entrance where the tunnel slopes to the steps, there's about a foot of water.'

'Show me.'

They led the way, and Murphy and Kelly followed. It was dark down there and, unlike the rest of the bunker, cold.

'Why is there no heat on, no light?' Murphy demanded.

'Well, that's the point, Brendan. The rest of the bunker's okay, but this part under the old farmhouse is on a separate system and the flooding must have screwed it up.'

'It's the rain,' O'Neill said. 'It's been terrible during the past two weeks.'

'I can tell it's the bloody rain, you eejit,' Murphy said. 'But if the electricity isn't working, that cocks up the entrance. There aren't any bars. They weren't necessary when it was electronic.'

'I've chained the handles and padlocked them,' Brosnan told him. 'I was waiting for you, Brendan. I know you would want someone reliable.'

'Exactly. Don't worry, there's that fella Patterson in Dundalk that builds the fancy houses. He knows which side his bread's buttered on.'

'I know who you mean.'

'You call him and tell him I'll see him at the Patriot for breakfast at eight-thirty tomorrow. Explain the flooding and tell him I expect miracles. He'll attend to it or he'll get a bullet in his left knee, and that's only for starters.'

They walked back through the storage areas. Mortars stacked neatly, the kind of missiles and heavy machine guns that could shoot down a helicopter, AK47s and Armalites still greased and brand new from the factory. Cases of Semtex.

Murphy lit a cigarette and said to Kelly, 'Look at it, Dermot. Just waiting to be used, and those old women in London talk peace.'

'You're right, Brendan.'

'Our day will come. I'll just check the office.'

It was at the end of the tunnel, small, functional, with filing cabinets, a computer system and a desk. He said to Brosnan and O'Neill, 'Wait outside.'

Kelly closed the door. Murphy knelt behind the desk and lifted a section of carpet. Underneath, set into the concrete floor, was an old-fashioned safe with a simple keyhole. He felt under the desk, found a key on a magnetic block, and opened the flap.

Inside were packets of currency, sterling and dollars, all wrapped in transparent plastic bags. He handled a few.

'You think this is cash, Dermot? It's not, it's power. With money you can do anything, and there's almost three million here.'

'What about Fox, Brendan? You know what I mean? What you owe him?'

'Hey, stuff Fox. Look what happened at Al Shariz. It was a total fuck-up, and all because of Fox. It must have been. I mean, how were the Israelis on to us? I know it wasn't me.'

'So you aren't going to pay him what you owe him?'

'Am I hell.' Murphy locked the safe and put the carpet back.

'What if he makes trouble, Brendan?'

Murphy laughed. 'Make trouble for me, the Mafia? Dermot, this is Ireland, the one place in the world where they're powerless. We're the ones with power, Dermot, you and me, so let's get on with it and go and crack a bottle and have a decent supper at the Patriot.'

* * *

They all sat round the saloon in the *Highlander*, a large-scale map laid across the table.

'Kilbeg village,' Dillon said. 'The abbey is quarter of a mile to the east. The bunker is underneath.' He tapped the map. 'There, where the site of a ruined farmhouse is indicated, is, according to Sean here, the exit to the bunker.' He looked at Regan, who sat on one of the bench seats, wrists manacled. 'Isn't that so, Sean?'

'To hell with you,' Regan said.

'So how do you intend to play this?' Helen Black asked.

'Well, according to Regan, there are only two caretakers in the bunker. I intend to act very quickly, very economically. Blow the exit door, go in, dispose of them, and leave a hundred-pound block of Semtex to take the place out. They're storing Semtex there as well as arms. It'll be like Bonfire Night.'

'Which, if I'm not mistaken, celebrates Guy Fawkes *failing* to blow up Parliament,' Hannah Bernstein said.

'Well, I won't fail.'

'What about me?' Billy asked.

'You can watch my back,' Dillon said. 'Guard the exit door after I go in.'

'Oh, great. So I'm standing around like a ponce.'

'Don't be a silly boy, Billy. I'll need you watching out for me.'

'So how do you intend to do it?' Helen asked.

'Right, there's the pier that used to serve the old granite quarry. Yachtsmen call in here occasionally and usually anchor in the bay, according to Roper's information. What we'll do is this. We'll take the boat in to the pier, you in charge, Sergeant Major. Billy and I will wear diving suits. We'll offload diving equipment on to the pier, in case we have to come back the hard way. You will take *Highlander* a hundred yards out into the bay, and anchor.'

'Fine,' Helen said.

'Billy and I will have transceivers, and so will you, so we'll be in touch. The farmhouse is what, a quarter of a mile away? This will be the ultimate in-and-out job. With luck, it'll be so clean that I'll call and bring you into the pier to pick us up.' He smiled and turned to Billy. 'No need to get your feet wet.'

'Well, that's nice. It's bleeding cold out there.'

Dillon turned to Sean Regan, sitting there, sullen, on the bench, manacled hands on his knees.

'Now we come to your part, son. Is there anything you haven't told me?'

'I've told you everything I know.'

'I hope so, for your sake, because if you haven't you're dead in the water. And that's not just a figure of speech.' He turned to the others. 'Right, people, that's the way it is, so let's get it done.'

It was nine o'clock and pitch dark when they drifted in, the engines a muted throbbing. Dillon left it to Helen Black. She steered one-handed, holding a pair of Nightstalkers to her eyes, and hardly touched the pier. In a second, Dillon was over with a line and ran it round a bollard.

'Right, Billy, pass the gear up.'

Billy wrestled with air bottles and other things and Dillon stacked them on the pier.

'All right, son, let's have you.'

Billy joined him. 'First time in Ireland, and what a bloody place.'

'The hob of hell, Billy.' Dillon called to Helen Black. 'On your way.'

The *Highlander* moved out and Dillon checked his transceiver. 'Hey, you still love me, Superintendent?'

'Don't be silly,' she replied, and then added. 'For God's sake, Dillon . . .'

'I know, take care. Well, here we go to save the British way of life. An Irish gunman and a well-known London gangster. Why is it that people like us have to do it?'

He switched off, checked his Uzi, and slung it across his chest. Billy did the same. Dillon checked his Walther, and, again, Billy did the same. Having heard Dillon talking on the transceiver, he said, 'Do you know the answer? Why *is* it people like us have to do it?'

'Billy, a great English writer once said – it's ironic that when it comes down to it – that it's men of a rough persuasion who have to do all the hard things that the general population are incapable of doing, and then the general population disowns them. It's called being a soldier.'

'But I'm not a bleeding soldier.'

'You're a gangster, Billy. It's the same thing, so shut up and follow me.'

On board the *Highlander*, Hannah obeyed Helen Black's orders and dropped the anchor. Below, Sean Regan sat on the bench, manacled, and thought about things. He was a practical man, and had survived for many years in the Irish struggle by being so.

However, try as he could, Dillon's reputation wouldn't go away and it was that of the ultimate hard man. The Brits used him on situations they didn't want to go to court. If he was on your case, you were dead.

With the best will in the world, Regan couldn't imagine a fate other than being tossed over the side into the Irish Sea, a convenient corpse, and there was no way he could risk that. A desperate plan came to him, and before he could hesitate, he acted. He knocked a tray bearing a teapot and cups off the table and fell on his knees.

A moment later, Hannah appeared. 'What is it?'

'My gut's killing me. I think it must be those seasickness pills.'

She crouched and checked him out. 'That bad?'

'I need the necessary. For God's sake, I might mess myself.'

She pulled him up and took him out to the lavatory. He held out his hands. 'Come on, you can't move in there. I couldn't get my trousers down with these things on.'

She hesitated, then took out her key, uncuffed

him, and pushed him inside. She stood against the wall and waited.

Regan sat down, breathed deeply, then stood up, shoved the door open hard, catching Hannah and knocking her against the wall. He went up the companionway fast, ran out on deck, past Helen Black as she emerged from the wheelhouse, and vaulted over the rail. The cold March Irish Sea took his breath away, but he struck out for the shore with all his strength and vanished into the dark.

Hannah appeared on deck. 'Goddammit, he conned me. I was such a fool.'

'Happens to us all.' Helen Black tried her transceiver. 'Dillon, are you there?'

But in the valley area up from the cliffs the signal was poor, and there was no reply.

Sean Regan hit the shore, colder than he'd ever been in his life, and immediately started to run, making his way up the cliff path and turning for Kilbeg. He burst into the Patriot fifteen minutes later. There were three drinkers at the bar, Conolly and Tomelty two of them.

He fell across the bar in front of Sullivan, and

Tomelty raised his head by his hair. Regan said, 'Thank God you're here. We've got trouble.'

'Well, tell the man here.'

Regan turned and saw Murphy get up from the bench before the fire.

'Why, Sean, I thought the Brits had you in Wandsworth. How in the hell did you get here?'

Suddenly, Regan realized he was in deep trouble here, too, and tried to recover. 'Never mind that, Brendan. Dillon's here, Sean Dillon. He's here to destroy the bunker.'

'Really?' Murphy said. 'But how would he know? Have you been shooting your gob off?'

'Please, Brendan. They took me out of Wandsworth. Beat the shite out of me.'

'Well, I must say you don't look too bad,' Tomelty said.

'We came over on a boat. Anchored off the old pier. I managed to get away. There are a couple of women on board, one Special Branch, that Bernstein bitch, the other is military police.'

'And Dillon?'

'He's gone to take out the bunker with another guy. He's going in by way of the exit at the farmhouse.'

Murphy shook his head. 'And how would he know about all that?'

'Jesus, Brendan.'

'No, you, Sean.'

At that moment, there was a rumble in the distance. Kelly ran out of the pub entrance, then came back in. 'It's the abbey. Some sort of explosion. Shall we get up there?'

Murphy cursed. 'No. It's a waste of bloody time now.' Murphy pushed Regan to the door. 'Let's get out of here, down to the pier.'

A few moments earlier, as Dillon and Billy had reached the exit door in the old farmhouse, Helen Black managed to get through.

'Dillon, for God's sake.'

'What?'

'We've got a crisis. Regan escaped. Jumped in the bay and swam for it.'

'Well, that's damn unfortunate.'

'Will you abort?'

'Like hell. We're at the exit now. We'll go in hard and get out quick.' He switched off.

Helen said to Hannah, 'He's still going in. I'll take the inflatable to the pier. Time could be crucial here.'

'Maybe I should go,' Hannah said.

'Not this time. Now I've got to get moving.'

At the exit door, Dillon stopped, took a magnetized block from his bag, and slammed it over the lock. 'Stay here and wait for me, Billy.'

He stepped back, the lock blew, and the doors folded inwards. Dillon ran in, took a smoke grenade from the bag, and rolled it down the corridor. The water considerably reduced its efficiency, but he ran on, pulling out a stun grenade, but again, swallowed by the floor, it wasn't very effective.

Behind him, Billy muttered, 'What the hell,' raised his Uzi, and went after Dillon.

Brosnan and O'Neill were having a late supper in the office when they heard the noise, grabbed their Uzis, and ran out. A certain amount of smoke remained from the grenade and they crouched from the half-shock of the stun grenade. A moment later, Dillon ran out of the fog headlong, and Brosnan rose to meet him, but Dillon was faster, his Uzi battering Brosnan back against the wall.

Dillon stumbled to one knee and O'Neill stood up in the murk. 'I've got you now, you bastard.'

He raised his AK and Billy came in on the run, firing his Uzi, and shot him to pieces. Billy dropped on his knees, breathing deeply, and Dillon stood up.

'Don't fall down on me now, Billy. This is the good bit.'

He kicked open the office door, produced five blocks of Semtex from the jump bag, took timers from the bag, and inserted them. He left one on the office floor and pushed Billy.

'Out you go. Three minutes.' He dropped the blocks one by one, as they ran through the bunker, splashed through the water, and made it out of the exit. As they went down the slope to the cliffs, the explosion rumbled underground.

Murphy was into the car, with Regan, Kelly, Conolly and Tomelty, and roaring out of the village within seconds of the explosion. When they reached the top of the road, he said to Tomelty, who was driving, 'Switch off the engine.'

They coasted down the hill and braked to a halt. Helen Black, sitting in the inflatable, heard nothing.

Murphy said, 'Not a sound. You go along the

strip of beach, Tomelty. You and I will take the pier, Conolly, and be very, very quiet.' He turned to Regan. 'And you be especially quiet.'

They moved out. Helen Black sat there in the inflatable. There was a footfall on the beach. She turned and took out her Walther, and a flashlight was switched on from the pier.

'Well, I know you're not Bernstein, I'd recognize her, so I suppose you must be the Sergeant Major.' Murphy frowned. 'You wouldn't be Black, would you? The one from Derry?'

'My God, you've got a brain.'

'Down you go, Tomelty,' Murphy said. 'Get her gun.' He turned to Kelly. 'You and Conolly take her out to the boat. If the Bernstein bitch argues, tell her you'll shoot this one.' He turned to Tomelty. 'You and I stay here for Dillon.'

The inflatable moved away. Tomelty said, 'What about Regan?'

Murphy said, 'Silly me. I was forgetting.' He turned to Regan and took a Browning from his pocket. 'You sold us out, you shite. You're lucky I don't have time to make it longer.'

The silenced Browning coughed and Regan went off the pier into the water.

* * *

On the *Highlander*, Hannah looked through the Nightstalker as the inflatable coasted in. 'Are you all right?' she called.

Kelly said, 'We've got your Sergeant Major here and I've got a gun to her head. If you're not sensible, I'll kill her stone dead.'

Helen Black called, 'Don't listen, Hannah, do what you have to do. You heard the explosion. We've achieved our object. To hell with these people.'

Conolly hit her across the side of her head with his pistol. She cried out. Kelly said, 'I mean it.'

'All right.' Hannah stood back, her Walther in her left hand.

A moment later, Kelly boarded, followed by Helen Black and Conolly, who took the Walther from Hannah's grasp.

'There's a good girl.'

Black was wearing paratroop boots with her jumpsuit. Stuffed into the right one was the Colt .25 hollowpoint. At that moment, she could have pulled it out in the darkness of the deck and shot both men. But what would that mean for Dillon and Billy? She decided to wait.

* * *

Dillon tried to get her on the transceiver and got no reply. On the *Highlander*, Kelly started the engines and moved in to the pier, and Conolly tied up. Dillon and Billy came down the hill on the run, and in the slight light of a quarter moon, the rain having stopped, saw the boat move in.

'They've come for us,' Billy said, gasping for breath.

'So it would appear.'

They hit the end of the pier, looked down at the deck with the light on, and saw Kelly push Hannah and Helen out, he and Conolly both holding guns to the women's backs.

Murphy came out of the shadows with Tomelty. 'They mean it, you bastard. You want them dead?'

'Certainly not,' Dillon said. 'Do as he says, Billy, guns on the floor.'

Billy complied, and Murphy lit a cigarette. 'Damn you, Dillon, I always admired you, but this time you've cost me money.'

'Not you, Brendan, Jack Fox.'

Murphy laughed incredulously. 'My God, is that what this is about, a personal feud?'

'You shouldn't have joined, Brendan.'

'Neither should you, Dillon. Now you and your friend get on board so we can move to where the water's deeper, because that's where you're going.'

Dillon and Billy went down the steps to the deck and joined Helen Black and Hannah; Murphy followed with Tomelty. Kelly was at the wheel, Conolly joined the others.

'You know what?' Murphy said. 'It's a waste of good women, but I'm going to kill the lot of you.'

He was looking at Hannah when he said that. Helen Black, close to the wheelhouse, pulled the Colt out of her boot and shot Kelly in the back of the head. The boat swerved, and everyone fell over. As Conolly tried to get up, she pushed herself upright, shot him dead, then ducked and dived over the rail as Murphy tried to shoot her.

At the same moment, Dillon grabbed Billy by the arm. 'Over!' he cried, and pushed him over the rail after Helen Black. As he tried to follow, Tomelty, still on the deck, grabbed his ankles, and Dillon went down.

'You bastard.' Murphy kicked him in the side. 'You're finally dead meat, Dillon, and you, bitch. Those two in the water aren't going anywhere. Fifteen minutes at this season of the year and it's hypothermia time. You two will get it quick, at least.'

Billy, close to Helen on the port side, said, 'I'm going to try for that gun in the wheelhouse.'

He didn't wait for a reply, simply jackknifed and went under the *Highlander* from port to starboard, scraping his back under the keel, surfaced, and reached up for the rail. As he pulled himself on board and slithered for the wheelhouse, he heard the exchange between Dillon and Murphy, unaware that, looking beyond Murphy and Tomelty, Dillon had seen him arrive.

'Come on, Brendan, why all the dialogue? In Derry in the old days, we didn't talk about it, we did it.'

On his knees in the wheelhouse, Billy dropped the flap and got his hand to the Walther, which Dillon had left cocked. He turned and shot Tomelty twice in the back, shattering his spine.

Murphy started to turn, shocked as Tomelty went down; Hannah kicked sideways at his left leg and he stumbled, which was Dillon's moment. He grabbed at the gun hand and came breast-to-breast.

'Now then, you dog.'

He pushed hard, Murphy staggered back, and they went over the stern rail.

And the sea was Dillon's, the master diver's

element, not Murphy's. They went down perhaps ten feet. Dillon got an arm around Murphy's throat and then the anchor on its chain scraped his back. He grabbed it with his right hand and held on fast. Murphy kicked and struggled and Dillon held his breath until he was bursting, and then Murphy stopped struggling. Dillon let him go and surfaced.

He managed the ladder and hung there and Hannah looked over. 'All right, Dillon? What happened to Murphy?'

He hauled himself up. 'What do you think happened? As the Sicilians have it, Brendan Murphy is asleep with the fishes.'

He sat on the deck, his back to the wheelhouse. Billy was there, and Helen Black.

'You okay, Sergeant Major?'

'I'm fine, Mr Dillon.'

'And you, Billy?'

'What the fuck did you get me into, Dillon?'

'Billy, you saved the pass, to use an old-fashioned phrase. You were fantastic. The SAS couldn't have done better. On top of that, you've given Superintendent Bernstein a severe problem. Try not to get arrested, because she'll feel terribly guilty if *she* has to arrest you.'

Billy grinned and turned to Hannah. 'What do I have to do? Take up good works?'

'Just don't give me a problem, Billy.'

'Trouble is, I've been giving people a problem all my life.'

Dillon said, 'Let's get the bodies over the side. And do me a favour, Sergeant Major – take us out. I'll do a quick change and I'll be up to relieve you.'

'Leave it to me.'

'Come on, you two,' he said to Hannah and Billy. 'Let's get into dry clothes,' and he led the way below.

An hour later, Charles Ferguson was in his Cavendish Square flat, enjoying a nightcap, when his phone rang. Dillon was at the wheel alone, the others below. Pushing out into the Irish Sea, he had switched to automatic pilot and lit a cigarette as he spoke.

'Is it yourself, Brigadier?'

'Dillon! Where are you?'

'On our way back to Oban.' Dillon was using his Codex Four mobile. 'We can talk.'

'What's happened?'

'Well, the Kilbeg bunker is no more, and the

Sergeant Major's proved a treasure. Killed two of Murphy's gang. Billy saved our bacon by killing another at the right time.'

'Good God! Is everyone all right?'

'Oh, right as rain, Brigadier. We're a tough lot.'

'Well, thank God for that. And Murphy?'

'Oh, I saw to him myself.'

'Well, you would, wouldn't you? So what now?'

'I'd say, six hours to Oban. The weather's not too good. If you could alert Lacey and Parry for a flight back to London around breakfast time?'

'Consider it done.'

'How's Blake?'

'A post-operational infection. Daz and Martha have it in hand.'

'That's good. Fox is really going to be mortified over this lot.'

'I like that, Dillon, a good choice of words. I'll see you tomorrow.'

Dillon sat there at the wheel, and then the door opened, there was a bacon smell, and Billy appeared, a plate of sandwiches in one hand and a mug of tea.

'There you go, Sean.'

Billy turned to leave, and Dillon said, 'Billy, you were great. Harry will be proud of you.'

'Yes, but he won't know, will he? What I mean is, nobody knows unless they've done it, been there, bought the tee shirt, isn't that what they say? Jesus, Dillon, this wasn't some punch-up in an East End pub. I killed two men tonight.'

'They shouldn't have joined, Billy, if they didn't want the risk. Remember that.'

'Okay, I suppose so. So – now it's the Jagos and Fox?'

'Yes. I suppose it is.' Dillon finished the last sandwich. 'Go on, Billy. Get some sleep. You've earned it.'

Billy left, and Dillon turned from automatic pilot to manual and took the *Highlander* onwards over an increasingly turbulent sea.

LONDON

13

Jack Fox had gone down to the Grill Restaurant at the Dorchester to enjoy an English breakfast. He was reading *The Times* and just finishing poached eggs, sausage, ham and toast, when Falcone appeared.

'We've got a problem, Signore.'

'What now?' Fox asked.

'I've just seen Sky Television's news programme. I think you should see for yourself.'

'That bad?' Fox asked.

'I'm afraid so, Signore.'

In the suite, Fox watched the next news update with horror. The story of a large explosion at Kilbeg in County Louth led the hour. There were pictures of the Irish police on site, and reports of some kind of IRA connection, although the IRA and Sinn Fein had denied it. One thing was certain — four bodies had drifted on to the beach, three dead from gunshot wounds. The fourth was Brendan Murphy, a well-known dissident who had left the Provisional IRA and formed his own group. The suggestion was that the PIRA had taken his men out. It was thought that the explosion had involved an underground arms bunker, and this was being investigated.

There was a ring at the door. Russo answered and returned with a waiter carrying a tray with fresh coffee. He was dismissed and Russo poured.

Falcone said, 'Murphy owed you money, Signore.'

'Well, we can kiss that goodbye,' Fox said.

Falcone said, 'Please forgive me if I overstep the bounds, Signore, but I've been loyal to you for so many years that I feel I can ask this question: How bad are things?'

Fox looked at him. 'Pretty bad, Aldo. But we still have one ace in the hole left. The White Diamond Company heist on Tuesday.'

'You said ten million sterling.'

'With four to the Jagos.' Fox smiled. 'And you disagreed.'

'I sure did, Signore. I say we take the lot.'

'I'm beginning to agree, Aldo, but afterwards.

Let these bastards do the hard work.'

Falcone smiled broadly. 'Excellent, Signore.'

'Okay, get in touch with the Jagos. I want a meet at lunch-time. Pick a quiet pub.'

'I'll arrange it, Signore.'

Falcone left to make the arrangements, but first he phoned Don Marco who, because of the time difference, was still in bed, but then, Falcone's instructions had been to call at any time of the day or night. The Don listened patiently.

Finally he said, 'Fucked again, my nephew. Fucked at the Colosseum, then at Al Shariz, and now in Ireland. You know what they say, Aldo? Once is okay, twice is coincidence, and three times is enemy action.'

'So what do we do, Don Marco?'

'Nothing. This is Jack's problem. He succeeds or fails on his own. But if he fails . . . Understand me, Aldo. I'll never let any physical harm come to him. He's my nephew. But the family needs a leader in whom it can be confident. This diamond heist is his last chance. If something happens to that, too . . . Jack's out. *Capisce?*'

'*Capisco*, Don Marco.'

293

In the back bar of the Horse Guards pub not far from St Richard's Dock, Harold and Tony Jago waited. It was misty on the river and a little rain drummed against the window.

Harold looked out. 'I like it like this, Tony, it's the way the Thames should be. England for the English, eh? Who needs Europe? A bunch of frogs and krauts.'

'You're right, Harold. Mind you, we're stuck with the fucking Mafia right now.'

'They don't worry me. We can handle them.' At that minute, Manchester Charlie Ford came in through the far door, Amber Frazer with him.

'Jesus, here they come,' Harold said. 'What a pair. I mean, if they want their own thing instead of a woman, that's all right, but I don't like blacks. They're nothing but trouble.'

Ford had the file under his arm and passed it across. 'Everything's taken care of, Harold.'

'Good. Let's wait for Fox. What do you want to drink?'

At Rosedene, Blake was feeling a lot better and greeted Dillon and Helen Black with enthusiasm when they turned up.

'Miller filled me in. We watched Sky Television. You really took them apart.'

'Which just leaves the White Diamond Company.'

'Hey, don't leave me out this time, Sean. I want to be part of that.'

'You can't be, because I won't be part of it, and neither will Bernstein or Ferguson. We've given it to Harry Salter. We're not involved, Blake.'

'Okay, but I can't just sit around here. I need to be with you.'

'Fine. If Daz will release you, that's okay by me.'

Daz agreed he could go, as long as Blake did not take part in any physical activity, so just before noon they repaired to Ferguson's office at the Ministry of Defence, Blake wearing a sling for his right arm. Hannah stood beside Ferguson at his desk.

The Brigadier said, 'I hardly need to say well done. However, we're left with the final nail in Jack Fox's coffin, the White Diamond Company job. What happens now, Superintendent?'

'Frankly, sir, the Salters won't talk to me. It's up to Dillon.'

'Well, according to Roper, tomorrow's the day

because that's when the big diamond consignment comes in.'

'What we do know is that they've cut open the old grille gate in the tunnel,' Hannah said. 'The thing we still don't know is, once they've smashed into the basement, how do they bypass the security to get into the vault?'

'That's what I'm going to see Harry Salter about,' Dillon said. 'I'll take Blake. You stay out of it, Hannah. I know you don't like our using a villain like Salter, and I don't want to offend your fine police morality.'

At the Horse Guards, Harold sat reading the file, then passed it to Tony. 'It's not only good, it's bloody good.' At that moment, Fox, Falcone and Russo came in. Harold got up. 'Good to see you. We're just finishing things.' They sat, but Falcone and Russo as usual stood at the wall.

'So, where are we?' Fox demanded.

'Hey, your file was sweetness and light,' Harold said, 'but Charlie here has put in some extras that will truly delight you.'

'Tell me.'

Afterwards, Fox nodded. 'Excellent. There's only

one change. I've just had more recent information that the take will be more like twelve million than ten. More for everyone, Jago. So keep our eye on the ball, people.'

'We sure will, Jack,' Harold said.

Fox got up. 'I'm in your hands. You're the experts, we'll keep out of it. Stay in touch.'

He went out, followed by Falcone and Russo. Tony Jago said, 'So we do all the fucking work.'

'Never mind,' Harold told him. 'For a payday like that, I'm glad to do the work.'

Ferguson went into the Dark Man with Dillon and Blake. Salter and Billy were in the end booth and Dora was giving them shepherd's pie.

'Smells good,' Ferguson said. 'Takes me back to Eton. We'll have the same. Blake needs building up.'

'Blake looks bloody awful,' Salter observed.

'Have you seen Sky Television, Billy?' Dillon asked. 'A terrible business in Ireland. An underground bunker blown up, bodies drifting in on the beach, one of them a hard man named Brendan Murphy. Everyone believes the Provos in Dublin were behind it. He wouldn't do as he was told.'

'Yes, I did see that,' Billy said. 'Terrible what goes on over there.'

Dora brought their food, and Dillon laughed. 'He did well, your boy, Harry. Saved my life by killing one bastard in the bunker and saved all of us, killing another on the boat.'

Salter was shocked. He turned to Billy. 'You never told me.'

'Yeah, well, you never believe anything I say.'

'My God, you are a chip off the old block, after all.'

'I'd say he's a chip off his own block,' Ferguson said and started to eat. 'Roper definitely thinks tomorrow. The big consignment arrives at the White Diamond Company from South Africa. And I'm told the stakes are higher. Twelve million, not ten.'

'Really?' Salter said. 'Then I'm sorry for them.'

'Why?'

'It's too big, Brigadier. I'm not an educated man, I go by experience, and nobody knows more about the London underworld and thieving than I do. What screwed up the Great Train Robbery was the size. Biggest criminal haul ever. There was no way society and the law could tolerate that, so they turned on the big guns.'

'That makes considerable sense,' Ferguson agreed.

Blake said, 'Yes, but Jack Fox is desperate. He has to be. He needs a big one.'

'Oh, sure, and Manchester Charlie Ford and his team are greedy and stupid and will all be back on landing D at Wandsworth before they know it,' Salter said.

Dillon finished his food and accepted the glass of bar champagne that Dora put at his elbow. 'Let's go over this again, Harry. They've got Manchester Charlie Ford, one of the best lock and safe men in the business; Amber Frazer, a heavy; and Connie Briggs, a hotshot on security and electronics.'

Salter told him, 'Did you know he went to London University? From a well-known family of villains. His mother was real proud, him doing that. Got this degree. What they call first-class honours.'

'My, that is good,' Ferguson said.

'They threw a big party. I was there. He gets a research job for British Telecom, but it's not worth enough money, so what does he do? Starts putting himself about.'

Billy said, 'He really is a genius where the electronics caper is concerned, Dillon.'

'I'm beginning to believe you. And Val French?'

'Well, he's a top man with a thermal lance,

cutting, all that. I'd say he'd have sorted out the gate and organized smashing through the tunnel wall into the basement.'

They'd all finished their food and Dora cleared the table. Blake was sweating, his forehead damp; he didn't look good.

Salter said, 'Bring him a brandy, Dora. You don't look well, my old son.'

'I've been worse,' Blake said. 'But thanks anyway.' He hesitated. 'I suppose someone should bring this up, for form's sake, and it might as well be me. Shouldn't someone be notifying the White Diamond Company that they might be in trouble, Brigadier?'

'I take your point, Blake. But we're not into ethics here.'

'We're into finishing off Jack Fox.' Dillon's voice was hard. 'As long as we ruin things for him, that's okay.'

'All right, all right,' Blake said. 'Just thought I'd ask. And while we're at it, how *do* we think they're going to get into that vault?'

'Well, it isn't the thermal lance man,' Dillon said. 'He'd be there all night trying to get into the kind of strong room they'll have in here. I'd say it's the electronics whiz kid.'

'I agree,' Harry said. 'But that doesn't get us any further.'

There was a pause, and it was Billy who said, 'What we need is more information, and the only way to get that is to pick up one of the team and squeeze him dry.'

Harry laughed out loud. 'My God, you really are learning. Who would you suggest? The one who's least important, the one whose absence wouldn't be a burden.'

'The heavy, Amber Frazer,' Dillon said.

'I'd say so.'

'Brilliant.' Harry Salter turned to Ferguson. 'We lift this guy tonight. Leave it to us. We'll deliver him to your safe house at Holland Park, then we'll review the situation.'

'This is illegal, of course,' Ferguson said. 'He hasn't done anything.'

'Not yet,' Dillon said. 'But I'm sure you could think of something. After all, isn't this why we didn't bring the Superintendent?'

'You're right, of course. It's in your hands, Harry. I may call you Harry?'

'You can call me any bleeding thing you like.'

'Excellent, then if your Dora can come up with an indifferent glass of red wine, I'll drink your health and leave you to it,' Ferguson told him.

It was ten o'clock that night when Amber Frazer and Manchester Charlie Ford emerged from a small Italian restaurant in Notting Hill. Harry and Billy had been waiting for some time, sitting in their car. Ford hailed a cab, patted Amber's face, and got in.

'Brilliant,' Billy said as Amber turned and walked away.

They trailed him and Billy pulled in at the pavement a little further along. Harry Salter got out. 'Amber, my old son, I thought it was you.'

'My God, Harry, what are you doing here?'

'Looking for you, so get in the car.'

Amber, alarmed, tried to turn away, and Salter pushed the muzzle of a gun he was carrying in his right-hand pocket against Amber's back.

'Is that a gun, Harry?'

'Well, it's not my finger. Yes, it's a gun, and it's silenced, so I could blow away your spine, leave you on the pavement and drive away and no one would hear a thing. Get in the car.'

Amber did as he was told and Harry got in behind him and took out the gun. 'Listen, Amber,

I know you like to think you're some kind of Mike Tyson, and you've got big muscles, but not with a bullet in your stomach. So do as you're told.'

Billy said, 'Evening, Amber,' and drove away.

At the safe house, Amber sat wondering what the hell was going on, Miller at the door. After a while, it opened, and Dillon and Helen Black came in, followed by Harry Salter.

'Look, what's this about?' Amber stood up.

Dillon kicked him very hard in the right ankle. 'Sit down.'

Helen Black said, 'Is this the man, Mr Salter?'

'Definitely. He's involved with a gang of known criminals: Charles Ford, Val French, Connie Briggs. I understand their intention is to rob the White Diamond Company tomorrow night of a very large consignment from South Africa. I also understand there's a Mafia connection, a man named Jack Fox.'

Amber panicked. 'Here, what is this? I don't know what you're talking about.'

Dillon said to Helen Black, 'Dear me, if this little caper goes through, he'll still be legally a part of it, am I right?'

'Absolutely.'

'What kind of sentence would he pull?'

'Minimum of ten years.'

Amber was sweating now. 'Look, for God's sake.'

'No, for your sake,' Salter said.

There was a pause, and then Helen Black said, 'If you help us in the matter, you'll be released within the next few days and put on a plane back to Barbados.'

'And if you don't, it's back to the shower at Wandsworth,' Dillon said.

Frazer had done a particularly nasty stretch at Wandsworth a couple of years earlier, and he had no desire to repeat it. He loved Charlie, but . . . Charlie could take care of himself.

'Okay.' Amber took out a handkerchief and wiped his face. 'Give me a drink.' Helen Black nodded to Miller, who went to the sideboard and poured a large Scotch. Amber swallowed it down. 'Okay, what do you want to know?'

On the other side of the mirror, Ferguson stood with Hannah, Blake and Billy. 'A good start,' he said.

'Depends on your point of view, sir,' Hannah said.

'Well, my point is getting a result. I'm like a lot of people these days, Superintendent, sick of the bad guys getting away with it, as our American cousins would say. War is war, and this is a kind of war. If you're not happy, go back to the office.'

'There's no need for that, sir.'

'I hope not.'

In the interview room, Salter said, 'All right, Amber. Manchester Charlie Ford, you, Connie and Val are going to hit the White Diamond Company for Jack Fox. We know you've already cut open the grille gate in the tunnel from the river.'

Amber was shocked. 'How do you know that?'

'We know everything, old son.'

Dillon leaned against the wall and lit a cigarette. Helen took up the story. 'The gate is open, you go up the tunnel, smash a hole through an old Victorian brick wall and you're into the basement of the White Diamond Company.'

'Only what we can't understand, old son, is how you're supposed to do the job,' Salter said. 'I mean, all that security, all those alarms.'

Amber didn't reply, and Dillon said, 'It's a waste of time, Sergeant Major. Ship him up to Wandsworth and charge him with conspiracy.'

'As you say, sir,' Helen Black said.

Amber said, 'No, for God's sake, I'll tell you. Give me another drink,' which Miller did. Amber swallowed it down just like the other. 'Okay, what do you want to know?'

'First of all, the security man?'

'No problem. He takes over at six o'clock from the other guy. Always gets coffee and a big box of sandwiches from the takeaway at the end of the street. There's a girl there who Charlie knows. She's going to put a couple of pills in the coffee. They take a while to act, but when they do, he's out for three or four hours.'

'But the security system?' Helen Black said.

'That's Connie Briggs. He's a genius at electronics. He's got hold of this thing called a Howler. When you switch it on, it screws up all electronic systems in a given area. TV video security, gate locks, vaults, the lot.'

'My God,' Helen Black said. 'I can't believe it.'

'Of course!' Dillon said. 'Oh, what an ass I am! I've seen those things. They work, believe me.' He turned to Amber. 'So it *is* tomorrow night?'

Amber nodded. 'Seven o'clock. It's got to be early because of the tide.'

'Will Fox be there?' Dillon asked.

'No way. It's all down to us and the Jagos.'

The door opened and Ferguson came in, trailed by Billy, Hannah and Blake Johnson. 'Thank you,

Sergeant Major,' the Brigadier said. 'Take him out and keep him secure.'

Black and Miller took Amber Frazer between them, and Blake said, 'Well, now we know.'

'The only trouble is, Fox isn't taking part,' Hannah said.

'Well, he wouldn't,' Dillon told her. 'He's too careful to get directly involved in a caper like this. We have to settle for foiling the robbery and banging up the lot of them, including the Jagos. The end result will still be that Fox loses his hope of a big killing with those diamonds.'

'His last hope,' Blake said.

'Exactly.' Dillon nodded. 'So how do we handle it?'

Harry Salter said, 'I've been thinking. My Joe, Joe Baxter, when he was doing a five stretch at Armley Prison in Leeds, did a learning programme. Did welding, all that stuff. You know, oxy-acetylene.'

'So what are you suggesting?' Ferguson asked.

'Well, it would run something like this, Brigadier,' and Harry Salter told him.

They all listened, and Ferguson burst into laughter. 'My God, that's the best thing I've heard in years.'

14

The following day, Fox was having a light lunch in the Piano Bar at the Dorchester, tagliatelle alla panna, noodles in a cream and ham sauce, just the way he liked it. The waiter poured him a glass of Krug, and Falcone came down the stairs.

'I've been to the Colosseum, Signore. Mori has laid off most of the staff. He's kept on Rossi and Cameci.'

'I know. That damn Ferguson. Any word from Ford?'

'No, Signore.'

'Today's the day, Aldo. Make or break time.'

More than you know, Falcone thought.

Manchester Charlie Ford had expected Amber for lunch, and when he failed to turn up he tried Amber's mobile. When it rang at Holland Park, Helen Black nodded, Miller stood behind and Amber answered.

'Hey, where are you?' Charlie demanded.

'Sorry, Charlie,' Amber mumbled. 'I've got a terrible toothache. I've only just managed to find a dentist who could give me an appointment.'

'You poor sod. Okay, I'll see you this evening.'

'I don't know, Charlie. This thing could knock me out of commission.'

There was a brief silence. 'Well, I suppose we can manage if we have to. Me, Tony and Harold. But be here if you can, okay, Amber?'

'I'll do my best, Charlie.'

'Well, you do that, darling. Stay well.'

Amber switched off the phone and looked at Helen Black. 'Was that okay?'

'You should be on stage, Amber.'

For some strange reason, he perked up. 'You really think so?'

'Absolutely. Much better than prison. Maybe you shouldn't go back to Barbados. Maybe you should get an education grant and try the London Theatre School.'

There was a final meeting at Fox's suite at the Dorchester: the Jagos, Ford, Briggs and French.

Falcone and Russo stood by, and Fox nodded to Russo, who got a bottle of champagne from the basket and thumbed off the cork. He filled glasses all around.

Fox raised his and toasted the others. 'To the big one. They'll all have to sit up and take notice.' He turned to Ford. 'Everything okay?'

'Amber isn't up to snuff. He's got some sort of tooth infection. He rang me up from the dentist.'

'We don't need the black,' Tony Jago said. 'We can manage. Enough of us as it is.'

'You know best.' Fox nodded.

Tony said, 'So you're sure you're not joining us?'

'Don't be silly. That tunnel would be rather crowded.'

'But you don't mind joining us to share out the loot.'

Falcone, leaning against the wall, straightened, but Harold took charge. 'You shut your mouth,' he said to his brother, 'or I'll give you a slapping.' He turned to Fox. 'Look, I'm sorry. He's young.'

'Well, we all were once,' Jack told him and smiled. 'Come on, another glass of bubbly, and then, as I believe the Irish say, "God bless the good work."'

It was six o'clock that evening when Hannah answered her doorbell and found Dillon on the step.

'Ferguson expects us at his place to wait out what's happening. I've got the Daimler.'

'I'll get my coat.'

She was out in a few minutes, he opened the rear door for her, and she climbed in behind the driver. Dillon leaned in through the open window and tapped the driver on the shoulder.

'Take the Superintendent to Brigadier Ferguson.' He smiled at Hannah. 'I'll see you later. I've got things to do.'

Hannah opened her mouth in surprise, but the Daimler moved away before she could reply.

Outside the Jagos' house in Wapping, a large white truck bearing the sign ELITE CONSTRUCTION drew up.

Ford was at the wheel wearing overalls, Briggs beside him, French in the back. The door to the house opened, and Harold and Tony Jago emerged, came down the steps and also got in the back.

'The moment of truth, boys,' Harold said. 'Let's get to it.'

At the same time, the night security guard at the White Diamond Company, having finished his sandwiches and coffee, sat back to read the *Evening Standard*. He kept blinking his eyes, yawned a couple of times, put the newspaper down, and checked the multiple television security screens. Everything looked normal. Suddenly, he leaned over the desk, put his head on his arms, and was asleep.

In the tunnel, Ford and French, each wielding a sledgehammer, attacked the wall at the right point. The old Victorian brickwork crumbled and fell backwards in large sections into the basement.

'Perfect,' Ford said. 'In we go, gents.'

They all scrambled through. 'Now what?' Harold Jago asked.

'The tide started to come in downriver fifteen

minutes ago. We're good for forty minutes. After that, the tunnel entrance will be covered.'

'Then let's bleeding get on with it,' Harold said.

Connie Briggs took an object from one of the carrying bags that resembled a television remote control. 'The Howler,' he said, and pressed a button.

'Is that it?' Tony Jago asked.

'Well, if it isn't, all hell will break loose when we go upstairs. If it works, the security system is fucked and all the doors will be open. Let's go and see.'

Dillon, the Salters, Joe Baxter and Sam Hall got out of a Transit. Baxter and Hall were carrying large canvas holdalls. Blake got out after them.

Harry Salter said, 'Look, old son, can't you stay in the Transit? You're not up to it.'

'No, it's important to me. Fox had my wife killed, Harry. I want to be there when he finally gets his. What happens now, if we succeed, will finish him.'

Strange, it was Billy who said, 'He's entitled. Let him be.'

'Well, you've changed, you young sod.'

'Damn right, Harry,' Dillon said. 'He's killed two men, and on the side of right. No going back on that.'

Salter said, 'Okay, let's get going.'

He led the way down the steps and started along the shingle to the tunnel entrance. When they got there, he turned to Billy.

'You checked with Handy. How long have we got?'

'Thirty minutes, and don't forget, when that tide floods in, it's what Handy means by St Richard's Force.'

'Right, let's get to it.'

As the Jagos and the others reached the entrance hall, they paused, observing the security guard sprawled across the desk, the security screens blank.

'There you go. Downstairs to the vault,' Connie Briggs said.

Manchester Charlie Ford laughed. 'I told you he was a genius,' and he led the way down a broad marble stairway to the vaults below.

*　　*　　*

The others, in the tunnel, had reached the grille door. Harry Salter said, 'Right, let's get on with it.'

Billy said, 'We could clobber them on the way out, Harry. I mean, twelve million.'

'Like I said, it's too much, Billy. They'd bring out the big battalions. Now, we go with my suggestion. I've never liked the Jagos, with their drugs, whores and pornography. Filth.' He turned to Joe Baxter. 'So get your gear out and let's hope the British prison system taught you a trade.'

Joe Baxter took out an oxy-acetylene welding torch from his holdall. From the other bag, Sam Hall produced an oxygen cylinder.

Baxter flared the torch and started to work.

The great vault doors opened, and the Jagos and their friends were into an Aladdin's cave. They opened their canvas holdalls, pulled out bags and poured in a stream of diamonds.

'Jesus,' Harold said. 'I've never known the like.'

There was an atmosphere of hysteria, everyone laughing, and finally, they were finished.

'Okay, let's be on our way,' Harold ordered and led the way back upstairs.

They moved down to the basement to the exit

hole they'd smashed, moved through one by one.

Tony said, 'Christ, there's water in the tunnel.'

'Well, there would be,' Harold said. 'The tide's coming in. We've got time. Let's get moving.'

It was already a foot deep when they reached the gate, Manchester Charlie Ford in the lead. He tried to open it.

'What the hell is going on? It won't budge.'

Val French pushed him out of the way and checked it. 'Christ! Someone's welded it together.'

'That would be me and my friends.' Dillon sloshed forward in a foot of water, Blake at his side. 'Sean Dillon, and this is Blake Johnson. I'm sure you've got a mobile. Call Jack Fox and give him the bad news.'

The Jagos grabbed the bars of the grille and shook them. 'Fuck you!'

Dillon smiled. 'No, I'm afraid it's you who are fucked, gentlemen. Now, if you'll excuse me, the water's getting a bit high.'

Dillon and Blake turned and waded away, the water already two feet deep and rising. They exited on to the beach, which was already flooded. Harry Salter and the others were at the steps, waiting.

Dillon took out his Codex Four mobile phone and called Scotland Yard, using the Special Branch number.

The officer who replied said, 'Special Branch. How can I help you?'

'The Jago brothers and a hand-picked team are trapped in the White Diamond Company building at St Richard's Dock. They can't get out the way they got in underground, because the tide's rising. If you get to the front entrance fast, you'll catch them with twelve million in diamonds.'

'Who is this?'

'Don't be silly, get moving.'

In the tunnel, the Jagos and the others shook desperately at the grille together, but Joe Baxter had done too good a job, and then the water rose and started to bore in very fast.

'Christ,' Harold said. 'It's that St Richard's Force thing. Let's get out of here.'

They turned and scrambled along the tunnel, the water foaming around them, got through the hole, and scrambled upstairs to the foyer and the security office.

'Listen,' Harold said, 'if that Howler works, then the front door's open.'

'That's right,' Connie told him.

'Okay, let's get the hell out of here.'

He led the way to the door, and there was a squeal of brakes as half a dozen police cars arrived outside.

Harold stood there, bitter and angry, and said to Connie, 'Close the door with your sodding Howler,' which Connie did. 'Let them wait.'

The police bunched together outside the glass doors, and Tony Jago gave them two fingers. Harold called through on the mobile to Fox at his suite at the Dorchester.

Fox said, 'Harold, how did it go?'

'Wonderful. I'm standing here at the White Diamond Company holding a bag worth twelve million and there must be at least twenty cops outside trying to get in at us.'

'What happened, for God's sake?'

Harold told him.

'Dillon?' Fox said. 'Are you sure?'

'And the American, Johnson. I think they've been on your case more than you know, Jack. The trouble is it's put them on *my* case.'

'I'll get you the best barrister in London.'

'Thanks very much. That's a great comfort, Fox. Sod you and your barrister!'

He switched off the mobile. Tony said, 'What the hell do we do, Harold?'

'Travel hopefully, Tony.' Harold turned to Connie Briggs. 'Go on, use that gadget and open the door.' Connie did, and the police rushed in and surged all over them.

Fox said, 'That bastard Dillon. He and Johnson, they've ruined the operation!'

'Signore?' Falcone said.

'God, I see it all now. It wasn't them just with the Colosseum, but Al Shariz and Kilbeg, too. And now this!'

'But how, Signore? How would they know?'

'The Johnson woman, everything flows from that. Somehow she found out and told them. God knows how.'

'So what do we do now, Signore?'

Fox turned to him with a hard light in his eyes. 'We exact revenge,' Fox said. 'That's what I want, revenge.'

'And how do we do that?'

'I'll tell you later. Right now, I want you and Russo to get down to the Colosseum and pick up Rossi and Cameci. Go on, do it now.' He was angry. 'And make it fast.'

'Signore.'

Falcone left, picked up Russo from his room, and filled him in as they went down in the elevator to get the car.

Russo said, 'He's too angry, and being too angry isn't good.'

'You don't have to tell me,' Falcone said.

In the car on the way to the Colosseum, he phoned Don Marco in New York and brought him up to date.

'Ah God, Aldo, can't he see? They're *looking* for him to come after them. He should just cut his losses, get out of there.'

'He won't do that, Don Marco. He's an angry man.'

'And insane to go after them. But then, Jack was always headstrong.'

Falcone hesitated, then said the unthinkable. 'Do you wish me to take care of him, Don Marco?'

'No, Aldo. No matter what he's done, he's my nephew, flesh of my flesh. I'm coming over there. I'll leave New York within the hour. You stay in close touch.'

'Of course.'

'Aldo. I need your total loyalty in this.'

'You have it as always, Don Marco.'

* * *

321

Besides the Gulfstream, the family operated a Golden Eagle twin-engine aircraft out of Bardsey Aero Club outside London. It was useful for local flights, the kind where you had to put down on short runways, so it was particularly good for Hellsmouth. Fox called the pilot now, an ageing, ex-RAF pilot named Swan, and got him at home.

'Mr Fox, what can I do for you?'

'I need a flight in a couple of hours to Hellsmouth. Can you manage that?'

'If you say so, Mr Fox. It might be a rough landing. It's pretty dark.'

'I don't care if you put us down on its belly, just so you get us there.'

'As you say, sir.'

When Dillon arrived at Stable Mews, Fox, Russo, Falcone, Rossi and Cameci were waiting in a large black van.

Dillon got out with Blake and gave him the key to the house. 'There you go. I'll be back later. I'll go and see what Ferguson wants.'

He got back into the taxi and it moved away. Blake walked slowly towards the door, and the van

drove up and braked. Rossi and Cameci were out
and had him in seconds. Blake tried to struggle but
had little strength. Fox leaned across Russo, who
was at the wheel.

'It's my turn now, Johnson. Get him in the back.
You know what to do, Falcone.'

They dragged Blake in and Falcone produced
a hypodermic. 'Now this will really make you
feel good,' he said and jabbed it into the right
arm.

Blake continued to struggle, but then everything
slipped away and he was still.

Bardsey operated a twenty-four-hour service that
handled the ever-increasing volume of private planes
and executive jets that Heathrow didn't welcome
any more. For internal flights, there was no particular security. Swan was waiting for them.

Fox said, 'We'll take off right away. I don't want
to hang around. I'm a little worried about my friend
here. He's had too much to drink.'

'Will there be a return, Mr Fox?' Swan asked.

'Not tonight. You wait at the airstrip for further
instructions.'

Swan, only too well aware of the kind of people

he was dealing with, said, 'As you say, sir,' and went and logged flight details.

Rossi and Cameci took Blake up the steps, Russo followed, and Fox turned to Falcone. 'Phone the caretaker, old Carter. Tell him I want the fireplaces lit, but I don't want him in the house. He can go home.'

'As you say, Signore.'

Fox boarded the Eagle, and Falcone got on his mobile and made the call. When he finished, Falcone followed and Swan pulled up the steps and closed the Airstair door. As he went up to the cockpit, Fox reached out to Falcone.

'Give me the phone.'

He took out a card, a digest of information Maud Jackson had given him, found Ferguson's number in Cavendish Square and dialled it.

'Charles Ferguson.'

'Jack Fox. Is Dillon there?'

'Why, Mr Fox. And how are you this evening?'

'Shove it, Ferguson. Give me Dillon.'

Ferguson handed the phone to Dillon, and he and Hannah stood up.

'Why, Jack, so sorry to hear your bad news.'

'Yeah, well, it's nothing compared to the news I have for you, Dillon. I've just grabbed Blake

Johnson, and I'm taking him to hell, but not, alas, back. I saw you clear off in the cab, Dillon, and I got him before he opened the door. If you use your brains, you might come up with where I'm taking him, and that would please me no end.'

He switched off before Dillon could reply, and Dillon turned to Hannah and Ferguson. 'He's got Blake. He said he's taking him to hell but not back.' He frowned. 'Hellsmouth, his place in Cornwall, it's got to be. Let me use the phone.'

Hannah said, 'Dillon, no, it's a trap. He made it easy for you to guess, and now he'll kill you, too.'

'That may be, Hannah. But I can't leave Blake there alone.'

He dialled the Holland Park safe house and got Helen Black. 'Bad news. The bastards have kidnapped Blake Johnson. Put the Major on.'

Roper said, 'Here I am, Sean. What's the deal?'

Dillon told him.

Roper said, 'Give me a couple of minutes at my computer.'

'Good man.'

Roper was back very quickly. 'Yes, besides the Gulfstream, the Solazzo family have a Golden Eagle. You know that plane?'

'I've flown one many times,' Dillon said. 'It's excellent for short runways.'

'Well, that's what they have at the Hellsmouth estate. There's an old RAF feeder station from the Second World War. The nearest decent airfield is RAF, St Just, twenty miles away. It's an air-sea rescue set-up, helicopters, long runway.'

'Thanks, old son.'

'You're going in hard, I take it.'

'You could say that.'

'I wish I could be with you. I'll stay on the computer, in case you need me. Just a minute.' There was a pause, and Roper spoke again. 'The Golden Eagle took off twenty minutes ago. The slot booked says Cornwall, Hellsmouth, six passengers.'

'And one of those is Blake. Thanks, Roper.'

Dillon said, 'Hellsmouth, they've gone down in a Golden Eagle from Bardsey. Six passengers.' He punched another number on the phone.

'Sean, what are you doing?' Hannah said.

'Well, I'm not phoning the Cornish police. They're a fine body of men, but not for a job like this. I'm calling Farley Field.'

'What for?' she demanded.

'Because he's going after them,' Ferguson said. 'I know my Sean.'

'He said to hell but not back,' Dillon said. 'Well, I'll follow him to hell.'

A voice on the receiver said, 'Farley Field.'

'Dillon. Get me Squadron Leader Lacey, if he's there.'

'Actually, I just saw him in the mess. Hang on.'

Lacey was there quickly. 'Is that you, Dillon?'

'We're going into action, and I mean now.'

'What's the score?'

'Hellsmouth, near Lizard Point in Cornwall. It's a small airstrip, so I need a parachute landing.'

'I know that area. RAF St Just is not too far away.'

'Exactly, so you drop me, then land at St Just.'

'Jesus, Dillon, you're at it again, saving the world.'

'No, saving Blake Johnson's life. Speak to the quartermaster. Brownings, AK47s, parachutes for two. I'd say six hundred feet.'

'You're mad, Sean, but let me get on with it.'

Dillon put the phone down and Hannah Bernstein said, 'Gear for two parachutists. What the hell are you talking about?'

'Well, not the SAS. There isn't time. I've someone in mind, and I'll go and see him now. If you want to see me again, it will be at Farley Field.'

'You're just going to execute all those people, aren't you, Dillon?' she said angrily.

Dillon turned to Ferguson. 'She's a lovely woman, Brigadier, but I've had it up to here with her morality. I'm more interested in saving a good man's life,' and he turned and walked out.

Hannah turned and said, 'He's mad, sir.'

'No, Superintendent. He's Dillon.'

Harry Salter, Billy, Joe and Sam Hall were in the end booth at the Dark Man enjoying large Scotches when Dillon came in.

'Sean, my old son,' Harry Salter said. 'Did we do it or did we do it?'

'Fox has kidnapped Blake,' Dillon said. 'Flown off to this estate he has in Cornwall with four of his heavies.'

There was silence. Salter said, 'What are you going to do?'

'I can't leave it, they might chop him. I'm flying down in an hour from Farley Field. I'll drop over the estate by parachute. Try and catch them with their pants down. It's got to be a drop, the landing field there is too short for a Gulfstream. The nearest RAF base is twenty miles away.'

Billy said, 'Fox and four makes five, Dillon, and you're going in alone?'

'No, Billy, I'm going in with you.'

'You must be bleeding mad,' Harry Salter said.

Dillon ignored him. 'Billy, you've heard of Arnhem in the Second World War, all those paratroopers going in? There was one major, an army surgeon, who'd never done a jump in his life, but they needed a doctor. He survived just fine and so will you. Billy, trust me. You jump out, pull the cord at six hundred feet, you hit the ground in twenty-five seconds, and that's all there is to it.'

Salter said, 'You're crazy.'

But Billy was smiling all over his face. 'I've said it before, Dillon, you're just like me. You don't give a stuff. Just show me the way.'

'Well, if he goes, I'm bleeding going,' Salter said. 'Even if I'm only on the sidelines.'

'Right,' Dillon said. 'Then let's do it.'

Hellsmouth

15

When Dillon, Harry Salter and Billy arrived at Farley Field, Lacey and Parry were waiting.

'Let's go into the operations room and make sure I've got it right,' Lacey said.

The quartermaster stood ready with Dillon's Brownings, two AK47s, parachutes and jumpsuits ready.

Dillon said, 'Have a word with Mr Salter, Sergeant Major, it's his first jump.'

'Is that so, Mr Dillon?' the Sergeant Major replied, face impassive. 'Then a word might be indicated.'

'Just show me,' Billy told him.

Dillon went to the chart table and started to check it out with Lacey and Parry. 'It's not as bad as it could be,' Lacey said. 'There's almost a half moon. One pass is all I'd recommend. There's no time for more, then we'll rush to St Just.'

'Sounds good to me.'

'The other chap,' Lacey said. 'He knows what he's doing?'

'Absolutely.'

Ferguson and Hannah Bernstein came in. When the Brigadier saw the Salters, he was astonished. 'For God's sake, what is this? You said two para-chutists, and he isn't a parachutist.'

'Well, I am now,' Billy said. 'I think I've got the hang of it, Dillon. I pull this ring and that's it. The guns are pretty obvious. I managed Kilbeg, I can manage this.'

'This is madness,' Hannah Bernstein said.

'No, it's trying to save Blake Johnson's life,' Dillon said. 'I'm ready when you are, Brigadier, unless you have other ideas.'

'No,' Ferguson said. 'It makes the usual wild sense where you are concerned, so let's get on with it.'

'Harry's coming along for the ride,' Dillon said. 'I suggest you lot board, and Billy and I will change and follow.'

'As you wish.'

Ten minutes later, Dillon and Billy, in jumpsuits, flak jackets, parachutes, shoulder holsters, AKs suspended across the chest, went up the steps and took their seats. Parry closed the door.

Salter said, 'Christ, Billy, you look like you're in a Vietnam war movie or something. What are you playing at?'

Billy actually smiled. 'I'm playing at being me, Harry, and it feels great.'

Blake sat down again on the stone seat in the tunnel, waist deep in water, hugging himself and trying to keep warm. Would Dillon come? Fox seemed to expect it, dangling him as bait. It was an impossible situation, but then, Dillon had always been master of the impossible. Somewhere high above, through the thick walls of the old house, he seemed to hear a noise, far off, something like an aircraft engine, but he couldn't be sure. The rat appeared and circled, swimming.

'I told you,' he said. 'Behave yourself.'

The noise of the aircraft faded quickly. Falcone said, 'What was that?'

'It could be normal air traffic at the RAF place at St Just,' Fox said. 'And then again, it could be Dillon. We'd better get ready.'

He was standing by the fire in the great hall with

Falcone and Russo. 'Get me a brandy first.'

Russo went to the sideboard, filled a glass and brought it back. Rossi and Cameci came in, holding Uzis.

Falcone said, 'Excuse me, Signore, but do you really think Dillon will come?'

'I gave him enough clues. He's smart. He'll come.'

It was Russo who said, 'But what if they send the police?'

'Dillon? No, it's too personal for that. He's not going to trust the police to do this for him.'

'But Ferguson is secret intelligence,' Falcone pointed out. 'What if he decided to use special forces, the SAS?'

'Same thing. He's operated this whole thing very close to his chest. Publicity is the last thing he wants, he won't change now. Low key, that's the way they'll do it. Like in the bullring, mano a mano, hand-to-hand, face-to-face.'

'As you say, Signore.'

Fox turned to Rossi and Cameci. 'Get out in the garden and keep watch. Check the doors.'

They went out and he drank some of the brandy. He was right in all respects except one. Dillon was already there.

*　　*　　*

As the Gulfstream throttled back to almost stalling speed, Parry ran back, opened the door, and dropped the steps. There was a rush of wind.

Salter said, 'Christ Almighty.'

Dillon turned and grinned at Billy. 'I'm an older guy, you young bastard. I'll go first.'

'Thanks very much. Get going, Dillon.'

Billy, feeling totally insane, pushed him out and dived after him.

There was rain, light mist, and yet the moon, the house and estate were clear below. Dillon hit in no time at all, punched the quick release after a perfect landing, not even a roll, and looked around. He saw the other parachute billowing like some strange flower, ran over, and stamped on it. Billy sat up.

'Are you okay?' Dillon asked.

'I think so. Went backwards and hit my back.' He worked the muscles around. 'But it feels okay.'

Dillon punched Billy's quick release. 'Then come on, move it!'

Billy was on his feet in a moment. 'Jesus, Dillon, I can't believe this is happening.'

'Well, it is. Kilbeg all over again, except this time there are five bad guys out there waiting to pounce, so be ready.'

*　　*　　*

Dillon trawled the gardens with the Nightstalker and saw Cameci over by the terrace. 'Take a look,' he whispered to Billy.

Billy nodded. 'Can't see anything else.'

'I'll go left, you right.'

'I'm with you, Dillon.'

Cameci was by the balustrade, looking out over the moonlit garden, when the muzzle of an AK47 nudged his back.

Billy said, 'Make a sound and I'll blow your spine apart.'

Cameci said, 'Is that Dillon?'

'No, I'm his younger brother.' Billy called softly, 'Over here.'

Dillon moved out of the shadows, and Rossi, on the other side of the terrace, stood up. It was Billy who saw him.

'Dillon!' he rasped.

Dillon turned, his silenced AK coughed, and Rossi went backwards, dead.

Dillon took Cameci by the jaw. 'Tell me who's inside and tell me now, or I'll kill you.'

Cameci, terrified, said, 'Signores Fox, Falcone and Russo.'

Dillon said, 'Excellent. Now what about the American?'

'He's in the tunnel in the cellars.'

'Good. Take us there.'

Cameci led the way through the kitchen, down the stairs and into the cellar system. They arrived at an old oak door.

'That's it,' Cameci said.

'Then open it.'

Cameci did as he was told. Blake, in the water, turned, the light falling across his face, and Dillon said, 'What are you doing, taking a dip? This is no time for fun. Get the hell out of there.'

Blake stumbled up the steps. 'What kept you?'

He was shivering and very wet. Dillon said to Cameci, 'Get your clothes off. The man's freezing.'

'But, Signore,' Cameci protested.

Dillon shoved the muzzle of the AK under his chin. 'Just do it.' He pulled the combat scarf from around his neck and gave it to Blake. 'Dry yourself a little.'

Blake did the best he could while Cameci stripped. Blake pulled on the clothes. Cameci was left in his underpants.

* * *

Meanwhile, Falcone, upstairs, had opened the French windows, gone out on the terrace, and found Rossi. He was back inside in an instant to Fox and Russo.

'Rossi's out there dead. No sign of Cameci.'

'Christ,' Fox said. 'He's here, the bastard's here. Spread out.'

At that moment, Dillon shoved Cameci into the room in his underpants, and startled by the sudden apparition, Falcone turned and fired. Cameci went down, writhing.

'Hey, you got the wrong guy,' Dillon called. 'It's me, Jack. Time to pay up.'

'Fuck you, Dillon,' Fox shouted.

They crouched in the hall, the great chandelier hanging from the ceiling spreading its illumination. Falcone whispered to Russo, 'Stick with me. Let's move towards the door to the kitchen quarters.' He saw Fox moving to the right.

'There's too much light,' Russo said.

Falcone fired his Uzi up at the chandelier and brought it crashing down.

'Not any more.'

He ducked, pulling Russo with him.

The hall was a strange place now, only the light from the great log fire picking out the suits of armour, the ancient banners, the great staircase to the left. Dillon, Blake and Billy crept in and crouched behind the great central table.

'Now what?' Billy demanded.

'Just wait, Billy, always hasten slowly.' He took out his Browning and passed it to Blake. 'Just in case.'

'How the hell did you get here, anyway?' Blake asked.

'Lacey and Parry did a low pass, and Billy and I jumped.'

'Dear God, what does this boy know about parachuting?'

'A lot more than he did a couple of hours ago. Don't worry, there are reinforcements coming.'

'A special forces team?'

'No. Ferguson, Hannah and Harry Salter.'

'Christ Almighty.'

'We can make it, Blake. Cameci and Rossi are down. That just leaves Falcone, Russo and good old Jack Fox.'

'So how do we do it?' Billy asked.

'I've told you. We wait, Billy, and let them come to us.'

There was quiet. Falcone and Russo had reached the green baize door leading to the kitchen. Fox had reached another door to one side of the fireplace.

He opened it and went up a spiral staircase to the landing, peered down at the hall, and saw a movement behind the table. Beneath his foot, a board creaked.

'The bastard's somewhere above us,' Dillon said. 'Slide off to the right, Billy.'

Billy moved away and Dillon called, 'Why, Jack, here we are again at the final end of things.' He pushed Blake away. 'Get over to the shadows on the other side.'

Up above, Jack Fox moved, crouching by the switches for the wall lights that normally illuminated the collection of paintings that hung on the wall. He paused and reached.

Below, Blake started to move, slipped, and cried out in pain as he fell on his arm. Dillon reached down to pick him up and Fox switched on the lights.

'I've got you now, you bastard.'

He raised the Walther in his right hand and shot Dillon twice in the back. To do it he had to stand, and so did Billy, over to the right. Raising his AK, he pumped ten rounds into Fox, driving him back across the landing. Fox bounced off the wall back to the balustrade and fell over. He lay there on the stone flagging, twitching for just a second. Then there was silence.

Falcone eased open the green baize door and said, 'We're out of here.'

'Where to?' Russo asked.

'The airstrip. We've got to get to London. Don Marco's due in, and we've got to give him the news.'

Russo said, 'Sometimes they kill the messenger.'

'Not now. This is too important.'

They slid back through the door, went down the steps and made the courtyard. A few moments later, they were driving away to the airstrip.

In the hall, Dillon had been thrown on to his face by the force of the bullets he'd taken in his back. Groaning, he forced himself up. Billy ran over, crouching.

'Dillon, are you all right?'

'Yes, thank God for flak jackets. I'll be a little sore, that's all.' He looked around. 'Anyone there?' he called.

There was silence. Blake said, 'Are you okay, Sean?'

'Yes, I'm fine. I think they've run for it. I heard a car leaving.'

He got up and walked to Jack Fox's body, and

Blake followed. They stood, looking down.

'Well, there you go, Blake. He's paid the price. You've got your revenge now.'

Blake said, 'Not really. Fox gave the order, but Falcone boasted to me that it was he and Russo who killed my wife.'

'And where are they?' Billy asked.

'Come with me and I'll show you,' Dillon said.

He went and opened the front door and stood at the top of the steps, and Billy and Blake followed. A moment later, there was the sound of an aircraft engine as a plane passed over.

'There they are, Billy: Falcone and Russo getting out while they still can.'

As they turned to the door, an RAF Land Rover drove into the courtyard, Hannah Bernstein at the wheel and Ferguson and Harry Salter in the rear.

Standing by the fire in the hall, Harry Salter said, 'Are you okay, Billy?'

'He's better than okay,' Dillon said. 'Fox shot me in the back twice. Only my flak jacket saved me, and Billy blew the bastard away.' He turned. 'That's three, Billy, you're an ace.'

'So what happens now, sir?' Hannah Bernstein

asked. 'Shall I notify the Cornwall constabulary?'

'I think not,' Ferguson said. 'Leave this for the caretaker to discover. Fox and these other two rogues are on Scotland Yard's intelligence information computer. This whole thing is obviously a Mafia feud, therefore it's nothing to do with us.'

'But, sir,' Hannah said.

'Superintendent, be sensible. That would be the best way of handling it, so don't let's argue. Now let's get out of here and back to St Just.'

On the Golden Eagle, Falcone called Don Marco on his mobile. The Don was about to board his Gulfstream in New York.

'Aldo, what news do you have for me?'

'Terrible, Don Marco. How can I tell you?'

Don Marco said, 'By getting on with it.'

Afterwards he said, 'Poor Jack, so stupid, so headstrong.'

'What shall I do, Signore?'

'Nothing at the moment. There is obviously a matter of family honour here, but we'll discuss that later when I'm in London.'

'As you say, Don Marco.'

* * *

On board the Gulfstream bearing Dillon and the others to Farley Field, Ferguson's mobile sounded. He hesitated, then passed it to Dillon.

'I think you need to deal with this.'

Roper said, 'I had a call from Hannah, so I know what's gone down. I'm glad you're still with us.'

'So am I.'

'I've trawled the Solazzo family affairs. The Golden Eagle just landed at Bardsey, with two passengers, Falcone and Russo.'

'Anything else?'

'Well, you'll love this. Don Marco Solazzo is en route from New York in one of the family Gulfstreams. Booked in at the Dorchester.'

Dillon laughed. 'Well, that really is going to make it old home week,' and he switched off.

LONDON

16

There was fog at Heathrow airport, and Don Marco's Gulfstream was diverted to Shannon in Ireland. It was several hours before it was once again in the air. It eventually landed in the private aircraft section at Heathrow, where Falcone and Russo waited with the Don's favourite car, a Bentley.

Falcone kissed the Don's hand. 'My condolences, Don Marco. Everything that could be done was done.'

'You don't need to tell me, Aldo. Let's get going, then we speak.'

Russo did the driving. Don Marco said, 'A little brandy, Aldo.'

Falcone opened the small bar in the rear of the Bentley, found the right bottle and a glass. Don Marco sipped a little and nodded. 'Fine, so now tell me – tell me everything.'

* * *

Later, in the Oliver Messel suite at the Dorchester, he stood at the open French window,
rain drifting across the Mayfair rooftops to his
terrace.

'Get me a cigar,' he told Falcone. 'In the croco-
dile case.'

Falcone nodded to Russo, who quickly opened
the case that was on the sideboard. He took out
a Romeo and Julietta Havana, clipped the end,
and gave it to Falcone, who warmed it with a
large match and passed it to the old man. Don
Marco lit up.

'Jack was stupid, Jack was greedy and headstrong, but Jack was also my nephew. Half of
him was Solazzo, flesh and blood. All men are a
mixture of things, Aldo.'

Rain swept across the roofs with considerable
force. The curtains billowed and Don Marco
nodded.

'Jack could be foolish. He was certainly a thief,
whatever you mean by that. But he was also a war
hero and served his country.'

'We all know what Signor Fox was,' Aldo said.

'And we all know how he ended, on his face at
the hands of these people. This Dillon, Johnson,
Brigadier Ferguson.' The Don turned, not even

angry. 'There is a matter of honour here. A debt must be paid. Money isn't everything in this world, Aldo.'

'Of course, Don Marco.'

The old man bit on the cigar, took out his wallet, and extracted a card that carried some phone numbers.

'I think the third one is Ferguson's office at the Ministry of Defence. Try it.'

It was two-thirty at the Dark Man and they were all there in the end booth, Harry and Billy, Baxter and Hall against the wall, Dillon and Blake, Ferguson and Hannah.

Hannah's mobile rang and she answered. 'All right, tell me.' She switched off. 'Priority intelligence at Scotland Yard, keeping me informed. It seems there were three killings in Cornwall, all known members of the Mafia.'

'Well, there you are,' Dillon said.

Billy was laughing. 'Surprise, surprise.'

Harry said, 'Here now, you watch it doesn't go to your head.'

'Billy the Kid,' Dillon said. 'In the Battle of Britain, he'd have earned a DFC.'

Dora brought a bottle of Bollinger and glasses on a tray, thumbed off the cork and poured. Billy said, 'That's it, then.'

'Not really, Billy.' Dillon took a glass. 'I mean, why is good old Don Marco Solazzo flying to London? To see his doctor, to get measured for a new suit in Savile Row?' He shook his head. 'Vendetta, Billy. Kill one of our own, we kill you.'

Harry said, 'You think that?'

'I think that,' Blake said.

'So it isn't over?' Harry said.

'Last act.' Dillon shrugged. 'You'd need Shakespeare to write it.'

'He's not available, he's bleeding dead,' Billy told him.

It was then that Ferguson's mobile rang. He listened, then switched off. 'The Ministry of Defence. Don Marco Solazzo wanting a word. He's at the Dorchester.' He turned to Hannah. 'Would you mind getting him for me, Superintendent?'

Dora brought her the bar phone, and Hannah called the Dorchester and asked for the Don.

'Solazzo here.'

'I have Brigadier Ferguson for you.'

She passed the phone to Ferguson, who switched

to audio so they could all listen. 'What a surprise.'

'I doubt that, Brigadier.'

'Condolences on the death of your nephew.'

'And congratulations to Dillon, I suppose?'

'Not at all. Your nephew was disposed of by an East End gangster from a family that isn't in the least intimidated by the Mafia.'

'Don't let us play games, Ferguson. This affair has gone on long enough, and my nephew is dead. I think it's time for us to meet and arrange a compromise.'

'That sounds sensible. When do you suggest?'

The old man was tranquil. 'That's up to you, but I think it should be just the two of us. I don't want Dillon and Johnson there.'

'I'll call back.'

Hannah Bernstein said, 'He's lying, sir.'

'Of course.' He turned to Dillon. 'Well?'

'He said he didn't want me and Johnson there. That means he does. If he knew Billy had killed Jack Fox, he'd want him there. This is a Mafia thing. Honour, family, revenge. He'll kill us all if he can. It's funny. We talk capitalistic values in society, but this kind of thing is the ultimate example of money being of no value.'

'So what are we talking about here?'

It was Blake who answered. 'I'd say a face-to-face meet where he'll have his people, obviously Falcone and Russo, and he'll take it for granted that you'll do the same. Not that he'll think I'm much help, but there's Dillon, and who knows.'

'There's me,' Billy said.

'Yeah, well just hold your tongue. You're getting too much of a taste for this, Billy. This isn't Dodge City,' Harry Salter said.

'It's better than Dodge City,' Billy told him.

'Fine,' Ferguson nodded. 'But what happens now?'

'You arrange a meeting,' Dillon told him.

'But where? Hardly the Piano Bar at the Dorchester.'

Dillon thought about it, then turned to Salter. 'Those boats of yours on the Thames, Harry? Something from Westminster to Chelsea or whatever.'

'The *Bluebell*?' Salter said. 'That goes from Westminster.'

Dillon turned to Ferguson. 'Choose one of the evening times. Arrange to meet him on board, just the two of you.'

Hannah said urgently, 'But he won't go alone.'

'Of course not, he'll have Falcone and Russo with him.' He smiled at Ferguson. 'He'll certainly expect me and maybe Blake.'

Blake was sweating again, his arm back in a sling. 'Not that I'm any good.'

'Yeah, well, I bleeding am,' Billy said.

'All right.' Ferguson nodded. 'So we meet and what happens?'

'He kills us if he can. It's the last act, you see,' Dillon told him.

Hannah said, 'Look, I think this is getting out of hand, sir. We've already breached all police codes by our behaviour in the Cornish matter.'

Dillon said, 'You're a good copper, and I've worked with you for some years, but we're talking about some of the worst people in the business and I want to finally put them *out* of business.'

'And I'm talking about the law,' she cried.

'Which people like Solazzo play games with. Lawyers are part of the law. The Solazzos are able to buy the best lawyers. Does that satisfy your fine moral conscience, Hannah, because it does nothing for me. I shall take those bastards out.'

There was a heavy silence. Ferguson said, 'Well, Superintendent?'

There was another pause. Blake said, 'Falcone and Russo killed my wife, and yet we'll never prove that.'

Hannah Bernstein was obviously distressed. 'I

know, and it's terrible, but without the law, we've got nothing.'

'Even if they walk free?' Blake said.

'I'm afraid so.'

Dillon said, 'Well, you've got me, and I'm going to play public executioner again.'

Hannah stood up. 'I can't manage this, sir,' she said to Ferguson.

'Then I suggest you take a couple of weeks' leave, Superintendent, and I would remind you that you signed the Official Secrets Act when you joined me.'

'Of course, sir.'

'Off you go then.'

She went out, and Ferguson said, 'Now how do we handle this?'

Rain increased in force as darkness fell and the Bentley arrived at Westminster Pier and Don Marco got out and walked up the gangplank. Falcone and Russo had joined the boat on its earlier trip, dressed in jeans and reefer coats, the kind of thing crew members wore. So did Billy and Harry Salter.

The fog was quite bad and rain fell heavily. The *Bluebell* nosed out into the river, and Don Marco walked out of the saloon, where there were only two other passengers, old ladies, and on to the stern, where there was a certain cover from the upper deck. He lit his cigar, and Ferguson moved out of the shadows.

'Don Marco, Charles Ferguson.'

'Ah, Brigadier.'

Fog swirled in. There was a seaman coiling a rope at the starboard rail. 'One of yours?' Ferguson asked.

'Oh, come now, Brigadier. All I want to do is bring this whole unfortunate affair to an end. My nephew was stupid, I acknowledge that.'

'He wasn't only stupid, he was murderous,' Ferguson told him. 'Having said that, don't tell me you don't want revenge.'

'What would be the point?'

'You know something?' Ferguson said. 'The older I get, the more obvious to me it is that life's like the movies. Take this situation. It's the gunfight at the OK Corral. Earp and the Clantons. Who's going to shoot whom? I mean, my dear old stick, why would an ageing Mafia Don go to all the trouble of coming here?'

The seaman at the rail, Falcone, stood up, and another, at the port rail, appeared, Russo. On the top deck, Billy and Harry Salter looked over, Billy holding a silenced AK.

Out of the shadows, Dillon appeared, Blake beside him, his right arm in the sling, sweating badly.

Don Marco said, 'You don't look good, Mr Johnson.'

'Oh, I'll get by.' Blake turned to Falcone. 'You butchered my wife.'

'Hey, it was business.' Falcone had a gun in his hand.

'Well, this is personal.' Blake's left hand came out of his sling holding a silenced Walther, and he shot Falcone, knocking him against the rail. Falcone spun round and went over head first into the river.

Russo raised his gun to Ferguson, and Billy, leaning over the rail on the top deck, extended the silenced AK and gave Russo a burst that sent him over the rail after Falcone.

Blake was really very ill, sweat all over his face. He said to Don Marco, 'Why the hell I don't kill you, I'll never know, but we ruined your nephew, killed the bastard and his men. I think I'd rather leave you to chew on that.'

He turned, and he and Ferguson walked away.

Dillon lit a cigarette. 'He's one of the good guys, Blake, wants to improve the world. Even Ferguson still tries, but not me. I've found life more disappointing than I'd hoped, so to hell with you.' He slapped Don Marco back-handed across the face, reached for his ankles, and tossed him over into the river. The fog swirled. A cigar butt floated smouldering on the water. It was over.

They were waiting for him in the Daimler on Charing Cross Pier. Ferguson said, 'Taken care of?'

Dillon nodded. 'Whichever gang took out Jack Fox and his men in Cornwall was obviously laying in wait for Don Marco here. Another Mafia execution. Very messy.'

'All in all, then,' Ferguson said, 'a satisfactory night.'

'Except for one thing.' They turned to the figure who sat slumped and ashen in the dark. Blake looked at them, his eyes burning. 'It won't bring her back.'

And to that, there was no answer.